HE TURNED. MARION WAS THERE,
CROUCHED LIKE A SUCCUBUS AT
THE END OF THE BED.

He watched without speaking, pleased
with what he saw. She was in her true
shape. She was beautiful, her musculature
picked out by moonlight, her flesh
sheened with golden down, her face
thrusting and strong. The scent of her
filled up the room, now that he was properly awake . . .

'Hallo, Stephen,' she said. Her voice was
husky, the words distorted by a mouth
not made for them. Moonlight glinted
coldly on her incisors.

(Liz Holliday, *Cover Story*)

THE WEERDE

BOOK 2
A SHARED WORLD ANTHOLOGY

DEVISED BY

NEIL GAIMAN, MARY GENTLE AND
ROZ KAVENEY

EDITED BY

MARY GENTLE AND ROZ KAVENEY

A ROC BOOK

PENGUIN BOOKS

Published by the Penguin Group
Penguin Books Ltd, 27 Wrights Lane, London W8 5TZ, England
Penguin Books USA Inc., 375 Hudson Street, New York, New York 10014, USA
Penguin Books Australia Ltd, Ringwood, Victoria, Australia
Penguin Books Canada Ltd, 10 Alcorn Avenue, Toronto, Ontario, Canada M4V 3B2
Penguin Books (NZ) Ltd, 182–190 Wairau Road, Auckland 10, New Zealand

Penguin Books Ltd, Registered Offices: Harmondsworth, Middlesex, England

First published by ROC, an imprint of Penguin Books 1993
1 3 5 7 9 10 8 6 4 2

Typeset by DatIX International Limited, Bungay, Suffolk
Filmset in 10/12 pt Monophoto Melior
Printed in England by Clays Ltd, St Ives plc

CONTENTS

Prologue

RAISED VOICES IN A READING ROOM: I

Roz Kaveney

_____

Snow fell on the colonnades of the British Museum, grey in the half-light of a winter afternoon. The country had sunk into the hibernation of the Christmas break, and into that paralysis which any variation on temperate calm traditionally inflicts on public transport. The streets of Bloomsbury had the silence of vacancy.

'The apes have been talking about us again,' a harsh voice said. 'And we need to be rid of their dangerous chattering. Their science and their bureaucracy will back us into a corner. The apes must die, now. And their own meddlings will give us the means.'

The streets of Bloomsbury were not as empty as they at first seemed. These were not streets where the homeless nested, and yet shabby men paced up and down Great Russell Street in unusual numbers; the shop where the Swedenborgians sold their apocalypses was dark, and yet a light shone on in its back office, and though the occult bookshop down a side street had finally gone bankrupt, a smell billowed from it, of incense and of attar. Shapes moved among the rooftops and there were eyes in the lime-tree in the garden of the house by the museum, where Trotskyites usually lived.

'That would be a little too drastic, my Lord of Stasis,' another voice said. 'Their civilization is quite fragile, really. Electromagnetic pulses in the right place at the

1

right time, and they would crumble. If, in the process, most die, no blood is on our hands.'

Over the preceding weeks, the British Library had migrated. Lorries had taken away its index cards and its microfiches, the Debretts of dead generations of gentry and the maps of countries that had changed their names and borders. Even the desks had gone – a few to be preserved in honour of those who had worked there, most to be disposed of. There was no need of their patina of dust and scholarship in the new, concrete library between the Euston Road and the great Northern railway lines; it was a product of a new age, and had no need of dust.

'Humans reduced to a few primitives, my Lords Man-hater of Stasis and Sweet Preytaker of Chaos,' a third voice said, 'would be humans on whom the wrath of the gods had descended. And the fear that would ensue is one we cannot afford.'

The lorries were all gone, and yet the streets were full of pantechnicons. Several of them had pulled into the courtyard of the museum and parked there. As Mr Chepstow walked past them, heading for the small door to which, as courtesy to a Librarian of the Library of the Conspiracy, he had a key, useful when the museum was temporarily closed, he caught a strong whiff of ammonia or some other nitrate. *The circus has come to town early this year*, he thought idly, as he walked down the steps to the small door.

'Like I said,' said the Lord of Stasis. 'Exterminate the brutes.'

The strange smell was omnipresent in the echoing galleries of the museum. On his way to the office of his colleague, the Chief Under-Librarian of the British Library Department of Curiosities, Chepstow was wont to take side trips. Librarians live in a world without time,

2

and are above mere punctuality, save in the matter of closing times and the return of loaned books.

There were wet footprints on the floor of the room that still contained the stolen marbles of the Parthenon and a cigar stub floating in the remains of a tumbler of brandy beside the statuette of an Egyptian hippopotamus god. It was a vulgarly large brandy glass, and it had been vulgarly full, Chepstow ascertained by running a finger round the upper rim.

'The only ways to be sure of getting them all,' said the third voice, 'would ruin the planet for us. And can we be sure that to commit mass slaughter would not attract – shall we say – attention?'

Chepstow's friend, Mr Glossop, was ill at ease when Chepstow remarked upon these departures from good museum practice.

Another voice piped up. 'We think you are all getting things out of proportion. The humans pay for their keep.'

'Of course,' Chepstow said, 'I lead a sheltered existence and am not answerable to the whims of visiting dignitaries.'

'This is all much too serious,' another said. 'I only came along for the party. Who ordered this double cheese with pepperoni?'

'It isn't the conference,' Mr Glossop said. 'I am told they will mostly be Arabs, and Arabs don't leave brandy around, or go looking at sculptures. It is their security men. They were most put out when I mentioned that you were planning to look in on the old place; I didn't tell them that you have a key, because I did not think that you would be especially pleased to have some jumped-up secret policeman knowing of the existence of the Library of the Conspiracy.'

'Even among us,' the Lord of Stasis said, 'corruption and decadence has set in. I have seen the effect on our

3

children of the apes' so-called fiction – a polite word, a scab over festering lies and cultivated delusions – and of their tawdry jungle rhythms.'

'I have met,' Mr Chepstow, 'in my time, secret police-men who were remarkably well-informed on such sub-jects.'

'So voting for killing the humans,' a quiet voice added, 'is actually a vote for giving Stasis unlimited rights to purge the Kin, again? If we vote with you, we give you the right to decide, as your next move, which of us has been corrupted?'

'Be that as it may,' Mr Glossop said, 'the place pullu-lates with them. I am not even sure that they will let you pay your respects – I understand that they are using the former Great Reading Room for this secret peace conference, and no one, not even the Chief Lib-rarian himself is admitted.'

'I move that we proceed to a vote,' the Lord of Chaos said. 'Deal with the apes first, as Manhater of Stasis says, then settle our own accounts afterwards, in the good peace and eternity that will be left to us.'

'If that is how things are,' Mr Chepstow said, 'I suggest that we pay our respects in another trad-itional manner. Let us find a public house, and I will sip mineral water and watch you drink your warm beer.'

'Nonsense,' the quiet voice said. 'If we are putting humanity on trial for its life, we should at least listen to some evidence.'

'They will not need evidence,' the Chaos Lord said, 'when they learn of us, and come for us. I was in Poland in 1943 and humans are as ruthless as they are efficient.'

'If we try and fail,' the quiet voice said, 'we ensure that they will come for us. And then we will need a voice to defend us, as they need one now, among us.'

*

4

It is not usual for a man to become a Librarian of the Library of the Conspiracy, or even to become an alcoholic who no longer drinks, without having, or learning, a fair measure of what friends call persistence and enemies obstinacy.

Mr Chepstow had spent many happy hours, in youth, under the dome of the Great Reading Room, and was not about to let the exigencies of politics, a class of affairs of which he and his colleagues had, after all, washed their hands, stand in the way of a decent last paying of respects. The small hours of the night accordingly found him returning, well-fed and with his warm gloves on, towards the small side door of the museum to which he had a key.

London always made him feel young again, and in the mood for a jape or an adventure.

When he walked down Great Russell Street, he felt eyes upon him, but he proceeded with the slow dignified tread and actions of a man who has every right to be where he is, as indeed, as far as he was concerned, he had. He ignored the watchers in the lime-tree and did not allow himself to feel hot breath on the back of his neck, or hear footsteps that dogged his own gently echoing ones. He almost missed the numbing of alcohol – Dutch courage has unpleasant consequences, but there are times when it is the only sort one has.

He had hardly stepped out of the staircase up into the main body of the museum from the underground complex of offices to which his key had admitted him, when he was firmly seized by two sallow men in a uniform he did not recognize. There was something in the particular firmness of their grip on his upper right arm, and lower left wrist, which reminded him of talons, and one of them produced a large gun of some sort and held its muzzle to Chepstow's forehead.

He had been ill-advised, it seemed.

The other guard reached into Chepstow's pocket, and checked his wallet for personal information.

'I am,' Mr Chepstow ventured, 'a great admirer of your people.'

'And which particular attribute of my people,' one of them said, 'might that be? Our calligraphy? Our exotic cuisine? Our wonderful sense of rhythm?'

'I was thinking, as it happens,' Mr Chepstow said, there being really no point in beating about the bush, 'of the Fifty Lives.'

It was at this point that he saw his first Ancient.

For a moment he thought that the curators had re-arranged the exhibits yet again, but what he took for an Assyrian bull-god came lumbering down the gallery towards them. Theoretical and empirical knowledge have odd gaps between them, and into that gap fear and surprise can, at a glandular level, creep.

'What have you here, children?' a large but quiet voice asked, from lips that seemed too heavily hung to move easily.

'A Librarian of the Library of the Conspiracy,' Mr Chepstow said. 'A neutral observer in all things.'

'In all things?' the quiet-voiced Ancient said.

'I invoke the Truce of Knowledge,' Mr Chepstow said, knowing that his neck could be snapped like a match between those teeth before he finished speaking.

'Do you, indeed?' the Ancient said. 'You are clearly quite remarkably well-informed.'

At a nod of the Ancient's titanic head, one of the two guards placed a blindfold around Chepstow's head, and they dragged him, with more force than was strictly called for, down the corridors and up a flight of stairs. From the changing quality of the echo, he deduced that they were in the main entrance hall, and a sudden kink

in their path, and a change from stone to carpet, indicated that they were entering the Reading Room.

It stank of cigar smoke, spilled red wine, manure and
the bitter sweat of sustained rage; the cacophony that
filled the dome like thick smoke could not be so readily
sorted into component parts. When the blindfold was
removed, Chepstow gulped slightly at the profusion of
flesh that stood, sat, squatted and towered before him,
scales and wet pelts shiny in the winter moonlight from
the skylights.

It is one thing to know that Weerde Ancients are the
originals of most human mythology, another to see in
the body Archangel and Titan, Dragon and Windigo,
Legba and Huitzilopochtli. Rugose and squamous they
were, and probably ichthyose as well if he could be
bothered to look carefully.

He was seeing more Ancients, he knew, than any other
human in history, or perhaps even in myth. There were
no books in the Reading Room any more, yet the accumu-
lation of knowledge was as great as it had ever been.

As the door swung quietly shut behind him, silence
fell, not the silence associated with the room in happier
days, but an altogether different silence of reined, but
imminently catastrophic, energy.

The Ancient who accompanied him looked around at
his peers, most of them, Chepstow deduced, his seniors.

'We have a Librarian of the Conspiracy among us,' he
said in that monumental yet quiet voice. 'And he has
invoked the Truce of Knowledge.'

'That is ridiculous,' a scaly specimen rumbled at the
back of the room. 'Obviously not meant to apply to the
apes.'

'No one ever said it couldn't,' a more gracile Ancient
tinkled in a voice like steel wire. 'That omission may
prove a useful legal fiction.'

'Precisely so,' said the Ancient whom Chepstow was already thinking of as his.

'What can the ape add to our proceedings?' the scaly one said in a temper.

'Knowledge, clearly,' Chepstow said.

There were howls of rage from some of the Ancients.

'The Library of the Conspiracy,' Chepstow said, 'has always encouraged its employees to conduct their own research. I am by way of being something of an expert in the interactions of your people and humanity.'

'We do not allow humans to know of these things,' said another Ancient, squat and hairy and seemingly eyeless.

'And yet we still know,' Chepstow said. 'And it does not matter at all, because those of us who know, also know the importance of discretion.'

'How much *do* you know?' the gracile one demanded.

'Enough,' said Chepstow, 'to know that this must be the largest gathering of Ancients since . . .'

Chepstow thought about when the last large gathering had been, and shut his mouth urgently and tightly.

'It is an intolerable affront,' the scaly one bellowed.

'I am a Librarian of the Conspiracy,' Chepstow said, 'and neutral in all things, save knowledge.'

'I accept that as generally the case, but I am sceptical about the present circumstances,' said Chepstow's Ancient.

'In all things,' Mr Chepstow reaffirmed, 'save knowledge, and thus the preservation of the Library itself.'

'And there you have it,' the Ancient said, 'for the preservation of the Library of the Conspiracy is predicated upon humans to staff it and humans to read in it and, for the most part, humans to proliferate the material it keeps on its shelves. And it is not certain that that precondition is one we are any longer prepared to countenance.'

'It is an experiment whose time has passed,' the scaly one said. 'The apes must die.'

'When you held your last Great Council,' Chepstow said, 'and decided that you could no longer go on destroying every attempt at human civilization . . .'

'We fixed the Towered City of Circular Canals,' the scaly one said, 'and we will fix you.'

'On *that* occasion,' Chepstow said, his voice raised above the hubbub and his glare managing to stare down even the angry scaly Ancient, 'you allowed humanity an advocate.'

'Precisely so,' the gracile Ancient said.

'And now that we have our counsel for the defence,' said Chepstow's Ancient smugly, 'I suggest that you produce your evidence.'

A couple of smaller Ancients at the back of the crowd looked up from eating a stack of pizzas.

'Courtroom drama,' one of them said, 'performing humans, all the scandals that we never get to hear . . . I told you we'd have a good time.'

'I'd still rather be watching *Terminator 2*,' sighed his companion.

The scaly one drew himself up to his full height.

'I summon my witnesses,' he said.

IMAGINARY TIME

Stephen Baxter

'We want you to assassinate Stephen Hawking.'

Harris, cradling a beautiful, antique vase, listened carefully to the voice. Even through the phone's tinny distortion he could distinguish a characteristic, resonant growl, a booming that came from a deep, old chest.

An Ancient, then.

He said, 'Payment?'

He heard the hiss of air through misshapen nostrils. 'Fifty per cent will arrive tomorrow. The rest will follow when Hawking is dead.'

There aren't that many Ancients. Their speech patterns, accented by their foreignness to the present, tend to be distinctive. Individual. Harris made it his business to know those patterns. Such information was useful. This was the female known as Gulliver. Eight centuries old or more; not one he'd dealt with before. He imagined the dragon-form, uncomfortable with age, huge and hulking in some deep room.

'Well?'

'If the payment's acceptable you will see the results,' Harris said. 'You know how to deliver?'

For a few seconds he heard the hiss of breath; then the dialling tone returned.

Harris learned about Stephen Hawking. Hawking was one of his generation's finest theoretical physicists.

Perhaps the finest. Harris, leafing through Hawking's popular writings, built up an image of an elegant mind, a vision of the universe like crystal clockwork. There was beauty in Hawking's vision, Harris saw. It was a type of beauty which Harris, used to the visual and tactile beauty of fine art, found oddly delicious.

But disturbing.

The payment was left in a safe-deposit box in a small local bank. Inside the box there was a small, flat package, wrapped in stiff card. Harris took it home and opened it. He found a sparse, elegant wooden frame about six inches square. Mounted inside the frame was a scrap of faded parchment the size of his palm. The parchment bore illuminated text. Harris held it close to his face.

> To the Child the World is Still
> To the Man the World Grows
> In the Eye of GOD the World Eternal is . . .

A pulse thrummed in his throat.

This was one of the more enigmatic verses of the Fifty Lives – perhaps it was some remnant of wisdom preserved from the archaic times of the reptiles. And so this parchment could only be a fragment of the Skye transcript, the result of one of the few attempts, by a cell of twelfth-century monks under discreet Weerde supervision, to transcribe the huge oral history of the Lives. Various factions had spent the intervening centuries trying to ensure that no scrap of the manuscript survived.

Maybe Gulliver had preserved this from her youth. It was beyond price, of course. But more than that: it was beautiful. Something moved in Harris's heart. He found a place for the parchment among all his other beautiful artefacts. He wondered why that particular verse had been sent to him.

Harris thought about Hawking, and Gulliver.

The Weerde were divided in opinion over the threat of human science. It wasn't easy for the Weerde to hide, in a society growing in technological sophistication. There was a grouping – clustered around the one known as Ancient of Days – that had grown concerned by the Human Genome Project. Perhaps the humans, in unlocking the secrets of their own genetic heritage, would expose the Weerde at last.

The conservatives among them were moving against the human scientific community, using methods millennia old. Harris had worked for this grouping.

Other factions, like the shadowy Organization, believed that human science would benefit the Weerde, overall. Perhaps human science would provide a way to challenge the Dark itself one day. The Organization believed that the conservatives' efforts to destroy human science and engineering by assassinating individuals were futile. Even dangerous to the species. The debate was bloody.

Harris had worked for the Organization. Surely one of the conservative groups must be funding this operation against Hawking.

Gulliver was not attached strongly to any one faction. Gulliver was old. The Ancients tended to exist in a web of old alliances, antique enmities, complex and fragmented beyond mere faction boundaries. And, if anything, Gulliver had a reputation as a supporter of the groupings who saw the development of human science as a benefit to the Weerde. There were tales, for example, that a century earlier she had discreetly encouraged the Darwinians, dribbling them fragments of Weerde prehuman memory.

So why should such a one as Gulliver now ally herself with a hard-line conservative faction? And why should she want Hawking dead? Harris frowned. He didn't understand Gulliver's motivation; it didn't make sense. Harris liked things to make sense.

Stephen Hawking was based in Cambridge.

Harris drove up from his London base. He arrived mid-morning. It was late October – term-time; the narrow streets of the old centre of the city were choked with cars, with bicycles.

He parked in a multi-storey, and bought a pocket map. He strolled past the Gothic elegance of the colleges, past lawns green with a patina of centuries.

In mid-afternoon he entered a college. He looked smart, white, in his early twenties; he wasn't challenged by the sleepy inhabitants of the porter's lodge. He walked into a hall of residence, a small, modern block within the college's old walls. At the entrance, fixed to a wall, there was a wooden frame; removable slates bore the names of students and their room numbers. Harris stood before the frame for a few seconds.

He climbed the stairs to the first floor. He passed a girl on the stairs; she smiled at him and brushed past. He came to Room B16. This was the room of a Mr P Walters, the slates had said. Harris walked up to the door and tried the handle. The door was locked. He walked on and tried the next door. B17, Mr G Berkhout. The door opened; a young man, sitting at a desk, looked up in surprise. The desk was piled with books and papers. An anglepoise lamp, brightly shining, loomed over the cluttered surface like a metal bird.

'Mr Walters?' Harris asked, smiling.

Berkhout shook his head, pointed with a pen. 'Next door. B16.'

'Thanks.' Harris closed the door.

He climbed to the second floor.

Room C32. Miss A Hinch. He tried the door. It was open; the room was empty, still. Harris walked in and closed the door quietly behind him. The room was small, lined with pine panels; there was a small, hard bed, a plain desk and a single chair. On the desk there was an anglepoise lamp like Berkhout's; books, papers and folders were stacked in ordered piles; pens and pencils peeped from a fur-covered case.

Beside the bed, on a shelf, there was a small travelling alarm clock. There was a picture of a boy, smiling, and a fat paperback. The book's spine was too cracked for Harris to make out the title. On another shelf there was a mirror, heated brushes, bits of make-up. There was a faint scent of hairspray, overlaying a deeper scent of furniture polish. The room was neat and tidy. Blonde hair was wrapped around the brushes.

Harris sat on the chair; he crossed his legs and waited. It grew darker.

Harris thought about the Weerde's evolving attitude to human science. The conservatives feared the specifics, the human scientists themselves and their bewildering technological toys. Like the Genome Project. Other Weerde, less fearful of change, sought opportunity in the new technologies. But beyond those straightforwardly opposing factions, Harris knew, there was a growing feeling among many Weerde that science itself had gone too far.

The Weerde had encouraged Bacon and some of the others – Descartes, Newton. They had liked the idea of the scientific method, of the universe as a piece of clockwork to be taken apart, shell by shell. Reductionist science, with its implicit belief that there was a law, a meaning, an explanation for all phenomena, had steadily removed the perception of gods, of supernatural beings, from human paradigms.

Some Weerde still believed that the Dark was attracted to minds dominated by mysticism. The Weerde observed that where science took hold, religion declined. The Weerde had imagined human minds dimming in the questing eyes of the Dark.

The Weerde were comforted.

Then, in the twentieth century, the Newtonian clockwork universe imploded. Suddenly there was relativity, a beginning to time. And quantum theory: uncertainty, the interaction of consciousness with reality. Daring, audacious, brilliant conceptions. The anthropic principle; the idea that out of a range of universes, some force had selected this one for humans to inhabit. The ideas of de Chardin, of the evolution of consciousness towards godhead at the end of time, at the Omega Point.

A new conception of God, of godhood, was emerging from the astonishing sea of ideas. The Weerde, the factions and Ancients, feared the Dark would be attracted once more. More and more of them concurred that scientific progress, and its influence on the evolution of human consciousness, had to be slowed, stopped.

Harris wondered what Gulliver believed.

At about five o'clock a key rattled in the lock of the door to the room. Harris heard a soft, self-deprecating mumble when the door turned out to be unlocked. The door opened. Miss A Hinch, swathed in a shapeless duffle-coat, bustled into the room. She was carrying a Sainsbury's carrier bag, awkwardly because one of the plastic handles had stretched and snapped. Miss Hinch closed the door behind her before she saw Harris. She gasped, fumbled with the bag.

Harris, still sitting with legs crossed, hands on his knees, gasped. Miss Hinch took an uncertain step for-

ward, brushing a ringlet of blonde hair from her forehead. She was about five feet two, a little plump, with a
delicate, pretty face. 'I'm sorry,' she said.

'I'm sorry,' Harris said.

The girl frowned. 'Who are you?'

'Who are you?' Harris frowned. Her accent was Home
Counties neutral, her voice flat and nasal. He repeated,
'Who are you? I'm sorry. Sorry.' Still not quite right. He
pushed his tongue further forward. 'Who are you?'

The girl's smile had gone. She was frightened now.
Still holding the Sainsbury's bag, she turned and
reached for the door handle. Harris was at her side. He
lowered her silently to the wooden floor.

'Who are you?' he said. 'I'm sorry.'

He would wait until night, and get the girl out of
here. And he'd need a change sleep. He sat at the desk
and crossed his legs. It grew darker.

'I'm sorry. Who are you? Who are you?'

Harris wanted to learn more about Stephen Hawking. He
found it useful to get to know as well as he could the people
he needed to destroy. It made it easier to be discreet.

The next morning Miss A Hinch was at the doors of
the Fitzwilliam Library as soon as it opened.

In the rows of purple-bound technical journals, Harris
found some of Hawking's original papers. Hawking, he
learned, had contributed much to the modern picture of
the Big Bang.

A century ago most humans had believed the universe
to be unchanging. Einstein, an earlier version of Hawking, had deduced that that couldn't be true. Static universes must be unstable. Einstein – a patent clerk – had
deduced this. Sometimes Harris wondered what it must
be like to be human, to have such a mind. It invoked
wonder in him; it frightened him.

The universe, not just matter and energy but all of space and time themselves, had blossomed from a single event: the Big Bang. Like the 'man' in his fragment of the Lives transcript, Harris thought vaguely, humans had put aside their childlike notions of a fixed, static universe. Their world grew now. But on immense time-scales, he realized; time-scales that dwarfed even the long traditions of the Weerde.

Everything, all the world-lines, had emerged from the initial singularity. The Big Bang. And the world-lines would merge again into a fresh collapse, a new singularity; or perhaps the universe would continue to expand, to push itself, purposeless, into emptiness; to define another boundary to space-time: the Omega Point, infinite age.

Perhaps God could be found in the Big Bang, men had begun to wonder. Or at the Omega Point.

The Big Bang model was beautiful, Harris saw. But there were problems still unresolved. Clarity of thought shone through Hawking's technical language, through the equations. Beauty shone through.

Harris, staring at the yellowing pages, absently brushed a blonde ringlet from his brow.

Another student died.

Harris, tall and dark, a wispy beard straggling across his chin and a college scarf around his neck, walked across the Market Square. Following his memorized street map he found the Department of Applied Mathematics. It was a ramshackle, rather dingy collection of buildings. Harris walked in unchallenged.

The corridors were narrow, the walls covered with notice-boards. There were wheelchair ramps here, unusual in a university not noted for its accessibility to the disabled. He found Hawking's office. There was a red postcard-sized sign pinned to the door. The sign said: BLACK HOLES ARE OUT OF SIGHT. Harris didn't try the door. Hawking, if he was there, was bound to be attended.

Harris looked back in time with Stephen Hawking. He learned about quantum uncertainty. He learned that there were scales – the Planck length and the Planck time – below which it was no longer meaningful to talk about 'length' or 'duration'. It gave a kind of graininess to reality, he thought. Stephen Hawking had wondered what the universe had been like when it was smaller than the Planck length, younger than the Planck time.

Uncertainty dominated, of course. You couldn't be certain that the Big Bang had occurred at this instant, or that; here, or over there. Maybe the universe had grown out of a virtual particle pair, a wrinkle of instability in the emptiness. In the intensity of Hawking's thought the initial singularity had melted away, into a hiss of uncertainty . . .

Harris, entranced, the scarf draped over his chair, read on, learning to see the universe through Stephen Hawking's eyes. It grew dark.

Harris learned, at last, of imaginary time. He closed his eyes and tried to hold the beautiful vision in his head. It was like cradling a vase in the palm of his hand: but the vision was at once more fragile, more rarefied, and more lovely for that. He hadn't imagined such beauty could exist.

Harris came to a decision. He stole a car and left the city. He found a hotel, and reverted easily to Harris's form. He left the car and took another. He extended his trail, then covered it over.

It took him some days to return to London. Some days after that, the phone rang.

'I know you have your methods,' the Ancient hissed.

19

As Harris had expected, she didn't sound angry. 'I know you take time, research your – subjects. But your sponsors are not infinitely patient.'

Harris ignored this. 'I'm not going to kill Hawking. You never intended me to kill Hawking,' he said.

Gulliver's huge, hollow breath resonated for long seconds. 'Is it so obvious?'

'You knew I'd research Hawking. You knew I'd find his material ... pleasing.' Harris clutched the phone tightly. 'You were able to predict my actions.'

There was a laugh, a sound dredged from time. 'Not entirely,' Gulliver said. 'I know you're not like others of your – profession. I know that your motives differ from theirs; that you do not share their vision, their devotion to the cause of the species. You're an aesthete. I know that from your preferred mode of payment. And that is your motivation to work. I had to gamble that your sense of aesthetics would extend to the non-tactile ... to the *intellectual*.'

'There is a faction that plans to kill Hawking,' Harris said.

'Oh, yes. And others. Penrose. Tipler. Some of the younger, less well-known ones too; the ones driving the whole enterprise now. They're getting too close to God.'

Harris knew that. 'Hawking believes there was no beginning to space-time,' Harris murmured into the phone. 'The world-lines are like lines of longitude, scratched on a globe; our lives, following "real time", are like journeys from North Pole to South Pole. And the Poles are the places where the world-lines meet: the singularities.' The Big Bang. The Omega Point.

But the lines were an illusion, the singularities artefacts of perception, Hawking taught. There were other times, 'imaginary times', like paths on the globe away from the longitudinal. In imaginary time there was no beginning and no end. The universe of space and time was closed and complete like the surface of a sphere, without boundary or edge in space or time.

Harris turned the vision in his head, let it shimmer. 'It is beautiful,' he said.

'Yes.' The Ancient quoted, '"To the Child the World is Still / To the Man the World Grows / In the Eye of GOD the World Eternal is . . ."'

'That's the meaning of the ancient verse,' Harris realized suddenly. 'It's Hawking's vision.'

'Yes. The same vision. *But transmitted through time, from archaic days.*' The voice of the Ancient grated with animation. 'Harris, the reptiles knew this too. That's what the Lives are telling us. The reptiles too went through evolutions of thinking: from the simple, static, childlike perspective of time to the exploding, dynamic vision of the Big Bang model – and finally to the vision that is emerging now, of motion, change; of beginnings and ends as illusions against a canvas of stillness. That's what the old verse describes; it's our last, imperfect echo in time of what the reptiles knew, and lost.'

Harris frowned. 'How could the reptiles know about the Big Bang, without radio-telescopes to observe the background microwave radiation, and –'

Gulliver laughed. 'They thought about why the night sky is dark.'

'You never intended that I should kill Hawking, did you?' Harris asked evenly. 'You allied yourself with this conservative faction in order to get yourself into a position where you could recruit the assassin – in order that you could manipulate the situation, manipulate me, to achieve your end. You even chose that fragment of the Lives, as a subliminal clue for me.'

Gulliver sighed; it sounded like waves breaking on

an old shore. 'The showdown with the humans is going to come anyway, I can't stop that. In a way the progressives are right to oppose us, we Ancients. We're doing too much damage to the human scientific community; we are impeding too many specific projects.

'We are coming to their attention. As soon as the humans understand what's happening, they'll come after us ... Maybe we'll win. At least we'll push them back. But I wanted to sabotage this assassination. Harris, listen to me. Over the last few years, as I've followed the work of Hawking and others, and as I've seen their new world-picture emerge, I've realized this: a beauty is returning to the world, a beauty lost for seventy million years, that we Weerde could never construct for ourselves ...

'Harris, you're an aesthete. You can understand how I felt when I saw all this, can't you ... the sense of *loss*?' She laughed again. 'Seventy million years of loss!'

'And the Dark?'

'Bugger the Dark,' Gulliver snapped. 'Why should we endure like this, terrified of the new, the strange, the beautiful? Let the conservatives fret over trinkets like the Genome Project ... But I can't bear to see Hawking's vision destroyed. You can understand that, can't you, Harris? Isn't all this wonder worth the risk? Isn't it? Harris?'

Harris hung up. For a few minutes he sat, reflecting. Gulliver had been able to anticipate his reactions, to manipulate him. He had become lazy. He had become predictable.

Harris, working alone and without support, had survived as an assassin for five decades.

He got out of his chair, walked out of his house, locked the door carefully. He drove away.

In the house, dust motes drifted over the abandoned things of beauty, over the crystallized deaths of human and Weerde.

THE GIRL WHO CHANGED EVERYTHING

Colin Greenland

———————

Duncan Turner was a solitary individual. Even in childhood he felt like a stranger in the world. He accepted that there were others, grown-ups and many other children, who had had the secret rules of life made plain to them; but they were never to be revealed to humbler creatures like him. He shrank from people, fearing to expose to them that he lacked the key they so obviously had. Duncan would cross the road to avoid three girls walking to his sister's school, a tableau of windswept mischief and mysterious clothing. Their laughter would echo after him as he ducked into the alley down beside the allotments, avoiding the trailing arms of blackberry bushes.

He spent the holidays indoors, with the wireless or a library book. He liked to read about boys of his own age who went to boarding schools, formed secret societies and caught surly men who robbed trains. Minute by minute, Duncan only seemed to be doing nothing. In reality he was a secret agent for a mysterious and very powerful organization, with many unexpected skills and concealed weapons. Or he was the actor in a television story, with hidden cameras on him every moment, and no one around him aware that they were being filmed.

In his later teens he would take himself off for days out, roaming the damp streets of some nearby town, looking for second-hand bookshops. In Bexhill and

25

Hastings Duncan felt adrift, self-conscious. The empty afternoon yawned ahead of him; he needed someone to tell him what to do next. He would loiter for an hour in a public library looking for sex in Colin Wilson and Mary McCarthy, then trail from newsagent to newsagent, leafing hotly through *Parade* and *Men Only*. From the pages of these magazines the sirens smiled at him, posing naked with a cuddly toy or half-dressed, sitting on the stairs with their legs apart, letting you look up their skirts.

In the park sometimes he caught a glimpse of the real thing. It was a small park – an oblong of grass, narrow flower-beds, a sundial – on a piece of ground where some houses had been knocked down. When it was warm Duncan liked to sit there and read, Hammond Innes or the new Ian Fleming. Sometimes women walked by, young mothers with toddlers on reins, or girls in headscarves wheeling bicycles. Sometimes a woman would sit down on his bench. He never said anything to them. He tried to smile once or twice, at girls plain enough not to take offence, but the smile felt horrible on his face, the tense grimace of a knife murderer.

When the girl who was to change everything sat down next to him, Duncan had no idea; which of us would? He was only aware of her body, a peripheral sense of a flowered dress and bare limbs a couple of feet away; and she was not old, he was sure of that. Duncan kept his concentration on the page in front of his eyes.

Then she said: 'What are you reading?'

Her voice was low, almost conspiratorial, and quite unhesitant. It was not a child's voice, nor an adult's voice, asking with authority that demanded an answer. It was the voice of someone his own age, who was curious. Duncan knew at once that she too liked to read: she knew his pleasure. He looked up. His first impression was of fair skin and fine blonde hair, and eyes as blue as slate. She was much closer than he had thought. Duncan felt the sun suddenly on his head, and heard a bird call, and that was all part of it somehow. He had a sense of being lifted up off the ground, like a small bird rising, or like a flower that someone has picked.

Duncan would have liked nothing better than to be able to answer the girl's question, cheerfully and candidly. But there was a problem.

What he was reading was a story about an ocean liner sinking in the Pacific, and about what happened to everybody. In one lifeboat there were two survivors, a man and a woman, drifting for days. The author went into a lot of detail about what they did to one another. It was one of the parts about them that Duncan was reading. He could hardly tell her that. He would have liked to say, It's about a shipwreck; but in the shock of her sudden address the word *shipwreck* had completely vanished from his mind. Wordlessly, Duncan closed the book and gave it to her.

She read the title and the author's name. She did not open it; she laid it in her lap. She said, 'Is it exciting?'

As she spoke she gave Duncan such a sultry look he realized she had been sitting close enough to read what he was reading, and knew perfectly well he found it very exciting indeed.

'It's all right,' he said. Duncan blushed frequently, but he did not blush now. In fact he felt himself go white, and there were butterflies in his stomach. He wanted it to be all right, but he was not at all sure that it was. He smiled a weak and apologetic smile.

Some satisfactory message was transmitted, at any

rate. The girl was still looking at him, and not at the book, and her smile was friendly. Duncan supposed he must be hiding his distress well, though of course he was doing nothing of the kind.

'My mother was in a shipwreck,' said the girl, easily, stretching out her legs in the sun. 'They hit an iceberg. People froze to death in the water.'

Duncan was horrified. His book seemed tawdry suddenly, its characters like little dolls jerked about for his entertainment. He felt guilty for reading it.

'Did she – die?' he asked, unable not to.

'Oh no,' said the girl, and laughed. '*She* was all right.'

Duncan felt relieved again, but confused. She seemed so contradictory, this girl, sitting there with his book still on her lap, coming out with all that about her mother. He wondered if she was teasing him, but he was sure she wasn't.

He had to get his book back before she opened it.

'Have you ever been on a ship?' he asked her.

'Me? Oh yes,' she said. 'Hundreds of times.' Then she smiled again, dipping her head a little, and said: 'Well, dozens, anyway.'

Duncan was sixteen. She looked no older. His eye passed from her face to the slight swell of her breasts beneath the dress. It was a light, white cotton print, and through it he could see her bra quite clearly. He looked away, at the sunlit grass. He couldn't look, not now that she was talking to him.

But her eyes drew him back, reassuring him, coaxing his gaze back to her face. Perhaps she was a year or two older than him. Girls matured earlier, he had read that. He thought about that word, *mature*, with all its mysteries.

'I've never been on a ship,' he told her.

She put her hands on her knees and leaned towards

him. 'You come here a lot, don't you?' she said, simply, expecting only confirmation. 'I've seen you here before.'

'I don't think I've seen you,' said Duncan. He was sure he hadn't. He would have remembered if he had. She was so pretty. Beautiful. She made his breath catch in his throat. His palms started to sweat. He wiped them surreptitiously on his trousers. He glanced at his book on her lap.

'It's a good place to read,' he said.

'It's a good place to be alone,' said the girl, echoing his tone of voice. She didn't make it sound like something to be ashamed of, wanting to be on your own. She made it sound desirable. 'You can't be alone at home,' she said, explaining. 'Your brothers and sisters won't let you.'

'I've only got one sister,' Duncan said. 'She's not in much.' He looked at her hands, then up at her face. 'My name's Duncan,' he said.

'You're a lucky boy, Duncan!' the girl said. She made it sound like an announcement, like a promise, almost; it made him nervous. He blinked helplessly and glanced around the park, glad no one was there to hear her.

Gravely she held out his book, returning it to him unopened. Then she laughed at him, wrinkling her nose. For the first time in his life, Duncan didn't mind being laughed at. He laughed too, shakily, and realized he was staring straight into her eyes. Her eyes were the most beautiful things he'd ever seen. He felt them wrap him all round with approval, even while she was laughing at him. Then she bit her bottom lip and put her head on one side, studying him mischievously as if he were a puzzle she was going to enjoy undoing.

And then she was gone. She rose up from the bench and brushed both hands down the front of her dress as if she thought she had crumbs on it, but more slowly, so the motion became something more vivid and meaningful; but while Duncan gaped at her, she waved and ran off down the path.

He watched her leave, a sliding flicker of pink and red flowers and a swirl of hair, up the steps and away. He wanted to shout after her, *Wait!*, but he had been brought up never to shout. He never felt at ease, shouting at anyone. What would he have shouted, anyway? He didn't even know her name.

He found he had got to his feet, far too late to run after her. Duncan hated to run, his knees seemed to swerve around all over the place. Again he thought, he should have shouted; but he couldn't blame himself for it. He was still feeling happy because she'd been sweet to him; blessed by her frank inspection. It was as though she had selected him for something wonderful. He felt like a prisoner released, standing outside at last under the blue sky. He clasped his book tightly under his arm.

No sooner was he walking back up the street between the tall red houses than apprehension swallowed him. She knew him by sight, and now she knew who he was. What did he know about her? Not a thing. Only that story about her mother and the iceberg, which she had made up, probably. She had just come out with it, then – stroked herself like that. Then she had run away. Duncan giggled to himself. Perhaps she was potty. Must be potty to sit down next to people and start talking about her mother. *Is it exciting?*

Duncan looked down at the book under his arm, and remembered how her hands clasped it, how they laid it in her lap. She was so beautiful. And he hadn't even got her name, let alone her address. He did not know what to do. He would have to come and sit in the park every day. He was convinced she would not come. No doubt he would never see her again. It was the safest thing to think, he told himself, and shivered slightly. How stupid he had been! By the time he reached his doorstep he had managed to smother the thrill in his memory under a light cloud of misery.

His father was listening to *Gardeners' Question Time* and reading the paper. His mother was ironing. Duncan ate his tea and went upstairs to read; but he couldn't read. The girl's face kept coming back to him, calling him until the words swam on the page. He saw her eyes, her blue eyes, steady and shining as pebbles under water. Was her forehead broad, or like this, narrower? And her nose, when she wasn't wrinkling it? Straight? Snub? Had there been little gold rings in her ears? How could he have failed to notice?

But he fell asleep with her eyes fixed in his mind. He did not dream about her. Still, he woke feeling excited, ready to return to the park. By the time he had had his breakfast and made his bed and cleaned his shoes, Duncan felt slightly silly about the whole thing, and ashamed of himself for hoping, especially after what he had resolved on the way home. He was ready to be disappointed.

He was. His mysterious visitor did not reappear. Duncan sat in the park all day, with nothing to eat but a packet of crisps he had bought along the way. He was there every day that week. Old people came with their sausage dogs, their pipes or their knitting. Little children stumbled into the flowers and tried to pull themselves up to see the sundial. Duncan finished his book and read another. The girl did not come.

Every word of their conversation, such as it was, was engraved in his brain. He replayed it, thinking of the things he ought to have said. In particular he blamed himself for not finding out anything about her. Did she have a job? Where? What did she do? When was her lunch-hour?

Why had she said he was lucky, if she wasn't going to return?

When the girl finally came down the steps in her miniskirt and suede jacket, Duncan hardly recognized her. His heart faltered when he realized she was walking towards him, she was looking at him – it was her, it was! She looked taller, her legs longer, and she moved with a confident sway in her step. Duncan glanced down at her feet; he thought she might be wearing heels. Then she stopped in front of him and he looked up into her smiling eyes. Her collar was turned up, framing her face, and she had her hands tucked in her pockets. 'Hallo, Duncan,' she said.

A warm glow spread down through Duncan, starting at his eyes and tweaking his lips into a smile, and slipping past the constriction in his throat to splash down and pour all over his heart.

'I thought I was never going to see you again,' he said; and hated it at once, because it came out whiny and complaining.

She wrinkled her brow. 'Did you *hate* that?' she asked seriously, and smiled at him artfully. Duncan realized she was making fun of him again; and again she melted his defences with the brightness of her eyes.

She sat down beside him, crossing her legs. She was wearing nylons. He had thought she seemed older when she came walking down the steps, but the impression vanished as they talked. She asked him a riddle, about a monkey and a concertina, and smirked when he groaned at the answer.

Her name was Marania. She said it was Russian, she had been born there, 'but we live here now,' she said, lifting her hand up nonchalantly. The way she spoke, the way she sat on the bench and raised her hand, two fingers bent into the palm, was like a queen on a throne, or Mary in the painting behind the altar at church. Duncan remembered what she had said about ships. Yet she did not look rich. Her shoes were cracked and the jacket was worn, the shine showing through where the pile had gone. Perhaps she was a Russian aristocrat in exile. Duncan would keep her secret. He was entirely in love with her.

'It's a very pretty name,' he said.

Marania seemed tired at first, but soon she became animated. She wanted to know where Duncan lived, and all the circumstances of his family. Were his grandparents still alive? Were his parents very rich? Or poor? Duncan stammered. He didn't know what she meant by these questions. It sounded as if she was measuring him for something. Part of him was uneasy about it, but he was happy just to talk to her, to tell her anything at all about himself, anything that might bind him to her. She did not speak about herself or her own life, not in any direct way. Duncan did not mind. He would have been happy with anything.

'My dad is like that,' said Duncan. He pointed to a man sitting on a bench reading a newspaper. There was a bright blue butterfly perched on a leaf, not an inch from his ear, spreading its shining wings in the sun. Marania laughed and softly clapped her hands. 'My dad is like most people. He never notices anything,' said Duncan. 'People don't really look at things. They don't notice what's all around them.'

Marania lowered her head and looked up at him through her fringe as though he had said something marvellously wise. Duncan could not think why he had not recognized her, on the steps. Her hair was different today, that was it. Longer than he remembered. And the way she moved was different, in her tight skirt, with her hands in the pockets of her jacket. It was very tight, her skirt, and very short.

She had not touched him, and Duncan could not touch her. While he talked, he could look into her blue eyes and bathe in the radiance of her incredible beauty, and that was all. He was stunned by her. Twenty minutes ago he had been resigned to never seeing her again. Her presence washed away that feeling, along with everything else that was past.

'Duncan,' said Marania at last. 'Have you got a girl-friend?'

A warm flush bloomed inside him. Duncan was remembering that boys were supposed to take the lead, and he didn't know what on earth to do. He couldn't have led a baby. His skin felt prickly all over, his hands were quivering. His heart was pumping hard and loud. All he could do was shake his head. Marania seemed content to let it go at that. Surely her breasts were bigger too today?

Duncan willed his quivering hand to lift from his knee and reach over to cover Marania's hand, which was perfectly quiet and still. His hand wouldn't move. Duncan was relieved. He was repelled by the perfection of her skin, terrified to touch her in case that was the thing that would break the magic spell and drive her away. Duncan was in love with her. But while they could sit there talking, not touching, not moving, it would remain safely latent, merely potential.

She started talking about pop music. Duncan hadn't heard of any of the people she mentioned, but then he found most pop music noisy and overbearing. He said he liked Lulu. It almost seemed like a betrayal, to mention the name of another woman in her presence. But Marania approved, as she seemed to approve of everything Duncan said and did. She nodded excitedly. She looked back over her shoulder, the collar of her jacket standing back from the curve of her neck. There was no one within earshot. She said, 'She's very sexy, isn't she?'

For a moment Duncan could not breathe. Lulu was his favourite fantasy. In newsagents he would imagine opening a magazine and finding pictures of Lulu taking off her clothes, baring her luscious breasts for him to admire. He could *not* say so. In confusion and shame he heard himself deny it. 'Lulu? You're joking,' he said, trying to sound heartless.

Marania leaned back, lifting one knee, wrapping her hands around it. Her skirt tightened across her thighs. 'Have you ever had a girlfriend?' she said. She said the word *girlfriend* delicately, as if suggesting something else.

Duncan hated her now. She was torturing him. He could not lie, not about that; not to her, whatever he might pretend sometimes at school. He knew that in the next moment, or the next, she would decide he was not worth her attention. She would say something that would bring all his wishes crashing down into dust; say it was time she went home, wish him good luck, and walk away with his heart. 'No,' he said, hollowly.

Her blue eyes gleamed brighter. 'Are you a virgin, then?' she said. Duncan blushed and glowered.

She said: 'A virgin! I knew it!' And she gave him a hug, rather more sketchy than Duncan would have preferred. She put her arms about him lightly and briefly, as if she was awarding him a Sunday School prize. When she let go his ears were burning hot and he knew his face was crimson.

Then she knelt up on the bench and said: 'Let's see what we can do about that.'

Duncan melted. His hand wavered up off his knee, as if fumbling for her shoulder, but all his sinews were cut, and the hand dropped back, irresolute. Duncan knew somewhere inside that what she was saying was exactly what he longed for, but he was full of dread. He was so frightened he could not remember how he longed every day and every night for someone, anyone, a woman.

He said: 'Here?'

Her eyes said yes. Then she leaned over and started to kiss him on the mouth.

It was not as he had read, that a girl's kiss would be soft and delicate and sweet. It was another person with her mouth on top of his. Her lips were mobile and wet, strong and sure. Her breath was on his tongue. He felt her hands on him, running down over his hips and stroking his bottom. In terror he felt himself struggle and pull away. 'Someone will come!' he whimpered.

She sat back, undismayed. Her mouth seemed very large on her face, as though it had grown by feeding on his.

'Tonight, then,' she said.

Duncan couldn't imagine how he might get out of the house at night. Right now, they had the park to themselves. Was he being silly? He thought of boys at school. What would they do?

Marania seemed to know. 'Come behind the bushes,' she said.

Duncan looked at the bushes. They were thick and rose close against the wall, with no space behind. The branches were many, and all twigs and leaves. If there was any room back there it would be dark and unpleasant and they would have to crouch. Still she was leading him there. He was frightened, he did not believe he could do whatever it was you had to do. He resisted her. 'No, no,' he said.

She stood still, waiting. At once Duncan felt ashamed. He had panicked and spoilt everything. He couldn't stay there with her. He was humiliated. 'No, I've got to go now,' he said. 'I've got to go home. I'll see you later, all right? Bye.' Then he turned and rushed from the park, not looking back though it tore his heart to go.

As before, his mood changed even while he was walking up the street. A woman was standing on a chair, cleaning her sitting-room window with a yellow duster. Ladders and dustbins stood silent in dark side-alleys. Duncan thought: *We could have gone anywhere.* He remembered a couple he had surprised once, screwing in a car under a railway bridge. He thought of what he was turning his back on and felt his cold prick begin to stir in his pants.

He ran back to the park, but Marania had gone. Duncan cursed himself aloud. Then he saw her, along by the shops, and he started to run after her; but something stopped him. He was sure she would be angry with him. She had offered herself, and he had spurned her. If she saw him coming she would run away, and avoid him for ever. Duncan hung back, keeping close to the railings, not crossing the road until she was on the other side. Between shuffling pedestrians her scissoring legs flashed messages to him, hurry, be careful, hurry, be careful. Duncan did not know what to do.

A bus pulled in and he saw her run for it, grabbing the chrome pole with one slim hand and disappearing inside. Duncan ran too, feeling jolted and clumsy. Diving on to the bus, he ducked his head as he went upstairs. He took the seat directly over the door, and every time they stopped he pressed his head against the window to see if she got off. He didn't see her. The conductor came to take his fare. 'All the way,' said Duncan, desperately. He had enough, luckily.

The bus went into a part of town Duncan didn't know. The shops were small and shabby; some of them were empty, with boards across the windows. People walked slowly along as though there were no place in particular they meant to get to. Duncan was convinced he'd missed her. Then he saw her getting off, and ran for the stairs.

Marania did not look round. He followed her to a dead-end street of two low, bare brick terraces, grey net curtains at the windows. Duncan glimpsed a face looking out at him warily from an upstairs room, a strange face, deformed somehow, he only saw it for a moment. In the road a gang of children were playing with a disintegrating grocery box. One was sitting inside with his arms resting on the rim, holes in the elbows of his pullover. They all turned to look at Duncan as he went by. All the children were wearing masks of different creatures: a frog, Duncan saw, and something that looked as if it was meant to be a turkey. They were very lifelike, even when they opened their mouths and started to shout.

The door Marania had come to opened and a woman in a slip appeared. Duncan turned about and started to walk back down the street, quickly. The children were still shouting, hooting and howling like the creatures whose faces they wore. Duncan kept his head down. *Marania*, he thought. Don't look back at her. *Don't*. At once he looked back. More adults were coming out on to the street with big hairy dogs. They were all standing looking at him. Duncan lost his nerve and broke into a run.

He thought about Marania a lot during the next week. Sometimes, when he recalled how he had behaved, he hoped he would never see her again. He lay on his back on the bedroom floor, clutching his cardigan to his chest and rolling from side to side in anguish and embarrassment. When he felt bolder, or simply lonelier, he wondered how he could win her back. He could never go to her house again. He felt he should purify himself. He stopped his habit of going into newsagents and leafing through dirty magazines. He tried to stop masturbating, but then he dreamed of Marania in black lace underwear which seemed to multiply while he tried to undo it, and he woke stiff and disconsolate.

It rained, off and on. When it cleared up he went and sat in the park. He took a plastic bag to sit on and a notebook in which to write down his thoughts. He wanted Marania to come, and see him writing a poem. She did not appear. Duncan went back to reading. He tried to read *Under Milk Wood*, but he found it hard to follow, and there was too much sex in it. He read *Ice Station Zebra* and *The Most Dangerous Game*.

One evening he was alone in the park. The summer was ageing, and the late sunlight glowed like honey among the leaves. Lulu came down the steps.

She did not take the most direct route, but walked around the corner of the lawn and then down a diagonal path towards him. She stopped at the sundial, resting one hand on it and looking straight at him.

'Hallo, Duncan,' she said.

He stared at her, almost rising up out of his seat. It was Lulu, there was no doubt about it, even in the crowding shadows of the park. She was shorter than he had imagined, but her legs were plump and her mini-dress was tight under her arms, and cut low to show the tops of her breasts.

'How do you know my name?' asked Duncan.

Lulu smiled her chubby-cheeked smile, full of sparkling white teeth, and sat down beside him on the bench.

'Your mother said I'd find you here.' She sat quite close. She said: 'You're a lucky boy, Duncan!'

Lulu's dress was green, to match her eyes. Her eyelashes were drawn out in little points with black mascara. She smelled of some kind of perfume. Her lips were pink and ripe. Duncan could hear her accent; the way she said 'Duncan' reminded him it was a Scottish name. He had seen her real name in one of his sister's magazines. He could not remember what it was. Marie Laurie, it kept ringing in his head, Marie Laurie. But that was someone else.

'Would you like to come with me?' Lulu asked him. 'Come on,' she said, bouncing to her feet again and holding out her hand.

Duncan stood up and let her take his hand. He was still gazing at her face, in shock, understanding nothing. Her eyes were blue now, blue as piled storm clouds. Duncan's own eyes grew wide; and then he knew. He screamed and jerked his hand free. He sat down, his hands spread wide, almost crawling up the back of the bench in his agitation. His horrified gaze never left her face. Because it was not hers, it was Lulu's. But this was not Lulu. Duncan sat and shook, and stamped his feet on the paving stones. Then he flung himself sideways and vomited over the arm of the bench.

Dizzy, he felt her hand on his arm. He lay there rigid and shaking and would not look round. 'Duncan,' she said. Her voice had changed. 'Duncan, it's all right,' she said.

He looked round then, full of fear: afraid to look, afraid not to. It was a monster squatting there at his feet, someone he didn't know, like a trick photograph, half Lulu, half Marania. He retched again and let his head hang down.

'I'm sorry,' he croaked. 'I'm sorry, I'm sorry.'

Eventually she calmed him down. She stopped him apologizing, gave him a tissue to wipe his mouth, and held him in her arms until he relaxed. In the dying light of the empty park she told him an incredible story, told it briefly and without any drama at all.

'I'm not human,' she said. 'We are another race. We can make ourselves look like other people. Anyone else at all.'

Another race. Duncan thought of Tarzan, of paperbacks they sold in heaps at Woolworth's, with yellow edges and crude pictures on the front. Men with unknown weapons and eyes like owls pursued a terrified woman in a torn blouse over black and scarlet rocks. Duncan thought his head would burst. 'Where do you come from?' he asked her.

'We were here before you.'

He refused to understand this.

She cradled his head. 'I've sat and watched you, over there, and you didn't know. You didn't know it was me.' She held his head to her breasts and rocked him to and fro. Duncan didn't want that. But he couldn't look at her face. He would not burst into tears, he would not.

'I'm sorry I frightened you,' she said, and he snatched a look. She was biting her lip as if she wanted to laugh and knew she mustn't. 'Will you forgive me?'

She was holding him. Her breasts felt real against his shoulder. 'Well?' she said. 'Duncan?'

'. . . Course I will,' he said huskily. In the ringing crater of his mind he groped for words. 'I just –'

'Shh,' she said, and laid a finger on his lips.

She lifted her head then, as if she'd heard something, or perhaps she was only gazing up into the darkening sky. He looked at the white curve of her throat in the twilight.

Quicker and quieter, she said, 'Will you be here on Thursday?'

Thursday was a week away. He stared at her, feeling her about to depart from him. 'Yes,' he said desperately, 'Thursday, yes.'

She blinked at him slowly, as if she were feeling slightly sorry for him; as if he were a dog she had hurt and wished she hadn't. 'You won't be ill again, will you?' she said, sceptically. Then she bent and whispered in his ear. 'Just think, Duncan. Any woman you like. Anyone at all.'

Duncan started shaking again. He gripped her hand tightly in his own. 'No,' he blurted out. 'No. I want you to be you.'

She sat back. The contours of her face slipped suddenly, the bone of her brow realigning itself like a rib straightening inside an umbrella. Duncan flinched, but made himself watch. It was nothing, he told himself, though it twisted his stomach and he began to sweat. It was soon over. Now she looked exactly as he had seen her at first, her forehead sleek as a child's, her eyes blue, her chin coming to a slight point.

'Like this?' she said.

'Yes,' said Duncan, and he kissed her. It took all his courage, but his love came rushing willingly, helplessly in, like the sea.

'All right,' Marania said. 'I'll try.' Then she stood and said softly, 'I'll go first,' as though there were a guard on the park, or somebody to be deceived. 'Till Thursday,' she said, and slipped away into the clotting darkness in Lulu's dress. It looked too big for her.

Reeling, Duncan went home. He told his mum he had a headache, and went straight to bed and slept for twelve hours. When he woke he wanted to shriek his secret from the rooftops. Instead he went running around here and there all week, talking excitedly about nothing and nursing the pride that billowed in his chest. His mother looked at him curiously, an anxious smile never far from her lips. Twice she felt his forehead for a temperature.

'I've got a girlfriend,' he wanted to tell her. But he could not tell anyone. He remembered his old daydreams of being a secret agent on an undercover operation, and he watched everyone he met to see if they too might be not human. He kept finding reasons to go past the park and just look in, in case Marania was there. She never was.

Thursday came and went, with never a sign. Duncan, who had been abstaining, masturbated ferociously all night, and later wept. She did not come the next day. All weekend, she did not come.

On Monday morning Duncan took the train to London. He liked going to London, though he couldn't afford to do it often, not as often as he'd have liked. He found comfort in the anonymity it conferred, the fact that no one knew who you were, or cared. In London, sooner or later, Duncan always ended up in Soho. This time he went straight there. For hours he roamed its crooked, confusing thoroughfares in a kind of frenzied daze. Here, they had whole shops full of sex mags. They had packs of black and white photos sealed in Cellophane bags: ordinary women, young housewives, posing in their underwear, getting out their breasts. In a public toilet Duncan paid them his tribute, with the hissing of the cisterns and the echoing scuffle of men's feet on the concrete floor for accompaniment.

On Tuesday, Duncan stayed at home and did some reading for the next term. On Wednesday he had to go out to the library, and do some shopping for his mum. Within minutes he met Marania, coming out of a clothes shop. She was with some boys, older than him. They looked Arabic, Duncan thought, or Italian. Marania stood with her feet apart and swung her handbag in front of her with both hands. 'Hallo, Duncan,' she said, happily.

'Hallo, Marania,' he said, as coldly as he could. He looked at her companions, wondering if she was going to introduce him. They put their heads back and looked at him.

'What happened on Thursday, then?' Duncan asked. It came out pitched rather high.

Marania considered. She rolled her eyes up and opened her mouth slightly, and ran the tip of her tongue around her teeth while she consulted her memory. Then she said, archly, 'You wouldn't believe me if I told you.'

For some reason the very phrase made Duncan angry. She was taunting him. She thought he was so innocent she could lead him by the nose. He had heard that some girls liked to try to do that.

Duncan put out his hand and took her by the sleeve. Instantly her brothers, or her bodyguard, or whoever they were, were standing around him in a crowd with their hands in their pockets.

Duncan ignored them. 'I've got to talk to you,' he said to Marania.

'Tomorrow,' she said.

'No, now,' said Duncan.

Marania moved her chin in a strange oval motion, flexing her shoulders like a cat. She looked at her companions. One of them said something terse in a foreign language. Marania gave him the smallest shake of her head, and a sweet smile. Then they turned and vanished, melting away into the crowd of passing shoppers before Duncan could see where they went.

She hugged him. For the first time it didn't thrill him.

He wanted to punish her for letting him down, and himself for going to Soho. Everything was going wrong. Duncan became utterly miserable. Everything was spoiled. They walked aimlessly through the streets.

'I think I'm going mad,' he said. 'I keep thinking I see you. Why didn't you *come*?' he said angrily, and his eyes filled with tears.

She stroked his cheek and down under his jaw, with the tips of her fingers. 'I'm here now,' she said, and put an arm around his back.

Duncan ignored it. 'I don't understand you!' he said. 'Are you trying to drive me mad?'

At one point he had her pinned against a wall, not touching her, but standing in front of her with his arms propped either side of her shoulders. He was demanding she change her face again. She wouldn't. She stood there with her hands folded, and a distant, insouciant expression.

Dimly Duncan knew he should have left her some while ago, but he found himself stuck. He couldn't leave without getting something said, but he couldn't seem to say it. 'What are you, then,' he demanded sullenly, 'if you're not human? I don't know what you are,' he said. 'I don't think you do either.'

She changed then, her face becoming harder and more lined. 'Oh yes we do,' she said, her voice suddenly grown very deep; and she laughed.

More miserable than ever, Duncan had hit her before he knew it. He had raised his hand and slapped her deceiving face. She looked straight at him, mute and level. By mistake or on purpose she had turned towards the blow, and his hand had split her lip. Duncan felt very detached from it all. He knew he was being cold and cruel. He watched himself thinking he could get out a handkerchief for her and deciding not to. Horrified, he put his hands to the side of his head, his fingers rigid, and started to grizzle.

Marania dragged him firmly into a shop doorway and stood there with him, shielding him from the street with her body, hugging him hard. 'You don't have to be so impatient,' she said. 'There's lots of time.'

She was speaking in an easy, matter-of-fact way, as if he had never hit her, as if he had hallucinated it. Duncan knew that in a moment it would be as if it had never happened at all. She would never acknowledge he had hurt her, and that he could not bear. 'I can't stand it!' he protested, sobbing.

'Be valiant, Sir Knight,' she said. 'Be strong. Be at the park at six o'clock.' She wiped her mouth and kissed him, fitting her mouth precisely to his. By the time he looked at it, her lip was healed. There was no mark there at all.

Wretchedly he trailed home, with no heart for the errand he was on, or hope for the assignation to come. He hated himself for hitting her. Should he even go at six? Was there any point? Even if she did turn up, all they could do was hurt each other. What sort of girl-friend could she be? Did he love her at all, any more, really? He simply didn't know.

Boys at school had girlfriends. They kicked footballs for their approval, or felt them up in empty classrooms. Duncan didn't want to be the one who was different, who had a girlfriend he couldn't even tell anyone about. Couldn't, even if there was anyone who'd believe him. For her sake. 'People get very frightened and hunt us down,' she had said, very positively. 'It's happened before, it'll happen again.'

While the clock struck six Duncan stood alone on the steps with his hands in his pockets, looking into the de-serted park. It was just coming on to rain. Witches, he thought. Werewolves. *Doppelgängers*. Gypsies. You could see them everywhere, apparently, fiends in human shape, once you started to look for them.

Marania wasn't in the park, though.

Then she was. She was standing behind the sundial; she'd been there all along and he hadn't seen her. He wondered if they could make themselves invisible too.

Smiling despite himself, Duncan started up the path towards her. He felt ashamed of the way he'd treated her earlier. He loved her, that was all. She must know that. She must forgive him.

It started well, with a kiss. He put his arms around her neck and Marania rested her hands on his ribs for a while. Then convulsively she slipped them around his back and pressed her body to his. She teased his tongue into her mouth and sucked it. He had to come up for air. He pulled back his head and arched his back as he hugged her hard. He saw she was wearing the same clothes as she'd had on that morning, black calf boots and a short black raincoat. The coat was buttoned up to the neck, the collar turned up.

Duncan shivered. Rain splashed on his ears and his neck. 'Raining,' he said, nervously.

'Good for you,' she said, slyly. 'Make you grow.' Then she put her hand most decisively on the back of his head, and her tongue in his mouth.

His hands explored her body, tentatively at first, then desperately. The coat was thick and muffled everything. He remembered her in her jacket and miniskirt. At the same time he remembered every picture he had ever seen in a sex mag, the bodies of a thousand women flickering black and white in the cinema of his mind. Would Marania be wearing a suspender belt? If she would be Lulu for him, what else might she not do?

'On Thursday I went to visit my aunt in hospital,'

Marania said, slowly, emerging from the kiss. In her mouth an utterly banal excuse could sound insulting, provocative, and maddeningly sexy, all at the same time. Duncan tried to stop her; he didn't want to think about Thursday. But Marania continued.

'She's not ill. She just lives there, in the hospital. She imitates one disease after another, just to keep them happy. Sometimes she does several at once. When anyone begins to get suspicious, she goes to another ward and pretends to be someone else. I pay her visits: kin visits and courtesy visits, but sometimes just visits.'

She slipped out of Duncan's embrace, took his hand firmly in her own, and walked him slowly down the path to a bench. It was not the nearest bench. It was the bench where they had first met.

'While I was there on Thursday at the hospital, a cord assassin from a Chaos flank caucus came in and tried to kill my aunt. She's not really my aunt, but that's the closest word you have. People are always trying to kill her. I had to grab this one and kneel on him until the nurses came with some reinforcements. The nurses went back to work, convinced a doctor had taken charge. Then we took the assassin to a place we go to, by the river,' she said, and she was coy suddenly, avoiding his eyes as they sat down, though sitting close to him. 'We read him his future in his own entrails.'

Her voice was soft and silky, and her breath steamed slightly in the cold wet air. She extended a gloved forefinger and ran it down his arm.

'I told you you wouldn't believe me,' she said.

Duncan could have made any effort she asked of him. Truth, madness, he didn't care, it made no difference what it was. Like spies, he thought. 'Are they trying to kill you?' he asked.

She raised her eyebrows and tilted her head to one side. 'Goodness me,' she said. 'Listen to him. Are they trying to kill me?' she repeated, and chuckled, shaking her head, dismissing his question. Duncan simply couldn't tell whether she meant they weren't trying to kill her, these Chaos assassins, whoever they were; or whether she meant it was all too much to explain.

He tried to kiss her again, and found her eager. This at least was true, this moist, mutual searching. What was more, it was beginning to be nice. And it might be snatched away any moment, if Marania was running true to form, so Duncan determined to put scruples aside and take advantage.

In a while they separated again. It was still raining, Duncan realized. There were raindrops on her face, tiny ones in her eyelashes. Her face was so clear, even in the clouded evening. She moved aside from him, shifting around three-quarters on the bench, with one foot on the ground. She pulled the little finger of her right-hand glove. Then she pulled the thumb. Then she pulled each of the fingers in between, and slid the glove off her hand, and gave it to him. Duncan held it. He put it in his lap. It held the shape of her hand for an instant, then seemed to sag. Marania was taking off the other one.

'Perhaps you are a Chaos assassin,' she said. 'Perhaps you are just pretending to be so – fixed.' And she pressed her hand to the crotch of his trousers, her fingers going straight to the tender underside of his erection. Duncan gasped, a fountain of silver light shooting up into his brain.

'So rigid,' said Marania, in a low voice curling with satisfaction. She withdrew her hand, and stood before him.

Her raincoat had three big buttons. She opened the

top one, the middle one, the bottom one. She flipped open the coat. She had nothing on underneath.

And she looked just as Duncan had always known she would look, just as he had imagined her in the solitude of his bed at night, firm uptilted breasts, flat stomach, the junction of her thighs a soft dark blur, a shadow of the encroaching night.

She sat him back on the bench, undoing his own coat, then pressing his chest lightly with one hand while opening his belt with the other. Duncan could smell the musk of her body, sweet as fresh bread, rich as the smell of mushrooms. She unzipped him, released his tingling cock into her hand. Her hand was very warm. She bent and kissed the end of his cock, as if she was blessing it; and she licked it lightly with the very tip of her tongue. It kicked in her hand.

'My valiant captain!' she said, fervently, as she straddled him.

Clasping her hips beneath her coat Duncan threw back his head and gasped. Rain fell in his mouth.

She moved on him, on the bench, holding his chin in her cupped hands, muttering aloud in a wiry, whistling language of her own. She kissed him all over his face. She was lithe and he was clumsy. Her muscles moved keenly under his hands, stretched and settled, stretched and settled.

He had thought, or feared, that if it ever finally truly actually happened he would come at once; but now that it was happening, happening, continuing, his climax seemed altogether remote, uncertain. The turmoil in his nerves, the friction of skin on skin, set his body stirring in a new and mysterious way, quite unlike anything he had managed on his own. But while Marania's moans and grunts grew more complicated and urgent, he felt no certainty he was ascending the gradient of his own release.

Photos of women cascaded in his mind again, and more dramatic images of his own, real little scenes, brightly lit, like excerpts from dreams. Girls he had seen in the library, Marania herself, in postures even more lewd than her present one. Duncan's erection hardened. Marania towered over him, ducking her head and sucking wetly at his neck. Blinded by her hair, he lost his way again. He lifted his hands to her neck, and felt it curving backwards from her spine. At that instant she reached her climax with a wild, high, breaking hoot of pleasure and despair.

They came then, gliding across the grass, her brothers, out of the shrubbery to reclaim her. Brothers, sisters, it was hard to tell. They still looked like people, except for their faces, which were long and pouchy, like the faces of fish. One of them threw back its head and pawed the air with its hand, crying in the same key as Marania, in a voice between whine of dog and yowl of cat. They stood in a semicircle on the grass and summoned their sister.

She slipped from Duncan's lap, brushing her hair out of her eyes. His cock felt cool and wet suddenly, shrinking swiftly. Marania kissed him quickly but tenderly on the mouth, and briskly slapped his cheek with her upright palm, a bizarre kind of salute. Then she went away with them, buttoning her raincoat. They paid no attention to him at all.

Duncan zipped up his trousers and straightened his clothes. Then he went up into the street and followed them. One of them saw him, and they flowed away up a side-alley, vanishing into the back gardens as quickly as they had that morning among the crowd of shoppers. It didn't matter. Duncan had remembered the number of the bus. He rode, following landmarks until he reached the stop where she had got off before, then walked, uncertain at first and then more and more quickly, until he came to the dead-end-street. The rain had left off some time before, but the street was deserted. Yellow lights glowed behind the curtains, moving here and there as if someone were carrying them around.

Duncan came to the door he had seen Marania open. It was an ordinary front door, four panels, painted dull green a long time ago. It had a combined letter-box and knocker in pitted chrome. Duncan knocked. There was a scurrying, slithering sound beyond, and then complete silence. Out of the corner of his eye Duncan saw the front window curtain twitch. He kept his eyes on the door. It opened, by and by. A thin man with long grey hair stood there, wearing a greasy suit.

'I want to see Marania,' said Duncan.

The man stared at him, dully. He looked over his shoulder as if for someone to consult, but there was no one behind him. He wiped his hand down his unshaven cheek and his lips moved inarticulately. He looked behind him again, this time over the other shoulder. Then he looked at Duncan, resentfully, Duncan thought.

'You can come in,' he said, as though it was Duncan who was delaying.

The house smelled of spicy cooking, and beneath that of something acrid, like a blocked toilet. The hall was filthy. Breathing through his mouth, Duncan stepped inside past the grey man, who closed the door.

A large hairy animal had come nosing into the hall from somewhere. Duncan supposed it was a dog. He didn't know much about dogs. When this one moved, suddenly, Duncan thought perhaps it had too many legs. He pressed himself against the wall, and followed his conductor. They went into the living-room.

That was what it was, presumably, though it was not

like any living-room Duncan had ever seen. It was dark and airless, cheap curtains taped shut across the window. Long scrolls of waxy yellow paper, illegible writing and small black shapes all over them, had been hung from the picture rail, and nets of herbs from the ceiling. There was obviously some furniture in the room, but it was difficult to say exactly what kinds because of the great number of its occupants.

They were all ages, it seemed, including one that was a babe in arms. Some looked like people, in ordinary clothes, and some like bald apes, and some of the apes looked like the fish-headed people that had taken Marania from the park. There were more big hairy dogs. The fireplace had been half demolished, but there was a fire in it anyway. The room was as hot and steamy as an oven, and smelled like a bonfire in an elephant house. There was straw and old food trodden underfoot, and young ones playing in it. In the corner beside the door, bizarrely, was a TV set, on spindly legs with a two-pronged aerial on top. It was turned up quite loud, tuned to a quiz game where the audience laughed when a man banged a gong. Duncan's family hadn't got a TV, so he didn't recognize the programme. In any case, no one was watching it.

Most of the eyes in the room were watching him.

The rest were turned towards a towering, bulky figure who was, if anyone was, the centre of the gathering. She – Duncan knew for certain it was female, though afterwards he could never think how he knew – was sitting by the fire with a frame of beads and knotted string propped on her lap. Her great thick body was wrapped in shawls and draped in sheets, her heavy head wreathed in a grubby turban, sparse white hair escaping from its folds. After everyone else, she too turned to look at the newcomer.

She no longer looked like a woman, though presumably she had resembled many in her time. She did
not look much like an ape or a fish. She looked more
like a giant lizard. What he could see of her face and
hands was blackened leather. Her skin was thick and
quilted like a crocodile's, creased into a million folds.
Her eyes were huge, big as drawer knobs, with no
white to them at all. When she looked at Duncan, he
knew she could see everything, everything and everyone
there had ever been in the world. She was the hidden
one; there was no hiding from her.

Gasping for breath in the stifling den, Duncan looked
round for the grey man, to let him out again at once,
but he could not see him there. He looked for Marania,
looked all around for her. There was no one in the room
he recognized. No one at all.

Duncan broke for the door and they let him go. He
never knew why. He never knew why they did not lay
hands on him and do away with him there and then.
They had no reason to trust him. Perhaps they did not
realize he was a human. (Duncan thought of the Old
One, and remembered her eyes, and felt this speculation
wither away.) Perhaps, whatever Marania said, they
were not hostile. Perhaps she herself had meant him no
harm.

But he never saw her again. He never looked for her.
He left her house (if indeed that was her house), and
didn't try to find it again. And though he lived in the
town all his life, he never again set foot in the little
park at the place where the houses had been knocked
down. He went to work or stayed at home, in all
weathers, and rarely went up to London for the day.

He turned it all over in his mind a good deal, through
the years. He never spoke about it to anyone, never a
word; and whenever he saw anything that made him

think they were near, that he was even, perhaps, talking to one, he would sit tight and say nothing and, at the first convenient opportunity, leave. He often thought what he would have said, though, if he had ever been put into the position of having to say something. How, Duncan would have said, could he ever have trusted her? Perhaps she had been in that hellish room when he came in, and said nothing to rescue him while he stood there sweating and twitching, in terror of his life; or perhaps she had not. And he would see again the way her companions had embraced her as they went out of the park – or had they been restraining her, taking her prisoner? He could never decide.

As time went by, there were other women, inevitably, who wished to associate themselves with him. Duncan did not encourage them, and none of them stuck, particularly. They could so easily have been her. Each of them could have been her. He could have let himself go too far with one and only then discover. It was unlikely, he supposed, as he turned out his bedside light, but then again, how on earth could you be sure?

DEEP IN THE NATIVE LAND

Michael Ibeji

When she dug the tunnels, her hair was still brown.
Today her head is white as snow . . .
The partridge in the night cries out the love of the
* native land.*
The Mother, she digs her galleries, defences,
Protecting each step of her children.
Immeasurable is our native land.
The enemy must drive his probes in everywhere.
Your unfathomable entrails, Mother,
Hide whole divisions under this land.
The dark tunnels make their own light . . .
Immeasurable is our native land.
Your entrails, Mother, are unfathomable.

Excerpts from *The Mother – The Native Land*
by Duong Huong Ly: translated by T. Mangold
and J. Penycate.

PHU MY HUNG, SOUTH VIETNAM, 13 AUGUST
1968   At 10.30 hours, Company A of the 1st Infantry
Division (The Big Red One), on an extended sweep north
of the Ho Bo Woods, was ambushed and engaged by an
unknown number of Vietcong. Initial contact revealed
the presence of a tunnel complex in the vicinity and,
accordingly, the area was secured while Diehard Six of
the 1st Engineer Battalion was notified. Alpha squad
was immediately dispatched into the area. Initial attempts to enter the complex at 12.45 hours resulted in
the wounding of Private Robert Barr, establishing that
the tunnels were 'hot'. Sgt. Pete Rivero volunteered to

take point, and began to probe the tunnel complex at 13.25 hours. At 14.07 hours, Sgt. Rivero encountered enemy within the complex, and was mortally wounded. When the other members of the squad went to his aid, they were caught underground in a grenade blast, killing two members of the team, and wounding the third, Private Dick Seward. After their bodies had been recovered, CS gas was pumped into the complex, denying its use to the enemy.

The After Action report stank. *Non gratum anus rodentum* in the words of the Tunnel Rats' own motto: not worth a rat's ass. Any veteran Rat could tell you that CS gas was useless in those tunnels, and I wasn't one hundred per cent convinced that all the bodies had been recovered. That's why I was in Rocket City talking to the survivor, Dick Seward, while the gooks outside the perimeter treated us to a pretty fireworks display and demonstrated how Lai Khe base got its nickname. They tell me that prior to Tet the base had endured over a hundred rocket attacks per day.

Seward was lanky for a Tunnel Rat, stretched out on the hospital bunk to a length of about five-eight, but he had the wizard's touch with explosives. I'd memorized his resumé, and it read like something out of the movies. The guy'd been blown out of more holes than Elmer Fudd, but if Bugs Bunny had ever gone up against him we'd be eating rabbit stew. He once lit the fuse on 300 pounds of explosive underground with a cigar, then calmly told his commander they had sixty seconds to get out before it turned them into ketchup. The blast had blown them out of the hole like corks out of a bottle, rupturing both his commander's eardrums, but leaving Seward with nothing but scratches. Where explosives were concerned, Dick Seward led a charmed life. That's why they kept him in the Tunnel Rats.

'So tell me about it,' I said, as another rocket made like the Fourth of July outside. 'How'd you get hit?'

I was a Special Forces Investigator, attached to Military Intelligence. I'd just returned from a tour up river, chasing some motherfucker who'd been sent after some gook general and had never come back. I could have told Pendleton what had happened even before I went up there, and saved myself a whole lot of hassle. Set a psycho to kill a psycho, and the best you'll get is one rogue psycho. Our agent had gone native, completely over the edge. I'd had to dig him out of his hole and kill him. He'd been falling apart long before he logged that mission, and he should never have been sent in the first place. I swear Pendleton's got worse since we transferred into Military Intelligence.

Pendleton's my boss, and he was turning into a bureaucratic asshole. Basically, he was losing touch. He was so far removed from the war on the ground, that he failed to realize what it was doing to his operatives. That was fatal.

He sat behind that big mahogany desk of his, with his hands steepled over his paunch, and he said: 'So, Arnold, what do you make of the report?'

I hate being called Arnold. Call me Ferret, call me Arnie, call me Lt Gertz, but don't call me Arnold, unless you're a fat rear-echelon motherfucker called Pendleton who's just about to land another pile of shit on my poor, unsuspecting head.

'Reads like something out of a textbook,' I said, ' "How Not to Go Ratting in One Easy Lesson." You ask me, the gooks are still down there, and they haven't even been mussed.' I tossed the report back on to his desk, already memorized. 'So what is it you haven't told me?'

Pendleton let a smile crease his fat lips. 'Very astute,

Arnold. That is why I am assigning you to this case. I need your quick mind, and your obvious abilities. You might like to cast your eyes over this.'

'This' turned out to be the transcript of a Hoi Chan debrief taken two days after the events described in the After Action report. Some gook had defected, claiming to come from the very complex that had been hit, burbling some crap about a *raksasa* and begging for asylum.

Pendleton was looking supercilious. He was beginning to get on my nerves. Recently, he'd got a big 'Need to Know' kick, which meant that screwing decent information out of him was like getting a gook peasant to give a straight answer. I, for one, had had enough.

'Look,' I snapped, 'why don't you cut the crap, and tell me what all this is about? Then, maybe, I can start doing my job.'

'Do you know what a *raksasa* is, Arnold?' he asked.

'No.'

'It is a piece of Eastern mythology: a jaguar spirit conjured by the soul of a great warrior who is unjustly killed. It seeks vengeance on those who have slain him.'

'And this Hoi Chan convert wants us to protect him from one, right?'

'Correct, Arnold. Specifically, he wants us to save him from the wrath of a *raksasa* which is haunting the Phu My Hung complex, and according to his testimony has already killed his cell commissar.'

'Oh brilliant,' I said, 'another fucking weird case.'

'I couldn't have put it better myself,' smiled Pendleton.

So here I was, dodging rockets in the base camp of the 1st Engineer Battalion, Tunnel Rats, talking to a loony who thought it was a big joke that he'd just been blown out of yet another hole with nothing but mild concussion, while his buddies had been turned into Jello.

'It was Barr's turn to go point,' he told me, 'so we lowered him down the hole, and all of a sudden he started kicking and screaming, and thrashing about on the rope like there was no tomorrow, and we tried to pull him up, but he wouldn't come, and he started screaming even louder. Then, suddenly, the screaming stopped. Charlie must have been waiting there for him at the bottom of the shaft, with a big bamboo spear which he shoved through his groin, pinning him to the wall. We couldn't drop grenades down there, for fear of hitting Barr, but we couldn't pull him back up without sending somebody else down first to cut him loose. And of course, Charlie was probably still waiting at the bottom. Well, that didn't bother Ratman . . .'

I interrupted. 'Ratman? That's Sergeant Rivero's nickname, right?'

'Yeah, that's right. The Ratman, he lived to go down those holes. There was nothing he liked better than a hot hole. When he got the smell of a VC down there, he just came apart at the seams. He'd start growling and giggling, and jumping up and down, all jittery until he got down there, and then he'd just go still. Fucking strange. He used to smell 'em. He'd just sit there for a while, and get accustomed to the tunnel, then he'd go after 'em. Hated torches, reckoned they made you a sitting target, can't say I blame him. We worked out a system where he'd sneak on ahead, one bend in front of us, and we'd follow behind making as much racket as we could. The noise would distract Charlie and cover the Ratman's approach, and he'd sniff 'em out and take 'em by surprise. He was damn good at it.'

I knew the feeling. I'd been a Tunnel Rat once, before they transferred me into SPEFINT. You could smell

Charlie down in those tunnels. You could smell his sweat, his urine, and his breath: and he could smell you too, taste the scent of fear borne on the carbolic tang of your soap. I stopped washing when our team was on call. There were times, down in those dark holes, when you could feel the flutter of his eyelid, and the two of you would stare at one another, face to face over the eternal gulf of the dark, and you knew he was there, and he knew you knew. Those ones you left alone. You edged back out, and you told them the tunnel was cold, and you lay awake at night, because in your nightmares he grinned at you as he squeezed the trigger.

'You OK, Lieutenant?' Seward was looking at me oddly.

I nodded. 'So the Sergeant went down the hole and freed Barr,' I said. 'What happened next?'

'Well, the Ratman, he refused to come back up,' said Seward. 'He just sat there in the dark and waited till we was ready. He was like that. When he knew Charlie was near by, he got real strange.'

'How long did it take to get Barr out?' I asked.

''Bout half an hour. The Ratman freed the stake and did what he could down there, but he couldn't take the stake out, so we had to lift Barr out real slow. By the time we got him to the surface, he'd lost so much blood, there wasn't much hope for him.'

'I doubt there was much anyway,' I mused. 'The Sergeant didn't encounter the gook down there straight away, then?'

'No. Charlie was long gone. He'd fallen back to his second position. That was the problem. When we finally followed him up, he was waiting.'

Weren't they always? I let Seward continue.

'We were doing everything by the book. Our book. It had worked before, so why shouldn't it work again?

The Ratman snuck ahead, as always, and we followed up, firing volleys at the floor with our pistols, and generally making as much ruckus as we could. I was third man, with the demos. Jim Thornton and Jerry Ellis were up ahead, which was lucky for me. All of a sudden, we hears this terrible scream, like a howl, coming from up in front, and we reckon that the Ratman's hit trouble.'

'This scream. Was it human? Did the Sergeant make it?'

Seward eyed me strangely. Fair enough, it was a strange question. 'Hell, damned if I know,' he said. 'It could've been coming from the Devil hisself for all I care. It just came echoing down the tunnel, and it was chased by this crunching and gurgling, and soft, squidgy sounds that bounced along the walls. It weren't very nice, scared the shits out of me.'

'What happened?'

'Looks like the Ratman got careless. He found a trap-door going up, and he must not have smelled Charlie through it, 'cos he stuck his head through the hole, and Charlie threaded another bamboo stake through his neck. He was hanging there, with his legs kicking, when we reached him, and just as we got there, Charlie rolled a grenade down through the trapdoor and blew the whole thing to shit.' He grinned. 'Lucky for me Elly and the Thorn was in the way, 'cos they took all the frags and the blast just shunted me ass backwards along the shaft. Me and the blow, we got an understanding. I give it a good time once in a while, and in return, it don't frag me. You dig?'

Like I say, the guy was a fucking loony, thought explosives talked to him. Apart from that, the last bit of his statement didn't add up. 'Did you say the Sergeant got caught by the old trapdoor trick?'

Seward sat up, his frog-like face jaundiced in the

pale lamplight. 'Yeah, looks that way. Not that I could tell that much. Elly and the Thorn was in the way mostly, all I could see was his legs, kicking and jerking through that hole. When I crawled back after the blow, they was all spread over the tunnel walls, and there weren't much left to see. You could've put what was left into a Willy-Pete bag.'

I could imagine it. In the confined space of the tunnels, the explosive force of a grenade gets concentrated, bouncing off the walls and ripping anyone in the centre of the blast to shreds. I'd seen it myself. I'd scraped more than one man off the walls in my time. The bags they kept white phosphorus smoke-powder in were little larger than a small satchel, but you really could pack the remains of a tunnel-blasted Rat into one. How Seward had escaped the blast, I didn't know, any more than I knew how Sergeant Pete Rivero, better known as Ratman, an experienced Tunnel Rat with over two tours' experience, had got himself pig-stuck by the oldest trick in Charlie's book.

Unfortunately, I could think of only one way to find out.

I woke up. It was night. The malformed moon hung bright in the sky, shining the colour of pus. It hurt my eyes. They would be all right down in the tunnels. Nothing moved. I didn't expect it to.

The Hoi Chan defector's statement had said the tunnels were cold, abandoned by him and his buddies once they realized a *raksasa* was in there. The Big Red One had avenged the attack on its Rat squad in the usual subtle manner, and bombed Phu My Hung into oblivion, not leaving so much as a blade of grass standing. I wasn't expecting company. Nevertheless, I'd been here five days and nights, waiting, watching, making sure no slit-faced little gooks were still hanging around. I hated going back into those tunnels. Out here on my own, unloved and unsupported, I wanted to be damn sure I had nothing but a folk memory to face down there.

It was clean. Nothing was moving. Charlie usually came out at night, to take a dump, to cook, gather food and generally get some fresh air that hadn't been breathed by at least three people already. I'd sprinkled talcum powder around the entrance, an old trick just to make sure, but no footprints had sullied it in the last four nights, so I was pretty certain the complex was cold.

The entrance had been easy to find. Usually they were a bitch: you could be within three feet of one and still not know where it was. You knew it was there because of all the frigging booby traps in the area, the gooks liked to protect their tunnel entrances, but finding the sucker was like looking for a clean whore in Saigon. However, this entrance had been blown off its hinges by the Big Red One, and the gooks' hasty repair job gave it away. The signs were obvious to anyone with experience. The stand of bamboo which camouflaged it had been newly planted, and was just a little too regular, a little too well-ordered to have occurred naturally. That was lucky.

I'd already located the booby traps and worked out my route. It went over a punji pit to the left of the trapdoor, one of those nasty little foot-sized ones with half the barbs pointing downwards so you couldn't pull your foot back out. It had been smeared with festering shit just to make it more interesting. This put me in position to dismantle the tripped crossbow set to go off when you lifted the trapdoor. Then I could lower myself into the hole.

It was pitch black down there, but like Ratman Rivero, I don't believe in torches. Even if you hold them as far from your body as you can, they still give the gooks too much to shoot at. I keep one handy, in case I need to dismantle a booby trap or come across something interesting, but down here in the entrails of Mother Earth, I rely on smell and touch and hearing honed to perfection. What they can't tell me is going to kill me anyway.

I was sweating already, as much through overheating as through fear. I'd taped down all the orifices of my clothing with masking tape, to keep out the fire ants. You couldn't keep out the Chiggers, invisible little bastards that got under your skin just by touching you and itched like shit, but you could keep out the fire ants and all the other creepy-crawlies that infested these tunnels. It was an uncomfortable way to do it, but not nearly as painful as having an ant nibbling at your crotch.

It was foul down there. It smelled of mud and shit and death and rotting things. You forgot what it was like, up there in the clean air of the jungle, where the smell of blood and napalm mingled with the scent of wood-smoke and the tang of cordite. Down here in the tunnels, the stench literally took your breath away. You just had to sit and wait while your nose got used to the olfactory war that was being waged against it and began to filter out the natural odours, making room for the dangerous ones that told you death was waiting round the corner. In a bad tunnel, it could take you forty minutes or more, just sitting still, your eyes watering, trying not to choke.

Eventually, I moved on.

The tunnel wove through the earth like the ripple of an anaconda. I counted the turns off in my memory: one left, one right, two left, two right, three left, and so on. The tunnels twist so much that ordinary grunts like Seward just take it for granted and ignore it, but I like to have some idea of how far I've come. Even with my memory, I didn't know where I was in relation to the surface. Down there in the dark, you lose all sense of direction. You just put one knee in front of the other, slide your hand along the earth, up the walls, across the roof, breathe a sigh of relief when you don't find anything, and repeat the process again and again and again.

I smelled it before I heard it. I could taste it on the air. A rat. It was sitting round the corner, malevolent, waiting. I eased my torch into my left hand, wrapping my fingers around it, and slid up to the bend as softly as I could. It let out a screech of fury when I flicked the beam on, rearing back on its haunches and punching the air, slavering teeth bared under an agitated snout. Its eyes were bright points of glistening yellow, darting to and fro as it strained towards me, pulling on its leash.

It was attached to the wall by a length of wire extending from a bamboo tube, and was completely blocking the passage. We had all heard rumours of plague-infected rats used to guard the tunnels. The story goes that the Tropic Lightning Division found an underground laboratory where the gooks had been infecting the critters. I wasn't going anywhere near that thing, but I didn't want to shoot it. The complex may have been abandoned by the gooks, but I didn't want to alert whatever they had left behind. I began searching the earth around me. The gooks had to have some way of getting round the thing, and the bamboo tube suggested that the leash could be retracted, pinning the rat against the wall.

I found the loop in the ceiling, but I wasn't stupid enough to pull it without checking it out first. Sure enough, those gooks had been double sneaky. The wire was set to trip a box trap, dropping a nest of scorpions on top of your head if you didn't insert a safety pin first. I set the pin, but I still wasn't taking any chances. I fixed a length of wire from my own supply to the loop, and played it round the corner before I pulled. There was no bang, no snap of sharp stakes, no thud of a crossbow or hiss of a deadly snake. I hadn't really expected one, but you didn't stay alive down there without being paranoid.

The rat had been pulled back to the tube, held there by the neck. I slid up to it, keeping the wire taut. It was still struggling to get at me when my knife nailed it to the wall, spilling its guts all over the floor.

I probed the area very carefully. I figured the gooks weren't going to go to all that trouble unless they had something to protect. I was right. I noticed it first because of the gouges in the floor. The rat couldn't have made those, no matter how big it was. Something had been here before me. Something big and mean which had torn at the earth with long, sharp tools. I shuddered, thinking of jaguars, but it could just as easily have been made with a knife.

It had exposed a trapdoor. Some attempt had been made to conceal it again, presumably by the gooks, and it would have passed any but the most rigorous examination: but it was there, bevelled into the floor, the sort you lifted with a finger and swivelled sideways. I checked it with a fine toothcomb. There had been a trap, a sneaky little trick with a one-step snake inserted into the most obvious fingerhole. They called them one-step snakes because that's about as far as you got after it bit you before you died. Someone, something, had slit its head open with a razor. The real fingerhole was more carefully hidden on the opposite side of the trapdoor.

On a hunch, I checked the rat-trap before I opened the trapdoor. Sure enough, there was an old bloodstain on the wall. Somebody, presumably Sergeant Rivero, had found this trap before me. The gooks had reset it since, replacing the dead rat with a new one. Presumably they did it during their clean-up, just before they found out about the *raksasa* and abandoned the complex.

I opened the trapdoor, and immediately wished I hadn't.

A wave of fetid air rushed out at me, dark and musty, carrying whispers on the wind, promises of death and torture, sinister secrets shared in a sea of pain. I slammed the door and sat on it, shivering violently. I knew what was down there. I'd been into tunnels like that before, the lower levels, where the ones who waited for you didn't blink, and fed on your fear, reeling you in until you were right on top of them and there was no escape but death: yours or theirs.

I would have to go down there. I knew I would. The gooks had protected that entrance with three different kinds of trap, so it was damned important to them. It was bound to hold the answers I was looking for, but I sure as hell wasn't going down there until I really had to.

I moved on, looking for any excuse to avoid going back to that hole. Two bends further on, I found the place where Ratman Rivero had been ambushed.

It was a small hole in the ceiling surrounded by tree roots. It probably led up to a spider hole; a marksman's firing-post overlooking the dead zone around the main tunnel entrance. The corridor carried on, but I had no doubt it led to a dead end, with a trip-wire intended to make that terminal strung across it. I didn't intend to find out. I checked for signs of damage. They were everywhere. The tree roots were smashed and blood-stained, with shards of bone and metal embedded all over them. In one cranny, I found the remains of a finger which the clean-up crew had missed on the hasty evac. This was where the team had been fragged. I took a couple of deep breaths, reminding myself that they said this place was deserted, then thrust myself up and through the hole, hoping to hell there wasn't any booby trap waiting for me above.

I emerged inside a hollow tree, bathed by the slimy light of the moon. Even as I spun round, a clammy hand clamped itself on my shoulders and a ravaged face thrust its nose into mine. I went ape: screaming, yelling, blasting and crying. Its head exploded, showering me with gobbets of blood, brains and bone; and all the while it kept on batting at me with its hands, until I ran out of bullets and it stopped jerking and slumped against the inside of the bole.

The stench this close was overwhelming. In a mixture of fear and revulsion, my stomach rebelled and emptied what little it contained over the corpse in front of me. It was the upper torso of a man, what was left of it, or at least I think it was. Its head had been blown away in my panic, making it impossible to identify, but close up you could see it wore the rags of a Vietnamese peasant. Its lower chest, stomach and legs simply weren't there, leaving it balanced precariously above the hole. When I came through, I must have dislodged it, causing it to flop forward on to me, and the force of my gunshots had kept it jerking after my initial fright.

It had been there for a couple of weeks, and the bloated flesh was now sloughing off the bone and turning into a grub-feast, but enough was left to reveal the marks of violence. Someone, or something, had cut this geek up pretty bad. The remaining shreds of its lower torso were consistent with the traumatic amputation of an explosion, but the upper torso was criss-crossed by deep, diagonal slashes which had peeled open the flesh. No wonder the other gooks had thought a jaguar spirit was on the loose.

Pieces were beginning to fit together: Ratman Rivero, the trapdoor behind me, the abandoned corpse in the tree trunk. I didn't like what I was thinking. I liked it even less because I was going to have to go down into the lower levels to prove it.

It was dark and fetid and sinister in the lower levels. The air hung lifeless in the black void, magnifying every sound, so that the nervous rasp of my breath sounded like the anguished wheezing of a dying man. Up above me, the pale hole of the trapdoor, with its dead rat and its box of scorpions, looked as inviting as the door of a dust-off helicopter.

I was ready. I didn't feel it, but I was ready. My body wanted to hyperventilate, but I wouldn't let it. Clutching gun and torch in sweating hands, I began to feel my way into the gloom.

I came across the first corpse almost immediately, filling most of the passage. Playing the torch over it, I could see at once that it wasn't human. I hadn't expected it to be. It was shorter and more sinuous than most of our kind, with a fluted bone structure adapted by generations of evolution within the tunnels, yet it was unmistakably Weerde. Its oriental features had become elongated in death, with a pronounced snout and a gaping mouth arrayed with sharp canines and carnassials, and the complex muscles of its limbs had reverted to a more feline physiology. I thought of jaguars.

The gooks didn't know what they nurtured deep underground. We have been fighting a secret war against the Mothers and their servants for centuries, even before the Mongols swept into Indo-China at our behest. The Americans are simply the last of a long line of human proxies helping us to root out their enclaves before they call the Dark upon us: the last and the most dangerous.

As I squeezed past the body, I could feel its skin peel from the flesh with the friction of my passing. The odour of death was so powerful that I almost fainted, and had to close my nostrils against the smell, holding my breath till I was past.

The corridor branched, but I followed the smell of death, and the taste of the dark. I pushed past more corpses, gagging on nothing, my stomach already empty. A little further on, a vertical shaft plunged into the earth. I took it. What choice did I have?

I was crawling through a corridor so narrow I was having to shrink my shoulders, when I felt the tingle along my spine which told me I was being watched. I stopped, senses straining against the dark, and it seemed to me as if the corridor moved. The whole shaft began to seethe and bubble, hissing and scrabbling, clawing at my face and limbs and body.

In a panic I switched on the torch, shining it on to the walls in an effort to find out what they were doing. The hole seemed to be darker than any I'd ever been in before, heaving in upon itself, then pulsing outwards like an artery. For a moment I thought I was losing my mind. For a moment I thought the walls were moving in on me, collapsing around me, and I was going to be buried alive. Purple spots danced before my eyes. I thought I was asphyxiating. Then I realized they were spiders, one huge, great mass of black spiders, each as big as my thumb, each with a purple spot on their back.

I was screaming and kicking and scrabbling to get out of there, flailing desperately forwards on a sickening, slick morass of crushed spiders. If they were poisonous, they didn't bite me. But there are times when such things fail to matter. I slithered out of the hole into a rough-hewn chamber, scraping bits of broken arachnid off my skin in great handfuls.

And in the darkness, it laughed.

I froze. I could hear it close by. I could feel the hiss of its breath. I still clutched my gun, a Browning .38, anything else being too cumbersome to take into the tunnels, but I had dropped the torch. It had rolled into a corner and was shining feebly at the wall. Its pathetic light was enough, if I widened my irises to see the creature I had come to face.

Crouched in the opposite corner of the chamber was the bleached and bloated body of a Mother. It was at least three times as large as I, slumped on all fours with its massive, ridged head sloping towards me, sightless eyes bulging uselessly from their sockets. Blood congealed in multiple wounds lacerating the front of its body. Its forehead was split wide open, revealing the flaccid, engorged tissue of its brain, upon which, feeding, was its executioner.

He still wore the uniform of Sergeant Pete Rivero and retained much of his human physique. Massive claws and teeth disfigured his hands and face, clotted with the gore of the dead Mother and her children. He glared at me with wide, bug eyes and grinned a slavering grin.

'You've come,' he hissed. 'I knew you would.'

Pendleton had fucked up again. The Ratman should have been sent home when his last tour of duty ended, but instead he had been allowed to stay on and I was having to clean up the mess. Down in the tunnels, slowly changing, hunting the human scum in search of the real prize, he had found one. It had been easy to dispatch the gook in the spider hole and dangle him as bait for his American team-mates. In the gloom they hadn't been able to tell Vietnamese rags from American combat fatigues until it was too late. Once fragged, he knew they would med-evac out. He knew they would gas the hole, but by then he was in the enclave and hunting. And here, deep in the native land, he had found his prey. When I got back, Pendleton was going to die.

'Lets get this over with,' I said.

This war humanized us too much. Pendleton was corrupted by bureaucracy; his agents in the field by brutality. The Gulf of Tonkin had been a mistake. It had brought the Americans into the war as intended, but had introduced bureaucracy and brutal technology into the highly personal mixture of death and heroism that was involved in digging out the Mothers. We couldn't cope with it. One by one, us motherfuckers were going over the edge.

Set a psycho to kill a psycho, and your best result is one rogue psycho.

I shot him as he came at me, deliberately aiming for the heart. Even so, it took three bullets to slow him down. A fourth stopped him, then he started going backwards. He was on the ground, writhing horribly, refusing to shift out of his human shape. Blood frothed on his maw. His staring eyes drilled into me as he scrabbled to pull himself upright. I put a bullet into each shoulder, just to keep him down long enough to empty the rest of the magazine into his brain.

I was shaking, quivering with shock and revulsion, disgusted as much by the humanness of my reactions as by recent events. The tunnels did this to you. They

warped us all. I had to get out of them, but I didn't
have the strength.

In the unfathomable entrails of her native land, I
sank to my knees before the dead Mother, buried my
head in my hands, and cried.

IGNORANCE OF PERFECT REASON

Roz Kaveney

There are pursuits conducive of relaxation, Charlotte thought to herself, but principal among them is not making love with an over-eager female werewolf, in the back seat of a stolen White Russian army staff car, while her five sisters prowl outside, slapping arms against sides in the steely cold of the high Mongolian plain.

'If you like,' Watcher said, earnestly, 'I could do *that* . . . And then *that*.'

'Honestly,' Charlotte said, kissing her on the lips and then caressing one of Watcher's moderately prominent canines with her tongue, 'honestly, you don't need to show off to me, and I can't see how, if you are going constantly to adjust your anatomy in ingenious ways, you can possibly concentrate on the matter in, as it were, hand.'

Watcher's bodily configurations ceased to flow under Charlotte's fingers, and she turned her attention to an intensification of her hitherto rather desultory nuzzling of Charlotte's left breast, and the emission of a series of rather gratifying short gasps of pleasure.

'You know,' she gasped eventually, 'this could be the beginning of a beautiful friendship.'

Then she started more delicious licking, all too soon interrupted by a loud cough from one of the sisters. I know they disapprove, thought Charlotte, but one had hoped that the family into which I appear to have married could conduct its disapprobation with a smattering more style.

'What is it, Singer of Songs of Vengeance and Despair?' Watcher said.

'I am sorry to disturb your connubial couch,' Singer said with a toothy grin that seemed entirely to dilute the verbal apology. 'But Sojourner in the Wilderness of Truth and Starvation found something rather disturbing a little further along this miserable apology for a road. You and your human friend really ought to unrumple your clothing, and come and offer your views.'

It was not really a road, merely a flattish track on which it was, with care, possible to drive. But there was enough distinction between the road and the scrubby grass of the plain it crossed that, as they drove the car along it, headlights shining, one could clearly see reasonably fresh marks where a lorry, or perhaps it was two lorries, had driven off the road. After all they were not, it seemed, alone on the eastern road from Urga, or the first to choose this approximate location to rest for a few hours.

The marks of tyres, the crushed grass and the spent ammunition were not the disturbing things, nor the excrement half-buried under soil kicked loose. The disturbing thing was the torn corner of paper that Sojourner had spotted among the spoil. A part of the paper was still legible, and Charlotte conquered her distaste to look at it more closely.

'Attention, even to small, and even unpleasant matters,' Sojourner said, 'has been a requirement of our lives, these many years of hunting and of vengeance. And the writing is in English . . .'

'It is, indeed,' said Charlotte with a moue of fastidiousness, 'and, as you presumably surmise, it is indeed the handwriting of my murdered brother. And what is a page of his journal doing out here on the plain, so many miles from where your enemies killed him?'

'Presumably,' Watcher said, 'it is part of the contents of this lorry – or lorries.'

'It was premature to hope,' Singer said, 'that we had managed to identify and kill each and every one of Darkcalling and Chaos that was in Urga.'

'The place was a rat-hole,' said Settler of Debts and Credits, 'with too much smoke in it to see clearly to kill.'

'I thought,' Charlotte said, 'that the whole point of killing my brother was to preserve the secret of your kind's existence.'

'It may have been,' said Mourner of Kindred and Hope. 'If he had been killed by Stasis, it would have been. We of progress might have chosen to kill him for that reason, since premature disclosure might complicate our plans. But the reasoning of Chaos is inscrutable, and the Callers of the Dark have many plans, most of them sinister.'

Charlotte looked coldly at the six of them. She was not going to weaken her already low prestige by actually asking for an explanation. Watcher looked entreatingly at her sisters – how charming her eyes were when she was abashed – and then took a deep breath.

'I suppose,' she said, 'you have gathered that the pursuit of vengeance for the deaths of our parents is not merely a personal matter, but one of politics as well.'

'I gathered that in Urga, my love,' Charlotte said, 'but I will admit to a degree of real ignorance as to what the internal politics of werewolfdom might be. But I am all ears.'

'It is partly a matter of attitudes to humans,' Tracker

of Scents and Spoor said, 'and partly a matter of the Dark.'

'Why,' Charlotte said, 'do you have the tendency to give the mere absence of light the dignity of an initial capital?'

'There is this Presence, somewhere in the void between suns,' Watcher said. 'And It comes when It is called, and It comes hungry.'

Charlotte looked even more coldly at her, and raised a sceptical eyebrow.

'I know, my love.' Watcher said, sighing. 'I know what this sounds like – the very rankest of superstitions, entirely inappropriate to the beginning of the third decade of your twentieth century.'

'That is my immediate reaction,' Charlotte said, 'more or less.'

'But when you come to know my kind better,' Watcher continued, 'you will see that we are not prone to superstition, or, alas, imagination. After all, there had to be a key to all your human mythologies, and it is this. There is something out there. It is hungry. It came, once before, when It was called, in the falling of stars. It ate the minds of the First, the people we once served and still remember, and It let us be. We do not know why. And we fear, most of us, that It will come again.'

'For humanity,' Mourner said. 'And perhaps for us as well. It has been a long time. We may have changed, or Its taste may have. But stars still fall.'

'But surely,' Charlotte said, 'if there are a group of you inclined to summon this Thing, allowing for a moment the hypothesis of Its existence, logic dictates that over several million years they would have managed to kill the right virgin or virgins. Mere random gabbling should have evoked It by now, assuming It comes to a call, like a faithful dog, or pigs at feeding time.'

'It doesn't work like that,' Watcher said. 'The Callers of the Dark can't actually call It. No Weerde could, we hope; our minds smell wrong. Imagination may be part of it; and religion; and the powers of the mind.'

'They call themselves the Callers of the Dark,' Sojourner said. 'But that is a boast merely. The First called It, and perhaps humans could. That is why most factions of the Kin agree on this – that we should do everything in our power to stifle religion in humans, and the powers of the mind.'

'Your brother's discoveries were a triumph of deductive reason,' Mourner said, 'and admirable as such. But even he worried that they might be a breach through which despair and superstition might enter. Imagine the effect if a supposed Tom Matthews were to arrive, showing his discoveries with glee in the capitals of Europe, and preaching unreason.'

'In that case,' Charlotte said, 'why on earth did you sacrifice one of your siblings to an attempt to kill and impersonate me?'

'We needed a Charlotte Matthews to play against their fake Tom,' Mourner said.

'We had not realized,' Sojourner said, 'even Watcher, who had a chance to observe you, the extent to which you were a person of resource and sense.'

'It was a risk that Dancer of Shades and Half-Seen Faces took,' Singer said, 'when we decided it expedient to kill an innocent. Innocence has teeth.'

Charlotte accepted that they were trying to put her at her ease.

Mourner had been facing away from Charlotte, into a wind as keen and rough as a file. Suddenly, she raised her nose into the wind and turned. She reached into the capacious pocket of her greatcoat and tossed Charlotte a revolver – Charlotte had, in the nature of things and a moment of amorous inattention, left hers in the car. Like Watcher and her siblings, she turned outwards, raising her gun. There were shadows out there on the plain, flowing in towards the headlights like ink across a page.

The sisters looked around them with the embarrassed air of those who realize too late that they have been too busy explaining things to take normal precautions. Even at the cost of all our lives, Charlotte reflected, it is nice to see that air of effortless, superior competence punctured just this once.

There came, from the darkness beyond the headlights, a series of snarls and barks that had the sententious, sarcastic air of being language.

'Our lineage's distant cousins,' Watcher said, 'the People of the Plains.'

Into the dazzle of the headlights, shielding their eyes a little, there strutted two figures of what were obviously yet another breed of Kin, but one that disdained the convenience of clothes in favour of a lot of hair and the odd useful strap.

'They say that they want blood for their blood,' Singer explained to Charlotte, before snarling back in the slightly diffident way that in other, human languages attempts to give verisimilitude to alibis. Particularly to those unlikely to be listened to.

'He said,' Tracker explained to Charlotte, 'that, to the People of the Plains, it does not matter that the killing here two days ago was carried out by our enemies. We are all as bad as each other. The factions and their quarrels are all disturbances of the calm of the landscape. It was strangers to the High Plain that killed Grarrl, and strangers who will die for it.'

One of the two snarled; it was a snarl that had clearly been practised with the intention of producing instant, terrified compliance and involved more facial muscles than Charlotte had guessed even the Kin's face possessed. How interesting to have exhibited for one the useful arts of primitive peoples.

Singer and Mourner barked back, their faces becoming more toothy and feral. Charlotte reached across and took Watcher's hand for a moment, noticing as she did so that it was becoming harder and its fingers more claw-like.

'I take it,' Charlotte said, 'that your cousins of the Plains can be killed.'

'We are a tougher breed than you apes,' Tracker said, 'but a bullet through the eyes, or a knife through the heart, or poison in the drink or the blood will none the less usually serve.'

Suddenly there came a loud baying in the middle distance and the naked Weerde fell back, abashed.

'There is no need,' a massive and articulate voice, out in the darkness, remarked desultorily, 'for alarm. The People of the Plain know perfectly well that their companion's death was not at your hands and they are a people noted for a tediously punctilious sense of justice. They are merely hurling accusations to oblige you to do them a favour; officiously, since it is I who require the favour of you, and my place to ask it.'

Out of the darkness there loomed a face. It was inhuman in any case, and its inhumanity was all the more utter for seeming set in granite, but what took it away from humanity more than its look was its sheer size. Heads are not normally that large, or that far from the ground, Charlotte thought.

Yet it spoke English with an intonation more perfectly that of London than the all-purpose Continental Berlitz precision of Watcher and her sisters. The mere fact that it was bothering to speak English seemed to indicate a certain disingenuousness, or abnormally good hearing.

'What's that? You have a human with you, I see. Good Lord,' it continued. 'Hardly wise, some might say, but I suppose you know your own business. Quite like humans, myself, and the People are positively besotted with them. What I say is, fire was nice, but what have they done for us *lately*?'

The two hairy snarlers turned towards Charlotte, observing her properly for the first time as their eyes grew accustomed to the light, and bowed their heads in what might be shame or worship. She for her part nodded graciously, and put the revolver she was holding into the pocket of her greatcoat.

'Two lorries encountered one lorry here,' the titanic face continued. Charlotte knew that there was a body attached to it in the darkness, but did not care to consider its size or its configuration. 'And the driver of the one lorry was compelled to join with the two. They, as Mr Belloc tells us, had the Maxim gun and he had not. Unfortunately, our late companion was seen, and they managed to wound him mortally; he struggled back towards our encampment, where he might have been saved. *Dis aliter visum.*'

'The gods wished otherwise,' Charlotte explained, helpfully.

'Strange as it may seem,' Tracker said, 'in the course of our misspent youth, we too found time for a classical education.'

The face's naked companions howled into the night.

'Hang on,' Charlotte said. 'I can just about swallow you six having found time amid your vendettas for a little light Latin. I am somewhat more amazed that the giant chieftain of primitive nomads should seem so well-informed on recent light verse and the scraps of classicism.'

Watcher and the others looked at her with the nervous air of schoolgirls whose friend has whistled in church.

'He's an Ancient,' Mourner said.

'You don't cheek Ancients,' Singer said.

Ignoring them, Charlotte continued. 'Well, I don't think it disrespectful to remark that he seems rather pukka sahib for a mysterious giant werewolf encountered in the steppes of central Asia.'

'Good Lord,' the voice said, 'that's never Charlotte Matthews.'

'It is, actually,' Charlotte said.

'Dear me,' the voice said, 'little Charlotte, well I never.'

Then it barked some orders and suddenly the headlights' beams were full of the naked hairy ones, all of whom insisted on shaking hands.

'I used to be your Uncle Wilfred's friend, Saunders,' the Ancient explained.

'Uncle Saunders! But they told me that you disappeared, oh, years ago, climbing in the High Pamirs, and I cried for two nights.'

'Requirements of Empire, originally. I was playing the Great Game, though Simla were not aware on whose behalf I was playing it.'

'What happened to you?' Charlotte asked.

'Dashed inconvenient,' said the former Saunders, 'chap usually gets some warning if this Ancient thing is going to happen, but there it is. Broke my leg in several places falling off some damned precipice, went into change sleep to get over it. When I woke up, there it was – I had started to grow. I had to limp my way practically across Central Asia looking for somewhere safe to hole up. I could hardly turn up at the mess – my regiment are not noted for brains, but they would have noticed something. The People of the Plains range widely, and had heard rumours; they haven't had an Ancient of their own for a century or two, and I agreed to travel with them, for a while. One avoids humans at such times, of course nothing personal – but one is a little conspicuous.'

As he moved closer into the light, in what was something between a lope and a crouch, Charlotte had more sense of his actual size. Not as big as she at first thought, but massive none the less – squat, muscular, fat, jowled, reptilian and as animal as an Egyptian god, yet still the traveller whose tales had frightened her in the schoolroom.

He was sufficiently dominant in his hairy near-nakedness that she found herself bristling into opposition at a purely glandular level; much the same level as that at which the sisters, even, she feared, Watcher, were responding with a rather contemptible fawning and respect.

'People of the Plain,' he went on. 'Now, they're fine fellows of course, salt of the earth, noble savage sort of thing; low on amenities though. Anything more than fire or a handaxe they regard as dangerously close to Darkcalling. Bit boring too – their version of the Fifty Lives is mostly a record of cattle-trails and useful oases.'

Watcher got her nerve back. 'Charlotte,' she said, 'are you telling me that the shaman Ancient of the People of the Plain is some sort of old family friend of yours?'

The former Saunders looked at her witheringly. 'I know,' he said, 'that Progress tends to appeal to the more counter-jumping tendency among lineages. But as humans go, the Matthews are a family of real distinction.'

'Besides,' he continued, after a pause in which he tried to make his glare at once more withering and more benevolent, in a doing-this-for-your-own-good sort of way, 'as it happens, I was also a friend of your family, years ago, before the unpleasantness in Siberia.'

'You knew our parents,' said Mourner anxiously.

'I corresponded with them, occasionally,' he said. 'I was less convinced than they were that radical parties were the best vehicle for progress, and they argued that colonial empires were doomed, in the long run. And of course, on the latter question, they were probably right. I can't see the British keeping India for more than another century or so; no time at all to do anything useful.'

'Look,' Charlotte said, 'this is all very pleasant, Uncle Saunders, but we have a little problem on our hands. The sisters and I formed an alliance, and settled the Darkcallers' hash in Urga, but a few survivors seem to be driving east with the fossil evidence my late brother, whom they killed, was indiscreet enough to dig up, and with God knows what else besides –'

'– Young Tom, eh?' Saunders said. 'So the Darkcalling rabble have killed Wilfred's godson as well as my good friend Grarrl. The vermin really are getting out of hand.'

He barked some more orders and the People of the Plain melted into the darkness, all save two who stood there silently, with expressions of concentration on their faces. They shivered as their faces and bodies altered towards the human and clumps of their body hair drifted to the ground.

'Still,' he said, 'it is an ill wind and so on. The lorries are still not going east – the People's scouts saw them turn south on a goat track some miles from here. Probably striking down to the railway – the late war tore up the track south of Urga, but some of it is operational, particularly once you get past the Chinese lines. We'd better head off in that direction. And the People will accept a modest vengeance as my fee for residing among them, just as you will pay me for my help by driving me to a more civilized location.'

'But there isn't room for you in our car,' Charlotte said.

'There is a lorry, parked some five miles away,' Saunders said. 'I had the People of the Plains steal it for me some months ago, in the middle of the war when things were not likely to be missed. The People may not use artefacts, but they are perfectly prepared to steal them, you know. They have this prejudice about mechanical objects, and I am myself these days indisposed for driving. I have just been waiting for someone who can drive, and now I have six of you.'

'Seven,' Charlotte said.

'Wilfred always said you were a bit of a tomboy,' Saunders said. 'Grew up to be some sort of New Woman, did you? I blame the war, myself. But we can't have you as a driver – never get past the border guards. I don't think you appreciate, with all the war lords competing for control, just how many borders we may have to cross. You, my dear, are going to have to be loot. Plenty of people driving south with the odd *ci-devant* White Russian gentlewoman slung across their back seats.'

Charlotte was getting progressively unhappy with the way that this oversized bully was taking over the whole enterprise and even more unhappy with the shamefaced way that Watcher and her sisters were letting him. They were standing there, looking up at him with great fawn-like eyes. Any minute now the ones that were quick to grow hair would grow forelocks so that they could touch them.

Watcher already knew her well enough to look at her in apologetic appeal.

'He's an Ancient,' Watcher said.

'What is that?' Charlotte said, 'Apart from some sort of glandular malfunction overcoming werewolves in middle age?'

'They live a long time, and they know a lot. Besides, he knew our parents. He's on our side, so we're supposed to do what he says. It's how things are. You'll understand, my darling, when you get to know a little better how things work among us.'

'Watcher, my sweet,' Charlotte said patiently. 'Herr Doctor Freud explained this sort of thing to me in Vienna last year. You personally lost your parents at an early age, so you need a father figure, to salve obscure guilt; your people lost the First, in the dawn of time, and so they need father figures of one sort or another. But wouldn't it be more mature? —'

Saunders limped over to her and fixed her with a glare. 'One of the reasons for not telling humans too much is that they will insist on arguing. You must be very tired after all your exertions, Charlotte.'

'How considerate,' Charlotte said, forced to look up as he loomed over her, his breath steaming rhythmically like an ox in a byre, 'but I am not tired at all.'

His breathing grew even louder, pounding in her ears like her own heartbeats.

'But you are tired, Charlotte Matthews,' Saunders said. 'You are very tired indeed.'

Suddenly Charlotte noticed that she had extremely painful cramp in her fingers and calves. As she waved her hands in front of her face, and kicked nervously against the seat in front, she noticed that it was daylight. The road they were travelling on was considerably smoother, and they were no longer surrounded by scrubby plain but jolting slowly across a metal bridge, behind a ramshackle lorry and an unusually slow ox-cart.

Visible in the distance ahead of them, out near the horizon, were some quite respectably sized mountains. The vast shallow river beneath them was succulent and stinking with mud and silt.

Charlotte was very hungry and thirsty, and there was a pronounced feeling of bruising around her left side and buttock, but she could tell from the feel of her underclothing that at least someone had kept her clean. One of the sisters handed her a water-bottle. Charlotte rinsed her mouth out, and then gargled a little of the water in her throat, both times spitting none too elegantly from the side of the car. Then she allowed herself to swallow, just a little.

'I see we got across the border all right,' she remarked in the most congenial voice she could manage, a little husky and cracked around the edges.

Watcher, she noticed, had reverted to the features she had known as Schmidt's, while the others were all looking desperately male and Chinese. A little more practice, she reflected, and I might be able to tell my sisters-in-law apart, but as things are ... They looked at her stonyfaced – one of them, she realized, was not one of the sisters at all, but one of the People. Something about his eyebrows ... The other sister must be in the lorry, which, presumably, contained Saunders and the other nomad.

They rattled off the bridge and on to the road, and joined a ragged line of vehicles that were being inspected, with the usual gross casual brutality of the officious, by a group of Chinese soldiers in scruffy khaki and an unlikely mixture of headgear. Their officer, a dapper young brute, whose hair was smoothed down with an overly-sweet pomade that Charlotte swore she could smell several yards downwind, inspected papers that were brought to him with a disdainful cursoriness.

One of the soldiers poked his head through the lorry

window and then proceeded to peer through the slats on the side, and to poke at whatever he saw there. A loud and convincing bellow followed.

'Surely not,' Charlotte said. 'I know his Grace the Ancient is large enough, but I refuse to believe you people can grow horns to order.'

'Misdirection,' Watcher clarified. 'It's the whole trick of it. People see what they expect to see; you just have to fade reality a little round the edges.'

'I see,' Charlotte said, trying very hard to convey her entire moral disapproval of such a procedure.

'In the old days,' Mourner said, 'Ancients just used to say that they were Beneficent Dragons of the Sixth Button and in charge of the Rains of the South Wind. And people used to swallow it. Progress means they have to pass as domestic animals.'

There was a sardonic edge to this, Charlotte noticed, but it was a little bit too much like the blasphemy of the true believer.

Evidently it had been successful, because the officer waved the lorry on, and the soldiers moved down the line to the car. Charlotte had already closed her eyes and slumped over to one side, as if still asleep, her hair straggling over her face. One may disapprove of deceit without rushing into the answering of awkward questions.

Watcher heaved a sigh of relief as they drew away.

'I didn't like the smell of that officer one little bit,' she remarked.

'His hair-oil was rather oppressive, wasn't it?' Charlotte said.

'That is not what I meant at all. Look, Charlotte, I really must apologize for what happened.'

'I don't think apologies are really in order. I cannot conceive of an apology that would be adequate.'

'There is little I can do, save kiss my beloved's hands in humility and hope in desperation for her forgiveness.'

'Why, Watcher, you say the sweetest things and, if I was not so furious, you might even succeed in turning my head.'

'I was hoping that I had achieved the soft answer that turns away wrath, but I would settle for turning your head . . .'

As they jolted along the rutted highway, a figure suddenly dashed from the scrubby bushes at its side and leaped on to the running-board of the car, ducking into a kneeling position and gripping the door with both hands. Instantly, there were shouts behind them and the biting sound of rifle-shots.

Whichever of the sisters was driving accelerated wildly, overtaking the lorry, whose driver instantly followed suit, after a while taking the lead again. The nomad sitting closest to the fugitive, who was hanging on as tenaciously as was possible with his head bent over, moved to hammer at the young Chinese man's hands with his fists; Watcher took his arm and made him stop.

'We are already in trouble,' she said. 'And we may as well find out precisely what sort of trouble we are in, before disposing of this inconvenient young man.'

'Can we not simply throw him to his enemies?' Mourner said from the passenger seat. 'It might at least buy us time while they do the unpleasant things they do to fugitives in these parts.'

'I would have thought,' Charlotte said, 'that they would be only too keen to postpone the disposal of a fugitive they have already identified as such pending discovery of exactly who his unsuspected allies are. That presumably would involve not merely questions, but interrogation of an unpleasant, physical kind.'

Several of the sisters nodded, and Watcher reached over and helped the young man climb over the side of the car and into the well between the seats, where he lay, among the boots of his unwelcoming hostesses, for their inspection.

He was a good-looking enough young chap, Charlotte reflected, though his face had a couple too many moles for her taste and his hair tended to the long and lank. The abolition of the pigtail had clearly not been followed by any tonsorial renaissance in these parts.

They continued to drive recklessly fast. What traffic there had been ahead of them had pulled to the side at the first rifle-shots or was driving with equal speed. As Charlotte watched, a lorry some yards ahead of them clipped the side of an ox-cart that had tried to pull out of the way and spun out of control into the ditch, fetching up against a telegraph pole.

A lorry full of soldiers, whose firing either lacked precision or was intended to frighten rather than maim, probably the former, followed in the middle distance. It seemed gradually to be gaining on them, and Charlotte had the distinct impression that the sister who was driving was, if anything, assisting this process by slowing down. As she watched, the nails of Watcher's hand grew longer, harder and more pointed.

Suddenly Charlotte realized that the pain in her side was in fact her revolver, and so she reached into her pocket and removed it. She turned, sighted over the back of the car and fired. To her disappointment, it took two shots before she hit a tyre and another before she managed to place a bullet neatly into the lorry's radiator.

As she turned back, Watcher and her sisters were looking at her with amused indulgence.

'That was very impressive, Charlotte dear,' Tracker

said, 'and I am sure that none of us could have managed it. But you really must try and conquer the urge to protect us from our enemies. It is redundant, and likely to lead to your getting in the way.'

'I was not trying to protect you from them,' Charlotte said. 'I was under the impression, knowing you as I do, that I was protecting them from you.'

The plain was interrupted by a small rise, on which the lorry with Saunders in it started to labour somewhat. On the descent, a barrier and several more soldiers, came into view, some of whom were already levelling their rifles.

Perhaps, Charlotte reflected, there is something to all this healthy living, because when she had seen the sisters dispose of their opposition in Mongolia, it was like watching a performance of some slightly recherché art; whereas when the two nomads, without even bothering significantly to change their human forms, flowed out of the moving vehicles, up to the sides of the road and down again, into and through the line of soldiers, it was like watching a high wind level corn.

The young Chinese man started to raise himself up to see, perhaps to enjoy, the slaughter. Charlotte looked at him severely and shook her head.

'What,' she inquired of Watcher, 'is the Chinese for "there are some things that humanity is not meant to know"?'

'I don't know,' Watcher said. 'I don't speak Chinese. Dancer was the only one of us that ever bothered to learn it. We were too busy in Siberia and the Ukraine ever to need it.'

The Plains nomad swung himself back into the car. Followed by the lorry, it passed through the barrier, which creaked gently on its hinges. The road block seemed deserted now; in their flow of violence, the nomads had put the bodies somewhere out of sight.

The road ahead was more or less deserted, and there was no sign of the lorry full of soldiers. Charlotte doubted that she had successfully disabled it for more than a few minutes, but presumably she had discouraged them enough that they had dropped behind in expectation that the soldiers at the road block, presumably warned, would do their work for them.

'I hesitate,' Charlotte said, her voice loud enough to carry to the other vehicle, 'to advocate delaying further. But the miracle of wireless telegraphy seems to be working to our disadvantage. If we do not do something about it, we are going to have to stop every few miles and kill people. This seems wasteful to me.'

The heavy door at the back of the lorry flung open, and with a thump Saunders heaved himself into the daylight. From somewhere he had acquired a large horse-blanket which he was using as some sort of improvised loin cloth. He waddled over to the side of the road. Charlotte noticed that his right leg was still lame.

He seized the telegraph pole by its base and proceeded to haul it from the ground. It came out with a slow gulping of the thick, rich clay which underlay the mild slope of the gravel embankment.

Suddenly, from the brow of the hill, there came a sinister swishing sound, the shouting of men and the firing of pistols. Charlotte threw herself down on top of the young Chinese man, who was mercifully somewhat on the plump side, followed expeditiously by Watcher, who was fumbling in her clothes for a revolver.

Down from the brow of the hill there swept some twenty gleaming bicycles, each of them ridden by a soldier, some of whom were trying to sight pistols over the handlebars, or steering with one hand while the other brandished a sabre.

Some of them braked rapidly at the sight of the

half-naked giant at the side of the road, but none fast enough to avoid the almighty effort with which he finally wrenched the pole loose from the soil and swung it, with a power that tore it free from its wires that lay sparking, in a low sweeping curve that sent half of the bicycles crashing to the floor in an instant, to be followed in a pile by the ones immediately behind them. Even those that had braked could not help smashing into the pile of crumpled machines and men.

At least one of them had got off a shot that had hit home, because Saunders was bleeding from his left shoulder and his right calf; this latter wound seemed to send him into a frenzy of temper, and he brought the pole down time and time again on the writhing mass of flesh, metal and rubber, pounding them to shreds like spices in a mortar. Then, suddenly, he turned away, and let the great pole fall.

There was blood, and worse, in pools in the dust of the road. Charlotte had seen the injuries of shells and machine-guns in Italy and had thought that she could not be shocked or disgusted ever again. Yet somewhere in that mass of offal there were still men with enough breath to be screaming. Watcher climbed from the car, as did her sisters, and walked determinedly across to the butchery.

Watcher fired three times and Mourner twice, and the screaming stopped.

Charlotte picked up a discarded rifle, opened the door of the shed and went inside.

There was a stove there, and some bedrolls, and a cold stove with a pan of millet broth on it. There was also a small table on which rested headphones and the rest of the telegraph equipment; she brought down the rifle butt on it until it was a heap of metal and glass fragments – but it did not relieve her feelings in the slightest.

There were also several jerrycans of petrol, that she carried out into the sunlight, one after another. Watcher saw what she was doing, and helped her distribute them between the car and the lorry. Waste not, want not, her governess had always said, and Charlotte imagined that petrol was not easiest come by, in China.

Then Watcher turned slowly and decisively and looked at Saunders. The expression that her Schmidt face wore was unreadable save for its narrowed eyes.

'You are an Ancient, and the friend of our parents,' she said. 'But we only kill when it is necessary. And we kill clean.'

'My old wound pains me,' Saunders said. 'And there is nothing so unimportant as the way in which one kills those one has decided to kill. I share your interest in killing the Darkcallers, and these soldiers stood in our way. This is a serious venture we are engaged upon. And vengeance is not a tea party.'

He waddled across to the car.

'This youth,' he said, 'has incommoded us far too much already, and seen appreciably too much for his own good.'

Charlotte closed the boot of the car, and turned.

'Watcher, I think I have had enough of all this. Saunders, for what little it is worth in your eyes, this young man is under my protection.'

Saunders continued to move forward, a look of cruel regret in his eyes.

'And Charlotte,' Watcher said, levelling her revolver at Saunders, 'is under mine.'

The two nomads started to move forward, only to stop when the sisters all raised their guns as well.

'This is all quite unnecessary,' said the young Chinese man.

'You did not say that you spoke English,' Charlotte said.

'No one bothered to ask the ignorant coolie,' the young man said. 'You took for granted that I was the object of conversation, not a participant in it. And I am accustomed to such, and find it useful not to speak the language of imperial oppression in front of the oppressors.'

'Who are you?' Charlotte asked.

'Personal names are irrelevant,' the young man said. 'I am the delegate from Hunan, merely. And we are wasting time. You have just destroyed a cadre of the bicycle cavalry of the Nationalist warlord Feng Yuxiang; and that makes you even more of a fugitive from this justice than I, whose death is merely a favour owed by him to the Comintern. He has ordered my capture, and I can expect little mercy if caught. But for one warrior, even an oversized crippled freak, to smash his best soldiers like an idle child's toys, that is to earn considerably worse than death. Forget all these quarrels, and drive as if death were behind you, because it is.'

Saunders stared hard at Charlotte, who refused to meet his eyes.

'That,' she said, 'is a trick I propose to let you work only once, Mr Saunders.'

Saunders looked around him and the faces of the sisters were all stony. He sighed, and turned away; he limped back to the lorry, reached inside and produced a flask of spirits. He took a sip from it, and poured more of it on to his two wounds. He put his mouth to one of his great hands and sucked out a splinter, then bathed the hand in the spirits as well. He drained the last drops, and then tossed the flask behind him into the lorry. He sighed again.

'What's an old man to do,' he said, 'confronted by all you decisive young people? I had hoped for a little consideration and respect ... Enough of that: very well, let us be off. And place this – ah – delegate's fate under consideration until we know more about him.'

'Of course,' Watcher said, as the cars drove onwards across the plain, speedily but without any obvious pursuers, 'of course, Charlotte, there is a very good case for what Saunders proposes.'

'I refuse,' said Charlotte, 'to have a private conversation about killing someone in front of them.'

'If I had not spoken English,' the delegate pointed out, 'you would have done so.'

'But you do,' Charlotte said. 'And if you hadn't, we would have had no option.'

'You could have bothered to learn the language of a country before crossing its borders. China deserves more respect than to be invaded perpetually by the ignorant.'

'We did not choose,' Charlotte retorted, 'to come here for personal pleasure or out of idle curiosity. We pursued our enemies from Mongolia and will continue to pursue them until we catch up with them or lose their trail altogether.'

'Your enemies?' the delegate said. 'Would these be two lorries similar to the one containing your large friend?'

'Three lorries,' Watcher said.

'I saw two, only.'

'But surely there were three,' Mourner cut in.

'There is much literary matter, and much advocacy of the brutal suppression of the people in the works of the master strategist Sun Tzu,' the delegate said. 'His emphasis on the importance of accurate observation as a prerequisite of leadership is a lesson to all of us.'

A silence fell, which seemed to last several hours. They stared at each other, and periodically the car would stop and a different sister would take over the driving or pour petrol into the tank from the dwindling supply.

Charlotte loathed inquisitiveness and small talk, but eventually she felt obliged to ask questions.

'What are you a delegate to? And what is your problem with the Bolsheviks? Are you an opponent of theirs?'

'Hardly an opponent,' the delegate replied. 'I regard them as my comrades. But there is a strategic disagreement of some importance.'

'So you are a Communist,' Watcher said with interest. 'I did not know there was a Communist party in China.'

'We started a year ago,' said the delegate, 'and I have already personally recruited sixteen members. I understand that there will be at least ten other delegates at the plenary conference in Shanghai.'

'I tried to read Marx, once,' Charlotte said, 'but I got bogged down in the Labour Theory of Value.'

'I haven't read Marx, yet,' the delegate said. 'I know that the Russian Communists think he is very important, but none of us have had a chance to read him yet. We stand for a programme of the abolition of unequal treaties, and modest amounts of land reform. But the Comintern have promised to provide us with some pamphlets.'

'Don't listen to Charlotte,' Watcher said. 'She is, bless her, an unreconstructed bourgeois. You really would find it very helpful to read Marx.'

'You are going to Shanghai,' Charlotte said. 'We seem to be heading in that general direction.'

Watcher looked suspicious.

'If you are going to Shanghai,' she said, 'and have come from Hunan, you have taken an awfully roundabout route.'

'I was warned,' said the delegate, 'that there might be an attempt to stop me turning up in Shanghai. Sometimes it is useful to take the long route round to get somewhere. It will have been useful to travel among the people.'

There was a certainty in his tone at once admirable and repulsive.

'Besides, there is so much of China it will be useful to have seen. A gazetteer will tell one how much soil is washed away by the Huang-Ho river, but it is necessary to see it to determine that one day systems of dams and catchments will change it from a menace to a benefit.'

Charlotte reflected how difficult it is to take a pompous young man seriously when you have recently used him as a safety cushion.

'You have travelled widely?' he asked.

'Reasonably so,' Charlotte said. 'In Europe and Siberia and Mongolia. But I have never been to China before.'

'Mongolia is China,' the delegate snapped, his eyes wide in anger.

Then, in a more conciliatory tone, he added, 'Eight years ago, when I was nineteen, I saw a map of the whole world. Even allowing for the lies of imperialism, I was truly impressed by how much there is outside China, even allowing for what would be rightfully ours, were it not for unequal treaties.'

'Aside from Mongolia, then,' Charlotte said, feeling an obligation to the social graces, 'I have never been to China. Is there much to see? Apart from potential irrigation projects?'

Watcher gave her an amused, but warning, look.

'There are many sights of historical interest,' the delegate said. 'Most of them have to do with feudal tyranny, but even those are often most important to the understanding of what it is to be a nation. Take the mountains to our right, for example.'

The suspension on the lorry was not entirely healthy, so they had taken the road across the narrowing plain rather than the more frequented road into the foothills.

'I was most impressed,' he continued, 'by the inscriptions on Mount Taishan. Most go there on the pilgrimages of superstition or on some mission to do with the arts, but I went there because the inscriptions, even as they glorify feudal rulers, tell us of power, and of responsibility.'

He struck an attitude, and intoned.

'"I am troubled by my lack of virtue. I am ignorant of perfect reason. I know not whether I have committed any offence against the gods or the people, and my heart is tossed on the floods as though I were crossing a great river. I deployed the power of my five imperial armies, I made the nine regions tremble with fear; the colours and standards were raised up; horses and soldiers were silenced. What majesty, what spectacle, what pomp! In this way did I arrive at Taishan and all was as it should be."'

He paused, then continued, in his normal voice.

'That is how it should be, you see; the ruler aware of responsibility, ignoring superstition, responsibility to the people. And none the less doing what is necessary, not in the name of personal glory, but in the name of the people. If there were a man in China capable of doing what needs to be done, he could build a new nation, like George Washington did, in the face of imperialism – but none of the warlords is that man. Dr Sun was briefly, but is now personally exhausted and politically spent.'

An awkward silence fell again.

'If it is possible to say so without seeming patronizing,' Charlotte said, 'you speak English awfully well.'

'Thank you,' the delegate said. 'It is not often that I get the chance to practise it at such length.'

For some time the road had been running alongside a railway, and, quite suddenly, they caught up with a train that was chugging gently south. Some of the carriages had roofs that were covered with people, some of them asleep, and some of them sitting with their feet dangling off the edge; some of the passengers were travelling in mere cattle-trucks. The road was so close to the line that the passengers started pointing at Watcher and Charlotte with a mixture of ridicule, hostility and incredulity.

The delegate stood up.

'You were discussing killing me,' he said, 'to preserve some secret or other. I have no idea what your secret is, and I care even less. There is nothing that human beings ought not to know, save what is unnecessary to their work. But try and kill me now, and these people will tear you limb from limb, even your giant. There are simply too many of them, and they do not like foreigners.'

He clambered over the side of the car on to the running-board and held out his hand; ten hands reached out to him to pull him on board the train. He looked down into the car from the roof of a carriage.

'It is often useful to have moved among the people,' he said, and leaped down into one of the cattle-trucks, disappearing like a fish into the ocean.

'Saunders won't be pleased,' Watcher said.

'But it is by far the best solution,' Charlotte said. 'You didn't really want to kill that silly little man with his silly schemes – he was much too busy making speeches to even notice anything out of the ordinary about the rest of you, and he thought Saunders was just a gland case. And now we simply don't have to bother with him at all, ever again.'

After a while, the railway swung away from them. The

road proceeded ever on through a plain of remorseless agricultural monotony, and Charlotte decided that after all, hypnotic trances are an overrated way of resting and it had already been a long and stressful day. She snuggled her head into the crease between Watcher's left breast and armpit, and fell gently asleep.

It was night when she awoke, and the car and the lorry were jolting through the streets of a small settlement at the edge of which the road they were on crossed another, rather more evenly laid-out one. In the far corner of the crossroads, slightly back from the road, there was a larger building than those they had passed in the town. It had shutters on the windows, in something that had once approximated the European style, though the paint had flaked and many of the slats were missing. From it, there came the unmistakable smell of ginger, hot vinegar and the sweet charring of pork.

Charlotte thought with enthusiasm of the possibility of dinner – she was not starving and so had presumably been fed something during her trance, but she did not care to wonder what it had been, and whether it had been cooked first. Saunders's lorry turned into the large courtyard and Mourner, who was now driving, followed suit.

Charlotte realized with mild disappointment that it was not the smell of roasting pork that had made them stop, but rather the presence in the courtyard, next to the roasting-pit, of an almost identical lorry, which stood, its back doors gaping open, clearly entirely abandoned. The two nomads, who had no trouble at all speaking Chinese, climbed from the vehicles and interrogated the plump, smiling Chinese men who came out to greet them. After a while, they came to the car and reported back in the high, barking Weerde language they had used on the plains. Presumably Saunders had good enough hearing to make out what they were saying, and the innkeeper, prepared to believe any strange noise to be the language of foreigners, would have been disconcerted had they chosen to explain themselves to some large domestic animal.

'He says,' Watcher said, 'that the other lorry left at daybreak – clearly the Darkcalling scum have dawdled, delayed by acts of random wickedness and we, almost uninterrupted, have made up a part of their lead.'

'But why have they left their lorry?' Charlotte said.

'We have experience, my love, of the Darkcallers and their Chaos co-conspirators. Rational behaviour, or anything we would recognize as such, is not to be expected from the Darkcallers. And the followers of Chaos, even if on the basis of rational premises, explicitly disavow rationality as a procedure.'

After a rapid conclave, held at a volume sufficient that Saunders could find a way of objecting, if he did, it was agreed that they pause and refresh themselves for a few hours. Charlotte was glad of the chance to wash herself, and rinse out her clothes. After she made signs to this effect, the sour-faced wife of the tavern-keeper hobbled off on her tiny, deformed feet and procured from some press or cupboard a none-too-clean robe of reasonably good silk. Charlotte took it and nodded her thanks. When the woman had left the room, Charlotte took a deep breath to rid her lungs of the sickly smell of the woman's feet, fungus-ridden inside their constraining bandages.

She slung her belt by its buckle from nails at the side of the window, and hung her blouse and her riding-breeches from it, to dry. There was a knock at the door and Watcher came in, with the apologetic expression that Charlotte was growing to know and despise.

'You do realize,' she said, 'that I am going to have to bring your food to you here.'

Charlotte looked at her coldly.

Watcher went on. 'This is not a very respectable tavern, and a European woman, whether dressed in a robe, or wearing what the Chinese are likely to see as rather masculine attire, is liable to cause comment.'

Charlotte did not say anything, and turned to adjust her clothes on their improvised line.

'Wouldn't you do better,' Watcher noted, 'to dry them an item at a time? Or spread them out more. I don't mean to be bossy, but I am only thinking about your best interests.'

Charlotte, pecked her on the cheek and then looked at her in a way that had little loving about it.

'I'm sure you mean well,' she said. 'But it is clear to me that whatever is between us is less important to you than the desires of that overgrown oaf with whom you and your sisters seem so completely infatuated.'

Watcher looked at her helplessly.

'You don't understand.'

'I think,' Charlotte said, 'that I understand only too well. I have worked in hospitals, and I have seen the giggling nervousness of young nurses when the chief surgeon does his rounds. I found it distinctly unattractive in them, and in you it seems uncommonly like a betrayal.'

She put her hand to Watcher's shoulder, then let it drop, and went across to the bedding where she sat with her head in her hands, next to the small pile of her possessions she had taken from her pockets.

'It is not like that,' Watcher said, 'and there is nothing in my relationship to Saunders that you need feel anything resembling jealousy about.'

'Jealousy of a sexual kind would be preferable,' Charlotte said. 'Either you would have tired of me, or I could compete. But I cannot and will not compete for your attention, when there seems to be something plainly pathological going on.'

'He is an Ancient. He is old and knows a lot, and I respect him.'

'I will not compete for your respect. I offered my throat to your teeth in love and attraction. I will not compete with anyone for you.'

'Charlotte, I love you enough not to mind if you want to think badly of me.'

'I don't want to blame you, Watcher; I want you to blame yourself.'

'You are impossible, Charlotte Matthews.' Watcher left the room, slamming the door.

After a while, she returned with a tray and some food, and had the sense to leave it and not say anything. Charlotte reflected that she was, after all, rather hungry, and ate her way through the roast pork and the rice and a few greens – the latter were unpleasantly fibrous but would doubtless help her digestion.

Her clothes were not entirely dry, but not so damp as to risk her getting a chill, so she dressed again, taking care to collect her possessions. She pushed the shutters aside, climbed up on to the window-sill and let herself down gently, hanging on to the sill with both hands and dropping the remaining seven feet or so.

It was dark in the courtyard save for light from one window, from which there also came the noise of people eating and drinking. Out of the corner of her eye, Charlotte saw a movement in the field beyond the courtyard – a large dog, or something.

She was somewhat surprised to see the back door of their lorry open, and the bonnet up; wherever Saunders had gone, he was clearly not there. Seizing a hoped-for opportunity, she clambered into the lorry, which stank of his sweat and worse, hoping to find what she was looking for. Her hand fell upon it almost instantly, where Saunders had tossed it into the lorry.

There was little light in the courtyard, but she hardly needed it. All she needed to do was remove the cap from the flask and run her finger across the initials that she knew were embossed on its interior. TM.

It was, as she had feared, her brother's flask.

She reached into the pile of straw at the back of the lorry, and removed the two petrol cans she had placed there earlier, putting them in a dark corner of the courtyard, in the shadow of a bench. She walked across the courtyard to the window that was showing light.

The innkeeper and his wife, several other Chinese men who were presumably travellers or local merchants from the moderate affluence of their clothing, and a young woman minimally clothed, sat stupefied in a corner, their eyes vacant and their heads nodding from side to side. Saunders was crouched in the middle of the room, tearing at a whole roast pig and feeding scraps of it to the nomads who sat cross-legged beside him. The six sisters sat opposite, deferentially listening to him, their eyes glazed in a way not unlike the vacancy of the humans.

'Fast,' he said, 'you must travel fast and on foot if we are to come up with the Darkcallers in time. We must overtake them before we reach Shanghai, or we will have to chase them through a warren where they have more lairs than I do. We are at Hicheng already, in Shantung province; we have not come up with them yet and we have not a moment to lose. The day after tomorrow, the road that we travel will be too near the city, too busy for quiet killing – you must travel the rest of this night and take to the hills by day. You must be my hounds, and I will set you on. Sleep now, sisters, and rise changed to take final vengeance on the slayers of your kin.'

She realized that the heads of Watcher and her sisters were nodding to the same rhythm as the innkeeper's and as she watched, Mourner, Singer, Sojourner and Settler slumped to the floor, gradually losing their specifically human features. Watcher stood, shaking her head to keep her concentration.

'This is not right,' she said. 'We cannot abandon Charlotte, and your plan lacks logic. And – and I cannot abandon Charlotte.'

She was staggering on her feet, and Saunders put down the pig, licked an excess of grease from his left hand with an excessively long tongue, made a fist and clubbed her to the ground.

'Four volunteers are worth one pressed man is what I always say. And do come in, young Charlotte, no point hanging around out there in the cold night air.'

Charlotte pushed a shutter aside and clambered over the sill. Saunders reached over and took the flask from her hand.

'I see you recognize it. Careless of me.'

He looked at her ruefully.

'It's not what you think,' he said. 'I had nothing to do with Tom's death. But a fellow can have his own interests, and his own plans, and the least you girls can do is be a little helpful, instead of selfishly pursuing your own pleasure all the time.'

Charlotte looked down at Watcher, who lay very still with a thin trail of blood trickling from her right nostril and from the side of her mouth. She dropped to her knees and kissed the quiet white forehead, just next to the depressed area where Saunders had struck.

'Murderer,' she said.

'Not in the least,' Saunders said. 'Her sisters went into the change sleep when I told them to, their natural deference to an Ancient's suggestions somewhat enhanced by the last of my opium in their rice wine. Your partner in viciousness – it is clear to me what is going on, Charlotte Matthews, and as a friend of your late uncle's, I feel some obligation to be shocked – needed rather more physical measures. But she will live – I know my own strength very well and precisely how much damage to do so that she will sleep until Shanghai.'

The two nomads started to drag the sisters out, but to the truck the Darkcallers had abandoned. Saunders saw Charlotte's inquisitive stare.

'Odd,' he said. 'But when we checked that one, it wouldn't go. Singer says that someone had taken out some of its parts; still, the other one was awfully bouncy for an old chap to ride in, and this one will be altogether smoother, now we've swapped the parts over. And we shall be taking the car as well. When I say we, I do not, of course mean you Charlotte.'

'Of course not,' Charlotte agreed.

'You really are the most vexing and irritating child,' Saunders said. 'Unnatural vice, questioning of authority, altogether too much curiosity. I really ought to dispose of you for good, but I think that leaving you here will serve perfectly adequately.'

Charlotte looked across the room at the fat, snoring innkeeper.

'He is not even as nice as he looks,' Saunders said. 'Last week, he sold his concubine and her child to the whoremongers, because the child disturbed his rest. When he wakes up, I think the innkeeper will be very distressed, and you will be here to take the brunt of his displeasure. If you survive it, it should be character-forming and may teach you some overdue lessons in manners.'

One of the nomads seized her by the arm and the chin, forcing her to meet Saunders's gaze.

'Goodbye, Charlotte,' Saunders said.

She awoke on her back, with something trying to force a bottle between her lips and someone else pawing at the fastening of her riding breeches, looking for her money belt, she assumed. She took a hefty swig of the fiery, violet-scented liquor into her mouth and then, as the landlord took the bottle from her lips, she spat the spirit into his eyes. His companions laughed as he tottered around the room, unable to see.

She reached up and shoved at the shoulder of the landlord's boon companion who was fumbling at her clothes, sending him spinning to the ground; sitting down, she looked around. Several more of the landlord's friends or customers were lounging against the far wall of what proved to be her room; all of them had identical, obnoxious male smirks on their faces.

The landlord had collapsed to the floor, frantically wiping at his eyes with an unclean sleeve. His expression as he looked at Charlotte was murderous.

Her revolver was gone from her belt, but they had not yet gone through her jacket pockets. Unhurriedly, she produced her two-shot derringer, that she proceeded to point at the innkeeper's low forehead. They might not appreciate, after all, that it had only two chambers. His friends laughed, and he got up. All five men left the room, locking it behind them.

She had left some of her food earlier, and she wolfed it, guessing that they would soon have the idea of trying to starve her into submission. The stench of the liquor that had spattered her clothes almost managed, but not quite, to diminish her appetite.

She went to the window. The car and the Darkcallers' truck had gone. The truck Saunders had ridden was still there. Two of the innkeeper's friends were there, watching her window, and one of them tossed a handful of mud to discourage her. She dodged it easily, and continued to watch the darkness at the entrance to the courtyard where, if she peered, she could see a shape dithering in the darkness, inching nervously in a half-crouch into the courtyard and behind a bench in the far corner.

After all, she reflected, when one bothers to think through the meaning of one's observations, the Chinese are not noted for the keeping of large dogs. The shape half-stumbled; there was the clink of one petrol can against another and a muffled noise of cursing. She whistled loudly, and the two men turned to look at her.

'I met a traveller from an antique land,' she said, at a venture. The two men looked up at her, as if she were mad.

She went on, 'Who said, "two vast and trunkless legs of stone / Stand in the desert."'

They continued to stare at her, oblivious of the shape that crept up behind them, picked up a broom that someone had left against the bench, and clouted them across the head with it. Charlotte clambered through the window again and dropped to the ground, her fall this time somewhat softened by the two men who lay groaning on the ground, to find herself confronting a somewhat undersized and seedy looking Weerde, who was shaking himself with a certain determination into a more human form.

He was entirely naked, save for a twist of cloth with something in it hanging from his neck. Charlotte reached down, tugged the jacket off one of the two semi-conscious men and handed it to him. He got the idea and helped her remove the man's shoes and trousers. The other man tried to get to his feet, and Charlotte kicked him smartly in the jaw without more than half-turning. On an afterthought she bent down and retrieved her revolvers from his belt, put one of them in her own, and stood watching the Weerde, who, as a human, was a small man with a weak chin and large, sensitive, untrustworthy eyes.

He barked at her. She recalled the conversations that the sisters, irritatingly, had continued to have around her and tried to follow suit, breaking out after a few moments into a paroxysm of coughing.

'We had better stick to English,' he said in a rather unappealing Hun whine. 'What with your accent and that nasty sore throat I can't understand a word you are saying.'

'I am Charlotte Matthews,' she said. 'And I believe that you have something that belongs to me.'

She did not point the revolvers at him, but held them ready, as an implicit threat.

'It was not I,' he said. 'I had nothing to do with it. I didn't even know what was in the crates.'

'Fine. You don't seem to have enough character to be a demon-worshipper. So you can take the distributor-cap and the rotor-arm from that piece of cloth around your neck, and you can fit them into this truck. Right this minute.'

'But the truck will not go. I saw them siphon the last of the petrol from it earlier.'

'You should have been paying attention, when you were loitering earlier,' Charlotte said. 'Or at least when you fell over the two petrol cans that I had the fore-thought to put behind the bench.'

The innkeeper and several of his friends came out of the door at the end of the courtyard, waving cleavers and an old pike. Charlotte fired into the dirt at the innkeeper's feet, and he retreated.

She climbed into the front of the truck, and continued

to keep a weather eye open while the seedy young Weerde carried out her orders. In a few minutes, they were ready and started to back out of the courtyard. As they did so, they noticed a crowd of people running from the settlement, led by the innkeeper with his cleaver.

'I think,' Charlotte said, 'that we have outstayed our welcome in Hicheng.'

They accelerated, leaving the mob to eat their dust. Suddenly, he looked at her.

'Scheiss, you are a human, is that not so? All I could smell before was the liquor, and I did not stop to think.'

'Yes,' she said. 'But I don't think either of us can afford to examine each other's pedigrees too closely.'

'You don't understand. They'll kill me.'

'Who will?'

'Everyone. I don't belong to a very exalted lineage or anything, but at least none of my Line has ever been dishonoured, and no one is actually wanting to kill me, Fritzi, specifically. Except perhaps a croupier in Odessa, but that wasn't anything to do with being Kin. But if they thought I was a Revealer . . .'

'I won't tell anyone, if you don't,' Charlotte said. 'And you may have gathered that I know a fair amount already.'

Fritzi started to gather the muscles at the base of his jaw and lengthen his features. Charlotte glared at him, and placed her hand on her revolver.

'Sorry,' he said, 'just a nervous twitch.'

She smiled at him reassuringly.

'You were going to explain what you were doing with my fossils.'

'I have not the slightest interest in fossils,' Fritzi said. 'There is no obvious profit to be made from them. I was only in Urga to get away from Irkutsk – I had to leave

Irkutsk because of a little misunderstanding over baccarat.'

'So you're a card sharp,' Charlotte said.

'Not at all. But I have a weakness for the tables, and have, on balance, been fortunate there.'

She looked at him sceptically.

'No, honestly,' he said. 'If only I had ever had a proper stake ... I have a real gift, when I am in a proper casino. I only ended up in Irkutsk because I was tired of marching across Asia with the Czechs. Anyway, Urga was full of Darkcallers and Chaoticists; not a healthy place at all, but no obvious way of leaving. Then I saw that they were loading a crate into a truck, with obvious care, and the truck looked worth stealing and the crate might have been.'

'And then they caught up with you?' Charlotte prompted.

'They caught up with me,' he went on in the tone of a man with a grievance, 'and they held their guns on me, and tied me hand and foot and slung me in the back of their truck. The Darkcallers wanted to kill me, but the Chaos couple said that it was random chance that had brought me there, and when the time came for sacrifice what better victim than a chance one? And what better chance victim than a gambler?'

'What sacrifice?' Charlotte said.

'I don't know. A sacrifice to the Dark, or to Chaos, I suppose; you have to understand that not all of us are interested in all this theology. It'll take place when they get to Shanghai, presumably. They are taking something there, apart from the fossils. It was important enough that, when the People of the Plain attacked them, they left one lorry and its contents to safeguard it.'

'This lorry.'

'I suppose so, and then nothing happened until we

got here and stayed overnight. They were busy carousing, so I untied myself, disabled one of the lorries and buried the bits, wrapped in some cloth, out in a field. I thought I might get a better chance to escape, so I tied myself back up, sort of. They just assumed the lorry had stopped working – I've noticed that Darkcallers tend not to be terribly mechanical. They think it's beneath them.'

'So you escaped,' Charlotte said. 'That was resourceful of you.'

'Not really. A few miles on from Hicheng, we met some travelling procurers, and they had a child with them – Shumeng, the daughter of the innkeeper back there – and her mother. They bought the pair of them, saying that they would do better; a woman dog and her child dog, the procurers said. They would have killed me, but the two from Chaos had taken my dice as a trophy, and they cast them, saved me from them, and threw me naked beside the road with my dice in my mouth, to die or be saved as chance decreed. And so I came back to Hicheng.'

'As chance decreed.' Charlotte handed him her last two squares of Swiss chocolate.

There was an old man with a bicycle standing in the rain on the less fashionable side of Nanking Road, opposite the Young Women's Christian Association Shanghai hostel and the offices of Flossing, Reeves and Matthews. The pouring rain had largely emptied the streets and laid the dust, and reduced the scent of incense, spices, sweat and dung to a mere water-shadow of itself. Native police were moving other street vendors along, but they left the old man to stand there, turning a grindstone that was mounted on the front wheel, with unpleasant-looking little sachets of herbs in a basket at the back.

Charlotte dismounted from the lorry and turned to say goodbye to the essentially harmless Fritzi, but the moment her feet had touched the ground, he slammed the door behind her and drove off as if the Dark were after him.

Charlotte looked at the old man with the grindstone and he looked back at her with interested, if filmy, eyes.

'Potions, Missy,' he said. 'Love potions.'

'Heavens, no,' Charlotte retorted. 'When I am unlucky in love, I handle the matter for myself.'

She turned to cross the road, then turned back to him, reached into her jacket pocket and handed him the straight-edged razor she found it useful to carry there.

'Now that I have returned to civilization,' she said, 'you had better put an edge on that for me.'

'Has Missy the money to pay for it?' he asked.

'Oh, I think so,' Charlotte said, passing him the very last of the cosmopolitan small change and notes that she found on a diligent search of the rest of her pockets.

He grumbled slightly, but proceeded to work on the razor slowly and steadily with the grindstone and some sort of jeweller's rouge that he produced from a small pouch. It glimmered dully when he had finished, but he pulled a hair from his head, split it, and then split the section he was still holding, before folding the blade and passing it back to her. She pocketed the razor, and then worked her way through the traffic to the other side of the road and entered the bank. A young Chinese clerk looked askance at her clothing and stepped decisively into her way.

'I would like to see the managing director,' she said.

'Do you have an appointment to see him? Miss – ah.'

'Matthews. Your name please?'

'I am Sammy White,' he said. 'I wish to cause no offence.'

'Good. I am glad about that, Mr White. And now, the managing director, if you please.'

'If there is a problem with your account –' White said.

'I do not have an account,' Charlotte said.

'I am sorry. The managing director is in a meeting just now, with a very important client.'

'White, my name is Charlotte Matthews and I own a sixteenth of the shares in this bank. No, of course, stupid of me, an eighth. And I wish to see my Uncle Gerard.'

White bowed alarmedly, and offered Charlotte his hand to shake. She shook it vigorously, if uninvolvedly, and then followed him through the bank to the back office. Uncle Gerard was making his farewells to a short Chinese man with an unusually bushy beard, who was wearing rather shabby trousers, and boots so well-polished that Charlotte suspected someone else had done it for him, and a black jacket with improbably large gold epaulettes.

'Good Lord,' said Gerard, 'Charlotte! Whatever are you doing here?'

He turned to the skinny pock-marked man who was serving as interpreter.

'Tell the General that this is my niece, an important shareholder. Charlotte, have you met General Feng Yuxiang?'

'No,' Charlotte said. 'But I have heard excellent things about his enlightened and modern rule of the areas he controls.'

The interpreter conveyed this, and the General smiled, and replied.

'The General wishes,' the interpreter said, 'that you bring your niece to dinner this evening. Even though she is too old to be marriageable, she shows a becoming sense of the proprieties.'

Then, with the usual bowing, the General and his interpreter left. White clapped his hands, and servants appeared with a pot of tea and some English biscuits. Charlotte slumped gratefully into one of her uncle's armchairs.

'Don't mind Wu Fang,' her uncle said, noticing the way she had narrowed her eyes as the clerk bustled around before leaving. 'Good lad, keen as mustard.'

'I thought he was called Sammy White,' Charlotte said.

'Goes by it. Spirit of deference, he seems to think. Lot of nonsense if you ask me, when a chap's got a perfectly good name and nation of his own.'

'Indeed he has.'

'How on earth,' Uncle Gerard asked, 'do you come to be here? The last I heard, you were pursuing your researches in the Bibliothèque Nationale.'

'I had news, bad news, about Tom.'

'Tom?'

'He is dead, Uncle Gerard, killed by wild beasts in Western Mongolia, and so is his friend Grobel, at the hands of the strangler-in-chief of the White Russian commander.'

'Are you sure?'

'Grobel told me that Tom was dead, a few minutes before he was killed himself. I tried to prevent Grobel's death, and was sentenced to death myself.'

'I gather things are a bit sticky,' Gerard said, 'up in Mongolia. This von Sternberg chappie who runs things at present seems to be an excitable sort of fellow, even for a Russian. You seem to have come through quite remarkably well, for a woman travelling by herself.'

'I had companions,' Charlotte said, 'part of the way.'

'Ah, well, that explains it.'

She sat, systematically and mechanically devouring

the biscuits, and charmed by the way he refrained from mentioning her travel-stained state. He went over to his desk, and worked on some correspondence while she slipped into a near-drowse.

After a while, he said, 'It will be a while before we can have Tom declared dead, you know.'

'The war will be over in a few months,' she said, 'and we will be able to check his grave.'

'Funny thing,' Gerard said. 'Coincidence, sort of, though I suppose it happens in troubled times. There were several cousins, but they never applied for him to be declared dead, and now he's turned up again, or so this letter says.'

'Who's turned up?' Charlotte said.

'Wilfred's friend, that loud-mouthed bore Saunders. He always kept an account here, and now he wants to clear it out. Not sure I can let him, just on a signature, but the poor old chap says he has some terrible disfiguring disease, and doesn't want to be seen. All most irregular.'

'Is he in Shanghai, then?'

'Seems to be. He always came here a lot, in the old days. Had some sort of interests here. Even when he was supposed to be dead, people kept on paying money into the account. Fairly disreputable bunch of people, come to that.'

'And he's here now,' Charlotte said.

'If it really is him. Says he's staying down the road, on Bubbling Well Street. In some clinic. Probably a glorified Chinese pox doctor, if my memory of Saunders serves me well.'

Charlotte wandered over to his desk with a satisfied smile, and memorized the address. Stupid male arrogance never ceased to amaze her.

*

She had been wearing her riding-breeches for so many days that it was almost a shock to wear a skirt again. She refused her uncle's offer of having a dressmaker produce some piece of frou-frou, and insisted on a sensible outfit. As a compromise to fashion, she put her hair up.

'General Feng does not want to look at my legs,' she said, 'but he may take a full view of my face for all the good it will do him.'

Her uncle's carriage took them to a large restaurant, full of gourmands and drunkards on each of several floors. They were shown to a large, European-style table, where Feng sat with a variety of business backers and local politicians. This was a male gathering, except for Charlotte, and Feng had already seen her uncle, so that they were, for the most part, ignored. This suited Charlotte, because it meant that she could concentrate on the first hearty meal she had had in she did not know how long; it did not really matter that it was the usual Chinese mess of rice and noodles and unidentifiable fragments of meat covered in thick goo – it tasted pleasant enough, and it was filling.

Her uncle of course insisted on showing off by using chopsticks. He tried to show Charlotte how, but she refused even to acknowledge the attempt. There was something she was trying to remember, and acquiring new dexterities would only confuse her.

After a while, the young officer who was sitting beside Feng came down and summoned her uncle to the far end of the table, to exchange a toast with Feng, who seemed to be ignoring most of the delicacies on offer in favour of a large dish of American ice-cream streaked with nuts and pastel-coloured, unhealthy looking syrups. He was shovelling this mechanically into his mouth, save when he paused to speak or to drink from a copious jug of lemonade.

Gerard came back and sat beside Charlotte.

'The General is not a happy man,' he said, 'and he wants to borrow even more money.'

'Why?'

'He had bad news after visiting us. Bandits massacred a crack platoon of his bicycle cavalry. There are plenty more soldiers where they came from. But he needs to buy new bicycles.'

Charlotte realized that the vague uneasiness she had felt when her uncle was summoned away had been prompted by the smell of hair-oil. The general and the young officer were talking to two Europeans who had just arrived and to whom Gerard had been momentarily introduced.

'Who are the Europeans?' she said.

'A Russian and a Dutchman. Vointsky, I think it was, and Hareng. Don't know who they are; Bolsheviks probably, though we are not supposed to know Feng keeps that company. Best be off, then; Feng wants to take everyone to the New World for gambling and dancing, and I am sure you wouldn't find that amusing.'

'Not tonight,' Charlotte said.

'The New World is a comprehensive den of the world's most depraved vices,' her uncle explained. 'It has gambling on five floors, and what is alleged to be music on most of them. There is only one place in the city that is worse.'

'Surprise me! What could be worse than gambling and loud music?'

'It's rival, the Great World, just around the corner from it, which is exactly the same except that it has opium and jugglers on the second floor, public suicide on the roof and unspeakable atrocities in the cellarage.'

'I would have thought atrocities in the cellarage more or less standard.'

'No,' her uncle continued, 'the cellars of the New World contain nothing more worrying than good French wines, though they tell me they are building an extension for the new vintages from California. Doubtless they will find room for unspeakable atrocities while they are at it.'

'What sort of atrocities are they?' Charlotte asked.

'I am sure I don't know, I have never considered a detailed acquaintance with such matters an essential part of good banking practice. Small boys, dead bodies, human sacrifice, that sort of thing, I would assume.'

'I would find night life a little strenuous after a long journey.'

'There is a spare bedroom in my rooms at the bank,' her uncle offered.

'I prefer a hotel. Less of an imposition, and it preserves the proprieties.'

'You ought to be under my roof, really you ought. Shanghai is a dangerous city, particularly for a scholarly spinster who spends her life in libraries, and doesn't know the world.'

As they left, Charlotte caught the young officer watching her in a considering sort of way.

Bubbling Well Street is merely a portion of Nanking Road devoted less to banks and offices than to shops and merchants of fripperies. There was a herbalist clinic at the return address on Saunders' letter, and it did indeed appear to be what her uncle had called a pox doctor's, but as she had feared, it also operated a profitable sideline as a poste restante.

She thought a while, and then wrote a short note on the back of one of the posters for the New World that were all the herbalist could offer her by way of stationery. It ran:

Dear Saunders,

You will be glad to know that I have arrived in Shanghai without too much difficulty.

I am sure that release of your funds can be expedited by the bank – in which, you may be unaware, I have a significant interest – if satisfactory proofs can be offered of your identity and your good faith.

You have something of mine that I wish returned.

This was not perhaps wise, but it was the best she could manage. If Saunders had killed her brother, he had presumably already killed Watcher and her sisters as well, and had lied to her; but the fact that she was still alive was not a wholly comfortable reminder of the possibility that he was telling the truth.

She handed the note to the herbalist, who allowed that it might in due course be collected, and tried to sell her leopard hairs, the gizzards of hunting birds and the stone teeth of dragons. None of these seemed to meet her current needs.

She was only notionally closer to finding Saunders, and even less so to finding the Darkcallers, assuming them to be distinct entities. She would, on balance, prefer to find them other than by their finding her first.

Thinking hard, and trying to avoid an impotent distress over Watcher that might cloud her mind, she paid little attention to where she was going. She paced the street, pausing occasionally to finger a roll of cloth, or buy small items from the exigent stallholders. The most amazing collection of the rubble of six continents seemed to have ended up on these stalls. On one stall she even found a London bobby's whistle that made her feel a momentary nostalgia for home, to the extent that she weakened and bought it.

Out of the corner of her eye, as she was haggling

with the stallholder, she saw the two Europeans from the restaurant marching down the street with fixed glares and determination. They turned off to the right, pushing their way through the crowds, off towards the French Quarter. She was watching them so intently that she was taken by surprise when someone took her by the arm, and placed what felt like a revolver in the small of her back. She could not see who it was, but there was a smell of hair-oil that she knew well.

'Miss Matthews,' the young officer said in a quiet voice, 'how convenient to find you here. It would not incommode me at all to shoot you here and now, but I would prefer you to accompany me to a place where your death will serve a greater purpose. Killing two birds with one stone, as you English put it, is a project of real elegance, I always find.'

There seemed little she could do for the moment save comply, so Charlotte allowed herself to be walked through the streets of the Quarter that combined, unappetizingly, the composite stink of a Chinese city with the unpleasant municipal architecture of a French provincial town. She noticed, ahead of them, Vointsky and Hareng turn into what appeared to be a girls' school, a vaguely ecclesiastical building in red brick into which, she noticed without surprise, her companion pulled her in turn.

The school was empty, presumably for the summer holidays, and their feet echoed on the polished wood floors of the empty corridors. Vointsky and Hareng did not look round, and turned into a classroom from which Charlotte could hear the voices of a number of Chinese men, arguing fiercely. Charlotte's captor pulled her into an adjacent room.

He pushed her to the floor, and put his hand over her mouth.

'The story of a politically motivated gang-rape and murder of a leading financial interest,' he said, putting his revolver to one side while he tore at her buttons, 'followed by a fatal quarrel between the deranged criminals will be most convincing if there are some signs of an attempt to violate you.'

She bit down on his fingers, hard.

The noise he made did not sound even like the Chinese version of profanity. His grip was still firm, though, and it was without any real surprise that Charlotte felt the blood that briefly flowed from his fingers dry up, and the fingers constantly shift and mend between her worrying teeth.

She kicked out wildly, and made a sudden connection with something solid. With a terrible clatter, the slate of the blackboard toppled from the easel she had kicked and landed on top of them. It was a heavy piece of furniture, and the young officer was lying on top of her. With a major effort, Charlotte wriggled out from under him.

The door opened, and eleven Chinese men rushed in, among them the delegate from Hunan. Vointsky and Hareng followed them.

There followed a loud argument in Chinese, in the course of which Charlotte picked herself up, brushed herself off and sat down on one of the desks in the front row. The delegate from Hunan looked at Charlotte with mild amusement.

'You have interrupted a most interesting debate,' he said. 'The fraternal delegates' – he nodded at Vointsky and Hareng – 'were proposing the dissolution of the party, and I was opposing them.'

'Fraternal delegates, are they?' Charlotte said. 'Last night I met them at dinner with General Feng Yuxiang and his messenger-boy here.'

The delegate smiled, turned and spoke volubly to his colleagues, who looked at the two European men suspiciously. Charlotte noticed that the unconscious young officer's face was drifting a little, but no one else in the room was paying him any attention whatever.

'I have told them,' the delegate said, apologetically, 'that you are reasonably trustworthy, for an imperialist, but they are not especially convinced. I think they are likely to return to the last motion that was put before the disturbance. As amended, of course. To take note of changed circumstances.'

'What motion?' Charlotte said. 'What amendments?'

'To ignore the majority given me by my block vote of sixteen members and kill me, as a left deviationist, whatever that is. And of course to kill you and this running dog of war-lordism.'

'I see.'

She reached into her pocket, pulled out the police whistle and blew a healthy blast. Then she sat back and smiled.

'Gendarmes are always, I have found, prone to prompt arrival and a fair degree of hostility towards covert political activity. Suggest to your colleagues that they had better leave,' she said.

The other delegates, and Vointsky and Hareng, looked at each other, and then ran quickly from the room. The delegate from Hunan looked at her with respect, as Charlotte picked up the young officer's revolver and pointed it at the man on the floor.

'The police will be here, in a moment,' she said. 'I trust it will be agreeable for me to explain to them that you are my hired interpreter, and nothing to do with any illegal meeting that may have been going on here. Indeed you merely followed, when I was abducted by a drunken officer with rapine on his mind. Oh, by the way, my name is Charlotte Matthews – I think they will expect us to know each other's names.'

'My name is Mao,' the delegate said, brushing a curlicue of long dark hair from his forehead, 'Mao Tsetung.'

'Fine.'

'Our friend on the floor appears to be coming back to consciousness,' said Mao. 'Another interesting glandular case, I see. I took him for Chinese at first, but this appears not to be the case.'

The young officer sat up and looked around him with some confusion.

'Very quickly,' Charlotte said. 'Who are you working for? Feng? The Comintern? Or someone else?'

'You have no idea,' the young man said, 'of the power of the organization I represent, Miss Matthews, and of the folly of trying to oppose us. And you,' – he glared at Mao – 'you are an insect on whom we shall tread.'

'I rather thought something of the kind,' Charlotte said, and shot him between the eyes at point-blank range.

'After all,' she explained to the somewhat startled young man, 'the French police are men of the world. And I shot an attempted rapist with his own revolver.'

The French police were easier to appease than her uncle, though he was somewhat mollified when General Feng sent round a large basket of flowers to Charlotte with a note offering his profoundest apologies that an officer of his army should have behaved so badly. Indeed, he further insisted that they should be his guests that night, at the New World.

Charlotte summoned a tailor to her hotel suite.

'But I don't want to wear a dinner-jacket,' said Mao Tse-tung.

'Come come,' Charlotte said. 'I saved your life this morning; the least you can do is help guard my back for an evening.'

'But I don't know anything about the decadent pursuits of such places.'

'Indeed I should think not, and that will make you all the more useful, because you will be attentive and not take anything for granted.'

'But I still don't want to wear a dinner-jacket.'

'What is good enough for me,' Charlotte countered, 'ought to be good enough for you. We are going to see General Feng, and one thing he will not be expecting is a Communist in a dinner-jacket. It was you after all who taught me valuable lessons about hiding in plain sight. Another thing he will not be expecting, of course, is a woman wearing one, but I shall tell him, not inaccurately, that it is all the rage in Paris. I detest skirts, and I need pockets.'

Mao had a surly expression on his face that seemed to betoken a lack of interest in such matters.

'In the meantime,' Charlotte said, 'I have a small job for you. You are, are you not, a professional agitator?'

He nodded.

'So go down to the New World in your present attire and wander around to the service entrance, and strike up a conversation with the waiters, or the cooks, or the croupiers.'

'What would I want to do that for?'

'So that you can agitate them. Exploit a legitimate grievance; incite class hatred; do whatever it is that you people do.'

He departed, less than wholly convinced.

She telephoned the gendarmerie and discovered, not totally to her surprise, that the body of the young officer had been handed over by the morgue to one of his brothers, also a captain in the forces of General Feng. At her request, Sammy White went to the pox doctor's clinic and checked that the letter had indeed been collected by, the herbalist said, an uncouth Northerner with bad manners and protuberant eyebrows. The herbalist had offered a potion that would remove this imperfection and had received a dusty answer; later, White returned with a letter which had been handed to him at the bank.

My dear Charlotte,

Imagine my surprise at learning you had made such good time on your journey to Shanghai. Our own journey passed without incident, you will be glad to hear, though sadly we failed to cross the paths of our errant cousins. Doubtless we will come across them soon. Like all great or wicked cities, Shanghai is a very small place.

It would be convenient were you to encourage the release of my funds without unnecessary officiousness; I have some information that may be essential to your survival.

As you say, I have something of yours, but it is not yet in working order and I am loth to let something of such sentimental value pass out of my hands without a consideration.

My congratulations on your recent intrepid adventure; you are indeed a formidable young woman. But you are still not immortal, and you have some very powerful enemies, among the least of whom, I number myself.

Frederick Saunders

Uncle Gerard made a terrible fuss when he discovered

that Charlotte was going to the New World in men's clothing.

'Anyone would think that you revelled in decadence, or that your head had been turned by your experiences,' he complained.

'Nonsense, Gerard, I am an independent woman, in command of my own fortune. And in a society like this one, to wear anything other than the clothing of privilege is to advertise yourself as a dependant. General Feng will just have to swallow any principles he may have regarding the matter because there is no reason for me to kowtow to him.'

'I suppose not,' said Gerard, resignedly. 'Can we rely on this Mao chap you have hired? Do we know anything about his people?'

'They are perfectly respectable farmers in Hunan,' Charlotte said. 'And he is himself a respectable married man.'

'Sturdy yeoman stock, eh? Offer him a job with the bank if you like. Ambitious young chap like that; should go far.'

'I don't think so. That is, I don't think he wants a job in the bank. I think he regards his people as having a prior claim on his time. And, speaking of the command of my own fortune, you will recall that Tom signed a power of attorney when he went off in '14. I may need to make some investments.'

You could hear the New World a block-and-a-half away. Charlotte reflected that it was bad enough going into what she assumed to be the lion's den, without being deafened at the same time. From the third floor came the discordant strains of a German band, a Chinese orchestra and a piano player, imported at considerable expense from New Orleans, who was playing some sort of ragtime. You could hardly see the full moon overhead for the blaze of lights from the nightclub's windows, and the flaming gas torches around its door.

In addition, from a block or so away the streets were crowded with rickshaws, carriages and parking cars. Charlotte and Mao had reluctantly allowed Gerard's chauffeur to drive them the few hundred yards to the entrance; Gerard had had a sticking-point – the prospect of the fearful shame of allowing Charlotte to arrive at the New World on foot.

'Good evening, Sir,' said the young man at the door, who wore an elaborate green brocade robe over black trousers, 'and good evening to you, – ah – Miss.'

'We are part of General Feng's party. I am Miss Charlotte Matthews, of the bank, and Mao here is my interpreter.'

'You have come at a convenient time,' the young man said. 'The General has just finished his prayer-meeting and is about to proceed to the roulette wheel.'

As Charlotte walked past him, she noticed that there was mud on the heels of his European shoes. Beyond the pink marble staircase that curved up to the principal gambling halls, there was an entrance covered by a brown velvet curtain.

She walked towards it.

'I will just avail myself of the cloakroom facilities,' she said.

'Ah, no,' said the commissionaire, catching up with her. 'They are upstairs. We will show you.'

'I don't understand you,' she said, 'speak more clearly.'

He started to pull at her arm, and she yielded to his entreaties. She had had time to see that behind the velvet curtain was a staircase leading down, and that the bottom of the curtain was stained with the same thick mud as his shoes.

The general was wearing a rather better pair of trousers, a resplendent purple cummerbund, a jacket whose epaulettes and orders dripped as bright as the chandeliers overhead, and a benign and fatherly expression. He looked askance at Charlotte's clothing and then pulled his face into its normal smile.

'He says,' Mao translated, 'he is glad to see that you have chosen to dress in a manner that could provoke no further attempts on your virtue.'

'May he live a thousand years,' said Charlotte, reasoning that politeness costs nothing.

'He wishes to present the brother of the man you killed,' Mao continued, 'who wishes to proffer his apologies.'

An officer almost identical to his brother, wearing a different but equally repellent hair-oil, drew them aside.

'The old man claims to speak no English,' he said, 'but there is no reason to trust his veracity.'

'Indeed,' Mao said, 'foreign languages are an accomplishment which I myself consider better exercised than acknowledged.'

'You do not,' the officer said, 'appreciate the seriousness of your situation. You are, both of you, doomed as soon as we can make the appropriate arrangements.'

'Revolutionaries,' Mao said, 'are dead men on leave.'

'Appositely quoted,' Charlotte said.

'I had thought it original.'

'Besetting problem of the aphoristic. Anyway,' – she turned back to the officer – 'what about this doom then?'

'You do not understand,' he said. 'It is our intention to dispose of all of these Bolsheviks. They are unlikely to disturb the endless peace of China, but it is as well to be sure. You, Miss Matthews, you seem to be altogether too inquisitive for your own good, or even too well-informed.'

'Just so,' she said.

The officer narrowed his lips, rather more perhaps than was normal in a human being expressing wrath.

'Avoid dark corners,' he said.

Charlotte and Mao bowed to him politely and walked back to the general and his party, who were about to leave the roulette table for a room on the next floor. Charlotte stopped to place a small bet, for luck, and found difficulty in getting the croupier to meet her eye. She was not surprised to notice that he had bushy eyebrows.

'Tell your master,' she said, 'that we need to talk.'

'No speakee English,' the croupier said.

'I think you do.'

She noticed with satisfaction that the young officer was still watching her; she stuck out her tongue at him, and then, with Mao dogging her footsteps, she sauntered up the stairs.

Halfway up the stairs, she paused.

'Mao,' she said. 'I know you are not enjoying all this very much, so go and talk to all the friends you have made here. Persuade them that they need an evening off; national holiday, or mass protest, or something.'

The very first person she noticed in the room upstairs, where a game of baccarat was in progress, was young Fritzi, whom she seized by the arm the moment she spotted him.

'Fritzi, darling, how nice to see you. Was it in Menton? Or was it in Venezia? I thought I might find you here, and I brought this for you.'

She drew him aside and thrust an envelope into his hand.

'You need a stake, don't you?' she said.

'I can manage,' he replied.

'You would like a proper stake.'

'Yes.'

'And I need a bargaining counter. We are surrounded by our enemies. I hope you are as good as you say you are.'

He tore open the envelope and looked inside. He gave a long slow whistle.

'Just be as good as you say you are,' she said, 'and we might all live out the night.'

Then she went over to the bar, and sat for an hour sipping fresh orange juice mixed with Vichy water. She had learned in Italy during the war that it was often possible, without the use of spirits, to abstract one's attention for a while until it was needed. The alternative to abstraction would have been to catalogue the lapses of taste in the room's décor, a long list, in which gilt dragons and red lacquer trimmings would have competed for priority.

After an hour, Fritzi took a break from the table, and tried to explain in tedious technical terms what he had done. Charlotte patted him on the arm, and sent him back to the tables.

When, after a while, he went down to the roulette tables, she followed him at a distance, just to be on the safe side. He seemed to be doing rather well, and she noticed after a while that General Feng, and various of the casino staff, were sweating.

The tension was increased by the gathering silence – the bands had stopped playing, and the *chanteuse* in a cheongsam who had been singing 'Tea for Two' and other risqué modern ditties packed up her music and went and sat at the bar. After a while, it became imposs- ible to get a drink – the bar staff appeared to have gone off somewhere, and a press developed at the bar of men unable to cope without alcohol. Charlotte finished her orange juice and wandered over to the table.

'I will see your boss, now,' she said to the croupier.

'Fritzi,' she added, 'you can take a break now.'

He bustled up, full of himself.

'I really would like to go on,' he said. 'I've never broken the bank before.'

'If you must,' she said indulgently.

'You can have your money back.'

'That will be acceptable.'

'And I thought I would make you a present of what I won from General Feng.'

Charlotte had a sudden feeling that things had got out of control, as the entire group of officers from Feng's entourage, including the one who had threatened her, walked up to her and Fritzi as a body.

'I may have need of you later,' Charlotte said. 'But you may reassure General Feng that it is in any case a loan, and you had better hang on to them, to protect yourself and the General. You, on the other hand,' — and she pointed to the officer who had threatened her — 'may come with me right away. I have a proposition to put to you.'

'I have nothing further to say to you,' he said.

'And I will say one thing to you. The enemy of my enemy is my friend, except when he is the enemy of all.'

The officer narrowed his eyes.

'I think you take my meaning,' Charlotte said. 'Sometimes, there is a need for truce. It is a full moon, for those who take account of these things, and a party of Darkcallers came here from Urga bringing something precious, and they brought a virgin child as well.'

'We have underestimated you, Miss Matthews,' the officer said. 'I had thought you knew too much, but this is intolerable.'

'In life there are priorities. I have priorities, and you have priorities. And the keeping of secrets may be a high one with you, but there are higher ones yet, are there not?'

He followed her up the staircase, then seized her by the arm.

'But how do you know that I am not one of them?' he said.

'You have the stink of hidebound, privileged, brutal reaction on you,' she said, 'of a pathetic desire to keep things always the same. But in Urga I smelled the stink of madness. They are surprisingly different.'

'And at the top of these stairs, what do you smell at the top of these stairs?'

'I smell the tired, corrupt stink of business as usual.'

They were on the top floor now, and the staircase led to a penthouse on the roof. In a sudden flurry of footsteps, Mao joined them.

'I have done as you asked,' he said.

'Good,' Charlotte said, and knocked loudly on the door that led into the penthouse. It was opened by another of the People of the Plain; they all really did have those eyebrows in common, it must be inbreeding or something, thought Charlotte. Inside, there was the noise of someone shouting very loudly, and in some distress, into a speaking-tube.

'Tell Mr Saunders that we are here to see him,' she said.

Against a far wall, shouting into the speaking-trumpet, the vast bulk of Saunders lolled on cushions. The air was thick with scent and incense, but it could not hide completely the animal stink of him. In such surroundings, he looked less human than ever, the green silk robe he had thrown over his bulk glimmering in the dim light like a serpent's scales.

Two more of the People of the Plains stood beside the cushions; one of them had a large and exotic curved sword, a yataghan, Charlotte supposed, or something of the heathenish sort, and the other a tommy-gun. Against the wall to her right, in what looked like extreme discomfort, the six sisters lay groaning in what would have been human shape, save that individual limbs were clenched and paw-like. A closer examination revealed that each of them had, around those limbs, a tight manacle too narrow to fit human shape. Watcher was nearest to Saunders, and her eyes were focused enough to signal extreme distress to Charlotte.

'I have come for what is mine,' Charlotte said.

'You have found me with your usual dispatch,' Saunders said.

'A person as large as you leaves large footprints. In the present case, large, ill-printed handbills at the herbalists where you have your mail sent. I know that it pays to advertise, but there are exceptions to every rule.'

'You have brought my money, from the bank?'

'No, on the contrary, from him that hath not, I have taken away even that which he had.'

More voices gabbled at Saunders through the speaking-tube.

'My agent has broken your bank,' Charlotte said. 'And my colleague here,' – Mao bowed – 'has spread social unrest among your domestic staff. I hold you, Saunders, in the palm of my hand. My uncle will never allow you access to my funds without seeing you, unless I assure him that I have seen you and that you are not an impostor. I do not know what egotistical game has led you to reduce my lover and her sisters to their present unfortunate state, but . . .'

'I needed them,' Saunders said, 'and I could not be sure of their compliance. You have no idea of how important . . .'

'I think I do. Otherwise I would not have involved the captain here.'

'Stasis,' Saunders hissed.

'Just so,' confirmed the captain.

'I think,' Charlotte resumed, 'that if we are to go through your little tunnel, we had better make a start now.'

'How do you know about the tunnel?' asked Saunders.

'It is merely basic prudence to know about a tunnel for which I appear to have paid.'

'The best of luck.'

'You will be coming too. This is too important for the most effective fighting-machine we will have to think of himself as on the staff.'

'But he must not be seen,' the captain said.

Outside and below, the noise of discontent had started to become almost a riot. Charlotte stepped to the door of the penthouse, drew her whistle from her pocket and blew three stentorian blasts.

She turned to Mao.

'Would you do the honours?'

'It's a raid,' shouted Mao Tse-tung, in several languages.

'Thank you,' she said.

Outside, the tumult grew and then gradually dwindled into the street.

'We have a few minutes,' Charlotte said. 'Your keys, Saunders, and be quick about it.'

'There is still a tommy-gun pointed at you,' Saunders said.

'Don't be childish. Your interests dictate that you transcend murderous spite, and that we all settle our grievances afterwards. Your keys.'

The guards handed their weapons to Mao, who retained the tommy-gun, and then they took the keys and released the prisoners. The sisters stretched and yawned, their tongues lolling over their teeth, and eased their cramped bestial limbs into a more human shape. Watcher tore the gag from her mouth.

'Charlotte,' she said.

'I said,' Charlotte reiterated, 'that we will settle our grievances later.' Then she softened, walked over to Watcher, and smiled and embraced her for a moment, moving her hands delicately over the much-loved body and the suit that travel and chains had worn almost to rags.

Below, the rooms had cleared, leaving little except a few overturned chairs, a bottle of champagne that dripped on to the floor and a cigar burning in an ashtray to indicate a passing human presence. Halfway down the stairs, the party was joined by the group of officers, Fritzi and General Feng.

Charlotte loathed speeches.

'More is at stake than I can discreetly speak about,' she said. 'One thing you need to know. There is a child in danger; that should be enough.'

General Feng looked at the vast, monstrous bulk of Saunders, tottered to the table where the champagne bottle was dripping and proceeded to gulp from its neck. This was no time for a breach of lifelong teetotalism, Charlotte thought, but refrained from commenting beyond a sour look. The old man was a valued client of the bank after all, and probably best left behind.

The young man with the muddy trousers had dispensed with his robe, and locked the doors of the New World; he stood at the curtain passing out extra firearms.

'You seem well prepared,' Charlotte said with surprise.

'We have an extensive Lost Property department at the New World,' said Saunders.

'Some people seem obsessed with collecting lost property,' Watcher said, almost sourly.

'And some of us,' Charlotte said, softening her words a little with a smile, 'do not relish being treated as luggage.'

Watcher smiled back, and laid her hand on Charlotte's wrist.

'I had some leisure to think, through the ache of my healing head, and you were right. I have cause to think ill of myself.'

'It does not matter,' Charlotte said. 'I am sure that, over the years, I will do things that you have to forgive, and it is best to establish a precedent of reasonableness.'

At the bottom of the stairs there was a wine cellar, which stretched under vaulting for some yards. At the end of the stone vaulting there were pit-props holding up a tunnel that continued in the same direction for twenty claustrophobic yards, took a short turn for six and then ended in clay.

'There is not far to go,' Saunders said. 'It is important that they don't hear us coming until the last possible moment.'

He took the lead and charged at the clay face, tearing at it with his vast shovel-like hands. He began to sweat, and Charlotte noticed how patches of his back had acquired a surface as much like scales as skin, though only moderately like either. With a cry of triumph he pushed aside hunks of masonry, that fell away from him with a splash. He dived forwards, wading up to his waist in the channel that lay immediately before the tunnel's mouth.

Opposite, rather than the blank wall of the storm-sewer, was a raised embankment with a high water mark near its brim, and beyond that a vast chamber that smelled of mortar gone to flakes, and stone worn to round evenness by the sheer weight of age.

The young man from the door had brought two large planks with him from further back in the cellar and these he proceeded to lay across the sewer. The party clattered across them with the best speed they could manage. At the far end of the chamber, they heard chanting. If it resembled the howling of wolves, they were wolves that had not only eaten carrion but smeared it on their muzzles, wolves whose eyes would have the yellow sheen of rancid butter. The figures stood around a great altar, a vast shape of stone, whose seeming formlessness had implications that chittered nervously at the borders of the unconscious mind. At its head stood a smaller stone that glimmered in the torchlight, and on the great stone lay a naked, but as yet apparently whole, girl child. As the interlopers rushed at them, they shrieked and turned; to her surprise, Charlotte recognized among them, their faces shifting into beasthood, both the herbalist and the knife-grinder.

What ensued was a whirlwind of teeth and knives, bullets and sudden rushes. Charlotte saw Mao firing his tommy-gun into the coming wall of constantly mutating flesh, but was whirled away by a clawed hand that seized her throat until discouraged by a bullet. She found herself briefly in the eye of the storm, and dived out of it on the other side, managing a reasonably accomplished rugby-tackle – how fortunate at such times to have had an aggressively athletic brother – on the Dark-caller with a large and unpleasant-looking knife, who seemed to be about to kill the child. In a wild scrabble for position on the stone-flagged floor where they had both fallen, he grabbed the knife he had momentarily dropped and turned to stab Charlotte, but she seized his arm, and was surprised to find it frail and all too human seeming.

Someone reached past her, and stove in the Darkcaller's head with the smaller stone that had been the idol by the altar's head; when she looked at him to give him thanks, he nodded, his face resuming a human aspect, and she realized that it was the herbalist.

Charlotte seized the child, who had begun the most frightful caterwauling, and took it out of harm's way in the shelter of the altar. She tried ineffectually to soothe it, and to stroke its hair into some kind of order; a somewhat battered Mao joined her on the floor.

'I have more experience with children,' he said. 'And I think you have other concerns. I am quite surprised at the extent to which I find myself taking your orders, let alone the extent to which everyone else seems to be.'

'When I first met Mr Saunders,' Charlotte said, 'I cited the works of Herr Doctor Freud, but after thinking a good deal about the giving and taking of orders, I have since decided that the works of Mr Jack London have greater relevance. There is always a struggle as to which wolf leads the pack.'

'Ah yes, I understand that London is a great favourite of Lenin's.'

Charlotte looked across the room at the battle, that was the usual mêlée; she paused to look at the idol, a black stone of possibly meteoric origin, that someone had carved rather badly into what might have been a walking lizard, or maybe a bird.

Saunders, in the middle of the mêlée, threw away from him two Darkcallers who had been hewing at the back of his neck with ineffectual hatchets, and they landed against a far wall with a fatal-sounding crunch.

'Get away from the altar,' he shouted.

Charlotte turned. With a slow, massive and decisive

effort, the nearer end of the altar raised itself from the ground, and looked at her with blank hideous great eyes. Mao raised his tommy-gun to shoot, and a huge paw batted it away and clubbed him to the ground; an eye turned from Charlotte to the child.

What had seemed shapelessness was merely a failure to think through logically how Saunders had been in her childhood, what he was now, and how, perhaps over centuries, he might continue to change. She remembered the destruction of Feng's militia, and reached into her pocket, producing the razor and flicking it open. If, she thought, one is to die messily, one may as well inflict a little pain in the process.

There was an echoing incoherence to the voice that then spoke, like sunken temples of evil reputation, or the bottom of poisoned wells.

'Ceremonies can be overrated,' it croaked. 'The Dark may yet come, if I take the child.'

Its open mouth stank and steamed in the cold of the cellar; vermin crawled among its scythe-like teeth. It reached for the girl Shumeng, but she darted beetle-quick away from its clutch, forcing herself into a crevice in the stonework.

'Leave her alone, you overgrown pond-spawn,' said Charlotte.

'Ay, yes, the redoubtable Miss Matthews. Doubtless, one virgin is as good as another.'

It reached for her with a slow, lazy paw, drawing back in sudden sharp reflex as Charlotte slashed the web between its finger and its titanic thumb with her razor.

'I am not precisely a virgin,' said Charlotte.

It reached for her again, and she slashed across its horny palm, drawing a thin line of blood.

'I am starting to find this annoying,' it said. 'You mindless little ape!'

144

Then, suddenly, a look of entire amazement came over its features. The vast maw that gaped across its moon-like features fixed in a rictus that showed its teeth, darkened by the years as by smoke. It raised itself up on its hindquarters, and collapsed on to its side with a resounding crash. Charlotte walked across and listened to the pounding of its mighty heart shudder and cease. She wiped the blood off her razor on to one of the few patches of fur remaining on its scaly flank and looked at the blade. It had returned to its usual bright sheen.

'Curare,' Saunders said. 'It gets them every time.'

Beyond him, the battle had ended. There were a large number of corpses, few of them identifiable by affiliation or species. Watcher limped across, with a vast bruise building across her shoulders, and a claw half-torn from her hand; the sisters followed her, Singer semi-conscious and supported by Mourner and Sojourner with her arms across their shoulders. The knife-grinder was there, the filminess of his eyes now less like cataracts than some quick smear of membrane.

Most of Feng's officers were somewhere in the pile of the slain, but the pompous little martinet who had threatened her earlier had come through with hardly a scratch.

'These cattle have seen too much,' he said. 'I invoke the Truce of the Lines. I really must insist . . .'

'Must, is it, little creature?' Saunders posed. 'I think you will find that matters will arrange themselves without further bloodshed, but if you insist, I can arrange for that bloodshed.'

'I really must insist,' the Stasis captain said.

'He means,' Charlotte said, 'that he can arrange for your blood to be shed. And Mr Saunders is so efficient in such matters that I would take him at his word.'

145

'Just so,' Saunders said.

'But the cattle . . .' the officer objected.

'The child will not remember more than a fever-dream,' said Mao Tse-tung. 'And I have other fish to fry.'

'And I,' Charlotte said, throwing her arm around Watcher with an abandon that forgot until too late the bruised state of her lover's shoulders, 'have my own reasons for discretion.'

'Go away, little creature,' Saunders said. 'Run back to Peking, and tell them that Shanghai is mine, mine utterly.'

Mao seemed about to say something demagogic and tactless, but Charlotte kicked him gently in the shin. The captain and his few surviving cohorts slunk away.

Charlotte nodded to Settler, who raised her revolver so that it pointed at Saunders. One of the People of the Plain had survived the battle, and also raised a revolver, pointing it at Charlotte.

Charlotte ignored this. 'As a representative of your banker, I think it is time that you settled your accounts.'

'My dear little Charlotte,' Saunders said, 'I must congratulate you on your skill. You are indeed a worthy huntress, a fine player of the Great Game. But presumably it will have occurred to you by now that every step you have taken, give or take the odd Chinese Bolshevik, was allowed for in my plans. The razor alone should tell you that.'

'The facts could indicate that we have all been walking around your web,' Charlotte said. 'Or they could indicate that you are an arrogant braggart with a certain gift for improvisation.'

'We have not forgiven him our confinement,' said Watcher, 'and there is a more sinister explanation for his actions. What group has been active in this affair that places everything in the hands of chance?'

'There is a lot of loose talk about Chaos,' said Saunders. 'It does not, as such, exist; there is merely a group of like-minded chaps who have taken notice of the extent to which chance rules in human affairs, and whose plans take account of it.'

'That is not good enough,' Settler said, maintaining her grip on the revolver.

'But it is. What can you accuse me of, Charlotte, save the same ruthless willingness to use that your lover and her sisters possess? And that you have so thoroughly shown? And both your sense of justice and self-preservation should tell you that it is best to assume I am telling the truth. Leave me alone. And let well alone.'

Charlotte nodded to Settler, who shrugged and lowered her revolver.

'Everyone wins,' Saunders said. 'The Darkcallers and their Ancient are gone from Shanghai, and the last of those who killed your brother and Watcher's parents are dead; you have proved again to your lover and her sisters that you are a worthy leader of the hunt.'

'So this is all supposed to have been some sort of colossal favour to me.'

'Of course, Charlotte. I have broken them to your leash. Hunt well.'

'But I love Watcher; I don't want her will in my keeping.'

'Of course. As you wish.'

A pause followed, in which Charlotte looked lovingly at Watcher, who looked back at her with a combination of devotion and suspicion.

'As for myself,' Saunders continued, 'I have added the Great World to the New as a possession – you realized, I take it, whose cellars these are. I have even, I suspect, acquired a useful manager in young Fritzi here; I have always regarded merit as more important than blood.'

'So we chased all the way here,' Charlotte said, 'to procure for you the command of a bordello?'

'The fossils will be broken up and sold as medicine by my herbalist here. Except for a few that will find their way into the possession of a Jesuit of my acquaintance; when I met him in southern England, he showed a rare gift for confusing things. The idol is interesting; it is one of the larger fragments of the Siberian meteor, sculpted into its present form by, I hope, pious fraud. I shall wrap it in old newspapers and ship it off to California, where, I trust, it will cause no further problems. I myself will vegetate here, devoting myself to pleasure and hallucination . . .'

Charlotte and Watcher looked at each other, shrugged, and joined hands.

'This simply is not good enough,' said Mao Tse-tung.

'I seem to have everything I want,' Charlotte said. 'And no one has died who was not trying to kill someone else. Usually you.'

'You,' Mao turned to Saunders, speaking in high rage and taking gulps of breath. 'I do not care who or what you are. These games of conspiracy and transformation are a luxury that one who aspires to serve the people cannot afford to reckon with. But it is intolerable. That you should have such power and use it all for selfish ends. To loll, smoking opium, and playing chess with human lives. Where is the responsibility in that? What of the people?'

'Those who rule men,' Saunders said, 'have no power, and do not rule. Chance rules.'

'I will not believe that.'

'Find me in fifty years and tell me so again.'

The child Shumeng had crawled from her hiding place and now stood with them by the great corpse, into whose dead open eye she now spat.

Mao turned to the child, and spoke to her in Chinese. She listened, evidently struggling to understand his dialect.

'I have told Shumeng,' he said, 'that I rely on her to keep me honest. She may come to me at any time, and I will listen to her advice. She is of the people, and who better to advise me?'

'You overestimate your capacity to combat destiny,' Saunders said. 'You had best ask her what name she will choose to bear as an adult. Shumeng is a child's name, and you would not wish to miss her advice. By chance.'

Mao turned to the child, and asked her.

'Jiang Qing,' she said.

'Now off with you,' Saunders said. 'Your comrades are reconvening at North Lake; you will lose the vote, but they will not press for your blood. I will arrange for the child and her mother to return home. They will be safe.'

Mao limped away, back to the bridge across the sewer. He turned then, his eyes filled with anger.

'I have remembered a line of the immortal Shakespeare which sums up my feelings.'

He paused.

'I'll be revenged on the whole pack of you,' he said.

Charlotte embraced Watcher even more tightly and the sisters huddled in around them. On the bridge, Mao passed the servant from the New World, who brought Saunders a pipe, lit it and handed it to him.

'Power, money, responsibility; honour, love and revenge,' Saunders said.

He drew deeply on the opium pipe.

And then he said, 'The stuff that dreams are made of.'

SOUNDS AND SWEET AIRS

Graham Higgins

BBC World Service news item:

The death has been announced of David Daniels, the actor and director. Daniels began his career as a singer, recording three internationally successful albums before turning his attention to acting. He was known in the industry as a supremely versatile actor, appearing in such diverse films as the award-winning Crime and Punishment, *which was also his début as director, and the* Arabian Nights *series made by his own production company, and for which he is perhaps best remembered. Many film fans were disappointed when he announced his intention to abandon his public career, and in recent years he became a recluse, devoting himself to ocean voyages in his private yacht. A close friend said of him: 'Like Sinbad, he sailed in search of treasure, which in his case meant privacy.'*

David Daniels' ashes were scattered at sea.

A close friend. That was me. The quote was his. I wouldn't have come up with something like that. He'd left me some helpful notes. Typical.

I've kept a little jar of sand from the island. Here on my window-sill, even on bright days, you get no impression of the colours of that shore: blinding white at noon, warm pink in the sunset, a blue whisper by moonlight. But what you can see, even with a half-decent magnifying glass, is that the sand is made up mostly of crushed shell and coral. Amongst these shattered fragments of ghostly architecture there are shards of delicate pink and amber, and a speckling of volcanic jet. The shore is sugary underfoot. When you lie by the sea you can hardly resist taking idle handfuls of sand; handfuls of time measured out in tiny lives, seismic torment reduced to pretty powder.

It was a few handfuls of sand I sprinkled with due solemnity on the waters. Why David should want this appearance of sacrament I can't say. Nor why he should choose me to officiate. The official story – his discovery of the island, the sudden and virulent tropical disease and hasty cremation – covered the contingencies, and I needn't sort out the loose ends because the lone voyager still maintained a staff to handle his affairs. I don't know who my version of events is for. Posterity? My bones will run through the fingers of posterity and crunch underfoot.

As soon as I picked up the package off the front doormat I could see it was from David. How he managed to keep a track of my addresses over the years has remained a mystery, but it comforted me, as no doubt it was intended to. I propped the package against a pile of bills and magazines on the kitchen table and lingered over breakfast, the better to enjoy the anticipation of breaking the seal. I could hear the rattle of a cassette inside, so I wanted to be ready to play it through uninterrupted.

The package was made up with rough, fibrous brown paper which hadn't travelled well. The stamps featured brightly coloured images of racing cyclists, a weightlifter, and a pair of Siamese twins joined at the shoulder. These last two were in soccer strip, so they may have been leaping for possession of a ball, now lost for ever beneath a slick of mauve franking-ink. David's even handwriting remained clear and legible on the scuffed wrapping, which had been carefully folded and sealed. Inside was another layer, this time of crimped maize paper, and inside that, the cassette.

The glinting perspex case and the crisp German manufacturers' graphics on the inlay made a curious contrast to the plainly handmade parcel. There was no track listing, only a telephone number written on the label of the cassette itself. I supposed it was a telephone number. No letter.

I hesitated between the telephone and the tape deck before I realized that's exactly what David would expect. His way of sending up my chronic indecision. His little joke. Like the tour T-shirt said: *David Daniels: Provocation = Evolution.* I opted for the tape deck and stretched out on the couch to listen. My fortieth birthday. That was the first time I heard the music.

So much has been written about David that I can't think of anything I could add. Our paths started to cross when he was David Daniels, Rock Singer. That was the phase before David Daniels, Movie Actor and David Daniels, Film Director and Designer. At forty-two, David quietly sold up his business interests and took to ocean-voyaging as a retirement hobby.

Maybe he kept in touch like this with lots of people, but I was always pretty flattered when I heard from him, partly because I was so far removed from all that. Not that I have any principles about showbiz. If I could've met up with a dark man at a crossroads offering some of what David had in exchange for my soul, I'd have had my plasma on the dotted line before you could cry mercy.

Instead I have what the music papers call 'a small but dedicated cult following' which means I've put out half a dozen albums, that a handful of writers think are soundly put together, and that an equal number of their friends buy to tape for friends. When you start to earn any kind of living you are said to 'leap' from cult status, a polite euphemism for 'honourable failure'.

The other title I hate is 'musician's musician', but I know what they mean. This flat was wired by an electrician's electrician; it's an admirable piece of work in its way, once you work it out.

It would be naïve of me to skirt around the fact that these are albums by a woman. Filtered through the Boys' Own world of music writing this reads 'Women's Albums'. Membership of a special-needs gender is not an asset to marketing, I gather.

The last three albums were made with my money and along the way cost me my marriage, a house, and some threadbare patches in my shop-soiled sanity. I can't complain.

I knock about on clarinet or drums with a rackety little trad-jazz band of Bix-fixated old maniacs, not so much jamming as preserving, doing the kind of clubs whose members will have us.

For money I do technical knock-ups on the desk at a local sound studio, and I get dead-time in return to do radio jingles and incidental music for industrial videos. These tracks go on to production companies' library shelves and have titles like 'Mellow Blue: floating synth theme over string and brass build. 2.27' or 'Prairie Highway: positive rolling piano, country rock backing. 1.43'. Officially they're by R. Porlock. (You know about the tradesman who interrupted Coleridge and stopped him finishing *Xanadu*. Coleridge says 'Where the hell did you spring from?' and the tradesman replies . . .)

When the other flats are empty during the day I can noodle away with my own little mixing-desk following the argument wherever it goes. I've never managed to take it for granted that you can drop a piece of plastic into a box of electronics and hear music from almost anywhere in the world and history. If I was a writer I might write about it, but for me it was easier and quicker to make records about it.

On my last album, say, (*1691*, Plumbob Records Pb003, at discerning record stores) there's a track called 'Nerval Quadrille'. It's a zydeco two-step version of a twelfth-century Breton troubadour ballad with a vocal arrangement based on evangelical gospel 'quartettes'. Really, it sounds better than it sounds. QED.

One writer described me as a musical de-ranger. As I said, the public isn't much impressed by my conclusion so far. I am the victim of wicked genes.

All of which accounts for my pleasure when I still hear from David, but not for why he bothers. I'm writing me in here because nobody else will.

The tape was beginning. It was a field-recording. Probably on an Uher. The music began with a bamboo flute, played so that the in-breath put down a rhythm, joined on occasion by spoken syllables. Then the tone changed so that I wondered if I'd been mistaken, because the treble of the flute seemed now to be more like a human voice singing counter-tenor. The recording-level was all over the place and for a while it occurred to me that far from being a raw recording it was a clever series of edits, another joke. Next time the music faded I listened for the splice, which didn't come. Instead the sound evolved into a set of hefty pan-pipes. If he'd edited it then he'd taken a lot of care over continuity in the ambient noise. If it was a practical joke, he'd taken some pains over it.

This was stupid. I wasn't listening at all except to the chatter in my own head. I rewound the tape, and for a second wondered if I should take it out and call that number.

Listen first.

I played the tape end to end twice before I picked up the phone and by the time I got through I still wasn't sure what I'd heard. I'd heard enough to want to call the number. You never knew what to expect with David. He said that people used neuroses like coffee granules so he liked to put them in hot water from time to time. He sounds like a tyrant king, but he'd also said how quickly imaginary fears dissolve in real predicaments. Some people who'd worked with him said he made them paranoid. During the ringing-tone I tried to expect anything and anticipate nothing.

I hadn't expected a firm of solicitors.

Mr Daniels had instructed them that my debts should be underwritten and my household expenses disbursed for a period of two months in the first instance, commencing on the date of my embarcation on a flight to Dakar (to be arranged at my earliest convenience). Mr Daniels would arrange for me to travel on, and there was a sum deposited with the firm to defray incidental expenses. My discretion was expected and appreciated. Did I wish the first tranche of this sum to be deposited in my account?

When I put down the phone I was in several minds, all of them belonging to someone who'd just won first prize in a competition he didn't even know he'd entered. She. Me.

So there were a few days of packing, and shopping (clothes! I'd forgotten what it felt like to be dressed head to foot in new clothes), and time on the phone, and unpacking and repacking. All the time there was nothing in the post or on the answering machine from David.

I had an idea about transcribing some of the music on the tape into notation and used some of David's money to get a book of Messiaen's bird-song transcriptions. Needless to say when I got to the airport I fell for a spy thriller, but I paid for that myself.

On the flight, I listened to the tape again. The thriller read itself while I helpfully turned the pages. The music became an unexpectedly effective soundtrack to the tribal feuds in the novel. Gradually there seemed to be a more plaintive tension in the music than I'd heard before. I closed the book and listened.

One of the things that had made me suspicious about the tape was the number of times a passage or phrasing would recall music I already knew. The discs I looked out made an unlikely heap: Bach, Toots Thielmans, Cootie Williams, Lully, Alfred Deller, Yma Sumac, Alessandro Moreschi . . . a tape I own purely on the strength of these four following words, '. . . the last Papal castrato' on the label. Those are some of the European–American stack.

Here in the gently thrumming sterile tube of the fuselage I was hearing something else. In my mind's eye I could picture the sleeves of the other records I'd have to add to the growing pile: Penderecki, Ligeti, Arvo Part, those polychromatic devotional chants from Russia and Tibet. Someone once told me Janis Joplin sometimes gave off those phantom harmonics too, but they never made it on to disc.

I shook off the earphones and got back into the novel for the rest of the flight.

There was an overnight stop at Dakar. I was booked into a place you were careful to call 'an' hotel: air-conditioned room with view and *en suite* facilities including a TV with a hypnotic Adult Video channel. Plus, when I slipped the floor porter five American dollars – I've played (sing it) for pennies on the street, so tipping was a hair-raising novelty – he matter-of-factly handed me a stick of herbal bojangles. After a meal garnished with piped Bert Kaempfert in the hotel restaurant, I retired to a memorable night out in my room. Never underestimate the potency of good pot and glossy porn. Later, as I drifted off listening to the tape, a little earlier than I'd intended, I was adding to the pile of records: Stax horns, Etta James, Robert Johnson, Son House ... And I told David aloud in the dark, 'I'm confronting my fears, David. I'm terribly afraid I might become a slave of luxury.'

I was picked up in the morning by a driver who shook my hand thumb-to-thumb and introduced himself as Duane? from Brisbane? We drove down the coast in a Chevvy Cherokee and Duane helped me finish the stick, telling me stories about how to get a taxi in Bali, where to find the best religious fanatics in Calcutta, and his girlfriend Shereen? whose face I might have seen on the video last night?

We were stopped once, at an army roadblock. A rangy officer in fatigues and a pair of cheap and cheerless shades leant in through my window. How he could see anything through those slabs of black plastic beat me, but his eyeless gaze scoured the back seats before resting on us. No, me. Beyond the clicking sounds under the bonnet from the cut motor, the silence stretched out for miles. He flipped open the door and while Duane lit a cigarette I stepped out into the heat. The soldier took my flight-bag from me and poked around inside. He took his time. What else was there for entertainment? Only a reedy radio I could now hear playing in one of the trucks. He pulled out the Messiaen and forced the book open with his thumbs, like a fig. He spoke for the first time.

'Music,' he said.

'Yes. Music by Oliver Messiaen. I'm a musician, you see, visiting a friend, another musician, who . . .'

'Sing this music.'

I looked at Duane, and at my pathetic reflection in the dark glasses, and whistled a few bars.

The soldier called to his partner and the pair of them stood in the dust and listened to me, with their Uzi's rattling on their webbing as they slapped their knees and laughed and laughed. A couple of times they caught their breath long enough to pat the book in my hand, their big hands slapping the spread pages, repeating in unison 'Mu . . . sic'.

I waved farewell as we drove off, and thanked Duane for keeping a straight face. He told me he'd been terrified. Words to that effect.

There was another stopover that evening at a beach house somewhere along Cape Verde while a motor yacht was made ready for the last leg of the journey.

Duane unloaded the Cherokee and made for the ocean to get in a little snorkelling. He said he needed to burn off some energy. I slumped on a lounger on the terrace and watched him saunter over the sand down to the ocean. The yacht gleamed peachy white off the shore. It was like falling into a page of the National Geographic.

I closed my eyes and found myself thinking about the flat. It was strewn with Stuff. Keeping track of the Stuff was a part-time job I tried to hold down between taking care of business and taking care of me. I tried to picture it as I'd left it, and thought about what I'd have to do when I got back. I made a start on the stacks of records that needed filing. What was I dreaming of? I realized that most of the records had only been lifted from the shelves in my imagination, so in my mind's eye I filed only the real discs back on the shelves. It was grey daylight in the flat; the titles were hard to make out, but I was certain sure that some of the discs weren't ones that I'd looked out.

I awoke to the sound of murmured conversation behind the glass doors to the terrace. As I sat up and rubbed at my face, the captain of the yacht stepped out into the darkness.

'Ah, Miss Pearce, you're awake. Sorry to disturb you. You'll be able to sleep on board.'

I watched the wake of the boat and behind it the lights of the house shrinking away. I hunched my shoulders against the cold night, and then turned in.

Lying in my berth, I wondered how David would look now, and how I'd look to him after all this time, and whether it would be a disappointment.

On stage David looked like Hendrix played by Elvis dubbed by Jim Morrison. And he used that voice as it had always been intended to sound, like a Vegas ballad-bruiser. I once spent an evening at David's watching a tape he'd edited together from concert videos – heavy metal, cabaret, opera, a few seconds at a time – arranged in a catalogue of stage gestures. '... one bar rest before the big finish. And ... he ... CRUSHES the flesh of the lyric in his fist, keeps a close watch on it as he raises it to eye-level and ... FLINGS it to the ground. See? Fingers spread out as if he were flicking the bloody remains off his hand.'

David knew his stuff all right. He made his well-cut black tux as rock'n'roll as black leather.

As an actor he got so fiercely into his roles that he appeared to change physically. He caught tiny inflections in the voice, subtleties of expression in the face and posture, and he made it look as though the character was sculpted by these habits. The public liked him best in his Adventure Film Hero guise. He pumped iron for the Sinbad films until he looked like a young Jim Brown poured into Steve Reeves' torso.

My last image of him was a photo in a letter from Padang. Dressed in white, waist nipped in with a thick webbing belt, peaked cap pushed back on his head, his smile was relaxed but his lean body was taut and muscular.

In the excitement of my adventure I'd not had time to think of this as anything more than a treat. David knew, as David would, that I needed a break, and he knew it before I'd admitted it to myself. I wished now I'd paced myself a little better over the past thirty-six hours. I felt very low and lonely in that cabin. I found the World Service on the bedside radio and fell asleep to a gardening quiz.

When I awoke the next morning the sun was already high and the morning's shipboard duties done. I could hear the crew playing backgammon under a linen awning on the foredeck. The heat and light and the sound of the dice and the sway of the deck made me lean on the handrail for support. I noticed these sensations in all their dreamlike clarity as though through the port-hole of a bathysphere. To starboard the island rose from the sea, flat and bounded by a margin of white beach where we were moored, rising away to the west to a peak, lush and hazy green. For a few minutes I wished I were back home again. If I could have been transported back there for say, ten minutes, that would have been enough.

I didn't feel hungry, but the skipper said I should eat before I went ashore, and while I breakfasted on apple juice, toast and cream cheese, a motor boat with a chugging Bevis outboard came out and drew alongside the yacht.

When the boat had been loaded I climbed into the bow with my flight-bag and suitcase. In the stern sat a salty-looking old codger who gave me a *look* as I settled and gathered my Stuff about me. He'd crossed his arms and hung them over the tiller while he looked. The look said in international Codger Code, 'I know where I'd rather be, pal. Somewheres else. And I know what I'd rather be doing, too. Nothin'. Any questions?' I sat down with the mound of supplies and provisions at my back. I realized I'd been expecting some version of *Aloha Hawaii*. Now at last under that homely scowl I began to relax and feel quite at home. I turned to wave to the crew, but they were already preparing to set sail.

Home, I discovered, was a village set back about half a mile from the shore, following a creek as it meandered idly between banks bursting with orgying flora. The local botany seemed to specialize in bright tongues and pouting succulent lips, inquisitive vines and silky priapic eruptions. And what began as a dizzying profusion of floral invention became after a few minutes oppressively relentless.

It was a relief when we rounded a bend in the creek and the tangle of greenery gave way to the sandy slope of a hillside running down to the water's edge. Between the trees, domed huts grew like dusty mushrooms. A tall kid dressed in a nondescript shirt and shorts introduced himself as Franklin, while a small crowd gathered to unload the launch, paying me scant attention except as an obstruction. Franklin led me away up the hill, lugging my suitcase while I panted behind.

My accommodation was a hut set a little apart from the others, a distance you felt more than measured. I couldn't tell if this was intended as hospitable privacy or . . .

'Franklin?'

162

He emerged from the hut where he'd left my case, smiling broadly. Down by the boat the ant-like activity of bearing away the cargo continued.

'Franklin, where is Mr Daniels?'

'He will come soon I think.'

'Does he know I'm here?'

'Oh yes.'

It was pretty clear that I wasn't going to get much more. Before I could give way to useless frustration my senses caught me unaware. I could say that I heard something, but it was hardly even that.

It was the music, a long way off, barely a tingle in the breeze, here and gone.

'Franklin, where is the music coming from?'

'Music? Oh ...' He lifted his arm toward the mountain. 'It is the old ones. I think they are talking about you. So ...' he shrugged.

'About ... can I see?'

Franklin shrugged again and led me up to the brow of the hill where a track led inland. The foliage was less dense here than it had been by the creek, and gave welcome shade as we walked, climbing steadily along the spine of the ridge until we came at last to the lower slopes of the mountainside.

I hadn't seen from the yacht that these slopes were cut into terraces. This is where the islanders grew a variety of grass related to rice, whose grains grow to the size of borlotti beans. Women and children work the paddies alongside the men, but only the men, it seems, run the risk of infection from a parasitic worm which lives for most of its life in the gut of the eels which live in the fields. Most of the men are unaffected by the parasite, a fact which induces the kind of fatalism associated in our culture with tobacco-related diseases. Normally the disease strikes the elders, who accept it with stoicism. The young men of course believe themselves invulnerable, immortal and favoured by the gods because they are young, and men.

The effects of the disease vary in individuals, but blindness is characteristic; the bones become heavier and the skin coarser, with a leathery grain and tufted with coarse hair. Though the features lose their mobility and take on an almost simian appearance, the change is symmetrical. I was never quite decided about whether this was less alarming than the baroque improvisations of neurofibromatosis. (I had to look up the word. It was the Elephant Man's affliction.)

No longer able to work, these elders sit out their days swathed in distinctive bedouin robes of black and red, on raised seats which reminded me of Wimbledon umpires' chairs set at intervals around the terraces.

They are the musicians. They pass on news and messages by passing notes to one another; fluting, trilling notes, sometimes on little reed pipes, but mostly by 'singing'. It is as if nature, in taking from them their physical dexterity compensates in some way with an astonishing vocal range, possibly achieved through the enlarged network of bone passages.

They live apart from the other islanders, hermit-like, only joining the community while they work. The islanders feed them, believing that in their new guise they embody the elders who first planted the ancient grain which in itself represents fecundity.

Here I'm compressing what I learned later with what Franklin told me that afternoon. As we walked along the terraces, the voices faded in and out just as they had on the tape, and the work in the fields went on as it must.

How is it that a single piece of information can induce a few impulses in the brain to fire a little differently so that your whole mood swings around? Hearing that this mystical, exotic song was the sound of an agricultural community's notice-board reminded me of the time when I first heard a record of Burundi drummers beating up a storm, driving each other on with salvoes of call and response.

Somehow I couldn't quite recover the first thrill after I was told that these were a bunch of wedding and bar mitzvah entertainers whose wild vocal outbursts amounted to: *Don't forget to thank the guy who's paying for all this! . . . Helluva guy! Generous? Let me tell you . . .* and so on.

By evening there was still no sign of David. Franklin took me to his mother's hut to eat: fish and herbs and giant rice. I was glad it wasn't eel, though Franklin had told me that the parasite was removed with the guts, and the flesh was perfectly safe when cooked. Tasty, too, I discovered later, but that first night I felt that small, vulnerable sensation creeping over me again.

Franklin and his mother, and some relatives and their children who dropped by were polite but reserved, and only Franklin knew any real English. One of the kids produced a reed flute which fingered pretty much more like a penny whistle, and I gave them a couple of lumpen morris tunes. They greeted this with the amusement and interest which I suspect they would have aroused in the Home Counties by demonstrating the use of knife and fork.

I was glad to turn in, finally. My hut was equipped with a truckle-bed under a cone of mosquito-netting, and I lay in the dark listening to the World Service on the earphones. Being the outsider in a society you understand is a conceit you can afford. Being truly an outsider, even amongst benign insiders, hit me worse, I guess because as well as the loneliness, I sensed the world sniggering as it called the career-outsider's bluff.

I awoke in the dark from dreamless sleep with the certainty that I was being watched; fumbling for my torch, I knocked the radio flat with a clatter on the board floor. I could hear the tinny rasp of a voice from the earpiece somewhere, found the off-switch and flicked it, sat upright and peered into the gloom.

'It's OK, Rachel.'

'David!'

'Glad you could make it.'

David's voice was a husky whisper in the dark, like Miles Davis's smoke and gasoline drawl, but it was David for sure. I lay back on my elbows, waiting for my eyes to adjust.

'Glad *you* could make it, baby. I was beginning to wonder. What's all this about, and it had better be good by golly.'

'What do you make of it so far?'

'How could I make anything of it, wise guy? If this is some sort of . . . I dunno . . .'

'I'm not sure that I know either, Rachel. I don't know why I thought of you or why I didn't think of anyone else. Maybe I thought you might be curious and you might have nothing to lose. As for me . . . I feel better already. It's good to see you.'

I could just about make out an outline by starlight. He was kidding of course. Doubt and caprice were not in David's make-up.

As if he were reading me, David gave a throaty laugh. 'You get some sleep now. We'll speak later.'

'Yes,' I said, and found myself smiling in the dark, 'yes we will. I'd like that.'

I heard David stand up in a single movement, sensed him towering over the foot of the bed for a moment, and for an instant I saw his outline as he ducked out of the door, clear against the star-blown sky. My happiness, my sudden sense of belonging, of self-assurance, crumbled as I took in a single inconclusive detail.

He was wearing a dark bedouin robe.

I need hardly say by this stage that David was nowhere to be seen the next day, or the day after, or ... Days ran, I guess, into maybe a couple of weeks? More? Franklin was no use at all, grinning and assuring me that *Mr Daniels come real soon* and not to fret. I didn't fret, but the truth of the matter was that I was a hostage on the island, with no means of escape, and no clear idea of where to escape to if I had.

I don't know if Franklin's mother thought I was out here to marry David, or if she just didn't think I should be out on my own, but she plainly didn't approve, though she fed me and suffered my presence when I watched her cooking. We got on fine. We couldn't talk much, and I wasn't sure what to make of what I thought she might be telling me.

One afternoon I was whistling a version of Big Boy Cleveland's 'Quill Blues', one of those snatches I'd remembered from the tape, and Franklin's Ma, Chori, took my arm and tried to tell me something. There was something about the old ones, how they didn't have much to do with them, how they lived or came from the mountain or some such, or was she telling me about how their affliction came from the fields up there? She patted her head and made steps in the air with her hand; something about children, many children? It seemed important to her briefly, but in the end she shrugged and turned back to pounding roots in a pestle.

I spent my days exploring the island, gradually extending my territory, fitting the pieces together. I knew that if I stayed huddled by my books and radio I would grow wretchedly mad, wanting to be anywhere but here.

As my confidence grew I went through a phase of feeling unpleasantly like the lady of the manor swanning about my estate, but I quickly grew out of that.

Maybe there was something in the food, or trace elements in the water, but in combination with long hours of sleep, exercise, and nothing to do but what I ordered myself to do, I was on a constant high after only a few days. Not the soupy euphoria you get from dope or mushrooms, nor yet the sprocketing can-do of speed. This was the thrill of unerring certainty which might easily have been paranoia.

Though I wasn't 'doing' anything in any sense that I was used to, I felt a growing sense of purpose, like surfing effortlessly along on the moment. My muscles relaxed, my breathing fell into rhythm with my movements, which flowed easily yet seemed to grow in strength. The sensation was like sustained *déjà vu*, which wouldn't evaporate even when I was conscious of it, and very soon it became irrelevant even to look for it.

I knew what I was about. I was hunting David across the island and through my memory's hall of distorting mirrors. I was beginning to realize how untrustworthy all that old information was. While I was scouring the island I was walking away from all that, like walking off a large lunch of candyfloss.

I saw him at last early one morning as I made my way down to the shore. The sun was already high, but still slanted through the tree trunks, illuminating and dazzling by turns. In his robes, at this distance, he was only a dark shape moving around a small skiff, preparing to cast off. A sudden impulse made me want to run on to the sand, to attract his attention and run to him, but an older instinct overtook me and I kept my cover and prepared to follow him along the shore.

He powered and steered the boat with a single oar mounted at the stern, and paddled towards the mountain. I tracked him, even amazing myself at the ease and quiet of my progress, until the ground suddenly rose up in a cliff ahead of me. I plunged inland, managing to find a gulley in the rock which gave access to the top of the promontory, but by the time I made it back to look down on the sea, there was no sign of David or the skiff. I stood and snarled and hissed like a cat in my rage, which may have looked ridiculous had anyone been there to see, but felt good and right.

I had come further in the past hour than I'd ever ventured before, and as I looked up to the peak and back along the island I was smiling deep inside.

I ranged over the mountain slopes that morning knowing I had no fear in me. David's effect again? Like the good weep that washes away the habit of hurt, I had dispensed with fear at last, dropped it like old baggage. No wonder the islanders had kept their distance. Like the weirdos on city streets, I had been invisible to them. They knew that paranoia is socially transmissible. In my society, and especially as a woman in my society, switching off the fear is as impossible as switching off literacy. You can't not fear the streets like you can't not read the Harpic tin.

I splashed down through the paddy-fields, hearing the music, listening for the impulse that would guide me to the musician I needed, and I found him as I knew I would. I wanted him to hear me coming, and I guessed they knew the core of certainty that had formed amidst the seething whirl of questions in my unclear mind.

I'd arrived on the island after a journey during which the thought of David had sustained me, blinded me even to possible dangers, and I'd mistaken this for confidence. It was dependence, and when he'd not been here for me, I'd felt betrayed. I'd felt he was hiding from me not because he'd kept his distance but because my one tantalizing glimpse of him had convinced me that his changing guise left me behind and shut me out. In recent days my memories of him had taken on a new aspect. A folk memory had stirred in my mind. A familiar object seen from an unfamiliar angle: the Enchanted Hill . . .

Like millions of punters I had his words in my memory and had confused them with my own thoughts. Like the big baby in the lyrics of 'Well' I'd thought often of David in the words '. . . I twist in tangled sheets / To see your face / In the tangled maze I trace / In my heart.' I wanted to look at his face now without that weak dependence. If there was any truth in my growing certainty then I was surely mad.

The old one must have heard me come, though he gave no sign, and sang on. I planted one foot on the lowest rung of his seat and said quietly but quite clearly:

'Who is David Daniels?'

His answering silence spread outward across the island like a shock wave. Work stopped in the fields and I felt the prickle of scrutiny on my neck. Fortunately I wore my cloak of invisibility, the immunity of madness.

He lowered his face to stare blindly at me.

I think the noise that escaped the thick, lipless mouth was laughter. I stared into the darkness under the ridge of his brow.

The single note which sprang from his throat was a tangle of tones and harmonics which made me wince, but I couldn't look away now. I was convinced he could hear me as I stared. My breath came deep and strong.

The note was taken up all around now, beautiful,

terrible. I didn't care, even when I heard my own voice caught up in it. My voice, screaming, crying, singing, calling, what the hell. My breath, deep and strong. My stare, deep and strong.

He reached out to me with his swollen, shapeless hands, calling me on, summoning my song.

We were calling David, together. I don't know how long we called.

I was drawing breath when the fields fell silent.

The old one dropped his hands into his lap and looked out over the island. We heard the answering note.

I started back toward the mountain, aware but heedless of the bovine stares of the islanders I was leaving behind. As I climbed I could not help but think of the Enchanted Hill. Its image had grown clearer in my mind's eye, more concrete in my thoughts. I was indeed the traveller lured into the faerie hill with promises ... After a while I heard the song resume behind me, but I could hear David clearly, calling to me. To me, clearly ...

The sun was blazing overhead, but it was no effort to follow David's clear voice as it went through its changes, like the music on that tape. I moved steadily through undergrowth that had so recently made my eyes and brain throb, and now seemed rich and vital. I wondered what sense I thought I could have made of the music back in the dark and dismal little flat. The world and time reduced to little slivers of plastic.

I found David seated cross-legged on a slab of granite which thrust out over the water-line, so that the swell echoed under it or slapped around it by turns. He faced the horizon, face lifted to the sun, his body swaying gently as he sang, a song so plaintively tender and a voice so strong that my back tingled. I walked to the edge quite close to him and sat down while he sang. I caught only a glimpse of his profile under his head-dress, and then closed my eyes and felt the sun on my face.

When he stopped singing we sat for a long time with our silence between us, and the sounds of the sea all around.

'Glad you could make it,' he said at last.

'Uh-huh?'

'What do you make of it?'

'Well ... you're not in the market for a recording engineer. Tell me this, David. Am I free to go?'

'It might take a couple of days, but yes, of course you're free to go, Rachel. When I decided to stay, I thought a transmitter might be a useful tool.'

I lay back on the warm rock and closed my eyes. 'Tell me about it, David. Which came first, the retreat or the dis...?'

'Disease? You can use that word. It's a retreat *from* disease. Don't you feel it too? I've not felt so comfortable with myself for years. You too I guess.'

His shadow fell across me and my eyelids flooded with violet light. I opened my eyes and looked into his face as he crouched beside me. I couldn't have prepared for that moment, and tried hard to look as if I had strength enough for it.

The eyes which looked steadily into mine were golden, their pupils tiny and (really?) vertical slots. His face and hands were covered with ochre hair and coarse skin stretched over jutting bones like threadbare coconut matting. The whole of his lower face thrust forward, but the lips, at least the margins of the mouth, remained ... yes, the word was *horribly* mobile.

'Oh David, I ...'

'How many of my faces have you seen? You know this is me don't you? Oh Rachel I'm so tired of wearing your masks. But how else could I have peered through so many doors, looked straight into so many carefully fashioned masks? My advantage is that I can hang up my mask and you can look me in the face at last.'

'You mean . . . the disease means you can't pretend?'

'Come along. You'll burn. Let's walk awhile.'

He led the way down from the rock platform and we walked along the shore below the mountain. Once again my strength had fled from me, along with that illusion of certainty which had sustained me on the island. David folded his bristly hands into his robe while he talked.

'I had to get out of all that. When I started pumping up for Sinbad I was already planning for escape. It was a shape I could drop easily, so I wouldn't have to live with it; so the character would carry on its own life when I was gone.'

Its own life. I could imagine how much that would mean to David. His characters appeared to have their own life because he chose and refined their characteristics with a watchmaker's precision. The Rock Star, Raskolnikov, Sinbad, David Daniels . . .

'When you know you're good at something it's not so easy just to let go. And it was so easy to do, that glamour thing. You wonder how far you can take it before you're found out. People are so hungry for dreams. I could've thrown the whole thing away with one good scandal, but it would have left its mark on the films. I didn't want to waste those royalties.'

If the outcome had been less horrific for David, had he simply gone paunchy and alcoholic, say, I would have smirked at his smugness. But to lose everything like this . . .

'Can you imagine what the press would make of this David? I mean, I won't say anything.'

'I don't think it will matter very soon. David exists in

your memories. It's what I'm becoming that's important now.'

'Oh god, I'm so sorry David.'

He smiled at me. It was difficult to take.

'I'm at rest now. My body is very strong. My mind is at rest.' He paused. 'I'm translating, of course, Rachel.'

'Sorry?'

'I'm trying to explain this in ideas that you can understand. "My" mind, in "its" body.'

'It's just a figure of speech.'

'OK. Then give me an alternative.'

'I . . .'

'Doesn't matter. "Your" mind is in "your" brain, or maybe it's the other way about, but where are "you"? You want to see mind-control? Do what they tell you in posture school. Straight back, head up, deep breath, relax. Just do it, and try to feel depressed. Really try. Look at me, Rachel, and tell yourself, "I seriously want to be miserable." Look at us, Beauty and the Beast.'

David uncovered his huge, heavy head, and his golden eyes blinked. How could . . . this . . . be so unmistakably David?

His gravelly rasp, threaded with stray harmonics, was still recognizably David's voice.

David's charm remained intact.

'Now we laugh.'

'We *what*?'

'Laugh, Rachel. We laugh.'

And he began to laugh exactly like a baby. Out of that cavernous mouth came a bubbling spring of laughter. It was such a good party trick, done with such deliberation that I giggled, and he laughed back, laughter begetting laughter, the way David lifted the crew backstage, when things were fraught, with effortless charm.

I laughed despite myself, and when it subsided, I shook my head and said, 'How do you do that?'

He shrugged. 'I am as I am. Nothing has changed, except some piece of your mind.'

He even looked a little different.

'It's the simplest flim flam. "Your" brain hears "your" body laughing and thinks "you" must be happy.'

Was it that I had, in the words of the song, just grown accustomed to his face? So quickly? It was after all David's face.

'Evolution gave you three brains, and divided them in two. Your consciousness is arrived at by committee, with voting cards dealt out by DNA.'

I loved his stupid face. His expressions were still the same as ever.

'What does that old saurian brain stem make of that flashy young cerebrum, trying its best to get a grip on the world with a handful of senses designed for life on the veldt? No wonder you find it so hard to concentrate, easier to imagine yourself somewhere else, in yarns spun from scraps of memories, most of them stuffed into the back pockets of your ancestors' hand-me-down genes.'

So David was into anthropology now. He used to go on like this about music. There was one time . . .

'That's what made it so easy to operate in your world, Rachel. And because you choose to live together and hope the world will be less confusing if you can only agree on the names of things, all I had to do was to tell you what label to see. Look at me, Rachel. Do I really look so different to you now?'

I shook my head. We had never been lovers. I guessed it was too late now.

'When you return, look at the faces of the ones with the leaders' labels – the salesmen, the priests, the politicians – all, notice, running their patch of the world like the skirmishing city-states under their skulls. Remember that crack about how your fortieth birthday brings you the face you deserve? Their faces are shaped not by wisdom but by their struggle to conceal what they think and control how they appear. Even when they're lying, they're judged by their skill at faking sincerity. When you can't control the thoughts that haunt your own brain, you need mummies and daddies who look like they know what to do, even if they send you to bed without supper. They all want you to see the world labelled their way.'

'Why are you telling me this? I liked it when we were just sitting on the rock.' I looked up, thinking of the Faerie Hill, where the traveller is entertained with tales, and feasts in magic company far into the night. 'I mean, you didn't bring me out here as someone to lecture.'

'No, I was telling you only that the ability to change your label is only a matter of intention. Some of us are more single-minded than others.' He smiled and tapped his forehead.

We were walking along the water-line. I pulled off my trainers and let the wavelets wash over my ankles. David's skiff was up ahead, and amongst the trees was a hut on stilts.

'Is that what you've been doing here? Building?'

'I'll live here until the time is right for me to join the old ones.'

'Will you be blind then?'

'They see visions. I think you would call it imagination. Is that blindness?'

'Will I see you again?'

'No. It's time to bury David. When I've told them everything David has seen, he'll live on amongst us. There's nothing magic about that. That's how he lives on in your race memory. Only our memories are longer.'

*

There's this jar full of sand, see. There was the burial at sea, the announcement released to the news agencies. The judgement was correct; David's death was a matter of record rather than mourning. The films were out on video and the radio played tracks from *So Long Pop* during the day, and still turn up amongst listeners' all-time top tunes.

It would be nice to be able to say I came back and made my long-awaited breakthrough album. Instead, life closed over my head without a ripple, an obscure footnote to the epilogue of a closed book.

It is possible to release the hostage from the Enchanted Hill by taking three turns around it by night, before halting with the moon at your back to play a slow air on the fife or flute. For the hostage, release is a mixed blessing.

Under the hill a hush falls on the revels as the footfalls without at first pound slowly, like a muffled drumbeat. The clatter of knife and spoon on gold and silver plate falls still, the pipe and tabor fail. All heads turn at the sound of far-off music, and as they do the hostage finds that the fine silks and damask are poor rags and tatters, the marble walls are mud, and the feast is heaped filth and twigs.

He or she sees the moonshine through the hillside and may tear it aside like a veil and so escape.

But the world has changed, and maybe many years have passed in a night. Time itself is but a flimsy veil, and the hostage imprisoned now in a body ill-made and weak.

I keep the cassette by the jar of sand, but I won't play it again now. Occasionally I remember the first time I heard the music. That will do.

SERPENT'S BLOOD

Molly Brown

Georgia Adams, five foot eleven, black, and American, stood to one side as Marcel raised his ebony walking stick and pounded on the door of a wooden shack. Her companion waited patiently, his deeply lined dark face showing no hint of expression. She had no idea how old he was – he looked at least eighty, but moved with a fluid grace she envied. Dapper in his white linen suit and panama hat – the top of which barely came up to her shoulder – he made her feel clumsy and ungainly by comparison. And there was something about his eyes, the way they shone with a feverish brightness, yet gave nothing away. She never had a clue what he was thinking. But so far, he had been extremely helpful, getting her into places she never could have gone on her own, as an outsider.

There was movement within the shack. The door opened slightly and a man peered out. From where she was standing, Georgia couldn't see much more than the man's nose and one bloodshot eye. Marcel and the man spoke in hushed tones for several minutes. Finally the man stepped back and allowed them to enter.

In the centre of a small, dim room full of cluttered shelves piled high with bottles and dusty bric-à-brac, a round-faced, round-bodied woman sat on a cane chair. She wore a voluminous white dress and no shoes. Her hair was hidden beneath a white turban. Three teenage girls, also dressed in white, sat on the floor at her feet. Two men stood against the back wall.

'This is Madame Marie Herard,' Marcel whispered in Georgia's ear, 'it would be wise to treat her with respect.'

Marcel nudged Georgia with his elbow. She stepped forward, bowed slightly, and began in halting French, 'I am a doctor from New York. I work for an American drug company, researching and developing new medicines. Marcel tells me you know about plants and herbs; I was hoping you could help me.'

'What help do you think I can give you?'

'As a student, I read everything I could of Macandal and the slave rebellion of the late 1700s. Macandal has always been my hero.' Georgia smiled. Marie Herard stifled a yawn. Georgia cleared her throat and continued, 'More than one history of the time mentions a zombie who lived in the mountains where the rebels had their camp.'

The round woman shifted in her seat. 'So?'

Georgia took a deep breath. 'They say he is still alive.'

Marie Herard snorted. 'You are very foolish, to speak of zombies in this day and age.'

'Why am I foolish? You don't deny that zombies exist?'

The woman shrugged.

'Oh come on, we both know they do. But they're not the dead called from their graves by a lot of magic and mumbo-jumbo, they're people under the influence of a plant-based drug affecting the central nervous system. That's fairly well established. But this is the first time it's been suggested that the zombie drug actually prolongs life. If what they say is true – that a zombie can live for hundreds of years – well, think of the implications!'

Marie Herard slapped one hand down hard on the arm of her chair. 'You don't know what you're talking about! Who has told you these fairy stories?'

'Some people I met in Limbé.'

The round woman chuckled. 'They must have seen you coming. Go home, little Doctor. And don't forget that those who spread lies often choke on them. I fear your friends in Limbé may swallow their own tongues if they're not careful.'

She sat down with Marcel in a sea-front tavern. 'Why would she deny the existence of zombies? Surely her livelihood depends on keeping the old myths alive.'

'I thought you wanted medicines,' Marcel said accusingly. 'If I had known you were looking for zombies, I would never have taken you to Marie. She may be *voudon*, but she is Serpent's Blood first.'

'What's Serpent's Blood?'

'A secret order, like the Bizango and the Cochons Gris. You do not want to cross these orders, they all serve with the left hand. And you never want to meet them by night. If you are wise, you will abandon all this. Forget about zombies, forget about everything, and go home before it's too late.'

'You've got to be kidding, Marcel. I can't give up now. I must be close to the truth, or you wouldn't be warning me off, now would you?'

'If that is your final word,' he said.

A sixteen-year-old boy approached her in the lobby of her hotel. 'You are American?' he said in English.

Georgia's eyes crinkled in amusement. 'Is it so damn obvious?'

'You have much money?'

The amusement drained from Georgia's face. She gave

181

the boy her steeliest expression. With her short-cropped hair and considerable height, she could look quite formidable when she wanted to.

The boy looked around before speaking in a low voice, 'They say you have been to Limbé, searching for the zombie who knew Macandal. Do you have money? I can take you to him, but you must pay.'

It was nearly midnight when Georgia turned the ignition in a rented jeep. The boy, who'd told her his name was Jean, sat beside her and pointed to the mountains outside the city. 'That way,' he said.

They drove in total silence. Georgia couldn't get more than two words at a time out of the boy; she'd finally given up trying.

Making her way along twisting dirt roads, winding higher and higher above the sea, she began – not for the first time – to have doubts. She was in way over her head, and she knew it: travelling alone with a total stranger, going who knew where to encounter who knew what? The canopy of trees above her head, and even the night air itself, seemed to take on an aura of palpable evil. Then she heard the sound of bells.

For the first time in over an hour, Jean spoke. 'Dear Jesus, it's the Bizango. Quick! Turn off your lights, they mustn't see us.'

'What?'

'Hide! They mustn't see us. And don't look at them or they will kill us both!'

Georgia drove off the road and into the forest, behind a cluster of trees. She shut off the engine and huddled down in her seat. Bells rang and drums pounded. There were voices, singing. The voices and the drums drew closer, grew louder. Georgia could hear some of the words they sang, but she couldn't understand them –

they didn't sound like English or French or any language she had ever heard. Beside her, Jean closed his eyes and lowered his head. He might have been praying.

Georgia's mouth dropped open. The road they'd just left became a moving stream of light. Grotesque figures, their faces obscured by masks portraying animals and demons, marched in a solemn procession, illuminated in the glow of flaming torches.

There were dozens of them. They wore flowing red and black robes; some wore horns on top of their heads, some wore crowns, one wore a tiny coffin and cracked a whip repeatedly against the ground. Some carried banners; others carried bells or drums. They all sang the same song. The music had a terrible beauty; it was strange and complex, yet Georgia knew that she could never forget it, it would haunt her for the rest of her life. She also knew her camera would be useless at this distance in the dark, but she reached for it anyway, pressing the shutter release again and again.

The song came to an end. There was a moment of total silence, as if the world was holding its breath, and then the marchers began to chant, repeating one word, ominously, over and over: 'djab'. The chant faded into the distance; the eerie procession had passed them by. Georgia breathed a sigh of relief and nudged Jean with her elbow. 'It's OK,' she said, 'they're gone.'

She felt a hand on her shoulder and screamed.

'Hush, ma cherie. It's only me.'

She gasped in shock. 'Marcel! What are you doing here?' She nudged the boy at her side again. 'It's OK, Jean. He's a friend of mine. Jean?' The boy slumped forward. 'Jean, are you OK?'

The old man gripped her shoulder more tightly. 'I told you not to go on with this, didn't I? I warned you.'

'Marcel, I think Jean is . . .'

'Dead? Yes, I think so.' He reached over and pushed the boy's head to one side, revealing a tiny dart embedded in his neck, below one ear. He crossed over to the passenger side, dumped the boy's body on the ground, and climbed into the jeep. 'He's fulfilled his purpose. You don't think our meeting here was an accident, do you? Now drive.'

Georgia did as she was told; Marcel was pointing a gun at her.

'What's all this about, Marcel?' she asked. 'What are you doing out here? Who were those people? And what are you going to do with me?'

'I could ask you one or two questions myself, ma cherie. Why did you lie to me? You said you were a doctor looking for medicine. Instead you are a journalist, looking for sensation. You work for a newspaper! Did you think I wouldn't check?'

'I wasn't lying. I am a doctor . . . of journalism. And I do know people in the drug industry who would love to get hold of a life-extending compound. And they'd pay very well for it. More money than you've ever dreamed of, Marcel. And you could have it all – I'd give it to you.'

'You're very generous, ma cherie. Turn left up here.'

'Where are we going, Marcel?'

'Where you said you wanted to go, ma cherie.'

Georgia turned off the main road, driving the car beneath a stone archway with the inscription: Order and Respect of the Dark. Beyond the arch, a cluster of huts stood in a circle. In the centre of the circle a bonfire raged, tended by several women in black robes. She stopped the jeep and they got out.

Inside the largest hut, a gigantic man lay across an

oversize bed. He must have been eight feet tall and nearly as wide. The only light in the room came from three small candles on a table near his head. Georgia found it difficult to see; she could barely make out the man's features. But she could see that his dark skin seemed to reflect what little light there was in the room; she decided he must be sweating profusely. 'What's wrong with him?' she whispered to Marcel.

'Nothing. He's just old. Go ahead, speak to him. He's the one you were so anxious to meet.'

'*He*'s the zombie?'

A low rattling sound came from the giant's chest. 'Zombie. That's a good one.'

Georgia jumped at the sound of his voice. She thought zombies were supposed to be catatonic. She hadn't expected one who could speak and hear. 'You're not really two hundred years old?'

'Older than that, my dear. Much older. But no wiser.' The man struggled to lift his head. 'Come here. Let me look at you.'

Georgia stood by his bedside, struggling to conceal her shock. There was something very wrong with his skin; it was covered with scales. And his eyes were too far apart – they almost touched his ears – giving him a vaguely reptilian appearance. He struggled to roll on to one side in order to see her better. She overcame her revulsion and leaned over to help him, pulling with all her might. He weighed a ton and he was ice-cold to the touch.

'You remind me of a woman I knew when I was young and handsome. I think perhaps she loved me.'

Georgia nodded. She had no idea what to say.

'And now I will tell you something important. When the Bizango take to the roads,' he told her, 'their rallying cry is, "Animals of the Night, change your skins!" But they cannot, nor can the Cochons Gris. They say that only those born with the blood of the serpent can truly change. These ones are known as the *loups-garous*, which some say means werewolf.

'The *loups-garous* believe that one day *djab* will come. Some say *djab* will destroy the earth. I say *djab* will save it. And so I call *djab* from the side of this mountain. Night after night I call him, while the sky above is dark.'

The old man reached out with one claw-like hand, holding Georgia by the wrist. 'I have enemies, Georgia Adams. Powerful enemies of my own kind. If you write or speak of what you see here, it will mean my death. Do not betray me to them.'

'Never. I wouldn't dream of it.'

The old man dropped his hand and closed his eyes. 'Marcel, do what we discussed.'

A group of thirty or forty people were gathered around the bonfire. A round-bodied woman walked up to Georgia, holding out a bottle. Georgia recognized her at once; it was Marie Herard. 'Drink,' Marie ordered her.

'What is it?'

'The Ancient wishes you to become one of us,' Marcel explained, 'thus binding you to silence. In order to join us, you must change your skin. The contents of that bottle will cause it to happen.'

'It's a drug.'

Marcel nodded.

'I won't take it.'

'Look,' he said, with exaggerated patience in his voice, as though he were talking to a small child, 'it's part of the ceremony. Everyone has some. *I'm* having some.' He put the bottle to his mouth and took a long drink. 'See?'

*

Stripped of her clothes, Georgia floated around the bonfire. She watched, entranced, as those around her changed. To one side, she saw a giant lizard with a huge flap of skin bobbing below its chin, to another, she saw a pack of wolves. She giggled at the sight of a man becoming a pig. Marcel was a sleek black cat, meowing and rubbing his forehead against her leg. She saw a unicorn, a llama, an elephant. She saw dragons and angels and demons.

She looked down at her arms and watched them turn into wings. She was a bird of prey; a night-hawk.

She watched the sun rise from a high cliff, overlooking the sea. She felt her hawk's wings beating. She left the ground and felt the rush of salt air through her feathers. She flew and she flew in a spiral down to the sea, for ever bound to silence.

COVER STORY

Liz Holliday

The house was full of the stink of human death. Stephen Audsley – he called himself that – walked across the darkened hallway. Moonlight caught the pictures on the walls, turning their strange abstractions dreadful. His nostrils flared. Beneath the stench of rotting flesh there was another very faint smell, that of citrus with musk. His lips pulled back into something that was not a snarl, but certainly not a smile.

Quietly, so that not a floorboard creaked, he walked to the stairs. A sound came from behind him, high pitched, mewling. He turned. In one fluid motion he scooped up the cat that had followed him in. It yowled, squirmed, flailed the air with needle claws. His fingers clenched on its neck. A muscle jumped in his cheek. Then, with a flick of his wrist he threw it away from him. It twisted as it fell, landed four-square, shook itself and bolted down the stairs, tail high.

'Stupid little cat,' he whispered. 'I didn't mean to hurt you.'

Then he went on upstairs.

He found the body in the bedroom.

The door stood ajar. Moonlight glinted off something on the floor by the window. He went and picked it up. It was a photo. The frame was dented, and the glass was cracked, but the woman in it was beautiful. Stephen grunted and set the photo on the dressing-table.

He flicked on the table lamp and took in with a glance the heavy velvet curtains, the book open on the stripped wood dressing-table, the flashing light on the answering machine. He ignored all these things and moved directly to the huddled figure on the bed.

There was a whisky bottle on the side-table, and next to it a pill jar. Both were empty. They told their own tale. Close to, the smell of alcohol almost obliterated the stench of decay. It was not until Stephen pulled back the sheet, revealing the dead body, that he smelled the other scent: citrus and musk, that unmistakable odour of the Family, clinging to the bedlinen.

'Who's been sleeping in your bed, little human?' Stephen whispered to the night.

The dead man, mute, stared across the room. His flesh was grey, already past rigor and softening into decay, but he was recognizably Daniel Harrington, the man Stephen had come to find. Had he been alive, Stephen would have found out what he knew about the Family, and to whom he had passed the information. Then he would have killed the human and burned down his house. He would have made it quick. He was not cruel, and unlike some of his Family he did not hate the humans.

With Harrington already dead, Stephen would have to find another way of discovering what he had known. Besides, Stephen was curious. What could be so bad that the prospect of living became worse than what lay on the other side of death? He shivered.

He was not an imaginative man. None of the Family were. Yet he had heard the tales when he was a child, the tales of the Dark that devoured minds, and worse things that might live in the spaces between the stars. He had learned of them as surely as he had learned who he was, and his lineage, and the deeds of all his forebears. As surely as he had learned how to hide his differences from the humans.

He began his search with the open book on the dressing-table. There were three envelopes lying across it: one was addressed to Harrington's parents; the second was his will, as Stephen discovered when he opened it. The third was addressed to a Paul Cunningham, care of Warnfield Hall Counselling Centre.

The first two envelopes contained no surprises. The will left Harrington's modest estate to be divided between his parents and his siblings and their children; his art was to be sold or not, at their discretion. Stephen opened the last envelope. The message inside it read: *You have to do something.* There was a photograph. Stephen held it up. It was a close-up of a face, smoke-blackened, twisted with fear and suffocation. Clearly, the face of one of the Family in the last stages of the swift, unstoppable reversion that came with death.

Stephen sighed. He put the photograph in his jacket pocket, next to an envelope containing other, similar pictures. They had been sent to him by Raymond Morant, an administrative assistant at King's College, London. He had intercepted correspondence between the head of the Zoology Department, Professor Hill, and Harrington. Hill had died in a car crash a short while after; police believed there was no connection between the accident and a break-in at his home a little earlier. They had not even realized that his office had been similarly raided.

Raymond was good, Stephen thought. A pity he was such a Family man. He sighed again, and moved on to the book. He stared at the words, all he might ever know of Daniel Harrington's mind, who had decided to face the Dark rather than live his life. He picked up the book and settled himself on the foot of the bed with it.

I can't go on. There are people who will say I've been a fool, that I've taken the easy way out. They know nothing. Nothing.

It isn't living without her, I think I could do that, if there were any point to it. No, it's the fact that if I carried on, I would have to face the failure of every other dream and aspiration I ever harboured, every hope I carried into adulthood from my childhood.

I dreamed of greatness, of my art touching people's souls. Of changing people's lives in a single moment of transformation.

And all my life they've said my work is trite, shallow, meaningless. I can see that they are right, now. Everything I do seems overstated, too polished, hopeless. I'm a victim of the shit-bird. Sits on my shoulder all the time I'm painting, screaming, *this is shit, this is shit, this is shit*. It touches no one, transforms no one, makes nothing new.

It is as hollow as I was. Until she came. She filled me up with light, with laughter, with happiness. She changed me. I was wrong. I can't go back.

Marion, Stephen thought. He thought also of the pervasive smell of citrus and musk, the far stronger traces that clung to the bedlinen. He skimmed backwards through the journal until he found the first mention of her name, then read forward from there.

Marion clearly had reasons for her actions, but Harrington had not understood them. In his journal he only told of how he met her, and came to love her; and then the devastation of being publicly betrayed by her.

'What's your game, cousin?' Stephen asked the quietness. Only the faint sounds of traffic from the street below answered him.

He shut the book, and turned off the light. Moonlight turned Harrington's flesh nacreous, flecked his dead eyes with silver, etched deep the shadowy places of his body.

Stephen stripped off his clothes and stood naked for a while, staring at Harrington, staring at himself in the wardrobe mirror. The other man was slightly shorter, broad with muscle, not fat. His hair was darker than Stephen's, his eyes lighter, but those things could be dealt with.

Stephen slid between the cold sheets. He heard the beat of his heart, the blood sighing in his ears; he was aware of the silence of the corpse beside him.

Sleep did not come. He turned. The message light of the answering machine was blinking. He pressed the play-back button, thinking as he did so that there would be a sample of Harrington's voice. But a woman's voice came from the machine, light with the merest trace of an Irish accent: *Dan? This is Marion. I just wanted to say that I ... well, that I'll see you around maybe. If you'd like. Take care now.*

Impossible to tell from a recording; impossible without the body language and the scent and the subtle stigmata of the Family. It would keep, he thought. First he would deal with the problem of Harrington's contacts, and then he would find out what game this renegade cousin was playing. He turned over and laid his head against the cold, dead flesh of the corpse, and folded his arms around its unmoving chest, and he slept the Sleep.

Sunlight and the sound of a vacuum cleaner woke him. He came awake easily, all his predator's instincts alive at once. The door stood open, as he had left it the night before. He rolled out of bed and into his jeans.

Cursing himself for a fool, he went to investigate, this time shutting the door firmly behind him. There was no lock, which he regretted.

He padded silently down the stairs in his bare feet.

Sunlight pooled on the thick carpet. The kitten regarded him suspiciously, then stalked away when he came near. The vacuum cleaner droned on.

He tracked the sound to the living-room.

'Good morning,' he said, pleasantly enough, to the woman he found there.

She turned. 'Morning, Mr Harrington,' she shouted, kicking the foot-switch on the cleaner. The noise died.

It was only then that he realized he had not so much as stopped to check his appearance in the mirror. He ran his hand through hair he hoped was dark enough.

'Look,' he said, 'I've got bit of a headache this morning. Why don't you take off early? It won't hurt this once.'

The woman smiled, bright red lipstick on narrow lips. She was thin and bird-like, and she reeked of nicotine. 'I was just going to do a bit of dusting, as it goes,' she said. 'I'll be nice and quiet. And I really should defrost the freezer. Smells like something's died in there.'

'Yes, yes, you're probably right,' Stephen said. It must be worse than I supposed, he thought, if a human can smell it.

'I'll see to it myself, a little later. But I really would appreciate it if you'd leave me to it.'

'Well, all right,' the woman said, allowing Stephen to herd her towards the door.

Once she had gone, Stephen made a thorough search of the house. He found an address book almost at once. There were phone numbers for both Marion Ryan and Warnfield Hall.

He dialled the Clinic number. A woman's voice answered. He asked to be put through to Paul Cunningham.

'I'm sorry,' she said. 'Dr Cunningham is on holiday until the twenty-third. Can anyone else help?'

'No,' he answered. 'I don't think so.' I hope not, he thought, and broke the connection. A moment later he thought better of it. He phoned back and made an appointment, the last available on the twenty-third.

He found a photo album. The final few pages were devoted to Marion. The last of them was a single large portrait shot. The woman in it was stunningly beautiful. Actresses would pay a fortune to gain a face like that, Stephen thought; but looks had never been important to the Family. Her hair was thick and lustrous, the chestnut highlights setting off her huge sapphire eyes and generous mouth. A photo on the previous page showed that her body matched her face. Stephen flipped backwards through the book. Little by little Marion grew more dowdy, until at the end – or the beginning – she was a round-faced mouse of a woman in a C & A skirt. The only question was over what length of time she had spread the transformation.

He rang her number, and got her answering machine. He listened to the message and put the phone down just as the bleep started. I *will* wait, he thought. There are other priorities; but then beware, cousin. Nevertheless he played her message back twice more.

After that he continued his search. Harrington was self-employed, and he kept thorough records. Stephen immersed himself in the accounts, the appointment diary and Harrington's journal. He practised the man's signature and listened to his voice on the answering machine. He found out that he had often met Marion at Hildebrandt's, a restaurant in Covent Garden; that they would frequently go from there to look around the galleries. Harrington was not very rich, but he had acquired a small collection of modern art. This surprised Stephen. He had thought all the work he had seen was Harrington's own.

The cleaning-lady was Mrs Bailey; she came in once a week, got paid at the end of the month. Harrington was seeing a counsellor once a week, but the man was on holiday. He ate often at a café round the corner from his workroom rather than cook during the day, if he was working. He was vegetarian. Stephen grimaced. He could live with it. He had done worse things for the Family. But not much worse. He hoped it would never find its way into the Song of the Lines, though.

He continued to assimilate Harrington's life, memorizing faces in photographs, names, dates; which critics had said what, which publishers he had worked for, was working for when he died.

He had taken on many identities in his long life, but Stephen had never before tried to impersonate anyone. He stared down at the diary. An entry dated 12 June read: *The Tower of Creeping Doom: Book 22 In The Antmage Trilogy* – COVER. Other entries followed. Daniel Harrington might have been panned by the critics, but he had a full order book.

Stephen had under a fortnight to turn himself into a creative artist, or to give a reasonable impression of being one. He was moderately old by human standards if not by those of the Family. He had lived in many countries and had been known by many names. He had killed in self-defence and he had killed to protect the secrets of the Family. He had even, once, refrained from killing and made the Family live with that decision. But he had never in all that time created anything, had an original idea or acted on intuition, though he deduced with a clarity that would have put most humans to shame.

'I can't do this,' he muttered. 'I can't do this.' Later, he wrapped the body in plastic and then in a large rug from the dining-room. He hauled the roll downstairs. It bumped on the treads, and he wondered if the noise would alert the neighbours.

He was strong – at sixty-one, he was in his prime – but even so he stopped for a rest on the half-landing. He thought vaguely that he was probably showing the body great disrespect by human standards. They had some strange ideas about what was essentially dead meat. *What the hell*, he thought. It was better than eating it, which he had also considered. Pity it was already on the turn.

He had intended to wait until nightfall, but the street outside was empty, and he reasoned that he would look less suspicious going out in the daytime. He brought his van round from where he had parked it several streets away. He heaved the rolled-up body on board, taking great care not to let the sheer weight of the package show. He had never worked out just how strong the humans were, but they were weaklings compared to the feeblest of the Family.

He drove down to his parents' house on the coast. He took great care to stay within the speed limits and to do nothing to arouse suspicion.

The house was large and ivy-covered, set away from the nearest village in its own grounds. Had it not been an old people's home, it would undoubtedly have been the focus of stories of ghosts and ghouls.

Stephen pulled up outside it. He left the body in the back of the van, and went inside.

Some of the more active humans were gathered in the old drawing-room at the back of the house. The television blared out. Mother Lena was bending over one of the old women, adjusting a blanket. He had considered going straight upstairs, but there were courtesies to be considered, and no reason to make himself even less welcome than usual.

One of the old women grabbed his hand as he walked in. 'I'm going to St Petersburg,' she declared. She stared up at him with watery blue eyes. 'I will go back as soon as the snow stops, and announce to the people that I have returned and their troubles are over –' She clutched at his hand. 'They killed my family, you know, but they didn't get me . . .'

Stephen pulled his hand away. The woman muttered something in Russian under her breath.

'I told you not to get up, Mrs Smith,' Mother Lena said, turning. 'Oh!' she said, and then again: 'Oh.'

'I'd like to see the proprietor,' Stephen said. The old humans spent their days floating on drugs. They would probably never notice anything odd about his sudden arrival, but his life had been built around eliminating or minimizing risks.

'Just go straight up,' said the cousin. 'The offices and staff quarters are right at the top of the house.'

'I'll find my way,' he said.

He found the others in the lounge. Only his blood-mother was missing. They were watching television. *EastEnders*.

'Hallo,' he said from the doorway.

Heads turned. There was a moment of startled silence. They smiled at him, but he smelled their irritation.

'Stephen! Good to see you, lad. Come in and sit your-self down!' said Father Albert, his voice full of fake cheerfulness.

'Shh!' said Father Jonathan. 'I want to hear what Sharon says to 'Chelle.'

Father Albert looked embarrassed. 'Just our little bit of research, that's all. Have to keep up with the times, you know.'

He got up and went to turn off the television. 'Oh,' he said, with his hand on the switch. 'There's that nice Nick Cotton. He's so good to his Mothers . . .' He stood watching the screen for a moment.

Stephen cleared his throat. Albert switched off the set, then turned to face him, looking embarrassed.

'Still killing humans?' Mother Julia asked. She was nursing again, probably the last litter the Family would have: a singleton, his twin having died a few weeks after the birth. Stephen pitied the poor lonely little thing. His own life had never been the same after his littermates had been killed.

He sat down next to her. The baby stared at him. I ought to get this over with, he thought. But he said, 'How old is he now?'

'Nineteen months. I'll be weaning him soon. You'd know if you came home more often.'

'Your Mothers miss you, boy. *I* miss you.' His blood-father's voice was a deep rumble from the depths of the Chesterfield chair. Father Geoffrey was the oldest male. Even when Stephen was a child he had been a vast brooding presence, and he was still the same now. Stephen expected him to go Ancient one day.

'Where is Mother Susan anyway?' he asked.

'Gone,' said Father Albert. 'She took the triplets up to your Aunt Cynthia's family for fostering. They sent Katriona back with a message that she had gone Walking. Pretty little thing Katriona's made of herself. She was asking after you, by the by.'

'Susan had the right idea, if you ask me,' said Mother Julia. 'I'll be joining her when William's old enough. Just you wait.'

'Don't say things like that, Julia,' Father Geoffrey said. 'Much more of this and we won't have a family left at all.'

'So what have you been getting up to, anyway?' Father Jonathan cut in. 'You never did say?'

He grinned at Stephen. If his tales were to be believed, he had been a rakehell in his day, leaving a string of broken Society hearts of both species and both sexes behind him. Then again, he would have it that he had played a triple game in the Great War, on two human sides and the Family's as well. Stephen had never known how seriously to take him, but at one hundred and forty he was still trim and boyish.

'Oh, much the same as usual,' Stephen said. With Father Jonathan, he always found a need to appear blasé. 'There's a body to dispose of, a girl to track down –'

'Nothing changes with you does it, boy? Still setting yourself up as judge, jury and executioner?' It was Mother Julia. When he had been a child, it was always her anger that cut to the core of him; not even Susan, his blood-mother, had been able to scare him as much as Julia in a rage. Now her voice was ice-cold.

'Let the lad alone,' Father Jonathan said. 'He'll settle down when it's his time to settle.'

'No!' Stephen said, and realized he had raised his voice. He went on more quietly. 'It isn't just a game. If we don't wash our own dirty laundry, one day the humans will come and do it for us, and –'

'All we want is what's best for you, son,' said Mother Lena. She always had been the peacemaker among them. When she goes, he thought, this family will fall apart. 'It's time you were settled, time you had a career. A *sensible* career.'

'If I were you, my lad, I'd pay a visit to that cousin of yours,' said Father Albert. 'She's as sweet a smelling little thing as you'll find anywhere, and of an age when a good –'

'Albert!' said Father Geoffrey. 'But you'll stay the night, at least, Stephen?'

'I can't, Father. I'll have to go straight back to keep my cover up. You will help me, though?'

'Yes, of course we will,' said Father Jonathan. He heaved himself out of his chair. 'Take no notice of this lily-livered lot. You do what you think you have to.'

'Thanks, dad,' said Stephen.

'Come on, I'll help you get the body round to the orchard. You can tell me about the girl on the way.' Father Jonathan led the way out of the room.

'Albert's right, you know. Katriona smells so sweet she's positively fragrant, and she has an excellent lineage. You could do a –'

'Don't you start,' said Stephen.

The next morning Stephen went round to Harrington's workroom, one of several cheap artists' studios in a purpose-built block. He nodded to a woman he met on the way in, and she smiled at him. Rock music blared from an upstairs room. He smelled clay and hot metal, felt the thrum of a motor in the soles of his feet. He let himself into Harrington's room.

The place was organized chaos that smelled of paint and photographic chemicals and Harrington. Canvases were stacked here and there, the strange abstracts Harrington considered his serious work mixed up with the realistic originals of his commercial painting.

A rickety table held a kettle and a miniature fridge, along with things for making coffee and herbal tea. Somewhat surprisingly, there was a phone on the wall by the table, but no answering machine. Stephen supposed it fit what he knew of the man: from his diary he was a social butterfly, but from his journal he was totally insecure. Work or not, he would never dare let himself be cut off from other people.

One end of the studio had been partitioned off to form a darkroom, and its outward-facing wall was plastered with photographs and sketches; a shelf next to it held two Pentax cameras and a clutch of lenses.

He stared at the cameras, at the photographs. Harrington's reputation lay in his paintings. As far as Stephen knew, the man had never sold his photographs or had an exhibition of them. The ones on the wall were an eclectic mix of portraits, landscapes and detail shots of architecture. Only when he had stared for a long time did he realize that Harrington had been using the photographs as reference material. Here, an old woman's face, shot in black and white, was reinterpreted in charcoal, in pastel, as a water-colour; there, a seascape was shot in saturated colours and then copied in pastel to form the backdrop for a mer-folk castle rising out of the waves.

Stephen grinned. Perhaps if he had to he could make a painting after all. The grin faded as he wondered how Harrington decided which photographs to use.

It was a question for later on. There was still a chance that he would find something here which would enable him to walk away from Harrington's life: something which would tell him whether Harrington really had passed material on to Cunningham; or something, perhaps, which would solve the enigma of Marion.

He searched the room thoroughly. He found the brief for the book jacket Harrington was working on, and the loose pages of the book itself, which Harrington had apparently scarcely begun to read, scattered all over the desk. He found rough sketches for the cover, none of them based on photographs.

Then, when he had almost given up, he found the

photographs pushed right to the back of the desk drawer. They showed much the same scene as the others: billowing smoke and flame in the background, while a woman of the Family underwent the rapid, automatic change to natural form that came only with death. Some of the photographs showed detail: the long muzzle, pointed teeth, hands malformed by human standards. These seemed to have been taken once the woman was dead. Others, a batch clipped together, depicted the change as it happened.

Bastard human must have had a motor drive on the camera, Stephen thought. He hunted through the drawer. There was nothing to indicate where and when the pictures had been taken. Nothing to say what Harrington had done with the negatives.

Harrington was cautious, then. Stephen's lips peeled back from his teeth in a smile that had nothing of the human in it.

Stephen went home by way of Oxford Street. He bought a dozen books, ranging from *The World of Chris Achilleos* and *Lightship* by Jim Burns to *Acrylics For Beginners* and *The Illustrator's Handbook*.

He was going to pay by credit card when he remembered seeing one of Harrington's portfolio albums alongside the Burns. He put the Access card away and paid cash.

When he got in there was a message on the answering machine from Marion: *Don't be a stranger, Dan. We really do need to talk, you and I. I'll see you at Hildy's tomorrow, usual time. We'll be fine. You'll see.*

He listened to the message twice more, trying to get some sense of who this woman was. Then he settled down with a glass of Harrington's good malt whisky, and began to read the book for which he had to produce some kind of cover. He had spent the whole of the afternoon examining Harrington's previous work. There was plenty of it around. Although he had sold many of his original paintings, there was a complete set of slides. He had also kept his working sketches and notebooks. Stephen wondered if he had thought they would be valuable one day, even though what Harrington considered his serious work had been routinely rubbished by the critics. Yet his suicide note had indicated that he had been dissatisfied in the end even with that. *It's shit*, he had said. *All of it.*

Stephen thought he understood. Harrington must have been obsessed, compelled to strive for perfection against all advice. The illustrative work, no matter how successful, had not satisfied him. It was the other, the need to communicate, that had burned in him. *I wanted to transform them.*

He had said that, but it had taken Marion to transform his life. Did that make her an artist? Perhaps by Harrington's definition it did. But then by his definition, Harrington was more of an artist for his paintings of overlapping red squares, which everyone hated, than for those of dragons arcing against the midnight sky, which brought pleasure to many.

It was beyond Stephen. He settled down to read the book. Perhaps something in it would give him an idea of what to do.

An hour later he gave up. The story was far too fanciful for him, full of elves appearing in New York, failing to do what they set out to do, and going back to some imaginary land, where they also failed to do whatever they had to do there. It was the twenty-second book in the series; Harrington had done covers for the last nine.

How could there be a land which did not exist? Why should humans invent elves, dragons, evil wizards?

Weren't there enough problems in the world? Stephen put the book down. Outside, twilight was deepening towards night. Cunningham, he decided. If nothing else, he could deal with him.

Warnfield Hall, despite its impressive name, was a converted end-of-terrace house that had seen better days. The others in the row all seemed to have been made into offices, so that at midnight the street was deserted. Stephen had considered changing his face slightly, so that if he were caught his position as Harrington would not be compromised. But he was more concerned that he would not be able to achieve a good likeness of the man again. Face dancing was never easy for him, but he had learned the skill out of necessity, as he had learned so many other undercover arts.

He disabled the rudimentary alarm system and entered through a first-floor window which yielded easily to his crowbar. His feet swung out over nothingness as he moved from the drainpipe to the window-sill. Adrenalin sent the blood singing round his body. This, this he understood! Let the humans have their books and their art. He wanted only to live in his body, to know that his people were protected, and that his name would live after him.

He moved through the silent rooms, rooms where countless humans had told their trivial secrets, and left them untouched behind him.

When he found Cunningham's office, he searched it thoroughly. He went through the filing cabinets memorizing everything in them that related to Harrington. He had no need to make copies – he despised such methods – what would do for the Lines would do for the less complex secrets of the humans.

Cunningham believed Harrington was paranoid; there

was even a suggestion that he might have fabricated the photographs in order to shore up what Cunningham referred to as his clearly delusional personal belief system. Cunningham also made plain that in his opinion, Harrington had been displaying symptoms of that neurotic paranoia for years, and that his apparently inflated opinion of his artistic ability was an overcompensation for deep-seated insecurity and anxiety about its actual worth; all of this resulting in his inability to relate adequately with others or form a stable intimate relationship. Cunningham believed the Kingsmead Hotel fire had simply triggered buried fears about ageing and death. Harrington had had a very happy childhood, unmarred by bereavement or tragedy. Paradoxically, this had meant he had never learned to deal with emotional pain. Faced with death in the fire, he had gone to pieces.

What would you make of my Family's attitude to death, Paul Cunningham? Stephen wondered. Are all of us then psychotic by definition? We all believe the rest of the world is out to get us, and our home life would seem very abnormal indeed to you.

He moved on to the most recent batch of files. As he opened them, he thought that if they were similar – if Cunningham had continued to think Harrington was just a little bit crazy – perhaps he would take a risk and leave well alone. He would kill where he had to, but that did not mean he relished it.

But it became clear that something had happened to change Cunningham's opinion. He made no further mention of the photographs, and where before there had been transcripts of his conversations with Harrington mentioning them, now there were none.

Something had happened, Stephen thought, something that had convinced him of the validity of those photos. He felt the hairs on his back stand up in that ancient fight-or-flight reflex he shared with the humans: suppose this had gone too far? Suppose he had shared this with too many others, others who could do something about it?

He had no time for politics, for debating the sense of Progress over Stasis, for intellectual arguments about the likely return of the Dark. He believed the greatest enemy of his people were the humans, their greatest safety in secrecy. He had shaped his whole life around maintaining that.

How could it be otherwise? As a child he had watched his blood-mother kill two innocent humans because they had seen his dead litter-mates revert to natural form. The images of that night had compacted down into a memory of driving without lights at night – some Family business had sent them out into the curfew – dodging Home Guard patrols and the police; rain on the windscreen and a shadow moving on darkness in the unlit road ahead of them; a squeal of brakes and blood on the tarmac: then the scent of fear, and the screams of his dying brother and sister. He blocked off the memory, as he had blocked it off for fifty years. All that remained was the scent of human blood on his mother's face, the sound of her soft voice in his ears, telling him it was all right, would be all right, the humans were gone. But Robert and Angela were dead, and after that it was never all right again.

In the treatment notes, Cunningham had said he intended to try hypnotherapy. Stephen had no idea if it would work on him or not.

'Over your dead body,' he whispered.

He continued his search. Forty years of covert activity had taught him much. When he had finished, the room looked just as it had when he had begun. But he had obtained Cunningham's home address, he had satisfied himself that none of the photographs were in the room, and he had copied the contents of his hard disk on to floppies. He had also found, hidden in the pot of a very large spider plant, the key to a bank safe-deposit box.

He locked the door behind him, and left the Centre the same way he had come.

When he slept he dreamed of rain and screaming, and the warm scent of Mother Susan corrupted by death and tears.

He woke drenched with sweat, and lay trembling in Harrington's bed. He had read somewhere of human dreams that were like fictions, twisted distortions of reality. He wondered if they were easier to bear than the memories retold that were the dreams of the Family.

He had believed once that if he could remember all of that night of death, he would banish it for ever. Perhaps he should consider hypnosis.

What would you make of me, Cunningham, he wondered aloud as the dawn light bled through the gap in the curtains.

And he slept.

Stephen arrived deliberately early at Hildebrandt's, despite Harrington's habitual lateness. He was concerned that he might not recognize Marion from her photograph, and so he waited in the cool white restaurant, with his black coffee and his newspaper. In truth, he was too tired to concentrate. He had woken late, with eyeballs that felt as though they had been sandpapered.

She would know what he was as soon as she scented him, of course. There was no hope that it could be otherwise. He did not much care, as long as he could get her out of the way before he had to deal with Cunningham.

She walked in as arrogant as a model stalking down a catwalk, all flashing eyes and jutting cheek-bones. Her waist-length hair bounced behind her. She sat down opposite him in a flurry of dropped bags and coat and scarves. She flashed a smile that belonged on the cover of *Cosmopolitan* as she ordered a Perrier. 'It's good to see you, Stephen,' she said. Her Irish lilt was soft, at odds with the calculated hardness of her exterior.

'I've missed you,' he hazarded. He stared at her, refusing to look away, though he was suddenly unnerved: he had never met anyone like her, human or Family. What does she *want*, he wondered.

She stared back. One long scarlet nail tapped the snowy tablecloth. 'Same old Stephen,' she said. Her smile was sardonic.

They talked, then, of many things, none of them important. The waiter came back.

'Steak, medium, with salad,' Marion said. Her lipstick was blood red. 'Same for you, Stephen?'

She isn't worried, he thought. What does she think is going on here? Does she know what I *do*? *Why isn't she afraid of me?*

She raised an eyebrow. He thought about Harrington's freezer full of Veggie-Burgers. 'I'll have mine rare,' he said.

'How's the work going, Stephen?' she asked him a little later. He could only bluster.

Afterwards, outside, he told himself he should kill her. The woman had clearly been set on Revealing herself to Harrington; if not directly, her game-playing would have done the job. Sooner or later he would have connected her with what he had seen in the hotel.

He should kill her. It was what he did. But the sky was the brilliant blue of high summer, and his senses were full of her chestnut hair and blue eyes, the scent of citrus and musk. He watched her walk ahead of him, heard the clacking of her heels on the pavement. He shook his head.

'Why don't you come back to the studio with me?' he said. 'I'll show you my work, if you like.' Get her alone, get it over with. Even as a child he had always eaten the despised vegetables first.

'I think I know your work well enough by now, wouldn't you say, Stephen?' she replied. She leaned forward and kissed him lightly on the lips. 'I'll be seeing you around, be sure of it.'

She walked off into the crowd. He watched her go, the taste of citrus still on his lips.

That night he raided Cunningham's home. He entered the flat as carefully as ever – it was a first-floor conversion in a terrace, and he watched until all the windows were dark; the people downstairs were out, those above, asleep.

It was simple enough, and he was expert. He went through the place like a quiet storm. When he had finished there was a pile of assorted junk in the middle of each room, and not a drawer still holding its contents.

He found no photographs and nothing to tell him whether Cunningham had passed his information on to anyone. He could have screamed then. He could have thrown china at the walls or torn the furniture to pieces. But to do any of these things might have brought the humans.

He did nothing, but stood in Cunningham's front room breathing deeply, letting the pain of his nails biting into his palms drive the anger from him.

When he left he took the video, television and hi-fi, along with a handful of jewellery and a few pounds in cash. He faked a clumsy entry. Then, to complete the illusion of a straightforward burglary, he did the same thing to the downstairs flat.

He let himself out of the front door. The fool humans upstairs had heard nothing. Impulsively, he lobbed half a brick through the window as he was leaving. Lights went on upstairs.

He laughed and ran. It was an idiotic thing to do, but it relieved his inner tension no end.

In the morning he paid a preparatory visit to Cunningham's bank. If it was large enough, he was prepared to risk taking in some identification and getting access to Cunningham's safe-deposit box that way. But as soon as he saw the place, he knew he did not dare try it. The place had a handful of staff on duty, even though it was lunch-time. He withdrew some cash and left, cursing inwardly.

For the next week he worked at the studio by day. He taught himself to copy any picture he saw. It was easy enough, a matter of fine muscle control and observation: nothing to a face dancer accustomed to sculpting the muscle beneath the flesh. Between drawings he studied how Harrington developed his ideas, but this he found harder.

In the evening he fulfilled Harrington's social obligations, hiding his unease with a kind of synthetic amiability his fellow-guests seemed to find natural.

Halfway through the week he admitted his unease to himself, and shortly thereafter realized it was because he was constantly looking for Marion. Every time one of the matriarchs who dominated things said, 'Of course you've met . . .' his heart lurched. But the women were never her.

He fell asleep at night with the images he'd worked on, perfectly remembered, burning behind his eyes. Why should a series of tree drawings be – apparently – the inspiration behind a sequence of spaceship illustrations? Why render the face of God, of all improbable human inventions, as polished bone?

Sometimes, drifting on the edge of sleep, he thought he almost understood. It was as if there was a void in his mind, an empty space waiting to be filled: and what would fill it would be something new in the world, never seen, never heard until he brought it into being. Then he would jerk awake and lie terrified, staring into the darkness, until the sound of his own rushing blood and the rhythm of his heart calmed him. Then he slept; but when he woke it was always with echoes of dreams fading in his mind, ragtag memories that would not come clear.

Always, when he came home, back to Harrington's house, the first thing he did was check the answering machine. He spent the early hours restlessly wandering from room to room with the stereo turned up, staring at the paintings.

I could call her, he thought. I could even visit her. Harrington would never do such a thing; he was weak, Stephen knew that much from the man's journals.

I'm not Harrington, he thought. Damn my cover to Dark and beyond. I *can* phone her. But he did not.

The next morning he slept late. He was still sitting in the kitchen with a cup of the heavy black coffee Harrington favoured when Mrs Bailey arrived. He heard her banging around upstairs. Any minute she would get out the hoover, and his head already hurt. He ought to go, but he would have to pass her, and she would want to chat.

He fed the cat instead. It twined itself around his legs, then attacked the cat food without delicacy. Stephen remembered the taste of rare steak. He realized he was once again thinking about *her*.

Mrs Bailey came in a moment later, surrounded by a haze of tobacco smoke. She put her cigarette on the lid of the cat-food tin.

'You ought to throw these things away. Filthy habit, Mr Harrington, I must say.' The cigarette sent little wreaths of smoke into the air.

Stephen sighed and took the post from her. The cat stopped eating and stared up at them. Then it stalked disdainfully from the room.

Among the bills and circulars were a couple of fan letters and an invitation to the celebrity launch party for *Winds of Change: a Book for Africa*, a coffee-table book Harrington had illustrated. A handwritten note paper-clipped to the card said: *Thought I ought to warn you – Marion says she'll definitely be there. Sorry the two of you aren't getting on so well. See you – S.*

Stephen found that his heart was racing and his fists were clenched. He was grinning like an idiot. He tried to slow his internal responses, but he had never been good at that; he had always been better at muscle control. He forced the smile from his face and left the kitchen rapidly, pursued by Mrs Bailey.

Stephen grabbed his coat from the rack. Mrs Bailey droned on. Just as he turned the doorknob, the phone rang. Reluctantly, he turned back. He went into the lounge and took the call on the downstairs extension. Mrs Bailey followed him in, and began ostentatiously dusting the picture-frames on the other side of the room.

If I were Harrington, I'd have sacked you long ago, Stephen thought.

He picked up the phone and identified himself.

'This is Southbrook Retirement Home, Mr Harrington.' It was Mother Lena. 'I believe you were inquiring about a place for your father? We have the information you requested, but we think it would be best if you visited us again before you make your decision.'

Stephen, with his back to Mrs Bailey, smiled. He arranged to go down to the house the following day. He put the phone down and turned. Mrs Bailey was no longer in the room. Stephen frowned. Pain began to beat at his temples again.

In the dining-room, the hoover started up.

Stephen leafed through the stack of drawings. They were Harrington's, sketches for the *Antmage* cover. He had decided that he still did not know how Harrington chose what to paint – and did not care. There were a variety of scantily clad, pointy-eared women in the sketches, all of them russet-haired, despite the fact that the elves in the book were uniformly white blonde.

Was this why Harrington's work was considered sentimental? Stephen still did not know.

He had to do something. Anything. He gnawed his thumb. He laid the drawings out, one by one, so that he could see them all at once.

They all looked equally good. He took a penny out of his pocket, shut his eyes and tossed it into the air. He opened his eyes. The coin had landed on a close-up of one of the elves, a female warrior wearing three loops of strategically placed chain. Her sword, also strategically placed, was taller than she was. It hardly made sense to Stephen, but he supposed Harrington had known what he was doing. He took a sheet of art board, fixed it to the drawing-table, and began to copy the sketch.

Once that was done, he laid down a wash of ground colour over it. After that, he would be able to paint in the background detail, and the figures. While it dried, he stopped for coffee. When he came back, the wash had obliterated every trace of his original sketch.

He started to look up what had gone wrong in the *Manual of Materials and Methods in the Modern Art Studio*, then shut the book with a bang. The hell with it, he muttered. Painstakingly, he sketched the picture in again.

Stephen wrapped his hands around his coffee-mug. He was cold despite the warmth of the night, with the shaky chill that only comes with absolute tiredness.

Night? he thought. But dawn had crept up on him, and it filled the studio with soft grey light. He looked at the art board. The painting, half complete, seemed much more garish than it had by electric light. *Must be right. Has to be, it's just like every other Harrington.* He drove the heels of his palms into his eyes.

It was 12 June. The cover was due at Quantum. He had to take it in, or they would know there was something wrong. But if he took it in they would see it was not good enough, not real, like nothing he ever did was good enough. And it wasn't even finished ... he found himself drifting, staring at the transforming face of his litter-mate Robert, with the blood tracing down his face; and all he could do was promise his mother that the humans would never find out about *him*, but he never was good enough, never got rid of all the danger –.

He jerked awake. The hell with it, he told himself. He had to get his priorities right. Marion first, then Cunningham. The painting was only important as long as it helped him get to them. Marion. Cunningham.

He shook his head as if he could get rid of the tiredness that way. Cunningham first. He had to remember that. He put his coffee down, then found that, irresistibly, his head was following, cushioned on folded arms.

He slept.

It was mid-afternoon when he woke. He did his best to smarten himself up, then set off for his parents' house. He stopped at a Happy Eater on the way. He had steak done rare, with chips and a dessert made of sugar and E-numbers.

Father Geoffrey was waiting for him when he arrived. He was in the front room with the patients, spoonfeeding Mrs Smith from a plate of mashed potato and finely chopped meat.

'You're late,' he said. 'I thought you were desperate.' He shoved a forkful of food in the general direction of Mrs Smith's mouth.

'I am. I had other things to do.'

'Things your poor parents might be proud of, I hope.'

'*Borzhemoi*, I want my food in my mouth, man, not in my ear,' said Mrs Smith.

Geoffrey scowled at Stephen, who replied, 'It's a dirty job, but someone's got to do it.'

'You've been watching too many old movies,' Geoffrey said.

'Just my little bit of research. How's Princess Anastasia today?' He gestured towards Mrs Smith, who was attempting to wipe a mashed-potato moustache away.

Father Geoffrey dabbed clumsily at the old woman's face with a tissue. 'Same as ever. Same as they all –'

'I am *not* Princess Anastasia,' Mrs Smith drew herself up in her chair. 'I'm Catherine the Great. Anyway, there's that nice Mr Yeltsin now, so there's no point going back, is there?'

'I'll come upstairs with you,' Father Geoffrey said. 'I have a few things to tell you.

'This Marion Ryan of yours is working for Her Ladyship,' Father Geoffrey said. 'You don't want to mess with her –'

'You should find a few nice girls to marry,' Father Albert said. He winked. 'That Katriona would make a good start. She always has been sweet on you, you mark my words.'

'Geoffrey meant Her Ladyship, Albert, as well you know,' said Mother Lena.

'It's about time I got back to the old girl,' Stephen said. He looked his blood-father in the eye, knowing it was no good, that his scent would make his sudden dread plain to everyone in the room.

'Nice try, boy,' said Father Jonathan. He grinned at Stephen from behind Geoffrey's back. 'But I wouldn't try to fool *her*.'

'It's a bit late for that anyway, dad,' Stephen said. 'Though I haven't had much to do with her lately.'

'The message we got said one of our children was already known to her,' Julia said. She smelled of milk and baby-shit. 'I might have known it was you.'

'Oh for goodness' sake, it's a bit late to be nagging him now,' said Mother Lena, without turning away from the television.

'At least the boy's got some go in him,' said Father Jonathan. 'I never should have let you talk me into getting married, Geoffrey old man. No disrespect, of course.'

'None taken. Nevertheless —'

'None of you need be involved any further,' Stephen said. His mouth filled with the copper taste of his own fear, and he knew his parents would certainly smell it. 'After all, I do have a long-standing arrangement with Her Ladyship.'

'Nonsense lovey,' said Lena. 'Geoffrey will go with you. With Susan gone, it's his place —'

'That's balderdash and you know it,' Geoffrey said. 'It's just storing up trouble for the future. Anyway, there's no reason it has to be me.'

'Well then, Jonathan could go,' Lena said stubbornly. She turned to him. 'You're *always* telling us how you worked for the Family in the war. This will be just like the old days.'

'Wouldn't miss it for the world, you know that,' Jonathan said, 'but as it happens I have an appointment with the bank manager in the morning.' He stopped and looked around at them. 'Well, one of us has to deal with the humans. Why don't you go, Lena?'

She looked flustered. 'By myself? A very good impression that will make, I must say.'

After that the talk turned to more inconsequential Family business — births, deaths and marriages. Especially marriages.

Next morning, while Stephen was sitting alone in the front room, Mother Lena's two girls came in. They were true twins, cornsilk blonde and cute in the human fashion. At seven they were already adept at changing.

They regarded him solemnly. 'Mother Julia says you're a sassin,' one of them announced.

'That means you kill people,' the other explained.

'Do you kill people?'

'Not often,' Stephen said, and smiled. 'But I could make an exception in your case.'

Lena came in and shooed them out. 'Sorry,' she said brightly. He wondered if she had heard, and was surprised how much it hurt.

Stephen drew up in the forecourt of Chevington House, alongside all the other tourists. He felt as if he were watching himself from a long way off as he got out of the car and found a tour guide. It was an effect of the absolute terror he felt at the idea of confronting Her Ladyship. He knew that.

It didn't help.

He told the tour guide he was a friend of the housemaid, and the man went off to find her. He came back far too quickly, and led Stephen round the back of the house.

The woman who met him in the basement kitchen was between his age and that of his parents. She smiled at him. Her name, she said, was Eileen. By her scent Stephen could tell that she was married, not yet with children though there were young in the group. He found the idea exciting. *Shit*, he thought, *I really am going fertile.* He clamped down on the idea, knowing she would sense his arousal.

'Come,' she said. 'We mustn't keep Her Ladyship waiting.'

Eileen left him standing in the corridor while she went in to announce him. He remembered the last time he had been there. He had been glad to get out with his life, let alone his freedom . . .

There was a rustling noise from inside the room. Eileen came out and ushered him in. The room was as huge as he recalled it. Despite its ballroom proportions the smell of Her Ladyship was overwhelming. They were in the cellar of the house, and the room was ventilated only by slits near the ceiling. The opulent drapes that hung on the walls covered false windows. The room was lit by candles, hundreds of them in a huge crystal chandelier suspended from the ceiling, more in wall-sconces and candlesticks on the heavy furniture that filled the room.

Her Ladyship was scared of electricity.

She was sitting at the back of the room on a scroll-back brocade couch. Even sitting, she was much taller than Stephen, and her hair added another foot to her height. She was broad in proportion, breadth made greater by the leg-of-mutton sleeves of her dress. Heavy make-up accentuated, rather than concealed, the thrust of her jaw and the roughness of her leathery skin.

'Stephen, how *delightful* to see you again!' she cried. 'Do come and sit next to me.'

Stephen went in, edging carefully around an aspidistra on a drum-table and a chair that looked as if it would collapse if any weight at all were put on it.

Tea things were set out on a low table in front of her. She smiled, revealing teeth as long as Stephen's thumb. She patted the seat next to her. Stephen perched on the couch as far away as he could from her.

'Do make yourself comfortable, dear boy. I so rarely get visitors these days.'

Stephen moved half an inch along the couch. He kept his hands clenched in his lap. Beads of sweat studded his face. He smelled terrified, even to himself. She must be able to smell it, he thought. She must.

'One shall be mother, shall one?' Her Ladyship said. 'After all, one has been housekeeper to the nobility.' She poured the tea.

She handed him a cup made of porcelain so fine he could see her fingers through it. He took it carefully, holding the saucer in one hand and the cup in the other.

'One lump or two?' she asked, with the sugar-tongs already poised.

Stephen sipped his tea. It was too hot, too strong, too sweet. The cup rattled against the saucer, loud as gunshot.

'I trust it is to your taste?'

'Fine. Fine,' Stephen answered. 'It's fine.'

'Of course, one can't get decent tea, now.' Her Ladyship picked up her own cup. It was as tiny as a doll's in her massive hand. She sipped delicately at the tea. Her fangs clicked on the china. 'Not like when I was a girl. It just doesn't have the time to mature in the chest on the voyage over any more.' She put the cup down. 'Tell me about this girl you are trying to find?'

'She is involved with a human,' Stephen began. 'One

I killed, and whom I am currently impersonating. I think
–' he took a sip of tea, aware that his next words would
surely trigger her rage. I'll never get out in time. I should
have stayed near the door, he thought, '– that she might
have been about to reveal herself to him.'

'Really?' said Her Ladyship. 'How simply *too* fascinat-
ing. Might I tempt you with a scone? A savoury? Perhaps a sausage roll? A waste of good meat I call it, but
Eileen's very proud of her pastry.'

'Not . . . not for me. Thank you.'

'Got a taste for vegetables, have you? You won't grow
big and strong if you keep eating up your greens, you
know.'

Stephen leaned forward and helped himself to a
sausage roll. He choked it down in two bites. Her Ladyship smiled.

'That's better. Now, I do have a smidgeon of a problem
with this situation. Perhaps you can help me?' She
picked up a chicken drumstick and ate it in one bite,
bone and all. Then she smiled at him. '*Can* you help me,
Stephen?'

'Yes,' he said, round a mouth full of pastry like wet
cardboard.

'Good. The problem is, much as I would like to help
you – much as I once thought you might have a place
with me – Marion already does work for me. Too many
of my . . . contemporaries know she is my protégée for
me to give her up. Not without proof, at any rate. The
embarrassment would ruin me. Do you have proof,
Stephen?'

'Yes!' he said too quickly.

'Think carefully,' Her Ladyship said. She glared at
Stephen. After a moment he looked away.

'No,' he said quietly. There was silence. 'But logic
says that was her intention –' he rallied.

'Logic never leads to Revealing,' Her Ladyship said. Her voice rose to a scream. 'Never!'

Stephen began to edge away from her on the couch. He could hear her taking deep breaths, smell her anger ebbing away, but he did not dare look at her.

'Forgive me,' she said. She fanned herself gently with her hand. 'I believe I might try one of those cream puffs. Would you . . .?'

Stephen tried out a smile, but regretted it instantly. He immediately found a plate piled with cakes being pressed into his hands.

'Now, as I was saying,' continued Her Ladyship, 'Marion is working for me. Indeed, I had sent her to deal with Harrington because of the Kingsmead Hotel fire business –'

Stephen stared at her. The plate tilted dangerously.

'– Oh yes, I know you've come to regard it as your own preserve, but we needed to move faster than that. Just how long do you think it would have taken the humans to work things out?' She licked cream off her upper lip.

'I had no idea,' Stephen said.

'That's the trouble with you young people today – you think you're the only ones who can do anything.'

'But Marion didn't kill him,' Stephen said. 'He killed himself because she was playing games with him.'

'More tea? No I thought not. You have to be going soon, anyway.' Her Ladyship poured a cup for herself. 'Let's spell this out plainly. I want Marion alive, but only if she's trustworthy. If she can prove that to you, well and good. If not, I want her dead with as little fuss as possible, and I want the proof brought to me.' She rang a little silver bell on the tea tray. 'Eileen will see you out.'

Eileen came and Stephen followed her to the door.

Just as he was about to leave, Her Ladyship called to him.

'I am depending on your discretion, boy. Don't fail me.'

The painting looked almost as bad in full sunshine as it had by the light of dawn. Stephen stared at it from across the studio. Terror had left him as exhausted as if he had missed a week of sleep.

Despite all that, though, he had intended to try and work on the painting. If he could not keep his cover intact, there was no hope for the rest of what had to be done.

'To hell with it all,' he growled to no one in particular.

He slammed the door behind him as he left. When he got home, he slept for ten hours straight.

It was not until he woke that Stephen noticed the light flashing on the answering machine. *Marion*, he thought. Then, remembering Her Ladyship, *Oh shit*.

He was wrong. 'Dan. Clive Thornton here. Remember me? The Art director at Quantum? The guy who gets your invoices paid? We may not be living in the same universe here, but in mine the *Antmage* deadline was yesterday. Get on it and get back to me, willya?'

Stephen rolled over, put the pillow over his head and made a good attempt at going back to sleep. All it got him was a headache.

Stephen stared at the picture. He had re-created Harrington's sketch faithfully, even positioning the figures in the same place on the art board. As *Commercial Illustration* had suggested, he had left a reasonable amount of space at the bottom for lettering, and an even more generous amount at the top. *You can always crop to fit afterwards*, said the book.

Perhaps that was why the figures looked so small, Stephen decided. He looked from the sketch to his painting and back again. There was too much space at the top. For the first time, he wondered if he ought to have scaled Harrington's drawing up. Hastily he reached for *Graphic Design for First-Year Students*, which informed him that it would be most convenient to make a series of half- or quarter-size working sketches in the early stages of any project.

He would have to do something, but there was no time to start all over again, and besides he could not bear the thought of it. Hastily, he grabbed the nearest sketch. It was the wrong size and shape. He flipped through the stack. Nothing, nothing, nothing. His eyes lit on the charcoal sketch of the old woman. As far as Stephen could remember, it had nothing to do with the book. Not that that had ever bothered Harrington very much, Stephen told himself firmly; besides, there was sure to be an old lady in there somewhere.

He was getting better. It only took him a couple of hours to sketch in the outlines.

The phone rang. Stephen dropped his pencil and hurried to pick it up.

'Hi, Dan,' said Marion. 'Aren't you the stranger?'

'I've been busy,' he said.

'And there I thought you'd been out of town. Visiting relatives, at a guess.'

He could see her so clearly he felt he would be able to touch her hair, if he only put out his hand. 'Oh. And who have you been talking to?'

'News travels. Anyway, I missed you.'

She would smell of musk and lemon, and her eyes were the blue of sapphires, of the sea. 'You surprise me.'

'I wanted to make sure you would be at the *Winds of*

Change launch. I'd not want you to be washing your hair that night, if you follow me.'

'I wouldn't miss it for the world. You'll be going to it, I suppose.'

'Oh sure. It would take more than some old woman to stop me.' *Aah*, he thought; but he remembered the way the sun caught the copper in her hair.

'Take care,' he said more urgently than he had intended.

'White or red, sir?' the waiter asked. Stephen was already regretting the double Scotch he had had before he arrived, but he took a glass of Riesling anyway. Then he wandered off into the crowd. He smiled vaguely at various people, hoping to chance on someone he recognized, if only from a photograph.

His bow-tie was unbearably tight. He resisted the temptation to scratch under it, or better yet to take it off altogether.

'Good to see you, Dan darling,' cooed a woman in a dress she was poured into. 'But I'd watch out for Clive if I were you.' She smiled sweetly. 'You know what he's like when his schedules get behind.'

He muttered something at her, all the while looking for Marion over her shoulder. He escaped from her and, realizing he had finished his drink, headed back to the bar.

'Hi, Dan.' Stephen nodded to a vaguely familiar man. 'Clive's been asking after you,' he said. He held two full glasses up over everyone's heads, and was away before Stephen could reply.

Stephen exchanged his empty glass for a full one. As he turned away from the bar, he spotted Marion on the other side of the room. For all he knew the man she was speaking to was Clive. *Hell with it*, he thought, and plunged back into the crowd.

By the time he had pushed his way to the far corner

she had gone. He cursed mentally and knocked back the wine. He grabbed another glass from a passing waiter. Someone in the crowd said, 'Well, Clive –'

Stephen backed off. A woman jogged his elbow, and his wine went flying: most of it ended up down her dress, but she apologized relentlessly anyway, dabbing at his shirt with a tissue.

He saw a flash of red. He picked up the woman's hand, removed it from his chest and went in pursuit. It took him a long time to get across the room; somehow everyone wanted to tell him how marvellous his work on the book was. He nodded, smiled, shook hands, signed copies. In between times he managed to acquire, empty and dispose of three more glasses of wine.

Naturally, by the time he arrived on the other side of the room she had gone – if she had ever been there. He leaned in a corner against a large potted palm. He stank of alcohol and fear, and the place stank of alcohol and far too many humans. He did not want to think of why he smelled of fear, or of the excitement that so clearly underlay it: that *frisson* he got only when he was closing in on prey. Most especially, he did not want to think of how the evening might end.

'The best thing about these dos is the free wine,' said a soft Irish voice beside him. He looked up. Marion offered him a glass of the red. 'So I'm told anyway. But then, you smell as if you've had enough for three, as *anyone* here could tell you.'

'We should talk,' Stephen said. He was getting a headache again. 'But not, I think, here.'

'True. We can go and sit out by the river, if you like. Mind you, there's some fellow named Clive asking after you. I can wait if you want to talk to him first.'

Stephen stared across the river. The wine had made him light-headed. He strove to control his internal responses, wished he were better at that side of things. Moonlight shone down on the river and the floodlit buildings. He wondered if it would make a good painting. *Perhaps I should ask Harrington*, he thought. *He'd know.* He giggled aloud.

But then he remembered the awe he had felt when he first saw Harrington's work, how he had yearned towards it. That was before he had learned it was worthless.

'Know-nothing humans,' he muttered.

He heard footsteps. Marion stopped beside him, with her back to the river. Her perfume enhanced, rather than disguised, her natural scent. The curve of her breast pressed against his arm. He felt it move as she breathed. He turned slightly, and saw that the reddish hairs on her arms were standing up, despite the warmth of the night. It was only then that he isolated the smell of her fear from his own.

'Why did you do it?' he asked.

'Come here tonight? Why, it's a good party, and I thought it was time we talked, you and I, Dan. Should I still call you Dan?'

'If you want. Why did you do what you did – instead of doing as you were told?'

Marion turned, so that they were facing the same way; but now she was pressed up close to him. He felt her hair brushing his cheek, the flesh of their arms separated only by a few thin layers of cloth. When she spoke, her breath was hot on his face.

'You're good, you are,' she whispered, 'asking me such things out here where anyone can hear. Or is it just that you're drunk, like any fool human might be?'

'There's no one to hear, and you know it.' He covered her hand with his. 'Now answer me. I have decisions to make, and I don't want to make the wrong ones.'

'Aah, so you have been talking to Her,' she said. 'I

wondered if I was just guessing well or –' Her voice deepened slightly, and swapped its Irish lilt for glottal cockney, '– whether I 'eard you right, talking to that lot up at Southbrook, weren't it?'

'You! But I never smelled you! The cigarettes couldn't do all that . . . could they?' The adrenalin surge cleared the last of the alcohol from his head. He sought to calm his panic. If she could do this, how many others might there be? How many feral, how many revealers or Dark-callers or outcast?

'Aah, you face dancers, you think you're the only ones with any skill, don't you?'

'You can change your smell? Your *smell*? That's not possible.'

'Not change it. Blank it out. That's why I needed the cigarettes. You'd think it bloody strange if I'd no smell at all, now wouldn't you? Not that it's easy, mind. I wouldn't do it for any old human who came along.'

'OK,' he said. She must know he was worried. His heart was still hammering, and his breath was coming fast and shallow. He gripped the stone wall. 'But why, Marion? Why didn't you just do as you were told?'

'There's more to life than following orders. I've always been interested in art. Studied it at college – oh, don't look at me like that! I studied art philosophy, art theory. That kind of thing. When Her Ladyship needed someone to deal with Harrington, I jumped at it –'

'She knew I was sorting out the Kingsmead thing. She told me so herself.' Stephen felt peculiarly aggrieved.

'So she did. But humans who clearly knew about us started turning up, and we traced them back to Har-rington. It was as easy for Her Ladyship to put me on it as it was for her to call you in and tell you – specially since you'd like as not have ignored her on principle.'

'That unreasonable old bitch –'

'You've spent your life putting yourself outside society, Dan. What do you expect? Anyway, you wanted to know why I didn't just kill him, and if you'll give me a minute, I'll tell you. It was the art, as I say. Have you never wondered how they take this, add that, mix in a little of a third thing – and then turn it into something *other*. I have. They have made me laugh, and cry, and wonder, when there had been no such thought in my head the moment before. And I have hated them for it.'

'Because you don't want them controlling you?'

She shook her head, setting her mane of hair bouncing. 'Because I can't understand it. I can't *do* it. But he could, however bad they said he was, however manipulative. He was an artist. Do you realize what that is? It means making things that are wholly new. It means making people see things differently –'

Stephen laughed harshly. 'Then you're a greater artist than ever Daniel Harrington was. Do you know, in his suicide note he said he had wanted to change people's lives. Transform them, that was the word he used. But he never did. It took you to do that. You made him see he could never have what he'd dreamed of.'

She stared at him. 'That can't be. All I wanted was to force him to make art. So I went to him. I was a dowdy little thing then, Stephen. You'd have recognized me, but he wouldn't. I changed myself, slowly. I became what he could not resist. I answered his every desire, echoed his every mood. When he was down, I cheered him. When he was happy, I intensified it. When he needed to tell secrets, I listened.

'I studied him as prey, and I caught him as a cat catches a mouse; and like a cat, I played with him. I set up the Mrs Bailey persona so I could watch him when I wasn't around. It worked all right. In the end, there was no escape for him. If you'd told him what I had done – even without the physical changes – he would not have believed you. He was happy.'

'A transformation indeed. Did it work?'

'I don't know. It all looks the same to me, anyway. The critics didn't seem to think so. The visual equivalent of candyfloss, one of them said. Anyway, that was only stage one of my plan. I figured I would only know if I was right afterwards, so I moved to stage two.'

'And Her Ladyship let you be while all this was going on?'

'I told her I was tracing his contacts. I was, too, but slowly. Having heard you tonight, I think perhaps I fooled her less well than I imagined. Anyway, it couldn't last for ever. When I realized that his art was as it had always been, I decided to shock him out of it. *Out of despair, great art.* Vincent Van Gogh said that. I thought if I could bring him low enough, he'd lose that edge of sentimentality they all said he had.'

'So you humiliated him,' Stephen said. Marion looked surprised. 'It was in his journal.'

'I did. I went to a party with him, a very swish dinner party with a lot of media types. I pretended to get drunk, and then I asked one of the art critics for a true opinion of one of his paintings. The man bluffed and blustered. Then I read out one of his critiques. It had been in the *Independent*, and oh, it was a piece of cruelty beyond anything of my devising. When I'd done, poor Dan was terribly upset. He begged me to stop, but I wouldn't. When he started shouting at me, I hit him. Not hard, not by our standards, but you could see the finger-marks. I told him I agreed with the critic, challenged anyone there to disagree. No one did. I left then.

'When Dan came to see me, I accused him of mental cruelty, of caring nothing for me, for my feelings. Perhaps that was true. I don't rightly know.'

'You do know what happened?'

'Yes. The morning after the row, I went round as Mrs Bailey, and let myself in. I had no real idea what to expect. Dan was an early riser, though, so when he wasn't around I went upstairs to find him.'

'I'm sorry,' Stephen said.

'Surprisingly enough, so was I.' She laughed shortly. 'Anyway, I saw him and you in bed, and figured you for what you were. Her Ladyship had told me to watch for you.'

'Would you have killed him?' Stephen asked. He could hardly bear to ask; if she said no –

'I don't know.'

Stephen wanted to grab her, to hold her and make her say yes; yes she would have killed Harrington, yes she was an obedient servant of Her Ladyship. Yes, she would go home with him tonight and –

'Did Her Ladyship tell you to kill *me*?' she asked.

'She told me to use my judgement. And that if she considers I got it wrong, well I suppose my name will be taken out of the Lives no matter what else I did right.'

'And what is your judgement?'

'Mostly that I couldn't kill you here and now and get away with it.'

'Would you believe me if I promised?'

'Maybe. Maybe not.'

'Words are just words. I could say anything.'

'Yes you could.' *Say anything*, he thought at her. *Give me a reason not to kill you.* 'So say something.'

She pulled away from him. Her hair haloed out around her, turned orange by the sodium glare of the street-lights. The smell of musk and citrus hung heavily in the air.

'Not tonight,' she said, and walked away.

*

231

The smell of paint did nothing to help his hangover. Stephen dabbed dispiritedly at the mer-folk castle with his paintbrush. It was the only sketch he could find that would fit the space in the right-hand corner. The only trouble was that *Antmage* was set in a desert. Maybe he could persuade them that the sea was blue sand.

That night there was an agitated message on his answering machine from Clive. He was desperate to have the painting, and demanded that Stephen phone him the next day.

On principle, Stephen spent the next day painting. Somehow he could not *quite* achieve Harrington's purity of line, and it irritated him. That, after all, was more a matter of muscular control than anything else.

About midday, the phone rang. He let it go on for a few seconds, convinced it would be Clive. Then he answered it.

'Dan? Marion. I've been thinking about our conversation.'

'Uh-huh. And you're going to tell me that there's nothing to worry about, you'll follow instructions from now on.'

'Something like that. I have a way to give you the proof you need. Something better than words. I know Harrington had contacted others. You'll have to deal with them. Let me help with the next one.'

'All right,' said Stephen. He felt the smile rising up inside him. 'I have a plan already, but another pair of hands is always useful. Meet me at Hildebrandt's the day after tomorrow and I'll fill you in.'

The next day Stephen took the painting down to Quantum. He was made to wait in the lobby of their offices, which were too modern to be imposing.

Eventually a secretary came down and took him up

to Clive's office. The art editor was a large, trendily dressed black American.

'Dan! I was beginning to think you were avoiding me!' Clive said, in a voice loud enough to turn heads.

Stephen smiled weakly. 'As if I would.'

'C'mon,' said Clive. 'Let's see this latest masterpiece.'

'Careful, it could do with another day to harden off properly,' said Stephen. Any minute now he's going to ask why it was late and I won't know what to say, he thought; my cover will be blown and that will be the end of it. His palms were wet. He almost wished he were human.

'You got it. I'll treat it like a Fabergé egg.' He unwrapped the painting, and carefully set it up on his desk. Stephen thought the light did not quite do it justice.

Clive was silent for a long moment.

'What do you think?' Stephen asked anxiously.

'It's sure ... different,' said Clive. 'I wish you'd asked me before you tried this collage effect, 'cause I'm not sure what the typographer's going to make of it. But yeah, I like it. It's so ... relevant. Really reflects the content of the book. Marketing will love it.'

'Oh good,' said Stephen.

Clive walked up to it and peered closely at it. 'This scumbling effect's neat too. I'm not sure about how it'll reproduce, though. Hell, we'll manage.' He turned and grinned.

Here it comes, thought Stephen. Here it comes. He got in first. 'Sorry it's so late, Clive,' he said.

'Don't worry about it,' Clive said. 'Besides, with you we know what to expect. I mean, I'd hate for you to think it was OK, but we know we always need to cut our Dan a little slack, you got me?'

Stephen stared at him. Cut him a little slack? He had

had nightmares about this painting. He had sweated blood trying to do what no member of the Family had ever done. Why hadn't Harrington mentioned in his journal that he always missed his deadlines? And then he thought, Well, would you want lateness remembered in your place in the Fifty Lives?

'Now, would you like to discuss your next commission?' Clive asked.

'Maybe later?' said Stephen.

'I won't be more than an hour or so, one way or the other,' said Stephen.

Marion twisted around in the driver's seat to look at him. 'Save some for me,' she said. Sunlight gilded her hair, turning the copper lights to brass. The heat drew out the smell of the vinyl seats, so that Stephen had to strain to catch her citrus scent. She patted his hand.

'See you later,' she said.

Stephen went to keep his appointment with Cunningham.

'So who did you send my photographs to?' Stephen asked. He was half an hour into his therapy session with Cunningham. *What do the humans get out of this?* Stephen wondered. He settled back and watched the human.

'Why do you keep going back to the photographs, Daniel?' Cunningham countered. 'You haven't mentioned them in a long while. Has something happened to upset you?'

How would Harrington react? It was the question through the whole therapy session. 'Obviously because they are important to me.' The light was deliberately dim; perhaps humans found it soothing. To Stephen it was merely unsettling.

234

'I know you feel that they are,' Cunningham answered. 'Perhaps we should talk about how you came by them.' He tapped the end of his biro on his jotter. He stared at Stephen from behind aviator glasses. His eyes were pale and watery, at odds with his physique. Stephen had found a membership card to a gymnasium in his flat.

'We've been through this before,' Stephen hazarded. *Come on, tell me. What happened to convince you they are genuine?*

'I know,' Cunningham said. He pursed his lips around the words as if they were lemons, yet his voice stayed soft. It was like the light: deliberately kept low in an effort to soothe. Like the light, it failed. 'But I feel it might help if you told me again.'

Tell me again, tell me again, Stephen thought. *Do you really think Harrington would have forgotten? Is that what making the world twist in your mind does to you humans? Makes you forget, makes you mad?*

He wondered, briefly, what Cunningham would say if he asked him for help: *I saw my mother kill a couple of humans one night during World War 2; I'd like you to help me remember it so I can tell the rest of the Family about it properly.*

'I saw creatures that changed when they died.' He strove to keep calm, though he was doing the thing most forbidden, the thing he had dedicated his life to stopping. He was telling a human about the Family, and he had to make the human believe him. He felt his throat constrict. Easier to kill him now, make a quick getaway, deal with the consequences later. But that would be leaving hostages to fortune, and it would deny Marion her chance to prove herself to Her Ladyship. 'Creatures that looked like werewolves.'

'Do you really think that's possible, Daniel?'

Cunningham asked. There was no hint of mockery in his voice. The man was a *tabula rasa*, clean of any hint of his own personality. Stephen wondered what he was like at home.

'Do you?' Stephen asked, and thought *You certainly do.*

'Let me have you hypnotized. That will prove what you saw, one way or the other.'

'I can do better,' Stephen said. 'I've got one of the bodies. I can show you.' It was hardly a lie. He felt the panic breaking out again. He stank of dread. He was sure even Cunningham could smell it.

'This is new.'

'I never needed to tell you about it before,' said Stephen. 'I always thought you were on my side then.'

'I am on your side, Dan. We have to work together to help you get better.' His expression had changed though, and so had his scent. His eyes strayed to the buzzer on the table; it was supposed to let the receptionist know Cunningham was ready for his next patient, but Stephen presumed there was an alarm code. He looked back at Stephen who realized that he had gone too far; Cunningham was almost afraid of him.

'I know that,' he said, allowing a trace of impatience to creep into his voice. 'The truth is, Paul, I've been thinking of going public with this. You're just the first person I'm showing.'

Cunningham relaxed visibly. 'That's good, Dan. That's very good. You must be excited.'

'Oh I am, Paul. In fact I was wondering – I know this is an imposition but I was wondering anyway – if you'd come with me to look at the body tonight?'

Stephen was quite prepared to use force if he had to. He had a revolver with him. Not that he would need it, but the humans seemed to behave better when there was a weapon involved. Otherwise they seemed to think they might win, which encouraged them to fight back. That inevitably got messy. Besides, a bullet in the brain was the surest way of making sure a Family member stayed dead.

'Now I really don't think that's on,' said Cunningham. 'I have other patients to see this evening.'

Liar, Stephen thought. 'I don't think so,' he said. He crossed the room in two strides. Before Cunningham could react, he had the gun out of his pocket and pressed to the human's neck. 'Now, you *will* come with me,' he said.

'Don't do this, Daniel. You don't really want to do this.' The man stank of fear, and his forehead was sheened with the first traces of sweat.

'But Paul,' Stephen said, 'you've always *said* this is my hour to use as I wish.'

They walked slowly down the road together. The receptionist had been startled when they left together, and there had been a dangerous moment when Cunningham might have spoken. But Stephen had pressed the gun into his back through the pocket of his jacket, and the moment passed.

He was holding the gun in the same way when they turned the corner to where Marion should have been waiting in Harrington's blue Rover.

The car was empty.

Stephen stared at Cunningham. The human's breath came in ragged little gasps. Blood trickled from his nose, from a split lip. His head lolled forward.

He had not dared go back to Harrington's. There were too many neighbours, too much chance they would hear Cunningham. Instead, they were in Stephen's flat. It was in a tower block in Tottenham. He had chosen it for its location. It was noisy enough and run-down enough that no one was likely to notice anything he did. There were already too many squatters and all-night parties and crack dealers.

'Don't,' the human mumbled. 'Please don't.'

'Who did you tell?' Stephen asked.

'I told you. I told you.' The man smelled of tears and terror and shit.

Stephen hit him so hard his head snapped back and his eyes rolled up. Blood dribbled from his nose. Stephen grabbed his hair, forced his head round, hit him again. And again. Suddenly his rage was uncontrollable. Marion was gone, gone when he would have trusted her, would have gone against his best instincts and the judgement Her Ladyship was testing –

He stopped. Cunningham was unconscious. 'Damn,' Stephen muttered.

He contemplated bringing the human round. Cunningham had already given him four names. There was a zoologist at Manchester University, an anthropologist in the USA and a popular science writer. Also Barbara Jones, a photographer; she was the one who had convinced Cunningham the pictures were not fakes. Stephen ground the heels of his hands into his eye-sockets. It was about as bad as it could get, and he had no way of knowing whether Cunningham had given him all his contacts. If he really believed the photos, he might have held out.

Stephen slammed his hand into the wall. He would start again in the morning. If Cunningham said the same tomorrow, Stephen would have to believe it.

He checked the ropes tying the human to the chair, then left the room. He locked and bolted the door behind him. It was the only exit from the room, unless you counted the window. The flat's eighteenth-floor location was another reason Stephen had chosen it.

Stephen's eyes flicked open in the dark. He heard a soft

susurrus of breath, and knew that someone was in the room with him. He tasted citrus and wondered if it was an echo of dream. He did not move. He counted a hundred heartbeats, and still the faint sound of breathing was there with him. Nothing but that, and the draught from a door he had shut before he went to bed.

He turned. Marion was there, crouched like a succubus at the end of the bed. He watched without speaking, pleased with what he saw. She was in her true shape. She was beautiful, her musculature picked out by moonlight, her flesh sheened with golden down, her face thrusting and strong. The scent of her filled up the room, now that he was properly awake.

He wanted to reach for her, to take off her human garments, to answer the urgent need of his body. He wished, most ardently, that he also was in the true form; that his senses were not dulled by their humanity. It occurred to him then that in true shape she was much stronger than he was. He wondered if that were why she had come to him in this way.

'Hallo, Stephen,' she said. Her voice was husky, the words distorted by a mouth not made for them. Moonlight glinted coldly on her incisors.

'You didn't wait,' he said.

'Will you work for Her Ladyship?' she asked. He felt her looking at him, taking in the sight of him.

He pulled himself upright. 'If she asks me, I suppose.'

'She's wrong, you know. You're wrong.'

'Explain.'

'You think it's enough to make sure the humans are ignorant of us. You think about today, maybe about tomorrow. But we have to look to the future.' Her gaze never left his face. 'We have to try to understand them, what drives them, what they want. That's the only way to protect ourselves.'

I want you, he thought. I want you so much. But he forced himself to say, 'And to do that we should reveal ourselves to them?'

'No! I never said that.' She moved forward on the bed until she was close enough to touch him.

Stephen was startled. He put out his hand towards Marion's face. She evaded it. 'But you would have revealed yourself to Harrington.' Flat statement: she couldn't deny it. He wet his lips. She wanted him, he could smell it. She must be able to sense his desire. What would be so wrong with that? Yet she was a revealer –

'Says who? Did Her Ladyship tell you that? Did she?' Anger flared on her face, in her scent. It only made him want her more.

'Well, no.' It was true. He really had no evidence for his belief, beyond the fact that she had changed herself injudiciously so Harrington would want her. 'But you didn't take a great deal of care when you *improved* yourself for him.'

'He thought I'd been on a diet, got a perm and some highlights. Don't overestimate the humans, Stephen. Just because they make art, make science, doesn't mean they see more than they expect to.'

'Would you have killed him?'

'Probably. In the end. Will you kill me?'

'No. Even if I could, which I doubt.'

'Her Ladyship will not be pleased,' Marion said, but he felt her shift on the bed as she relaxed slightly.

'She will trust my judgement. I will make her.' He put out his hand to her, and this time she took it. He pulled her towards him. 'Come,' he said.

'Yes,' she said, 'I believe I shall.'

They got up late the next morning. Marion kept her true form. She refused to tell Stephen why, and he did not know if she could sense his unease with that.

'You did a job on him, didn't you,' she said. There was a hint of disapproval in her voice.

Cunningham turned his head heavily to look at her. His eyes went wide. Stephen realized that only exhaustion kept him from hysterics. Even so, there was a sudden acrid stench of shit and urine.

Marion went and stood in front of the human.

'Christ, get it away from me! *Get it away from me!*' he screamed. He twisted against the ropes so violently that Stephen thought he might actually manage to break them.

'You see how we scare them, love? They're so weak.' Marion took Cunningham's face in her two hands. She forced him to look at her. 'There are easier ways than brute force,' she said. She lowered her face to Cunningham's and kissed him gently on the lips.

The man gagged. The room filled with the hot metal stink of human fear.

'You said I was an artist because I transformed Harrington's life,' Marion said. 'Perhaps you were right. But what have you done to his?' She put one sharp talon close to Cunningham's eyeball. The man squirmed in her grasp. The talon tracked along, never going more than a quarter of an inch from the human's iris. 'There does have to be some artistry involved, after all. I've always found this very effective.'

'*Please.*' Cunningham whispered. 'Get it off me. I'll tell you anything you want to know. Anything.'

Stephen touched Marion on the arm. She released Cunningham.

'Tell us,' Stephen said. 'Or I will let her practise her art on you.'

'For pity's sake,' whimpered Cunningham. 'I told you. There was Wilkinson at Manchester Uni, and then Sherrington in the States. That pop science writer Gina

Mitchell. And the photographer –' he stopped. 'You're going to go after them all aren't you?' His eyes were wide. Marion took a step or two towards him. He started to struggle against the ropes, but he stopped before she got there. 'Don't. *Don't*. Her name was Jones. Like I said yesterday, Barbara Jones.'

'See,' Marion said. 'There's no real need to hurt them.'

Stephen nodded. He went outside and came back in with the revolver.

'Oh no, oh no! I told you what you wanted! Don't do this, don't *do* this!' The human's voice was a constant whine as Stephen loaded the gun.

He went over to Cunningham. As he put it to the man's temple, Marion said, 'Don't.'

'Oh, thank God. Please, I won't say anything to anyone,' Cunningham's voice started again.

'There's no need for that, love,' Marion said. 'You wanted proof. I'll give it to you.'

She took off her human clothing piece by piece. Then she knelt in front of Cunningham. His face, watching her, was a mask of horror. She placed her hands on his chest. Stephen listened to the syncopation of their hearts. He wondered how much Cunningham understood, if he knew why he had to die. Marion placed her lips with utmost delicacy on the human's neck. His scream began, sharp in the silence, and ended in the fountain of blood that burst out over Marion.

With the human's body still jerking against its bonds, she turned to Stephen. She held out her hand to him. Blood dripped from her nails. He licked her fingers clean, and then her lips.

Later, they took the bones down to Southbrook. The parents were not pleased, but they accepted it in the end. Marion and Stephen buried the body themselves.

They stood in the orchard piling old leaves over the freshly turned earth. Marion had gone back to human form, a different appearance to her last.

The smell of new-turned earth and last year's mulch mingled, but it could not hide the new smell of her. 'You're fertile, aren't you?' he said. He had noticed the night before.

'Yes,' she said, 'but don't worry, I'm not pregnant, yet.'

'Will you marry me?' he asked her, without ever having consciously formulated the question.

'Settle down, have babies? It's not a future I ever thought of. I like my life as it is.'

'Would you have to? We worked well together, in the end.'

'I'll let you transform my life, if I can transform yours,' she said.

'There are still babies to consider. We aren't human, after all. We won't be able to hold out for ever.'

'Just the two of us, like a human couple?' Marion asked. She cocked her head on one side. 'I never meant to take the research so far.'

Stephen caught sight of Father Albert standing by the French windows. 'I believe my parents know someone who might be interested,' he said.

THE IF GAME

Paula Wakefield

If wishes were horses
Beggars would ride;
If turnips were watches
I would wear one by my side;
And if ifs and ands
Were pots and pans,
There would be no work for tinkers.

Children's Nursery Rhyme

Your letter, asking for a reconciliation, arrived yesterday, and then the police came and told me that Maria and Philip are dead. Two gut-busting shocks in one day – in less than an hour.

I'm still in shock, perhaps – but I have spent twenty-four hours remembering, and after all I've decided not to tell the police anything other than what they already know or guess.

Maybe you know about Maria and Philip ... I think that in some way you do – you must – and part of me calculates that I ought to be ... wary, if not frightened, but I'm not. I could not be, because I have loved you. And because I have loved you – still love you, I suppose, I want to warn you.

It is me I am afraid of.

And as it is so long since any sensible communication took place between us, I want to explain some things too. Besides, who else do I have to grieve to?

The men who came to see me yesterday know that we were together during that time, before Maria and Philip died. At the very least the police might call on you, (and your agent certainly wouldn't be happy about that sort of publicity) and I am sure there would be questions that you could not answer ... like I said, I've loved you.

I was shocked to hear about Maria but not surprised. I hadn't seen, or heard from her since I'd visited them in Nova Scotia. That was our first publicized split, remember? It was one of the last times I allowed you to be unfaithful to me (though, I guess you'd still deny it) and I'd flounced off (trying to disguise my pain), disappearing with my jealousy and humiliation, yet again.

But even what happened across the Atlantic – even what I saw in Maria, and him – couldn't compete with the burning images I had scorched on to my imagination: those other women tasting your skin, other women testing you, invading my pleasure-grounds, robbing me of the power that exclusive rights over another's body and emotions confer. And though I hate to admit it, the memories still hurt, a little. If love (human love) makes you like that, Jack, then I loved you ... to distraction. And I was distracted when I went over there to see Maria and him, and for a long time I attributed my view of the things that happened there to my own distress, my own sickness, madness.

Of course, you hardly knew Maria. You met her just the once, but I don't suppose you remember that either ... She came down to tell me she was getting married. And it was too late when I realized she had wanted to see me on my own, to share the news, her big one-time news, properly, privately ... to celebrate as only two friends, two women, can. But I had to have you there. I couldn't bear to be parted from you. I had to show you off, and my glow, my sparkle.

Did you know she met Philip at about the same time I picked you up in that wine bar? They were working at the same school and I had just won my first big ad account. Have you noticed, the company is still using my slogan? Anyway, that was why I was in the bar, celebrating. And it was one of those rare moments when you really are on top of the world – on top of everything – in control, the whole thing spinning around you, sparks flying, and everything within your grasp: as it was for me that night, when I saw you, wanted you, and knew that I only had to breathe in your direction and you'd be there, like magic, and of course I did, and you were, and that was the start of you and me.

I don't know how it happened with them, Maria never got the chance to tell me. Or, perhaps, in the end, she decided not to.

And I don't know when they started planning to go abroad or when the decision to leave was made, but now I do know why. At that time (when you met her) they were scouring the countryside for antiques (if you can call the bits and pieces they collected, antiques); those ugly remains of other lives that the rich and the dealers never want. Philip was at some farmhouse sale when Maria came down to us. We took her to that swanky café-bar for lunch. Christ, how she must have hated it! I only realize that now. And it's only now, after all these months of missing you, and not communicating with her, that I have thought about her at all, thought about what happened, about any of it. Now she's dead.

It never occurred to me then that she wanted to see me for some particular, some special, reason. I suppose

I believed it perfectly natural and inevitable that the whole world should gravitate towards you and me. Anyway, we insisted we all went to that place – whatever it was called – and we loved it; the best place, at the time, to see and be seen. We were still at that point in an affair when visibility, as a couple, is one more aphrodisiac.

We ignored the fact that Maria hardly touched the expensively unpalatable *nouvelle* food. Poor Maria, she was far too dull for the way we were then. We ignored her. She was, after all, a distraction from ourselves. The less she said the more we could chatter about our successful careers, our enviable acquaintances, our fashionable politics and the pretty, pompous people who paraded about that place waiting to be discovered. I wouldn't say I was happy, or proud, so much as – excited ... constantly exhilarated; showing you off again in the best setting available.

And I know you were puzzled about my friendship with Maria. But she could be tenacious. She held on to our friendship long after I was ready to let go of it. And I was to witness how determined she was to hang on to Philip, regardless of the cost.

By the time you met her I saw very little of her and our communications were generally limited to Christmas and birthday cards. And I was as intolerant as you of all that quasi-romantic hippy stuff about 'getting back to nature' that she wanted to bury herself in. I have always loathed Laura Ashley frocks.

But you see, Jack, Maria and I were still linked by those bonds that teenage girls forge between themselves, and I suppose we held on to those old loyalties, though at the time Maria's grip was firmer than mine. And as the police said, I was really all the family she had, apart from Philip. God, Jack! It's only now that I realize how little you know about her, about me. What did you and I talk about? Just us?

But I am forgetting. If I am right, you do know something of kinship, although your notion, your experience may differ, is bound to differ, I guess, from mine – ours.

Anyway, back in that different land of Then, we excluded Maria simply by taking her to that bloody awful bar, and it wasn't until you went to the loo and I was ostentatiously paying the bill that Maria had a real chance to speak.

'Actually, Sue, I have some news of my own.'

'Oh?' I was indifferent to anything that might possibly compete with the glitter of you and me. Besides, the waiter was flirting with me and I was wondering whether she had noticed.

She fiddled with a bit of her badly permed hair. 'That was really why I wanted to see you. Philip, my friend, the one who has gone to the sale – well – he's more than a friend ... he's – well, actually – we're getting married.'

She stuttered and stammered and I got hot with embarrassment and the shame of realizing why she had come.

'Oh, Maria! Oh, God! Wow!' And then, stupidly, 'Why didn't you say something earlier –' and making it worse, '– we could have had champagne!' And then the crass, automatic afterthought, 'You're not pregnant are you?'

'Sue.' It was only then that she showed her disappointment in me. She glanced awkwardly at the neighbouring tables, checking to see whether anyone had overheard.

I tried to be blasé. 'Don't worry about them, they're probably pregnant every other week!' She looked as though she might cry.

'Oh, God, Maria, I'm sorry! I wish we could have met him. Is he nice? How long have you known him?'

Poor Maria. She had wanted to share her happiness, one of the few significant moments of her grown-up life, with me, and I – we – had spoiled it. She was just a minor character, stuck in the wings. I had dictated the script, chosen the stage and cut her out. There was room only for you, my star performer.

'Well, I think he's nice.' She was looking strained and clearly wanted to be out of that place and her discomfort, at last, made me want to escape too ... but where were you?

'Well, we must all get together sometime. We must meet him ... Philip, – oh, I think Jack's on his way back, God, he'll be so pleased when I tell him your news –'

'Sue, please don't make a fuss ...'

She was being polite. And my concern about your absence made it easier for me to ignore what was going on between me and Maria. We went and collected our coats and I thought my neck would break with the strain of looking for you. When I did see you (head and shoulders above everyone else, as usual) meandering beautifully back through the crowd, I relaxed a little.

'So, what about the big day? When is it? You must let me know the arrangements.'

'I'll write to you, Sue. Oh, hallo, Jack ... I'm sorry Sue, I really must go. I told Philip I would meet him at three.'

It was already half past ... and she was the one who was apologizing.

The Pouilly-Fuissé had turned sour in my throat and I was desperate to turn things around. 'You will write won't you, Maria? Promise.'

'Of course I will. Goodbye Jack. Thanks for lunch, Sue.'

She didn't promise, and I watched her go, pulling on

some woollen gloves and bowing her head to the wind. Then I started a row with you about the blonde in the green dress I'd seen you talking to at the bar.

She did write, but it was months later when I got the card telling me they were leaving. I've still got the card. It's here, beside me now. It asks me to go and visit them.

I was surprised about the planned move ... Maria had never lived anywhere else before, and I was suspicious that it was her house and possessions they were selling, and that he – Philip – had contributed nothing.

Anyway, I didn't go and visit them. It wasn't just that I still found it hard to go back to that provincial world with its prospect of duty visits to my parents, brother, and sister and her never-ending string of kids. It was mostly because I was too busy thinking about you, and who you might be screwing. You were doing a short run in Sheffield – Doctor Faustus. At the time I bitched that you had been miscast.

I caught a train and travelled it seemed for ever to get there for your opening night and knew as soon as I saw you with the B-movie actress that you would take her to bed. I knew it the way we always know these things; I'm not sure if it's the same for you – whether you have the same sense – that special ability one has when one is in love. All the senses are so receptive that the combined sensitivities are capable of detecting the slightest tremor of change in the beloved's attention-range. Believe me, Jack, when a woman is so smitten she can *smell* her lover's desire for another woman. So I knew that you would have to have whatever-her-name-is – who was playing a very voluptuous duchess – just as I knew, or felt, or imagined that I wouldn't like Philip.

But, as I said, I was far too preoccupied with you to spare any attention for Maria, for them. I ignored the card, this card, and I dare say would have lost touch with Maria for good, had it not been for her nerves or fear, or whatever it was that prompted her, months later, to call me.

Hoping it was you, I was disappointed to hear her voice at the other end of the line, where yours was supposed to be.

'Sue? It's Maria. I've only got three ten p's. We're on our way to the airport. I'm sorry we haven't been in touch – we've been really busy – and I'm sure you have too, but we're leaving today – I wondered, could you – would you come and see us off, Sue? It might be years before I see you again.'

I felt like I do when my mother asks me to visit at Christmas. 'Oh, Maria ... I wish you had let me know sooner. Things are terribly tight at the moment. There's a new account up for grabs and –'

'Oh, I know how hectic your life is. And you've got Jack to think of – I wouldn't normally ask – I know I'm a nuisance, but please, Sue. There's no one else to say goodbye to.'

How could I say no to that? Besides, I had already begun to think my absence from the flat might serve as a punishment for you on your return. It wasn't until I was on the tube to the airport that I realized that on finding me gone, you would simply go out and find another pretty face to discuss your performances and notices with.

But that was later. 'What time does you plane leave?'

'Twenty past nine.'

I was already imagining the look of disappointment on your face. 'OK. I'll meet you by Tie Rack, you'll be able to find that, won't you?'

'Yes, yes, I think so. Thanks Sue. It wouldn't have been – right, without saying goodbye –'

I was glad the money ran out.

By the time I was on the tube I had worked out that you would have left again by the time I got back and that I would be the one who was hurt. I spent the whole journey re-mapping your body in my mind: your unfathomable musculature with its ever-shifting masses, your tantalizing length, and your smooth, smooth skin, with barely a hair to hide in, even in the gulleys of your armpits and your groin. In the first days, after we had made love, I would underline my pleasure, my achievement, by searching the ligaments and fillets beneath your skin. You never commented on my fascination, just as I never admitted to my disappointment at finding you gone from my bed in the morning. You would be lying on the sofa, or showering, or already making breakfast, but never there next to me, never with me, the way I wanted you to be.

'I'm not used to sleeping with someone else,' you said, the first time I mentioned it, and to my raised eyebrow added: '. . . sharing a bed all night.'

Afterwards it was always: 'I couldn't sleep.' Or else: 'I had some lines to learn.'

You never apologized. I don't remember you apologizing for anything. But then, why should you? You are superbly suited to this time. You will always expect admiration, adoration, love. And you are unquestionably qualified to receive it. Just as the camera loves your face with its unique combination of smoothness and lines, the ability of your jaw and cheekbones to realign according to character, so will women and men. I have hated you for that.

'If only you loved me better,' I thought then, rattling and swaying towards Heathrow. 'If only you would trust me, give me some commitment. Ah, if only you could feel how I love you.' I didn't understand then. Couldn't, and carried on mentally fingering the self-inflicted wounds in my belly.

I know better now. About you and about games like that. I don't even find it odd any more that I played that game with myself about you. I had never done it before. But with you I couldn't see – did not feel – that I had choices.

Recalling all this reminded me of something Maria said the last time I saw her. I had forgotten until yesterday. Now, I think you should know about it. But I must take my time. You must believe me. And I am not sure you will, unless I tell you all the things I . . . censored, before.

The airport was heaving with people so I made straight for the store where I had arranged to meet them. I waited there for more than an hour, occasionally sipping some scalding liquid from a machine close by.

I saw Philip first. Not that I knew that the hulk towering above everyone else was Maria's husband. Her tiny frame was hidden among the crowds.

Like everyone else in Philip's vicinity I tried to ignore his compelling vastness. Even taller than you, he appeared to have a girth to match his height. The man was huge. I shrank back a little into the display stands in the doorway of the shop so that I could watch this giant's progress without being thought a voyeur – by now, he was close enough for it to be obvious he had some kind of illness. The body lurched slightly to one side as if the spine was twisted and one leg dragged a little as he persisted along the concourse. It was hard not to stare, he did look alien, and I imagined all the mothers of the children near by desperately trying to divert the fascinated and horrified gawpings of their offspring. I couldn't school my own attention away from the panels of rough skin that looked as if they had been nailed to the superstructure of his face. Inevitably his eyes met mine in mid-stare and I shrank further into the displays, concentrating on a tie you would have hated.

When I heard Maria's voice my stomach dropped.

'Sue! Thank goodness you're still here. I am sorry we're late. There were terrible traffic jams on the motorways and then, when we did get here, we went to the wrong terminal and I was sure we'd never find you but I told Philip what you look like, and he spotted you as soon as we got to the top of the steps – oh, I'm sorry, blabbering away, nerves I suppose, let me introduce you. Philip this is Sue, the Sue I've told you so much about, the friend who looked after me at school ... and when gran died –' she smiled, a tight, wistful, blink of a smile and added, 'and Sue, this is my husband.'

She craned her neck to look up at him, rather as a child does to reassure itself of its elder's presence and mood.

I had expected Maria's husband to be small and wiry, rather like her, but Philip was a giant and, beside him, Maria was a moppet.

With some effort I forced myself into social action and stuck out my hand. 'Philip, pleased to meet you ... I'm, er, sorry I can't say "I've heard so much about you" – my fault, I've neglected Maria, and you –' he shook my proferred hand which felt vulnerable between the rough plates of his palms and fingers. I forced myself to meet his gaze and, unaccountably, my skin burned just as it did when you held my head between your hands the moment before kissing me very slowly and deeply. Oh, yes, I was confused. I think I said: 'No excuses. I am sorry, and now you're going.'

'Don't be silly. You lead a busy life and you've got Jack to think of and anyway you're here now, that's what counts.' Maria was excited and nervous and obviously (I thought) had no idea what the mention of your name, at that moment, was doing to my insides.

Automatically, I took refuge in time. 'Maria, it's getting very late, what time did you say your plane was?'

She checked her watch against an elevated digital display unit. 'Oh, you're right! Oh, no, Philip, this is so silly, we'll have to hurry. Oh, Sue, I've dragged you down here and we've hardly got time to say two words to each other –'

The three of us were already shuffling in the direction of their departure lounge, Philip on one side of Maria, me on the other. Philip and I were content or relieved to let Maria carry on talking.

'But you musn't think that just because I'm married – oh, Sue, I'm no good at making speeches, you've always been the one who's good with words, what I mean is, we'll always be friends, and you really must come and see us. Bring Jack! I've told Philip all about you. I'm sure the two of them would get on.'

She sounded silly and trite, and I didn't know whether it was because of my mood, or Philip, or what. She prattled on, triggering long forgotten images of two girls listening to an old woman's collection of seventy-eight records, talking clothes and memories, and boys and futures . . . Maria helping me with my maths homework, me helping her with her English. And most of all, if I am truthful (and what point is there in not being truthful now?), me continuing the friendship for the quiet refuge of her grandmother's house, after the noise and congestion of our overcrowded bungalow.

Anyway, at the airport, Maria was enjoying her role of wife: arguing with staff about a special seating arrangement for Philip, exhibiting a proprietorial, even slightly bossy, air I had never recognized in her before. Perhaps, I thought, marriage had given her an assertiveness she'd never found elsewhere. Philip did not speak but continued to look as if he was permanently in pain and making an effort to contain it ... to control himself. I did not like him – and my dislike had nothing to do with his appearance. I was glad when they had gone. But I hung around for a while, stupidly hoping that if I left it long enough, fatigue might have carried you home to the flat before me.

Eventually I pulled myself together and caught the tube back. Unable to make room in my head for analysis about Maria and Philip, I took the easy, painful option and let an image of you settle behind my closed eyes.

I didn't tell you about where I had been and you didn't ask when you came quietly in just before daybreak and I was ready to crack open with desperation for you.

There are moments, spaces, events that can be altered, suspended I suppose, by need, by desire. For a time the slights, the wounds, the betrayals don't matter, nothing matters for a time – like that time – until the body and the heart are comforted. And for a time I was all right.

But in the morning you were dressed and drinking orange juice and I saw you had slept on the sofa again and I was depleted: frustrated. Hurt. Mad.

Oh, Jack. You must remember how I screamed at you? After a while we were both throwing things, and through my taunts and your justifications and the broken crockery all I recognized was the renewed ache for your body; I knew it was all I could have of you. The act of love was better than nothing, and as you are now proving to the world, you are a consumate performer. So, through your sweat, and my snot and tears, we tore into each other and transformed the anger.

Afterwards I went to work and when I got back we rowed again. We rowed and fucked for weeks.

And then, quite suddenly, you were becoming famous. A colleague of mine told me he had seen you in some hotel with that gossip columnist. So I had to escape. Either that, or break. I needed sleep and someone to confide in. I wanted to forget. Not you – your treasons. I wrote to Maria, taking her up on the verbal invitation I had ignored at the airport. I had packed my bags and run before I received a reply, confident at least that Maria would meet me in Halifax.

And she did. Philip was with her, waiting for me at the gate in the clinging heat of what was going to be an unusually hot and humid Nova Scotian summer. He looked better than I remembered – still pained but not quite as grey or tortured.

'I hope you've brought more practical clothes than those.'

They were Philip's first words to me. If I had found him taciturn before, I had put it down to the awkwardness of the situation, or his discomfort, or concern at the prospect of a long flight. I had acknowledged my dislike of him but it never occurred to me, until this moment, that he would not like me, or that he might have recognized my feelings. Maybe it wasn't that. But these words were punched at me and I felt as unwelcome as I later discovered I was. It was all the more disconcerting because his voice was not gruff or deep as I suppose I had imagined: neither was it light, and there was a concord to it that must once have bent itself to seduction.

Their new existence, it struck me, although agreeing with Philip, had metamorphosed him into a wild man. He was just as big, and possibly heavier, and since I had first met him he had grown a great fleece of a beard.

Then there was Maria with a tired smile on her face.
It would have been obvious even to you that she was
finding her new life cruel. She was much thinner than
ever before and dripping with dull rags. The busy wife
buoyant with her new status and the prospect of a
semi-dependent husband had disappeared. Next to
Philip, she was a wraith. It upset me to think that you
would have found it impossible to hide your shock and
distaste at the state of her. I grinned, and shrugged for
want of another gesture, and she let me hug her in the
old way and I smelled the grease and dirt in the string
of her hair. But, you know, if I wanted to cry then,
whatever had happened – was happening – there, to
my oldest friend, it was still for you. For me.

Philip broke us up. 'Maria, we must get on with those
vegetables. At least the extra hands will be useful.'

Maria helped me with my bags while Philip preceded
us across the car park. It struck me then that he looked
slightly less awkward, not so constrained and uncomfortable in that landscape which, even in the confines
of the airport, bragged a vastness that dwarfed England
with its chaotic cities and busy countryside and
crowded, cloud-filled skies.

'There are only two seats in the van, I'll sit in the
back, it's a bit mucky,' Maria apologized, looking at my
clothes.

'No, no, it's OK. A bit of muck never hurt anyone and
these will wash!'

Anything, even chicken-shit, as it turned out to be,
was better than travelling next to Philip.

'I've been thinking we might get a cart. We don't
really need the van and with no proper income we can't
really afford petrol. A horse might be cheaper.'

Was Maria hinting that they needed cash for fuel?
I made a mental note to give her some money but I

couldn't answer her. I was already reeling from culture shock, so I climbed in and held my breath, trying not to think about the stench I was sitting in, or what lay ahead.

It was a silent journey that I spent, watching the unfamiliar territory roll by. There were two small windows in both sides of the van's back panels, so it was like watching the landscape on a piece of film, or looking through those little viewing boxes that people used to put slides in. We travelled for miles, very slowly. Despite the heat, the sky was a grey roof and its uninterrupted paleness only served to emphasize the blatant expanses of land, and the long, empty roads we moved along. At other times we drove through acres of pine forest, grown tightly as a crop, but much of it scorched and blighted by acid rain. It was in the middle of one of these huge plantations that I dozed once and when the scrape of a gear roused me I wondered if we had moved at all. Philip negotiated two towns, one not much more than a mega-shopping mall. Even in those places the people looked lost. Out in the wilderness there was just the occasional roadside store – God knows who those shopkeepers ever speak to – with the more entrepreneurial displaying handwritten signs for maple syrup by the pint.

The cramps in my shoulders were murderous and the only reason I didn't ask Philip to stop, so that I could stretch and gulp a breath of fresh air, was that a break would only prolong the journey.

But the sight of the smallholding brought me no relief. We had travelled maybe the last ten miles on a dirt track, walled in by yet more pine. Their land was all that was left of the original farm, the rest was completely given over to the dense trees.

Stranded in the middle of the clearing was the house. It was long and low at the front, rising to what must have been once handsome gables at the side and back. Now it was ugly, despite an eager and uneven coat of white paint smeared across its wooden walls. Philip parked the van on a patch of scrub in front of the house and Maria let me out.

'We'll take your things up and then you can come and help us with the vegetables.'

She started telling me about the history of the place and how they had cleared out the well. They had cleaned up the inside, she said, but they were not going to buy a generator (it was too isolated for wired electricity or piped gas) because there was so much wood around, and they liked candles, and it was getting back to basics – rejecting all the things they had escaped from. That was when I began to wonder exactly who had escaped and what freedom had been won.

A concession to modernity was a black lead range where Maria cooked, and I began to panic when I guessed there would be little, if any, hot water to spare. But like a good house guest I followed her, without a word, across the cold tiles and up the bare wooden stairs, listening to the boards creaking their disapproval at my heels.

My room, my box, was just that and despite the curtainless window it was as dark as a church. There was a mean bed that Maria said Philip had made, a washstand with a jug and a basin, and a candle on a little wooden table beside the bed.

'I hope it's not too primitive.' Maria's murmur could have been a question or a comment.

I replied as truthfully as I could. 'It's fine. Anyway, I've come to see you, not assess your house.' Already it was impossible to refer to that place as a home.

'I'll see you downstairs in a minute. Sorry to throw you in at the deep end but Philip's determined to get all these peas in for drying by the end of the week.'

She gave me the tired smile again and went away.

I pulled on some old tennis shoes, but as my clothes were already filthy there seemed no point in changing. Clearly this was going to be a working holiday. Then I went and joined them and picked bloody peas.

The day felt as if it would be endless to spite me, and there was no time to talk to Maria. After a supper of soup and bread, Philip wandered outside and I helped Maria clear up. She was very quiet but then so was I, what with the journey, and that wretched pea-picking. I thought my back would break.

'I'll show you over the house, if you like,' she said, when the last dish was stacked, and lit another candle.

Yes, I did wonder what was the point in trailing around a house in almost pitch darkness, but Maria's mood was so peculiar and, believe me, I was too tired to openly question any of it, so I followed her.

The sitting-room was full of ugly furniture they had taken with them but there was nothing else remarkable about it. There was no bathroom either upstairs or down. A tin bath hung just outside the kitchen door but all the time I was there, no offer of filling it was ever made, and from the smell of Maria, I doubt it was used at all.

I followed her across the carpetless floorboards, once or twice stubbing my toe on boxes of books that hadn't, even after those few months of living there, been unpacked.

Upstairs their bedroom was much the same as mine but slightly bigger. I was a little surprised at the two single beds but assumed that, what with Philip's size and his disability, it was probably the most comfortable sleeping arrangement.

We traipsed along the landing, missing a room, and then climbed a narrow flight of stairs to what was the attic bedroom. When Maria opened the door I gasped. Even in the limited light of the candle it was obvious the contents must have been worth a small fortune. But I couldn't even recognize – let alone name – most of the ancient musical instruments arranged across the walls and floors.

'Maria! Does Philip play all these, or is he just a collector? What a shame they are all hidden away up here, they're amazing, beautiful!' I meant it.

But she wasn't pleased or enthused, just indifferent, tired. 'He used to play most of them, I think. He's been collecting them for years, but his hands, you see . . .'

Yes, I did see. The thought of those great stiff paws made it impossible to imagine Philip fingering these delicate pieces.

'Do you know who he is, Sue?'

'What do you mean . . . you mean his other name? I don't understand, Maria, he's a teacher like you, isn't he?'

She stood in the doorway staring at the instruments. 'Oh, it's so very complicated. There's so much to tell you . . . I've wanted to tell you for ages –'

'Maria, I'm really sorry. I should have been in touch sooner. I'm to blame –'

'It doesn't matter now anyway.' She paused then announced: 'Philip Wittenberg. Do you know the name? He was quite famous, once. He conducted and composed and everything, once.'

I was struggling to take in what she was telling me and for a minute or more the name meant nothing, and it was only when she started speaking again that I dragged out a hazy recollection: big brittle records on an old lady's gramophone, a dark red label showing a little dog and the name, Philip Wittenberg.

'He's never been a teacher. He was working as care-taker at the school I was teaching at and ... oh, that's not the beginning – you're not the only one who can land a big catch you know – but I don't know where to start, and it doesn't matter now anyway ...'

I thought she was just babbling and she certainly looked as tired as I felt.

'Let's go back down,' I said, with half my mind on Philip's likely anger should he find us there, though I did wonder how often he forced himself up those stairs.

Back on the landing I stopped at the door we had ignored earlier. Imagining that it was a room they hadn't got round to cleaning up, and thinking I could lighten the atmosphere with a conversation about decorating, I tried the handle. The door was locked.

'Oh! What's in here, Maria? Come on, what are you hiding?' I teased.

It's odd how desperate humour is often unintentionally accurate. She looked at me as though she were questioning all our years of acquaintance and then she sighed resignedly and pulled a key from her pocket and opened the door.

It was much more of a museum than Philip's room and its contents would ever be. But I didn't think that then. This room had had more attention and care lavished on it than the whole house, or the land, was ever going to get. There was a cot as well as a beautifully carved crib. Lace curtains disguised the windows and pretty hand-made rugs were scattered across the floor. Draped across a rocking chair was a colourful antique quilt and, here and there, on the shelves above the cot, were old books and toys: neat, tidy, preserved.

Partly to hide my surprise and confusion I exclaimed. 'Wow! Maria! Did you do all this? It's beautiful! Well! I should be congratulating you, Mrs Wittenberg – you

should have let me know, I would have brought something for the –'

'Sue, don't!' She pushed me out of the room and I
listened to her fraught breathing while she locked the
door after us.

When she turned she dropped into my arms like a
tree being felled, and despite the stench from her body I
held her, squeezing out a little love from my badly
diminished reserves. Her bony body shook against me
and I could feel the wetness of tears through my shirt.

'I'm not pregnant Sue. I can't be. I won't be . . . Philip
doesn't . . . we're not even married.'

That was when I realized . . . the smell, mixed in with
her sweat, was stale menstrual blood. I badly wanted to
vomit.

Oh, Jack, it was awful, dreadful. I had to force myself
to be practical. I helped Maria downstairs, cleaned her
up and tied her hair back, and made some tea. We sat
quietly for a time with just the clock ticking as it had
done in her grandmother's house until, eventually, I
suggested she went to bed before Philip got back.

We had been avoiding each others' eyes but that was
when she looked at me again, as if from a huge distance
beyond her retina, and said, 'He won't be back. He
doesn't sleep here, with me.' She looked out of the open
door into the deeper shadows of the outbuildings. 'He's
always slept in the barn but more often now he goes
down to Rushfall, it's a little settlement down the road.
We didn't pass it earlier – it's in the opposite direction.'

I was too tired to take in any more. At that moment I
felt more alone than I had in all the hours I'd spent
waiting for you. Perhaps it was the realization that
Maria couldn't help me – save me? – she could barely
help herself. Or perhaps, for the first time ever, I was
half admitting that there was something in Maria's

personality I did not like – and yes, I felt guilty. Perversely, having just escaped from you, I wanted to run to you then; escape to your treacherous arms. And if that had been possible, I would have. Instead, I persuaded Maria upstairs again and tucked her into the sheets that must have been her grandmother's. Then I crawled into my own bed, anaesthetizing myself with the duty-free gin I'd crammed in my bag.

Thankfully, I didn't dream, but my sleep was as heavy as the weather and I didn't feel refreshed when I woke the next morning. When I felt able to go downstairs and face my hosts again, I found Philip already lumbering outside and Maria doing something with the dough that was destined to become our next loaf of bread. I emptied the cold water from my bowl and helped myself to some biscuits and maple syrup.

'I want to go to Rushfall. I want some more booze.' I was in no mood for prevarication.

Maria looked across the table at me. 'There is a liquor store there. You can only buy alcohol from the government-run stores.' She glanced across to the barn. 'But it's about ten miles the other way and you know I can't drive.'

'I'll drive, or we'll walk. Leave the chores until we get back.' And before she could argue I'd snatched the van keys from their hook and half run outside, quite prepared to take Philip on should he confront me.

But he was either in the barn or one of the other sheds and we didn't see him, though he probably saw us.

The van wasn't all that difficult to manoeuvre but Maria had to keep reminding me to drive on the other side of the road. Rushfall was probably more like fifteen miles away. But the forest on that side ended after five or six miles and Maria cheered up once we were out of the pine walls. She started pointing out the scattered maples whose leaves were colouring early and even agreed to let me do her hair and nails that evening . . . a sort of girls' night in. In fact, she was more like her old self until we got to Rushfall and, I suppose, she remembered Philip and his visits to the place.

I parked at the roadside and Maria seemed unable to decide whether it was better to stay in the van, alone, or risk exposure and join me in the liquor store.

'It's your fault, you made me come!' She was suddenly vicious with hatred, contempt.

I took a deep breath. 'Maria, what's wrong? You seemed quite happy to come with me. I thought you would feel better for getting out for a while.'

'Happy. Ha! You know about "happy", don't you? Don't you understand? They'll see me! It's humiliating!'

I looked about, bewildered. 'Maria, there's hardly anyone here.'

'Oh, you . . .! You're so stupid!' She stopped and grabbed my arm, turning red-rimmed eyes on me. 'Oh, Sue, please don't leave me on my own here. Let's go. Let's go back. We'll go to the mall or somewhere, instead. Please, Sue, please!'

The mood-swing was as violent and unexpected as the outburst but I refused to give in to her. In the end she chose to stay put and I wandered down the almost deserted street that was the town, wondering why Philip came here and telling myself to stop imagining watching eyes.

And again you were with me. Walking with me. Your fully animated image filled my head; hurt my heart. Did Philip come here to whore? Was that it? Was that why Maria went crazy? Was she embarrassed, about herself, or some predilection of the man she lived with? At the liquor store door my stomach lurched as I feared lone women might not be served booze in this backwater that resembled a hastily constructed film set.

But it was OK. The men, who were almost as big as Philip, did serve me and one even touched his cap as I left.

As much to convince myself I wasn't unnerved by the town as a desire for decent food, I stopped and bought two huge lobsters from a place that had them swimming about in a tank. I would have sworn, as I left, that it was Philip across the street, playing checkers – or whatever that game is – until I got halfway to him. The stranger's hair was lighter than Philip's, but apart from that slight difference, the similarities he and his opponent, in fact all of them, shared with Philip were remarkable. I turned away, retracing my steps. I had seen no women or children but I reasoned they must be about somewhere, and had half convinced myself that Rushfall was Philip's birthplace, and that the people I had seen must be relatives of his, when I walked into a wall of black serge. I stretched my neck back as far as it would go before I met the cataract-covered eyes in the large domed head. I side-stepped, startled, apologizing, noticing Maria frantically waving at me, calling, wondering why she hadn't told me about the people here.

I hurried back to the van, hearing her screech turn into a scream when she saw the lobsters. She was in the driver's seat and revving the engine before I got to the door.

'I'll drive! I'll drive! Get in! The other side – get in! Quiiick!' She was shrieking, drumming her fists on the wheel. She accelerated, shouting at me all the time, even when we were out of the town and she was braking, ordering me to get out and drive. She didn't leave the van but crawled across to the passenger seat while I ran round. It was Maria who frightened me but I had no time to deal with her hysteria then. And I hadn't recognized the lie. I just wanted to get out of there.

So I drove, Jack. I drove back to that terrible small-holding that was less threatening than that hick-joint town, furious with everything and wondering whether home and you wouldn't be easier after all.

Philip's face was like the thunder that had begun to roll along the ridge in the distance at the front of the house. He was angry about the van and about us going to Rushfall but he was pleased with the lobsters and threw them into a pan of water on the stove, slamming the lid on, severing a quivering antenna.

Then it was time to get back to the vegetables, though I had no idea what it was we were cutting and hacking at.

For three days we all worked together on that land: Philip dishing out orders, Maria deliberately silent. On the fourth day, despite the ever-present pall of cloud, it was hotter than ever. I eased my abused limbs out of bed and pulled on some shorts and sandals, and an old T-shirt of yours that I had packed by mistake, and made my way outside to the lavatory. It was an earth closet by the way (there were few compromises there) and the stench was becoming unbearable. I perched myself on the edge of the wooden bench, holding the door open with my foot, watching the silver arcs of lightning fuse into the branches of the pines at the very top of the hill, convinced by the hairs on the back of my neck that Philip was watching me.

The heat was leaden, but by the time I had convinced my bowels to be civilized again, Maria was already back in that bloody garden, cutting and chopping. I sat on the porch for a while, shelling the last few peas Philip had pulled, into a jar. My hangover was competing with the thunder that was now permanently

grumbling through the forest and when Philip appeared
with his knife I rounded on him.

'What do you do with all this?'

Philip was contemptuous. 'We eat it, Susan.'

It was the child's name. It was the trigger and I was
ready to let rip at him anyway: for turning Maria into a
drudge, for the joylessness of their existence, for his
enormous selfishness, for my god-damn aching back,
and of course, my still seething anger over you.

'Isn't it a waste of time? It can't taste better than the
stuff you can buy! Why don't you grow something commercial – make a profit, enjoy yourselves? I can't see
what you are achieving!'

Maria carried on hacking at the green heads.

'That is not the point. We wanted to get away from
all that. We wanted a better life.' There was no condes-
cension but he sounded authoritative.

Nevertheless, it was claptrap; not for the usual
reasons but I followed the usual logic anyway. 'Better?
Is exhausting better?'

All the time he had been straightening up, straining
to force himself completely upright. 'It is productive,
unlike advertising. Everything we do is productive.'

I waited for a minute, enjoying my own anticipation,
then I went for him. 'Oh? Like reading? You read, don't
you, Philip? I've seen your books. Writing, singing, playing music, composing – your argument dictates we
should give them up. They are not productive in the
way you mean!'

I savoured every syllable of sarcasm. Then I watched
the knife slip and slice through his hand.

It was one of those flesh-wounds that look worse
than they really are but Maria screamed and trampled
through the vegetables, grabbing at Philip's bleeding
fingers. He made no sound at all and appeared unmoved

by Maria's distress and her ineffectual attentions. I swear, to this day, that it was the sight of me watching him that brought his fist across her head.

'Leave it!'

He lumbered away while Maria lay crumpled and breathless in the dust. That was when I started shaking, when the anger left me. I kept hearing the sound of bone hitting bone; imagining the crack that must have crept along her skull. Perhaps it was only a few minutes before Maria struggled to get up and I half carried her to the scrubland where we propped ourselves up against a tree-stump. There was nowhere else to go.

'Maria, I'm sorry. I shouldn't have provoked him. I'll go and get some water and a cloth, OK? Maria?'

She was very dazed and she should have seen a doctor. Eventually she said: 'No. Don't go. Not yet. Not just yet.'

'It's all right, Maria. I'm sure he won't come back now.'

She coughed, then sighed through a weak grin. 'You still don't understand.'

I was sure she must be concussed. 'Has this happened before, Maria? Has Philip hit you before?'

'No! No, of course not.' She was offended, indignant. And, predictably, I did not believe her.

'You mustn't blame yourself, you know. It's not your fault.' The words – those words, that I had repeated to myself so often like a mantra, reminded me of you. 'Has he ... has Philip ever been unfaithful to you? Is that why he goes to Rushfall, do you think?'

'No, no, no! It was me he needed. Nobody else could help him – had wanted to help him – I was the only one. It was me.'

I pulled her hair away from her face. 'Why did you come here, Maria? Perhaps you should move away from this place – start teaching again.'

Two small semicircles of sweat were staining her dress, spreading from under the fleshy flaps that had been her breasts.

'I loved him, Sue. I would have done anything. Gone anywhere. He was gentle and kind and he listened to me. He *listened*.' She turned a mask of sudden resentment towards me and the bitterness poured out. 'It had been a long time since anyone – any adult – had paid me any attention, real attention – had listened to *me*.' She looked away again.

'We were going to be married. He promised. It didn't matter to me that he wasn't famous any more. It wasn't important to me what had happened to his money. I felt safe with him. He was interested in me – in *me*, he really was. I wanted him so badly. I would have done anything for him, anything.'

She swivelled round, staring at me, daring me to contradict her. 'You do know what I'm on about, Sue. Despite your fancy job and clothes and all that show, I know you know what I'm saying.'

And yes, I did know, Jack, of course I did. Back then, you were where I belonged. The poets and the pop stars have it right: *It's you, you, you.* But I pushed the thought of you away.

'And did Philip choose to come here? Did you sell your grandmother's house to get here? Was that it, Maria?'

'Yes. Philip said he had found an advert somewhere. He wanted to be here more than anything.'

I flapped at some gnats gnawing at us and said, 'Perhaps if you hadn't come here . . . if you sold this place, you could find somewhere else, less depressing, away –'

Maria was looking at her hands, tracing the drying patches of Philip's blood along the lines. 'You don't understand. This is where he has to be.'

I was completely baffled. 'Why, Maria? Was he born here?'

She stared out at the track, beyond the outer ranks of trees, and was quiet for some time, as if she was listening for the answer. She still looked puzzled when she replied: 'I don't know. I – I hadn't thought about that. I haven't worked that out.

'But it was – what I wanted, and I wanted what he wanted. I thought I knew what he wanted – needed – you see, but I was wrong. I got it wrong.' She was shaking her head. 'It can't be any different now. And don't say I can go back. There's nothing for me to go back to.' She laughed, 'Besides, you shouldn't play the If Game, Sue, it doesn't work.'

I understood that there was nothing for her in England, not even me, especially not me. There was nothing I could do to help her. She had made that clear. By the time I had packed she was kneading more dough with her unwashed hands.

'You won't see me – us – again. Goodbye, Sue.'

And through all of that I carried you with me, Jack. You were in my head even as I was witnessing Philip's violence and Maria's despair.

Someone from Rushfall was waiting to take me back to the airport. A crater-faced youth with a gangling body who seemed more wary of me than I was of him. Once or twice I tried to question him but he refused to speak, and cynically I guessed that Philip had arranged my chauffeur, and thoroughly drilled him about not conversing with the enemy. The truck was more comfortable than Philip's van and the last conclusion I vaguely formed, before ennui finally muffled my brain, was that I had been . . . tolerated.

But it wasn't until yesterday that I understood, fully.

I think I was tolerated, not because of my friendship

with Maria, not even because of Philip, but because of you, Jack.

I am sure I'm not wrong on this. You see, I'm trusting my instinct, Jack and, God knows, where you're concerned it hasn't let me down before.

Anyway, I was almost glad to get home to the turmoil and trauma of you and me. But it had been so long since we had shared anything other than anger, jealousy and resentment, that I never told you about my visit, or why I had left early and of course, you did not ask.

We dragged on, becoming jaded, tardy.

People were surprised I survived when your agent insisted your public image was of a single, high-profile hero and pulled you out of the flat, my flat. I had no choice in the matter but now I'm – not glad, but aware that I was lucky that that decision was made for me. That was what helped me wean myself from you; eventually changing jobs, moving. I shudder to think of how, despite my status, my style, how like Maria I was, perhaps still am.

Oh, there's one more detail that helped me work things out about Philip. The forestry worker discovered two bodies, one large, the other small; he guessed, one male, the other once a woman – both were badly mutilated. When the police went back to the smallholding they found only the woman's corpse, but forensic tests proved the forester wasn't lying and I gather he has now been cleared of suspicion, even though the other body has never been found.

My guess is that Philip was taken back to Rushfall, though the police wouldn't understand that. Trapped in England, little England, he used Maria to get out there, to that huge country where there were others, like him, waiting. The police wouldn't understand that Philip had gone to that place to be near his kin. You see, Jack, I know he was waiting to die.

I asked the police, very obliquely, about the things in the house. Apparently, no musical instruments were found but Maria's museum was still locked up and intact. I've told them (should it come to it) that I don't want anything of hers.

Do you know, it is only now that I have allowed myself to ponder the lies she told me? And it is only now that I realize she was as emotionally manipulative as Philip was intellectually domineering. They had used each other; the only difference was that once out there, Maria had been abandoned. And she knew, in the end. She knew. And still she would not betray him, even to me.

But as you will appreciate only too well, there is simply no point in telling the police that I think Maria killed Philip and then set about butchering herself. It wouldn't make sense to them.

And I've told them very little about you, my love. For although you were wowing West End audiences at the time Maria and Philip died, you never know where those questions might lead.

So there you are, you see? I do love you, still. But I cannot allow myself to love you like that again, Jack. That is what I'm afraid of. I could never betray you. But I could destroy you – us.

And the danger would always be there, because I have never been sure, never could be, of you, your love. Which leaves me with my other puzzle. Why me, Jack? Just as I'm learning to sleep without longing for you, just as I'm learning to wake without thinking of you, why do you want me again, huh? What makes you think I'm the one?

I am not like you, Jack – not one of your kind, and even if I were, well . . .

In your letter, you play the If Game, Jack. You say things would have been different for us, if . . .

And that really is the point. None of us can go back, not even you. Neither Maria nor Philip had any choices left about the future. Philip's fabulous life was all but over anyway, and Maria had severed herself from anything other than him. Nothing could change that.

We have new lives now and that is why I wanted to tell you about Maria. She was right about the If Game, Jack. You shouldn't play it. I won't.

THE LIONS IN THE DESERT

David Langford

'... *further information on the elusive topic of poly-morphism is said by some sources to be held in the restricted library of the Jasper Trant Bequest (Oxford, England).*' (Various references, from about 1875 onward.)

'How shall one catch the lions in the desert?' said young Keith Ramsey in his riddling voice, as he poured hot water into the unavoidable instant coffee.

After a week of nights on the job with him, I knew enough to smile guardedly. Serious proposals of expeditions, nets, traps or bait were not required. Despite his round pink face and general air of being about sixteen, Keith was a mathematics D.Phil. (or nearly so) and had already decided to educate me in some of the running jokes of mathematicians. It could be interesting, in an obsessive way. The answers to the riddle were many and manifold.

'I thought of a topological method,' he said. 'See, a lion is topologically equivalent to a doughnut ...'

'What?'

'Well, approximately. A solid with a hole through it – the digestive tract, you know. Now if we translate the desert into four-dimensional space, it becomes possible to *knot* the lion by a continuous topological deformation, which would leave it helpless to escape!'

I have no higher mathematics, but dire puns were

allowed, 'parallel lions' and the like. 'Er, geometrically the desert is approximately a plane,' I suggested. 'With the lions on it. Simply hijack the plane, and . . .'

He groaned dutifully, and we both drank the awful coffee supplied by the Trant to its loyal security force. Keith had converted his to the usual syrup with four spoonfuls of sugar. After all my care in dosing the sugar-bowl, I was pleased that he took the correct measure.

'Deformation,' he said again, with what might have been a shiver. 'You know, Bob, I wish they hadn't shown us that picture. For me it's night-watchman stuff or the dole, but every time I put on this wretched imitation policeman rig, I can feel things crawling all over my grave.'

'I never feel things like that – I'm too sensible. The original Man Who Could Not Shudder. But I sort of know what you mean. It reminded me of that bit in *Jekyll and Hyde*, if you ever read it . . .?'

He looked into the half-drunk coffee and sniffed; then snapped his skinny fingers. 'Oh, ugh, yes. The awful Mr Hyde walking right over the kid in the street. Crunch, crunch, flat against the cobbles. Ta very much for reminding me. Yes, I suppose it was like that.'

'They say down at the Welsh Pony that the turnover of guards here is pretty high for a cushy job like this. I have the impression they last about six weeks, on average. Funny, really.'

'Hilarious, mate. Look, what do *you* think happened to that bloke last year?'

'Maybe he opened one of the forbidden books,' I offered. 'A hell of a thing when even a trusty pair like us gets told to keep clear of Area C.'

A grey man in a grey suit had hired me on behalf of the Trant Trustees. Amazingly little was said about career prospects, union representation or even – the part I was naturally curious about – the precise nature of what the two night guards actually guarded. Books were said to enter into it.

Instead: 'I should warn you, Mr Ames, that certain people are intensely interested in the Trant Bequest. Last year, just outside the ... that is, outside Area C, one of your predecessors was found like this. His colleague was not found at all.' He showed me a photograph without apparently caring to glance at it himself. The spread-eagled remains did not slot handily into anyone's definition of how a corpse should look. Someone had, as Keith would have put it, tried bloody hard to translate him into two-dimensional space.

'How shall one catch the lions in the desert?' he repeated, now badly slurred. The sugar treatment had taken longer than I had expected. 'The method of the Sieve of Eratosthenes is to make an exhaustive list of all the objects in the desert and to cross off all the ones which on examination prove ... prove not to be ... To cross off ...' Abandoning thought experiment number umpty-tum, he slumped to the table, head on arms, dribbling slightly over the sleeve of his nice navy-blue uniform. I thought of hauling him across to his bunk, but didn't want to jog him back into wakefulness. With any luck he'd reach the morning with nothing worse than a touch of cramp. I rather liked young Keith: some day, maybe, he'd make a fine maths tutor with his games and jokes. If he could rouse interest in a dull pragmatist like me ...

Certain people are intensely interested in the Jasper Trant Bequest. I am one of them. I slotted my special disk into the sensor-control PC and moved quietly out of the room.

*

Area A of the big old house on Walton Street is mostly an impressive front hall, crusted with marble, chilled by a patterned quarry-tile floor too good (the Trustees said) to cover up with carpeting. Maggie, the black, shiny and very nearly spherical receptionist, reigns here from nine to five, Monday to Saturday – grumbling about the feeble electric fan-heater, nodding to the daily Trustee delegation, repelling any and all doomed inquiries for a reader's card. I had yet to research the turnover time of Maggie's job. The 'guardroom' and a small, unrefurbished Victorian lavatory complete Area A.

Once upon a time, it was said, Jasper Trant saw something nasty in the woodshed. The people who strayed into the bequest between nine and five had often gathered as much from odd sources – a footnote in Aleister Crowley, a sidelong reference in (of all places) H. P. Lovecraft. They came hoping for secret words of power, the poor fossils. Modern spells are written in bright new esoteric languages like C++ and 80486 Extended Assembler. This was the glamour I'd cast over the real-time monitoring system that logged all movement in Area B.

'It's like something out of fucking *Alien*,' Keith Ramsey had said the day before. 'All those narrow twisty corridors ... it's *designed* to make you expect something's going to jump out at you from round the next corner, or chase you through the bits where you can't run because you've got to go sideways.'

Naturally I'd been thinking about it too, and had replied: 'My guess is, it was designed that way to make it hard to bring in heavy cutting equipment. Or a trolley big enough to truck out the library. Assuming there really is a library.'

'Mmm ... or maybe it was just fun to design. Everyone likes mazes, and why not old Trant? He was a maths don, wasn't he? You know there's a general algorithm for solving any maze. No, not just "follow the left-hand wall", that only works without unconnected internal loops. To find the centre as well as getting out again, what you do is . . .'

I was fascinated, but Area B isn't quite that complex. It fills almost all the building, winding up, down and around to pass every one of the (barred) windows, and completely enclosing the central volume in its web of stone and iron. You might get lost for a while, but there are no actual dead ends, or only one.

'You wouldn't get planning permission for *that* nowadays,' Keith had said gloomily. 'Bloody indoor folly.'

I moved along the eighteen-inch passageways now. The dull yellow lamps, too feeble and too widely spaced, bred a writhing mass of shadows. (When the gas-brackets were in use, it must have been far worse). Our desultory patrols were set to cover the whole labyrinth, with one exception: the short spur where the sensors clustered thickest. Daily at 10 a.m. the grey-headed Trustee and his two hulking minders went down this forbidden path to – consult? Check? Just pay homage to? '*Feed* the Bequest,' came Keith's remembered voice, now artificially hollow. 'His expensive leather briefcase, Bob, simply has to be packed with slabs of raw meat. Flesh which is . . . no longer of any human shape!'

Remembering the photograph of a certain ex-guard, it was possible to feel apprehension. I thought also of my reconnaissance down at the pub off Gloucester Green, where it was almost a standing joke that people didn't wear a Trant guard's navy uniform for long. They did not all suffer freak accidents: that would be absurd. By and large, they merely tended to leave after that average six weeks. You could speculate, if you chose, that something had frightened them. The heavy, regulation torch was a comfort in my hand.

Somewhere the real-time watchdog system dreamed its dreams, fed a soothingly 'normal' pattern of patrol movements by my rogue software, registering nothing at all in the dense minefield of IR and ultrasonic pick-ups that guarded the way to Area C.

Left, right, left, and there in the torchlight was the door: big, grim, banded with iron, deep-set in its massive frame, with a lock the size of a VCR unit. I was half inclined to turn back at that point, because it was a joke. Modern burglars flip open those jumbo Victorian lever-and-ward efforts almost without breaking step. As part of my personal quest, I'd entered other restricted libraries (including sections of the BM and Bodleian known to very few) and had never seen such a lumbering apology for a lock. But after all, and hearteningly, there was the maze and the electronic network . . . something here was surely worth guarding.

'How shall one catch the lions in the desert?' I quoted to myself as I felt for the lock-spring, remembering one of Keith's sillier answers: the hunter builds a cage, locks himself securely in, and performs an inversion transformation so that he is considered to be outside while all the lions are inside, along with the desert, the earth, the universe . . . Perhaps Jasper Trant had liked mathematical jokes. He was here at just about the right time to have known Lewis Carroll, another of Keith's heroes whom I must look up some day.

I was here because of a rumour that Trant's preoccupations, Trant's bequest, had a personal connection with – well – myself.

Click and *Click* again. The door swung ponderously inward, and the first torchlit glimpse swept away half my uncertainties. Area C, where the movement sensors did not extend, was indeed a library – a forty-foot square room with wooden bookcases scattered along its iron walls. Ceiling and floor were likewise made of, or lined with, dull iron. A vault.

All this profusion was a disappointment. I had flicked through libraries before. The literature of the occult is stupendously boring and repetitive ... it may contain many small secrets but I had very much hoped that dead Jasper Trant knew one big secret.

Musty smells: old books, old iron and a thin reek of what might have been oil. Keeping close to the wall, I moved cautiously clockwise to the first bookcase. An average turnover time of six weeks. Easing out a random volume with a cracked calf spine, I shone the torch on its title-page to find what blasting, forbidden knowledge ...

The Principles of Moral and Political Philofophy by William Paley, D. D.: The Twelfth Edition, corrected by The Author. Vol. I. MDCCXCIX. Crammed with edifying stuff about Chriftianity.

Jesus Christ.

The next one was called *The Abominations of Modern Society*. These included swearing, 'leprous newspapers' and 'the dissipations of the ballroom', and the author didn't approve of them at all. Then another Volume I of Paley ... sermons ... more sermons ... numbing ranks of sermons ... a *third* copy of the identical Paley tract.

The Bequest library was a fake. Not even a volume of dear old Ovid's *Metamorphoses*.

On the other hand, where does the wise man hide a pebble? On the beach. Where does the wise man hide a leaf ...?

Perhaps. In the centre of the far wall, opposite the door, my circle of torchlight found a cleared space and a long metal desk or table. On the steel surface, an old-fashioned blotting-pad; on the pad, a book like a ledger that lay invitingly open. Cautiously, cautiously, now. There was something almost too tempting about ...

What I felt was minute but inexplicable. I might have put it down to nerves, but I never suffer from nerves. A sinking feeling? I backed rapidly away, and my boot-heel snagged on something, a slight step in the floor. The floor had been smooth and even. Now the torch-beam showed bad news: a large rectangle of iron had sunk noiselessly, with the metal table and myself on it, just less than half an inch into the floor. I thought *hydraulics*, whipped around instantly and blurred towards the door faster than anyone I have ever met could have managed. Too late.

It was all very ingenious. Victorian technology, for God's sake. The 3-D maze construction of Area B must have concealed any amount of dead space for tanks, conduits and machinery. Now, tall vertical panels within the deep door-frame had hinged open on either side to show iron under the old wood, and oiled steel bars moved silkily out and across, barring the way. By the time I reached the door, the closing space was too narrow: I could have thrust myself a little way in, only to have neat cylinders punched out of me. The heavy rods from the left finished gliding into their revealed sockets at the right. And that was that.

The space between the bars was about four unaccommodating inches. I thought hard. I still knew one big thing, but was it needed? 'Well, I was just curious,' I imagined myself saying with a slight whine to Grey Suit in the morning. 'It's a fair cop. I don't suppose, ha ha, there's any chance you could keep me on? No? Oh well, that's the luck of the game,' and bye-bye to the Jasper Trant Bequest. Everyone gets curious after a while. Practically anybody would end up overcome with curiosity after an average time of, say, six weeks. Thus the staff turnover. Thus . . .

No, I don't pretend to be an expert on human psychology, but surely sooner or later the Trant would end up hiring someone too loyal or too dull to take a peep, and they'd duly hold down the job for years on end.

For the sake of form I tested the bars – immovable – and went back to learn what I might from the disastrous ledger. It was all blank sheets except for where it had lain open. That page carried a few lines of faded blue-black ink, in the sort of clerkly hand you might expect from Bob Cratchit.

> Jasper Trant says in his Last Will and Testament that once, as a magistrate of the Oxford court, he saw a shape no man could believe, a thing that crawled from a cell window where no man might pass and left nought behind. All his life he puzzled over this and sought a proof. Here is his bequest.

Here was what bequest? Was this slender snatch of gossip the root of all those rumours about Trant's secret lore of shape-shifters and changelings? Something was missing. Or perhaps I had not thought it through. The path seemed clear: wait till morning, own up like a man, and walk out of the building for ever. No problem.

It was then that I looked properly at the steel table which supported the book. It was dreadfully like a medical examination couch. Two huge minders always accompanied the Trustee on his morning visit to Area C. Suddenly I was sure that no errant security guard was allowed to say goodbye without being carefully prodded and probed. Which would not do at all.

The Trant Bequest had circulated its own damned rumours, and fed the fires by refusing any access to its worthless collection. Bait.

How shall one catch the lions in the desert? There was one answer that Keith repeated with a tiny sneer because it wasn't pure maths but mathematical physics.

I know even less physics than maths, but swiftly picked up the jeering tone ... protective colouration. The theoretical physicist's answer: build a securely locked cage in the centre of the desert. Wave mechanics says there is always a tiny but non-zero probability that any particular wave/particle, including a lion, might be in the cage. Wait.

With the long patience of the dead, Jasper Trant had waited.

Shit, I thought, seeing another facet. After six weeks on average, if they hadn't given way to curiosity, each successive Trant guard would be sacked on some excuse or another, to make way for the testing of the next in line. No one who wanted to infiltrate the Bequest would have to wait for long.

I sighed. Four inches between the bars. This would take time and not be at all comfortable. I could not stay around for a possible medical examination: every instinct screamed against it, and I trust my instincts. The Trant Bequest had nothing more to tell me about myself.

So. Off with that smart uniform. The dull, painful trance of change, writhing to and fro on that death-cold iron floor, in the dark. Bones working as in a dream. Muscle masses shifting, joints dislocating, rewriting the map of myself. The ribs are one thing; the pelvic and cranial sutures are very much harder work to part and rejoin. It went on and on, until at length I was a grotesque flat parody of the Bob Ames who had entered an eternity before. Even so, it would be a long hard wriggle. By now I must look like ...

Well, specifically, like the dead and flattened guard in that photograph. Could *he* have been —? No, it wouldn't make sense, there was a real autopsy and everything. But I did examine the bars more closely, in fear of some hidden trap. Then I stood back and glimpsed the trap too obvious to be noticed.

Jasper Trant himself had seen something slip from an Oxford gaol cell, through the bars, no doubt. Bars, no doubt, set just as far apart as those now blocking the Area C door. There was another subtlety here. If this was a snare for people like myself, set by his long-departed curiosity, why the loophole?

I could almost hear Keith's voice, the eager voice of the mathematician: Didn't you read the mention of 'proof' in the book? Wasn't I telling you last night about the austere kind of maths reasoning we call an existence proof? Trant wasn't collecting for a zoo ... he was a mathematician and all his Trustees want is the existence proof. Which they'd certainly have, if after walking in there and triggering the hydraulics you got out through that impossible gap. Don't you *see*?

I saw, and was profoundly grateful to Keith for the patterns of reasoning he'd shown me. It was heady stuff, this reason. I couldn't stay and I couldn't go. After the long years' trek from the orphanage in search of more of my kind, whatever kind that might be, I did not propose the betrayal of confirming to these ... others ... that my kind existed. Which left me caught, like the lion in the desert who ('Ever heard the psychologist's method, Keith?') builds around him, deduction by deduction, the bars of his own intangible cage.

Yes, I owe a great deal to young Keith. Education is a wonderful thing; he taught me how to be a lion. And at the last I remembered one more thing that he'd explained to me, sentences falling over each other in his enthusiasm ... the technique of reducing a difficulty to a problem that has already been solved. All else then follows. Q.E.D.

It was solved, I think, last year.

Caught in this exact dilemma, what did my anonymous cousin do then? He could escape the cage, but at the cost of leaving the Trustees their proof. I salute him for his splendid piece of misdirection. Then as now, there was a second guard, no doubt asleep back in the control room. No live man could have slipped through those bars after springing the trap, but a dead man, topologically equivalent but stamped and trampled and flattened . . . In the morning, outside the barred doorway of Area C, there lay an object that might just have been – that to any rational mind must have been – hauled and crushed with brutal force through one narrow space. Hauled from outside the cage. A bizarre and suspicious circumstance, but not one which quite *proved* anything.

So logic points the way. I'm sorry to be doing this, Keith. I'm truly grateful for all our conversations, and will try to make quite sure that you feel no pain.

THE MISSING MARTIAN

Marcus L Rowland

———————

That morning the sky was the colour of cotton candy, pink with white streaks. I had a feeling we might be due for a bad storm. As usual I stashed my car in a garage a few blocks from my office, and rode the rest of the way by streetcar. I've made some enemies, and leaving my car outside the office all day might just have put a little too much temptation in someone's way.

Clients weren't forming a line to see me, so I propped my feet on the waste-paper basket and settled down with the *San Francisco Examiner*, which had another boring story about the stupid things people did during the *War of the Worlds* panic. You'd think that after a week they'd be tired of it. Two hours later I was working on the crossword when the door opened.

'Mr Ginsberg?'

I dropped the paper into the basket, sat up straight, and tried to look more alert. She was blonde, about twenty-five, attractive in a quiet way but not a real looker. Well-dressed, but dressed for work, not a night at the opera, with medium heels and a small plain purse, topped with one of those expensive little hats with a silly scrap of lace veil. No rings. She had good legs, and the shoes were expensive. Her complexion should have been peaches and cream, but she had a deep suntan. Her tone of voice said Vassar or some other fancy college, the scent said Paris.

'What does it say on the door, sister?'

'Lou Ginsberg, Confidential Investigations.'

'Then who do you think I am?'

'For all I know you could be the janitor, and I don't have business with a janitor.'

'I'm Ginsberg. What can I do for you?'

She came in and shut the door. 'Prove it.'

'Prove what?'

'Prove you're Ginsberg.'

I dug out my wallet, and showed her my investigator's licence.

'Good enough. I wasn't expecting a fake.'

'Then why ask?' I wasn't sure if I should be amused or insulted.

'The Ginsberg I'm looking for is supposed to be a professional. I don't expect cheap sarcasm from a professional.' Ouch. Game, set, and match to blondie.

'OK, sister, you win. I'm Ginsberg, who are you and what can I do for you?'

She sat down in the good chair I keep for visitors, angling her legs so that I didn't see anything interesting except some reasonable ankles. 'My name isn't relevant at this stage. I represent someone who wants to talk to you, but can't come to your office.'

'Can't?'

'He thinks that he may be followed.'

'And what do you think? Is he nuts, or is his wife on his trail?'

'Neither. I'm sorry, I'm not prepared to answer questions. This is an extremely delicate matter. We must be sure that you won't talk to the police or reporters, or describe this case in your memoirs.'

'I don't do that sort of thing. Bums like that guy Spade who writes for *Black Mask*, or that geek Goodwin who shills for Wolfe and puts every detail in his god-damned memoirs, they give this business a bad name. It says "confidential" on the door, and confidential is what you're buying. Even the cops have given up on trying to make me talk about my clients.' That last was a little exaggerated, because only the week before Detective Monroe of San Francisco's finest had been in the office making a nuisance of himself, but I meant the rest of it.

'Good. Very good. Are you prepared to spend an hour or so out of your office, and earn fifty dollars even if you decide not to take the case? Two hundred a day if you take it?'

'I'm like the Boy Scouts. I'm always prepared.' Business was lousy. People didn't even seem to be getting divorced any more, and I had no special reason to stay in when I could be out earning fifty bucks. For two hundred a day I'd think seriously about going to Outer Mongolia.

'Splendid.' She pulled a small roll of bills out of her bag, peeled off five tens, and put them on my desk, then gave me a small card. 'Be at this address at one, and ask for John Sloan. Show him this card. He'll take you to meet your client.'

The address on the card was one of the largest banks in the city; the only other thing on it was Box J131, handwritten in black ink. She got up and headed for the door.

'Wait a minute. How do I know this isn't some sort of hoax?'

'What have you got to lose?' She slipped out, and closed the door behind her. I waited thirty seconds then followed, intending to see where she went and find out a little more, but all I saw was the indicator on the elevator, going down. By the time I reached the lobby she was long gone.

*

Sloan looked like he worked in a bank; if that isn't much of a description, it's because I can't honestly remember much about him. Short, thin, and balding, I think. It's only in the movies that detectives have perfect memories, and he really wasn't important enough to matter. He was obviously expecting me.

He led me down stairs that had more marble facing than a mausoleum, past the vault, then through a door marked 'Employees Only' and up two flights to some extremely fancy offices. Eventually he showed me to a door that had the name of the chairman of the bank on it, held it open while I entered, then bowed himself out so inconspicuously that I hardly knew he was gone. Most of my attention was on the man on the other side of the office.

'Good afternoon.'

'Oh. Good afternoon, Judge Dell. What's this about?'

She'd said it was delicate, and she hadn't been kidding. Dell was one of the top judges in the city; in the country, for that matter. Everyone knew he was headed for the Supreme Court. He looked about forty, was pushing fifty-five, and I'd never heard anyone even hint that he could be bought. I'd testified in his court once or twice when I was on the force. He was as impressive up close as he was in court. A massive bull of a man, the type who looks like he can walk through walls if he really puts his mind to it. His handshake was surprisingly gentle.

'Please, take a seat. Have you eaten?'

'Now you mention it, no.'

'There are some sandwiches here. Nothing kosher, I'm afraid.' He gestured to a trolley, loaded with trays of food.

'That's all right, I'm not religious.' I took some ham and pastrami on rye. 'Why all the food?'

'I'm here for a working lunch with the directors of a charity for the dependants of bank guards. I've arranged for us to spend a few minutes alone before the meeting begins.'

'What's this about, Judge?'

'Hmmmph.' He looked at me for a few seconds. I felt like a dishonest accountant when the auditors start looking through his books. 'Mr Ginsberg, I suppose I must trust you.'

'It's usually a good start.'

'My son has been kidnapped.'

'How old is he?'

'Eighteen months.'

'Jesus. What the hell do you need me for? Every cop in the city must be looking for him, not to mention the FBI.'

'I haven't told them.'

I choked on the sandwich I was biting, spluttered a little, then got my mouth closed and my mind back into gear. 'Isn't that a little ... umm ... unusual, Judge? Considering your position, I mean.'

'The circumstances are unusual. He isn't being held for ransom, but for the release of a prisoner, Claude R Worlsman. You may know the name.'

'The shrink.'

'The murderer. If he's convicted, of course.'

I knew the name, all right. Worlsman was scum, a crooked psychologist who'd earned big bucks getting more criminals off the hook than any five attorneys. Then he got really greedy, and hit on the idea of blackmailing some of his former clients. One of them was Mark Lee, a psycho who really should have been locked away in the funny farm. Lee took it badly, and went after Worlsman with an axe, but Worlsman got him first, with a syringe full of strychnine. The cops stopped

Worlsman's Buick, and found the body wrapped in an old blanket, with Worlsman's fingerprints all over the syringe.

'I thought it was a foregone conclusion.'

'Any judge can disrupt a case. For example, the defence will undoubtedly protest the evidence of the officer who found the body. He was actually after another Buick and stopped the wrong car.'

'I thought that accidental discoveries were admissible as evidence. Umm ... Weeks versus the United States, back before the big war, I think. That case only ruled out deliberate illegal searches.' I felt proud for remembering that one, maybe the Police Academy really had taught me something.

'You know your law.' It was a compliment, coming from him. 'Even so, Worlsman's lawyer will undoubtedly object. Normally I wouldn't hesitate to accept the evidence, but the District Attorney would have serious problems if I ruled it inadmissible. There are other points at which I could intervene.'

'So who's got your boy? It can't be Worlsman himself, he's in prison, and I never heard he had any partners.'

'Worlsman has apparently threatened to ... ah ... "spill the beans" concerning some of his patients if he's convicted. This would appear to be their response.'

He got out a piece of paper, with a few lines of neat typing, double-spaced with no corrections.

WE HAVE YOUR BOY, JUDGE. HE'S UGLY, BUT WE'RE SURE YOU WANT HIM BACK. IF WORLSMAN ISN'T FREED THE KID GETS IT. IF YOU GO TO THE COPS, DELAY THE CASE, OR DO ANYTHING THAT ISN'T PART OF YOUR NORMAL ROUTINE, WE'LL SEND YOU SOME TOES TO PROVE WE MEAN BUSINESS. DON'T CROSS US, WE ARE WATCHING AND WILL KNOW IF YOU GO TO THE POLICE.

The typeface looked like a new Remington, but I could have been wrong.

'It isn't a bluff. I'm fairly sure that I was followed here this morning. A black Packard has been parked across the road since I arrived.'

'Great. When did you notice your son was missing? And why the insult?'

'His nurse left him in a play-pen in the garden just before nine this morning, and came indoors to get a cup of coffee. When she went out again he was gone. The note was left on the sand.'

'How long has this nurse worked for you, Judge?' Naturally I was thinking that she had to have been planted by the mob.

'Nurse Jukes has worked for us since my daughter was born in 1913. She's nearly sixty, and has taken this very badly.' So much for that idea.

'Any new employees?'

'No.'

'What about old ones?'

'We have a chauffeur, a cook, a maid, and my secretary. All of them have worked for us at least ten years.'

'Fired anyone recently?'

'No. My household hasn't changed in many years.'

'Any other family members live with you? Your wife, of course, and you mentioned a daughter, but are there any others?'

'None.'

'That was your secretary that came to see me this morning, was it?'

'No, my daughter. Rowena lives on the campus at Stamford, and it seemed safer for her to make the initial contact.'

So blondie was Rowena Dell. I'd never have guessed, though maybe there was a slight family resemblance.

'Was she at home when the kid was snatched?'

'No. I called her and told her what to do.'

'How do you know they weren't tapping your phone?'

'We spoke in Latin. If they understood that they're better educated than any criminals I've ever encountered.'

'Oh. Anyway, write down the names and addresses of anyone who might be familiar with the layout of the house, and their connection to you.'

He wrote a few lines on a big legal pad.

'Any other kids?'

'None living. One other son, stillborn, in 1925.'

'Sorry. You never know when these things might be relevant. Now, you didn't answer part of my original question. About your kid's looks.'

'Is it relevant?'

'I think that there's something you're not telling me, and that's no way to do business.'

He hesitated for a while, then looked down at the floor. 'Richard is deformed. He suffers from a condition called acromegaly. His bones are growing too quickly, and it affects his looks. You'll appreciate that this is another reason why I would prefer to recover him before there is any publicity.'

'How bad is it?'

'At the moment his face looks ...' he hesitated '... rather odd. His jaws, teeth, and cheek-bones protrude, and he seems to find it hard to talk. Our doctor hopes that surgery and hormone treatments will eventually correct the condition, but he must grow more before surgery is possible. Fortunately it doesn't appear to be painful.'

'Hormone treatment? You mean something like insulin? Does he have to take it regularly?'

'Something of the sort. And no, he doesn't need regular treatment at the moment.'

'I'm sorry, Judge, I didn't mean to upset you. By the way, put your doctor's name on there, and anyone else that might have seen the kid in connection with the treatment.'

'As suspects? I must admit that I hadn't thought of them. It's very unlikely, my doctor is an extremely old friend.' He added three more names.

'Who knows? Look, Judge, I think you ought to go to the police, no matter how much publicity you get. The kidnappers are probably bluffing, and you need more help than I can give you.'

'And if they're not bluffing?'

'If not, they'll probably kill the boy even if you let Worlsman go.'

He winced. 'I'm aware of the possibilities, but there is no question of my letting Worlsman go, even if I wanted to. You must understand that the kidnapping disqualifies me from trying this case, regardless of the result. Fortunately the case has been adjourned because his attorney has influenza. On Monday we resume. I'll carry on until the jury are ready to deliberate, if it will keep my son alive, but at that point I'll have to declare a mistrial, explain the circumstances, and call in the police and FBI. I've spent most of my life serving the law, and I am not prepared to compromise it now.'

'And if your son dies?'

'I'm hoping that you can prevent that.'

I thought it over for a couple of minutes, then said, 'You just hired yourself a detective.'

I left the office, and wondered what to do for a lead. If Dell's house was watched I didn't dare go near the place. Ditto the people on the list. If one of them had fingered the kid for the mob, they'd soon pass on the word that I was on the case.

There was one possibility. Dell thought that he'd been

followed. If he was right, there might be a way to use the tail. I found Sloan and got him to show me out through the staff entrance, then crossed the road and strolled back towards the Packard. I casually glanced in as I passed it; the driver was a ratty little guy with pebble glasses. I had an idea that I'd seen him when I was a cop, but I couldn't put a name to him. There was someone else in the back, but his face was turned away from me. I walked on to the corner, found a call-box, and asked a friend to check out Dell's doctor. It was a long shot, and nothing ever came of it, apart from an extra item on my list of expenses.

I looked down the road. The Packard was still there. I made another call, and told the police that someone was casing the bank. I hung up when they asked my name, and hopped a cab to the local precinct house. Halfway there two police cars went by, headed towards the bank.

Detective Monroe wasn't delighted to see me, but for once I had something to give him; the address of a guy who was fencing hot cars near the docks. I'd been saving the information for a rainy day. While we were talking, the patrol cars returned with the pair from the bank, now handcuffed together.

'I know that bozo from somewhere,' I said, as casually as I could manage. Monroe isn't Einstein, but he really does have the sort of memory dime-novel detectives dream about. There was no way he could resist the challenge.

'Which one?'

'Pebble glasses, looks like a rat.'

'Easy. Wallace Rosen.'

'Never heard of him.'

'Drum Rosen, the door-to-door salesman.'

'Oh. Umm . . . the guy who used to sell encyclopaedias on a five-dollar deposit, then change the cheques to read fifty before he banked them?'

'That's the one. Really small-time. We nabbed him when the regional supervisor of the Fuller Brush Company spotted him as a phoney.'

'Yeah, I think I saw him at the line-up. What about his friend?'

'Porky Pig.'

'You're kidding.' The guy was as thin as a rake.

'Spelled P-I-G-G. Real name Harold. He was in prison when you were on the force, serving a ten-year stretch for armed robbery. Got out last year. Hangs out with the Cream mob. I'd heard he and Rosen were buddies, they shared a cell or something.'

Waldo Cream was a bad bastard, who ran one of the largest vice rings outside Chinatown. Four years ago Worlsman helped to get him off a charge of aggravated assault, one of the last cases I worked on before I left the force. The memory still gives me nightmares.

'What have they been doing?'

'Why are you so interested?' As I said, Monroe isn't an Einstein, but he usually gets there in the end.

'It never hurts to know what's going on.'

He strolled over and exchanged a few words with the arresting officer, then came back to me. 'Someone spotted them casing a bank, and Porky was packing a concealed weapon. That's a parole violation, maybe more if we can prove they planned to rob the bank.'

'Good work. One of these days they'll promote you to Lieutenant.'

'Fat chance.'

I chatted a minute or two longer, then glanced at my watch and said, 'I've got to run, a client's coming to see me this afternoon. See you around.'

He watched me leave, and I could feel the little wheels turning in his head, ever so slowly. Fortunately he likes crooks even less than he likes me, and there wasn't a chance that he'd tell them that I'd been interested. The danger was that he'd sweat them so hard that they told him what was going on, then all hell would break loose. With any luck one of Cream's lawyers would spring them first.

When I left the precinct house it really was starting to rain. I pulled down the brim of my hat, turned up the collar of my coat, and looked for a cab. Before one came along, a battered old Ford stopped by the kerb and the door swung open. 'Get in, I'll give you a lift.'

It was Rowena Dell.

'Where to?'

'Just drive, and tell me what you want.'

She put the car in gear, and drove off a little jerkily, then said, 'What the hell do you think you're doing? They said they'd kill my brother if the police interfered.'

Dell's daughter worried me. When I saw her that morning she'd acted way too cool for someone whose little brother was kidnapped. Now she was apparently much more concerned, but I wasn't sure why. Dell wasn't a millionaire, so far as I knew, but with an address on Russian Hill he had to have money. From what he told me she'd been an only child most of her life, but now there was competition for her parents' affection. To add insult to injury, the kid wasn't even pretty.

'How did you find me?'

'I knew when you'd be with my father, and waited to see you leave. I wasn't expecting you to go straight to the police.'

She'd followed me five blocks without me noticing. That implied training, or considerable natural talent.

'Don't worry about the police. I haven't told them anything, and I've got a lead on the man behind the kidnapping.'

'Oh! Who is it?'

'Why should I tell you?'

'But he's my brother . . .'

'That doesn't mean I have to trust you. For all I know, your boyfriend is holding him. You certainly didn't seem too worried about it this morning. Whoever snatched the kid had inside help.'

The note must have been typed in advance, and they knew what he looked like when they wrote it.

'I don't have a boyfriend. Look, he's my brother, but apart from that I don't really have a lot in common with a child that age. I've been in Egypt most of the last year, so I haven't even seen him much. I'll be upset if something happens to him, but being emotional won't help to get him back.'

'I can think of reasons why you might want a brother out of the way. Inheritance, for example.'

'Don't be stupid. My father's will leaves fixed bequests to members of the family, and the rest to charity. I wouldn't gain anything if Richard died.'

That killed that idea. I tried another.

'What were you doing in Egypt?'

'Archaeology. That's what I teach. There was a big German dig near Cairo a while ago, but they abandoned the site for some reason, and left a terrible mess. We were helping to record the inscriptions before the sand buried them again.'

'We?'

'Oh, I went out with a team from Marshall College in Connecticut. One of their professors visited the dig while the Germans were there, and suggested the expedition.'

There was nothing for me there. I never could see the attraction in digging up the past, though come to think of it that's what a detective mostly does. I decided to try another tack.

'All right, let's assume that you're clean. Who would you say was their inside man in your house? Someone must have described the family's routine, and told them when they'd be able to snatch the kid.'

Her knuckles went white. 'I can't believe that anyone would do that. Everyone loves him.'

'What about your mother? How did she react when she found out her kid was a freak?'

She slammed on the brakes, and slapped me as soon as we screeched to a halt. I was too busy fending off the windshield to stop her.

'You despicable ... you revolting ...' She tried to slap me again, but I got my arm up first. Just as well, she packed quite a punch.

'Just asking. Some parents would hate a kid like that.'

'Not my mother. She loves him, truly she does.'

'When I was on the force most of the killings I saw were in the family. You have to know someone well to hate them.'

'That's a horrible thing to say.'

'Yeah. It's a horrible world, sister, and there are some horrible people running around in it. When you feel like driving again, turn left at the lights.'

She started the car again, and soon had us moving through the traffic. By now the rain was heavy, and I had to peer past the wipers to watch where we were going.

'Where are we going?'

'You're going to drop me on the next block, then head back to Stamford. I'm going to visit a cripple and ask a few questions.'

'A cripple?'

'Just stop here.'

'This is a convent.'

I climbed out of the car. 'They call it a hospice. Scram, you won't be welcome here.'

'What do you mean?'

'I'm going to see a girl who hasn't got much of a face. The bastard who did it might be the one that has your brother.'

'I'm not afraid to see her.'

'Don't be stupid. You're no Garbo, but you aren't that bad. How do you think she'd feel if she saw you?'

'I'll wait out here.'

'No you won't. If she helps me I'll want to move fast, and I won't be able to protect you.'

'I can take care of myself.'

'Nuts. I have enough to worry about without pushing you out of the way of bullets. Go home.'

She seemed to be ready to argue, but I slammed the door and headed for the entrance. I half expected her to come after me, but she put the car into gear and drove off. I would have been happier if she'd reversed first, because she was headed the wrong way for Stamford.

Sophie used to be a beautiful girl, before she made the mistake of holding out on Cream. After he was finished with her she had one arm, one eye, no face, and legs broken so badly she'd never walk again. You had to listen closely because he cut her tongue to stop her talking.

'Ginsberg. Long time, no see.'

'How are you, Sophie?'

'How you think, asshole? Got any booze?'

I took a look around. There weren't any nurses in view, so I slipped her my hip-flask. She took a quick snort, coughed, and pushed it away.

'Can't take that like I used to. What you want?'

'You remember Worlsman?'

'Do I ever. Creep tried put me away for saying was Cream that cut me up. Hear he's in the slammer.'

'Maybe. He's got some powerful friends. One of them is trying to help him beat the rap.'

'Which one?'

'Who do you think?'

'Bastard. Hope they rots in Hell, both them.'

'Maybe you can help me send them there.'

'How?'

'Cream has a lot of girls in his string, and some of them must get pregnant occasionally. What does he do when that happens?'

'What you think? There plenty doctors in city to fix a girl for fifty bucks. Cream takes it out their hides.'

'What if it's too far gone for an abortion? Did that ever happen?'

'Now again. Give me another shot.'

She took another long gulp from the flask.

'So what did he do?'

'Sell kid, maybe cuts momma if she pretty no more.'

'What do you mean, sell the kid?'

'He know someone runs baby farm. Take kids, pretty them up, sell to folks that want a child. Money in it, 'less you gets careless, lets them die of measles or something.'

That had to be it. Someone in that racket wouldn't think twice about hiding a child. After all, that was half their business.

'Got a name for me? An address?'

'What's worth?'

'What do you want?'

'When Cream in jail, an' Worlsman, you gets me a big dose horse, or some sort pills, 'nough to see me dead. I hide it till you long gone, keep you out trouble.'

'Are you sure that's what you want?'

'Yeah. Only way I'll stop them nuns prayin' over me.'

'Done. As soon as the bastards are out of the way, I'll pay you another call.'

'OK. Doctor usually Dan Mosler. Not real doctor, but he good. Fix girls real quick, no trouble.'

'Mosler like the locks?'

'That him.'

'Where do I find him?'

'Dempsey Bar and Grill, Market Street.'

'What about the baby farm?'

'That I don'know. Mosler was front man for that. He take care of things.'

'OK, you've earned your fee.'

'Fuckin' right. See you soon, sugar, an don' forget my gift.'

I left a twenty-dollar bill in the collecting box in the lobby, said goodbye to a couple of nuns, and headed out into the rain.

I thought that Rowena might be waiting outside to follow me, but the only woman around was a stranger, one hell of a lot more attractive, who was looking at flowers outside a nearby shop. Maybe a relative of a patient. I gave her the eye, and she sniffed and went inside while I went on my way.

I was soaked by the time I got to Dempsey's Bar and Grill, and the barman tutted as I dripped on to his nice clean carpet. It wasn't quite the dive I'd expected; it was only a few years old, and the decor ran heavily to padded leather and chrome. The prices were chrome-plated too, or maybe they used a little platinum. There weren't many customers; a couple of smart businessmen in a corner, talking percentages, and a solitary drinker working his way through his third or fourth boiler-maker. I ordered a Scotch, helped myself to a few nuts, and asked the barman if Mosler was around.

'I'm afraid I don't know the name, sir.' He had a fake English accent, which I suppose was meant to give the place a little class.

'Mosler. Dan Mosler, I heard he's always in here.' I tried to sound just a little drunk, without making it obvious.

'I can't recall anyone of that name, sir.'

'Look, I have the name from a friend. Dan Mosler, like the locks.'

'I really don't know ... oh, I believe that there's a Doctor Mosler.'

'That's the one. He drinks here, does he?'

'No, I'm afraid he doesn't, sir.'

'Then how come you know his name?'

'If I'm right, he has an office on the fourth floor.'

'Oh. Maybe I got it wrong, I thought they said the bar.'

'Above it, perhaps? Would you care for another drink?'

'No, I've gotta see the doctor.' I picked up my hat and headed for the door.

Naturally he was right. The bar occupied part of the ground floor of a five-storey block; if I'd kept my eyes open I would have seen the lobby entrance next to the bar. The notice-board said that D. Mosler DO had an office on the fifth floor, not the fourth. I couldn't remember what DO meant, but I decided to take a chance and go upstairs anyway.

There were a half-dozen diplomas from the American Osteopathic Association on the wall of his waiting-room, which was all the help I needed. Doctor of Oste-opathy. His receptionist should have been a looker, with peroxide-blonde hair and a build like Jean Harlow, but she was eating a doughnut when I came in, and I got an idea that her figure owed more to Maidenform than nature. She asked me the usual questions, and I gave her a fake name and address, and said I had a persistent pain in the small of my back. I was vague about where it hurt. Doctors love that sort of thing, they can spend hours poking around, then charge you even if they don't find anything wrong. While we were talking I noticed a covered typewriter behind the desk; I couldn't see the trademark, but it looked about the right size for a Remington. She asked me to wait while the doctor finished with another patient, so I spent a few minutes reading some medical magazines. You wouldn't believe some of the things that can go wrong with people's bones. It was educational, and some of it was very surprising.

After twenty minutes or so I heard a door click, and the doctor buzzed her on an intercom. She told me that he'd finished with his patient, and showed me into his surgery.

Mosler couldn't have been more than thirty, and looked like the sort of doctor you see on the cover of those medical romance magazines; the kind where the guy has a stethoscope round his neck, a mirror strapped to his head, and a nurse in his arms. Handsome, and then some.

He had a lot of equipment, including a sterilizer and other stuff I wouldn't have expected to see outside of a hospital. Maybe that was normal for an osteopath, but it was the sort of stuff that would fit in well with a sideline as an abortionist.

He asked me the same questions, and I gave him more of the same lies until his receptionist shut the door. Then I decided to take a chance, and said, 'Get rid of her, Doc, Cream sent me over to see you, and he doesn't want any witnesses.' I opened a button on my coat, and let him see the butt of the revolver.

'Cream?' He licked his lips nervously. He knew the name all right.

'Come on, Doc, cut the crap. Cream's upset, and if you mess him about, things'll get one hell of a lot worse.'

He looked around, a little wide-eyed, then pressed the button on the intercom and said, 'Take an early afternoon, Monica. I'll see to the rest of my appointments myself.'

'Are you sure, Doctor?' the intercom said.

'Quite sure.'

'Don't forget Mrs Jones at four. I'll see you tomorrow.'

I heard movements outside, then a door closing.

'That's smart, Doc. Now, Cream wants me to get the kid. Seems he's a little unhappy with your arrangements. Someone got too talkative.'

'Who ratted? Bates? Chalker?' No pretence that he didn't know what I meant.

'I'm just a messenger, Doc. I don't know the whole situation, I just know I'm supposed to get the kid.'

'Maybe it's just as well. Let me get my coat. Have you got a car?'

I thought fast. 'No, Cream said you'd drive me.'

'Oh. Well, we'd better get going if I'm to be back by four.' It was just after three now, so the kid couldn't be too far away.

He led the way out of a door that opened directly on to the hall. I followed and something heavy and hard hit me behind the ear.

'. . . bastard bit a lump out of my hand when I tried to make him eat his mush. I'm telling you, if the Judge doesn't play ball I'll ice the little brat myself.'

'Shh. I think he's coming round, Gladys,' said Mosler. I kept my eyes shut, and pretended I was still out.

'Who cares? Kill him now, Cream won't mind.' I recognized the voice of Mosler's receptionist. Calling her

Monica must have been some sort of code, and of course she'd been waiting in the hall when we came out.

'Cream will want to have his fun.' Something poked into my eye, and I pulled my head back before he put it out.

'Ah, I thought you were awake.'

We were in some sort of cellar, and I was wedged into a corner with my hands behind my back. It felt like they were cuffed to a pipe. Naturally my gun was gone; I could see it in Mosler's belt. I wondered if the cuffs were the pair I usually keep clipped to my belt, or the pair from my pocket. There was a difference, but I couldn't find out while Mosler was watching.

There was a big machine to one side of the room, that looked like a boiler for a hot-water system. It made a deep throbbing noise, and I felt fairly sure that it would drown out any screams or shouts. The only other features of the room were a couple of rickety chairs and a heavy-looking steel door in the far wall. I wanted to throw up, but managed to keep the impulse under control. My head felt like she'd slugged me with a ball-peen hammer, but it was probably just a sap. With any luck I didn't have a skull-fracture.

'Where are we?'

'Not far from my office, Mr Ginsberg. Mr Cream was very pleased to hear that you were ... available.'

'That the Dell boy I heard you talking about? You must be out of your mind to snatch a judge's kid.'

He kicked me in the stomach, not particularly hard, but enough to make me puke over his nice shiny shoes. They were dry shoes, until I spoiled them, which either meant that he'd worn galoshes, or that we were in a basement of the office building. He kicked me again, much harder, then said, 'It wasn't my idea, but in principle I agree with it. Doctor Worlsman is a fellow professional, and it would be unfortunate if he were executed. If the Judge cooperates the child will be released unharmed, if not I'm sure that we can find a use for him. As dog food, perhaps.' He was a real sicko. Gladys wasn't turning a hair, and I guessed that she was as deep into the racket as Mosler. Sophie hadn't said he had an assistant, but I'd forgotten to ask her.

'If you let me go, I can get you off the hook.'

He didn't buy it, of course. 'If we let you go you can undoubtedly find enough evidence to interest the police, then I'm afraid we would probably be facing several decades in prison. Killing you should be a lot safer.'

'Wonderful, add murder to kidnapping.'

'Don't say any more, Danny. Cream might want to leave him alive, and we don't want him talking.'

'Don't be silly. Even if Cream does leave him alive, he won't be in any condition to talk.'

I thought of Sophie, and I felt sick again.

Mosler said, 'Check the child again, and do try to get him to eat something. For the moment we really must keep him healthy.'

She grumbled, and went out, giving me an uninspiring glimpse of a passage with rough brick walls. I strained to listen for any sign of the boy, but there was nothing but the rumble of the boiler. Mosler turned one of the chairs to face me. I gave the cuffs a quick tug while his back was turned; they felt much too solid for comfort, but I couldn't give them a real test while Mosler was in the room.

He sat down, put the gun on his lap, groped in his pocket, and stuck some gum into his mouth.

'Any chance of a piece of your gum?'

'No, I'm afraid not.'

'How about a drink of water?'

'Later, perhaps.'

'Come on, my mouth tastes like a cat's sandbox.'

'Tut, what a shame.'

Gladys backed into the room, with a nasty-looking little automatic in her hand. She said, 'Look, we've got company.' She stepped away from the doorway.

Mosler said, 'Do come in, my dear,' and pointed his own gun at the entrance.

Rowena Dell stepped into the cellar.

'I thought I told you to go home.'

'I'm sorry, Ginsberg, I thought I might be able to help, so I followed you here.'

'Amateurs. That's all I need.' My professional pride was hurt. She'd been able to follow me twice without me noticing. I wondered how she'd done it, and how she'd found her way to the basement.

Mosler laughed, and said, 'What a touching scene.' He tossed a pair of handcuffs on to the floor. Mine, I guessed – I hoped. 'Pick these up, very slowly, then move over to the other corner.'

Rowena did as she was told. 'Now put one cuff on your right wrist.' Eventually she was cuffed to the other pipe, with her hands behind her back.

'Who is she, Ginsberg?'

'My secretary.'

'How did she get into the cellar?'

Gladys looked up from the handbag she was examining, and said, 'She bust the lock with a tyre-iron. I took it off her before I brought her in. By the way, the ID says she's Dell's other kid.'

Mosler said, 'You shouldn't tell lies, Ginsberg, your nose will grow like Pinocchio's.'

Gladys laughed, and said, 'Cream will love her. Maybe he'll want to keep her. A judge's daughter ought to fetch big bucks, especially if he lets people hurt her a little.'

Rowena said, 'Better let us go, the police will be here any minute.'

'Really? And what did you tell them?'

'Everything.'

I twisted my wrists, and strained at the cuffs again. Still no result, though I couldn't use my full strength without them noticing me moving.

'Indeed? Well, then we'd better kill your brother, hadn't we? After all, that was what we said we'd do if the police became involved.'

I said, 'She's lying.'

'How would you know, Ginsberg?'

'If she was telling the truth she would have waited for the cops to get here. Besides, I didn't see any public phones in this building, and she can't have had time to use a call-box.'

'That may be true. Gladys, go up to the office, and see if you can see any signs of police activity. Bolt the cellar door behind you, and put the padlock on. I'll use the other way out if it's necessary to leave. Call down and let me know the situation.'

That meant there was a telephone somewhere down here. Gladys went out. This time I thought I heard a noise like a kid crying, but the pitch was higher than I would have expected from a child that age. Then I remembered that there was supposed to be something wrong with his face, which might affect his voice.

'If she has called the police I'll find the time to make you feel very, very sorry before I leave.'

Five minutes or so passed, then I heard a bell ring; not the steady rhythm of a public phone, but an irregular jingle. Probably an old hand-cranked bell. 'Perhaps I'd better get it, I think you're both a little tied up.' Mosler tittered, and went off down the passage.

I gave him twenty seconds, while I made a last try at

pulling my cuffs apart, then whispered: 'They're trick cuffs. Pull on them, as hard as you can.' She nodded, and did as she was told. For a few seconds nothing happened, then there was a loud click, and a broken link flicked across the room and pinged off the boiler. Mosler was still talking, though I couldn't hear what he was saying. 'Get over here, I've got the key for this pair in my shoe.'

She started to get up, then crouched again and put her hands behind her back. Smart girl. Mosler came back into the room.

'Well, it appears that you're right, Ginsberg, Miss Dell doesn't seem to have called the police. Gladys says that Mr Cream has just called, and will be arriving shortly. We'll have a little party, I think.'

'You won't laugh when my father is through with you. You won't laugh at all,' said Rowena.

'Miss Dell, I'm pleased to find you in such good spirits. So many young women in your position would faint or start to scream. Your faith in your father is touching; mistaken, since you do seem to be my prisoner, but touching.'

'Let me go. I'll pay you.'

'I don't see any money, and I'm sure that you'd try to kick me if I were foolish enough to come any closer.'

'It's under my sweater. A gold crucifix with diamonds.'

'Is it, indeed. We'll have to take that little trinket at some point, there's no point in leaving it with you. Later, perhaps.'

I decided that it was time for a diversion, and pretended that I was trying to break out of my cuffs. Mosler stepped towards me. 'If you don't stop I'll shoot your balls off, Mr Ginsberg.' Behind him Rowena silently rose, picked up the chair, and smashed it over his head. I hardly noticed, because the chain of my cuffs broke and I was busy falling on to my face.

By the time I got up again Rowena was making goo-goo noises at the kid, in a poky little nursery down at the other end of the corridor. I checked Mosler. He wasn't dead, but the side of his skull was smashed. If he ever woke up it would be a miracle.

I took a peek at Rowena and the kid. His father was right about his looks, any circus would have paid a fortune to have him as their dog-faced boy. Ugly, and then some.

The rest of this story doesn't take long to tell.

We didn't find Mosler's other way out, and we didn't have the tools to open the door from the inside, but I did have my gun. When Gladys and Cream arrived fifteen minutes later we were ready for them. I was through playing games, and had an old score to settle for Sophie. They came in looking the wrong way; I shot Cream before they realized that we'd escaped, tried to make Gladys surrender, and ended up having to shoot her twice before she dropped her gun. Cream and Mosler were dead by the time the police answered my call, Gladys was still in a wheelchair when she came to trial.

I expected to spend a few nights in jail, while the police decided whether or not they believed my story, but Judge Dell packed a lot of clout. They found four other children buried in the cellar, so no one was too concerned about anything that we'd done to get the kid back.

The Press was there in force by the time the police were finished with us, and I couldn't stop them getting a few shots of Rowena and her brother. He looked a lot more normal by daylight, no worse than any other screaming kid with a dozen flash bulbs exploding in his face. It was mostly me they wanted to talk to, which suited the Dells just fine. I kept quiet about some details that weren't really relevant to the kidnapping, and we went back to the Judge's place for supper. Afterwards I told him the whole story.

'. . . I think I was wrong about an inside man. I took a look through Cream's coat while we were waiting for the police, and found a notebook with a timetable of your family's movements. There were pictures of your garden taken from above the street. There's a telephone pole in the road. Was anyone working up there in the last few days?'

The Judge's wife thought for a moment. 'Yes. We had a lot of trouble with bad lines last week, and there was someone up there two or three times.'

'He was probably listening to your calls too. The police will want a full description, though I'd guess it was just one of Cream's hired hands. The police have pulled in a few already.'

'Undoubtedly. Well, Mr Ginsberg, you've done a wonderful job, and I think that you've earned a substantial bonus . . .' The Judge reached into his pocket and pulled out his wallet.

I said, 'There's something that's still bothering me.'

'What's that?' asked the Judge.

I got up and walked over to the fireplace, and stood with my back to it. I wasn't feeling cold, I just wanted to be sure that no one was behind me.

'Years ago a cop I knew was chained with his own cuffs, then they set fire to him with gasoline. I remembered that, and I didn't want it happening to me, so when I quit the force I bought a pair of fake magician's cuffs. I keep them on my belt, where it's easy to find them, and a real pair in one of my pockets. Mosler cuffed me as soon as they knocked me out, and he used the first pair he found. The trick pair. I just wasn't pulling the right way at first. Rowena was wearing the real pair.' I fished the broken link out of my pocket, and tossed it across to her. 'Toughened steel. You bent it like it was a paper-clip.'

'A poor weld, perhaps?' suggested the Judge. He looked a lot warier. So did everyone else in the room.

'Not a chance. Then there's the door she broke, and the way she smashed Mosler's skull. Normal women aren't that strong.'

'I get a lot of exercise,' she said. I ignored it.

'Your son's face was another clue. The shape of his bones was odd, and it seemed to change once Rowena calmed him.'

'Acromegaly. I told you this afternoon.'

'You did, Judge, but Mosler had some magazines in his waiting-room. Medical magazines about bone diseases. One of them had an article about acromegaly. It messes up the faces of adults, but children don't have that problem. They just grow extra tall.'

'I see.'

'Put it all together, and the answer I'm getting is rather odd.'

The Judge said, 'What answer would that be?' He rose to his feet, and poured a drink.

'Rowena is stronger than any human has a right to be. Your son's face changes shape, unless one of you tells him to stop it. I didn't see Rowena following me, but I did notice a woman outside the hospice when I headed for Mosler's place. Her coat looked a lot like Rowena's, only the face was different. Maybe the kid isn't the only one that can change his face. You gave me that story about acromegaly, and it's nonsense. You're reluctant to have the police or the Press investigate your affairs. Any other judge would have gone straight to the FBI if his kid was snatched, and that makes me wonder what else they'd find if they really started looking at you. I can't think of a rational explanation that covers all the facts, so I've settled for one that's downright silly. I think you're Martians, or something of the sort.'

'Martians?' His face was blank, completely impassive.

'Like *The War of the Worlds*?' said Rowena.

'No. If I thought that my gun wouldn't be in its holster. You work for a living, you love your children, and you don't seem to be doing much harm to anyone who doesn't deserve it. You're stronger than us, and you can change your looks, but I don't think that you're super-powerful. If you were, you wouldn't have needed a detective.'

The Judge's wife laughed. 'A peaceful invasion. What an odd idea.'

'I don't think you're invading. Maybe you just like living here, and want things nice, or maybe you're out to civilize us a little. I don't care. You've put away scum that needed it badly, and you gave me the chance to ice Cream. There's no way that Worlsman will get off now, even with another judge running the case, because everyone knows who set the ball rolling. I'm not complaining, and I couldn't prove anything if I wanted to.'

'I'm pleased to hear that . . .' said the Judge, relaxing a little, '. . . but it leaves me wondering what you propose to do with this peculiar theory?'

'Nothing. I told you when you hired me, I don't rat on my clients. I just want you to know that your stories need work. Think about it, because I'm not the only detective in the world, and some of them are as good as me, and much better equipped. Give me my fee, and that bonus you mentioned, and think about what I've said. And if you ever need a detective, find someone else. You lied to me, and that's something I don't like.'

'I'm sorry you feel that way, Ginsberg. Honourable men are hard to find.' Dell gave me seven hundred and fifty dollars, which was rather more than I'd expected, and shook my hand. His grip was still surprisingly gentle.

Rowena offered to show me out. In the hall she stopped and said, 'Wait a minute,' then took my hands. Her face started to writhe. I wanted to get free, but I might just as well have tried to break out of my handcuffs. The real pair. When her face settled down, a half-minute or so later, she was a dead ringer for Garbo. She pulled me close and kissed me, and I tasted blood as her teeth nipped my lip. I thought of vampires, but she pulled away after a few seconds.

'Now that's a neat trick,' I said.

Her face writhed again, and her looks returned to normal, but she kept hold of my hands. 'You'd be amazed, but perhaps I'd better not demonstrate. Thank you for helping to find my brother. He means a lot to all of us.'

'It's my job.'

She smiled coldly. 'My parents are too relieved to worry about anything you might do. I'm not quite so sentimental, although I feel some gratitude. I've just shown you that I can be anyone, Ginsberg. A woman you meet in a bar, or one you pass on the street. Think about it, and think about how easily I can get to you if I want to. I know your voice, I know your scent, now I even know what you taste like. If I ever think you're becoming a threat, I'll find you wherever you hide, and then you're dead meat.'

'I'll bear it in mind.'

'See that you do. Goodnight.'

She let me go and opened the door, and I walked out into the drive. Monroe was still there, talking to a couple of his men, and I talked him into giving me a ride back to my car. Along the way I started to feel shaky, and decided that I wanted a change of scenery.

Worlsman never did get sentenced: he rocked the boat too badly, and someone made sure that he wouldn't talk – the hard way. They found his body in his cell, a couple of days before they sent Gladys down for twenty. A week later I said goodbye to Sophie, and moved to a little town in Nevada, where a small detective agency was advertising for a new partner.

I never saw any of that family again, but I did keep tabs on them through the papers. Dell never made the Supreme Court; they don't like judges with odd reputations, and his use of a private detective raised just enough doubts to keep him out of contention. He retired last year. Rowena still teaches archaeology. She publishes a book every two or three years, but I don't know enough to say if they are any good. So far as I know, Richard Dell is still in school.

As for me, life in Las Vegas wasn't as quiet as I'd hoped. But that's another story.

THE DECONSTRUCTION OF
THE KNOWN WORLD

Elizabeth M Young

The jam sandwich came hurtling down the street as if driven by a poltergeist. It did a pirouette around a microdot roundabout and jerked to a halt. The policemen flowed out and stood around helplessly, like flies round a broken ice-cream. The siren kept screaming and passers-by, having slowed down to stare, covered their ears in protest. What was happening? No one seemed to know. Slowly, the steady drift towards the underground station was resumed. The day was darkening. The siren suddenly died away and the moment of disruption passed. It had just started to snow and one could hear all the city clocks striking five.

When will you pay me, said the bells of Old Bailey?

It was at that moment that Bobby Fever approached the professor.

'Got a light, sir? Please?'

'As it happens I don't smoke. But – look here –'

Instantly they both recoiled. In all that busy street there were only two non-humans and each recognized the other's alien status. Apart from that they could not have been more different. For a start they were on opposite sides of the law. Bobby Fever was very well-known down at West End Central. Dr Marvin Vonderhyde was known to nobody. Bobby recovered first and shrugged. What the hell. He smiled his sweet,

321

professional smile. The professor was thinking fast and distractedly. (What's the harm, what's the harm ... a cup of tea, a cup of tea ...) 'Look here, you're frozen. Let's get you warmed up.'

Bobby Fever allowed himself to be led through the thickening snow towards the warm, melting lights of a Burger King. He could always spot a closet case, human or not.

Both Bobby and Dr Marvin spent their lives, as they saw it, slumming amongst humans, although for very different reasons. If they were disconcerted by this unexpected encounter with one of their own kind they were not going to show it. However, even had they kept to their own species, their paths were unlikely to have crossed. Their families were at opposite ends of the Weerde social scale. Really, of course, anything might have happened to Bobby who lived on the wild side. He may have wondered briefly why an adult male like this guy could not satisfy his desires amongst his own people without trolling through the rush-hour crowds on the Embankment (a closet case, right?) but he wasn't going to dwell on it. His focus was the wallet not the psyche. Leave that one to the shrinks. However, for Dr Marvin, this was the first time he had ever initiated a social encounter – of any kind. And, as he limped and puffed up the hill, casting sidelong glances at Bobby through snow-crusted lashes, he was already having doubts.

Snow had fallen, snow on snow, sno-o-o-w ... *on snow* ... Marvin could remember another white city by a river. Bremen. Before the war. *In the bleak mid-winter* ... long, long ago. The Vonderhydes, along with a million other refugee undesirables had been driven across a blighted, frozen Europe by the *Übermensch*, the Nazi devils. They had escaped on one of the last Save the

Children Fund boats out of Holland, with Marvin, an anxious, pale-haired little scrap, tucked beneath his mother's greatcoat, next to her heart. It was so cold her pet parrot froze during the crossing and fell like a stone into the sea. His brothers and sisters had all been caught and sent to the camps. The remains of the family blew like soiled rags, or fallen leaves, into North Kensington where they collapsed. They were a notoriously decayed branch of the tribe anyway and the war had finished them.

It had been left to Marvin alone to surmount the general despair and go out into the world again. He was a success.

Bobby, looking across at the plump, fair man in the baggy tweed suit, would never have guessed it. With hair-oil cascading stickily down both sides of his face and eyes darting around like nervous fish behind his enormous, round redwood-framed glasses, he was a joke.

'And so,' Marvin retained precise European pronunciation. 'What is it that you do, young man?'

Bobby smiled emptily. 'Oh, this and that.' He gathered his energy for the pitch. 'It's hard these days. I'm like, you know, homeless.'

'Yes, yes. It is a tragedy, this government.' Marvin looked deep into his coffee-cup. He cleared his throat. 'Perhaps I can help?'

Marvin was now in a panic. The boy — so young, so pitiful. *So beautiful, so seductive.* He needed help, that was clear. *He needed love; someone strong, someone gentle.* What were his family thinking of, letting him wander around like this? Marvin could give him some money and send him on his way. That was enough, surely. *Marvin is singing Lieder, songs of love and loss and yearning. Bobby is drifting past in a swan-shaped gondola. They are eating strawberries together on a*

*carpet of warm grass; the heavens open, cherubs up-
end silver conches and shower them with pearls and
white marshmallows. Laughing, they run hand-in-hand
through a rainstorm, Bobby spills a bouquet of wild
flowers as Marvin draws him into an urgent embrace.
They stand beneath pastel umbrellas at a garden party,
Bobby is in a white suit, he has an erection, there is
a crash of thunder, they are on a turbo-charged fuel-
injected bed above Rome, Marvin is tearing at
Bobby's thin jeans with his teeth, the whole world
smells of piss –*

'Why are you singing?'

'Was I? I am distracted. I have terrible problems – at
work.' Marvin stood up. His legs were shaking. A sensation of doom overcame him as he gasped out, 'Shall we –
would you like to come to my house?' He fumbled for
his asthma inhaler.

Bobby uncoiled himself and stood over Marvin. The
harsh lights had drained away his colour. His eyes
were crystalline, silver-white. 'I have to see someone
first. I – owe them some money.'

'I'll come with you.' Resigned, Marvin followed him
out to the pavement, his eyes fixed on the tight buttocks
outlined by ageing, clinging denim.

If Marvin had known Bobby's surname he would have
understood much more. It was the Weerde equivalent
of Lowell and Cabot in America or Howard in England.
Few families have ever named themselves so unequivoc-
ally after their greatest triumphs as Bobby's arrogant
relatives. The Rickets and the Clapps, the Dengues and
the Shingles – the branches of the family were spread
all over the world and together, comprised a true aristo-
cracy. One could trace Bobby's ancestry back through
the centuries. His French mother, Bernadine Peste was

particularly high-born and closely related to the first known family of the tribe, the still patriarchal Cankers. The whole tribe were purists. Throughout known history they had all steadfastly opposed humankind and done everything they could to spread suffering and disease throughout their ranks. They isolated viruses, they supported right-wing dictators and left-wing tyrants, they poured money into the pockets of capitalist despoilers. They had helped exterminate some of Marvin's own family who'd just, unfortunately, gone down with the flood in the Nazi holocaust.

No true Canker ever let the small-scale pathos of their own kind detract from their long-term aim which was to smash every last filthy little human biped off the face of the planet and establish Weerde hegemony. The twentieth century had been a battle of Titans. Penicillin had been met with the atom bomb, contraception with sexually transmitted disease. The entire Canker tribe was at its most powerful and influential, privy to all the secrets and conspiracies that wreathe Weerde politics at the very highest level. The individual families, worldwide, were all enormously rich and relentlessly well-organized, and somehow, overall, depressingly reminiscent of Mormons.

Bobby's own family, the Fevers, had been in London since the seventeenth century and were exceptionally fine, upstanding members of the proud Canker tribe. On reaching adolescence everyone had to undertake a lengthy spell of community service before retiring to research and breeding. Bobby had to choose between resettling mental patients in local communities or joining the 'Just Say Yes' faction of the vast 'War on Humans: Drugs Division'. Detesting social workers, he became a drug dealer. All too soon he was hanging out with clients, night-clubbing in Brixton, wandering around like a zombie, seemingly forgetful of everything he'd ever been taught. Priceless bibelots and Clichy paperweights started vanishing from his mother's bedroom. He gave one little cousin, Joey Warbles, some E and he was sick all over a pure-bred Sharpei. Another, Mario Rubella, he sexually abused in a greenhouse, amongst the sun-dried tomatoes. By then, Bobby was down and out as far as the Fevers were concerned. He was excommunicated, denounced and disinherited.

Now, leaning back in the cab as it flew down Queensway, Bobby lit a Gauloise. He imagined his mother standing next to the great swagged drapes in her cool, grey drawing-room, gazing out mindlessly at the snow whirling through Campden Hill Square. *I did everything for that boy, everything. He had my heart's blood. Come back,* mon petit. His great-aunt Agnes comes in and starts playing some mournful Chopin on the Bösendorfer. His mother cries. Bobby glanced over at Dr Marvin, wheezing and sucking on his inhaler in the corner of the seat. Another day, another dollar. It's too late to stop now.

By the time they climbed the steps to the tall, narrow house near Kensal Green cemetery the wind had whipped up a blizzard. Chunks of snow and ice were pouring down from broken guttering. Bobby noticed that the house was unlit and several of the windows broken and stuffed with newspaper. He drew back, looking anxiously up and down the deserted street. This guy couldn't have any money after all. In fact – and Bobby started to turn around – he was probably a maniac. Marvin laid a hot hand on his arm. 'It's OK. Really. It's just my family. A little eccentric, you know?'

As soon as they stepped into the hall Bobby did know. A familiar smell assailed him, remembered from childhood visits to primitive relatives. Fur and feathers, blood, meat and straw. And beneath it, the rancid scent of age and unreconstructed feral beings. The professor's family were just ... like – *antique*. He smiled, even as he banged into a brimming dustbin in the gloom. Glass and cans clattered out and the hall filled with the angry screeching of awakened birds and the rush of their wings. Bobby untangled a small owl from his hair as he squelched forward on what seemed like layers of damp cardboard and newspaper.

'My mother – she is fond of birds,' offered Marvin, holding open a door at the end of the corridor. Bobby felt his way past tallboys and wardrobes into what was evidently a kitchen. At least it was lit, by small blue gas jets. Marvin was filling a tin kettle at a flat scullery sink.

'Have some Ovaltine?' he said.

'Don't you have a drink?' Several huge hounds had risen from their nest around a paraffin heater and were all nosing damply at Bobby's crotch. A row of parakeets were perched above an Aga range and their droppings hissed like eggs on its surface. Marvin produced a bottle – no cobwebs, no ancient seals. Thank Christ, thought Bobby.

'This place – it's a fuckin' fire-trap.'

'Better than the streets, surely?'

Bobby cast his eyes upwards. If this jerk didn't realize that someone who looked like Bobby never had to sleep on any streets – well, he just didn't know anything.

'It's a dump. A tip. They'll turn you out – for hygiene or something.'

Bobby was secretly amused. So this was how the other half of his people lived. The lower classes.

'I grant you it's unmodernized but we own it.'

'Psycho City,' said Bobby. 'You do have a bathroom?'

Dr Marvin wrenched open a back door, allowing a furious blast of snow into the kitchen. 'In the yard.' He wrestled it shut again. 'No way, Jose!' Bobby unzipped his fly and turned towards the sink.

Marvin modestly averted his eyes and started feeding Cheezits to the small owl that was perched on the back of a rocking-chair. 'Groo,' it said, several times while Bobby peed.

'Well, hey – you must have a stylish little boudoir tucked away somewhere.' Marvin flushed. 'I have a room, yes.'

Marvin was very proud of his room, reclaimed from the general decrepitude, but he wasn't at all sure, now, that he wanted to expose it to someone who seemed less wounded and vulnerable, more smart-assed and high-toned by the minute. Sighing, he put the glasses, bottles and Cheezits on a blackened silver tray and added a candle-sconce to light the back stairs. Bobby Fever glided behind him, parting a grey sea of dog.

They were unlikely to meet any of the Vonderhyde relatives. Most of them had long regressed into saurian prehistory, rooting and snuffling in their dreams of countless aeons, behind padlocked doors. Marvin fed them from the pet-shop stall in Shepherd's Bush market. Only his mother, Alice, could still pass in public but she was a heavy drinker and rarely seen. Marvin worried incessantly. He knew that he alone, respectable and rotund, and his status as Associated Professor, stood between his monstrously decayed family and bureaucracy, publicity, razing and ruin. He paid his poll tax, locked the doors and hoped for the best. Repairs were impossible; he couldn't get into many of the rooms as some of his uncles no longer recognized him. Alice too was aggressive and determined to re-create the comforting conditions of her peasant childhood.

Marvin had seen few rooms outside his home, so his was modelled on his university office. The bare brick-work, wooden shelves and metal waste-basket gave him a warm, familiar sense of academic cut-backs. There was a typewriter on the desk, surrounded by books and small hurricane lanterns. A Calor-gas heater breathed hot air from a corner. A poster for Young Guns II was sellotaped to the wall above a rough shelf containing a huge vase of canna lilies and another lan-tern. The monastic bed with its tartan cover was ob-scured by a fur rug of softly intertwined cats.

Marvin lifted a limp Siamese and sat on the bed, the cat on his knees. Bobby stood by the unsteady mantel-shelf, shaking the damp out of his dark hair which shone black and auburn in the lamp's steady light. He took off his leather jacket and dropped it to the floor. To Marvin he seemed clothed in heavenly light, his white cotton shirt and thin black tie giving him the look of a depraved schoolboy or a raped angel. Bobby turned around and ran his fingers along the shelf of books. 'Barthes, Baudrillard, Derrida . . .' he read aloud, with difficulty. 'Who are they?' Marvin was gazing, stunned, his mouth hanging open, at the frail shoulder-blades and narrow hips.

'Oh – just . . . my work.' He tried to pour some drinks, his hands shaking, the bottle rattling against the glasses. Bobby moved to the bed and laid out the spoon and cup of water he'd brought from the kitchen on an adjacent crate. 'You don't mind if I get comfortable do you?' The boy-whore's phrases came easily to him. Marvin sprang up as if electrocuted.

'No. No. Do what you like.' He knocked back a tumbler-ful of vodka. A gust of wind shook the house. He could hear Alice singing a sea shanty, faintly, next door. Marvin paced around in anguish.

'Bobby ... Bobby – there is something I must tell you.'

Bobby looked bored. Well, yes, perhaps it was a slightly embarrassing situation but what was there to say? Sex is sex, right? The prof had said he'd a good job – he must have plenty salted away. He certainly didn't spend it on upkeep. There couldn't be a cash problem. So – why the fuss? Why didn't he just get on with it? Bobby went on heating the powder and water in his spoon with a Bic lighter.

Marvin clenched his sweaty hands together. He unclenched them. He leaned forward awkwardly, hugging himself tightly. How could he possibly confide in a stranger? How could he explain that he was not only a virgin but that he – he couldn't even trust the boy! He might do anything – out of malice, or carelessness! He might talk. Word would get around. The authorities would descend on the family. Raze the house to the ground. Publicity, terror. Oh dear, oh dear, oh God, oh God. Marvin had a position to maintain. Careless children cost lives. On the other hand how could Marvin refuse what was being so casually offered?

I'll have him and then I'll kill him. The atavistic whisper from his unconscious horrified Marvin.

Bobby put the spoon down carefully and looked up at Marvin, smiling slightly.

'I don't care what your problems are. I couldn't give a shit.' He started to suck up the liquid in the spoon through a cigarette filter into the syringe. 'Don't you even want to know my name? It's Bobby Fever.'

A Fever! A Canker! An infamy! A scion of the loathsome, power-mad renegades who would put them all in jeopardy. But Marvin, turning away to hide his expression, could not prevent a rush of hysterical joy. He would – *he would* – bestow his precious virginity upon this aristocratic execration. He would subjugate him – subjugate them all. They despised his kind, his family. He was poor but he was honest and he would fuck Bobby till he cried tears of blood, till he begged for mercy, till his rectum split. *He would get his own back.* Marvin began to tear at his tie.

'Don't thump about.' Bobby's own tie was around his arm and in his mouth and he spoke indistinctly, his pale eyes focused on the crook of his arm. Marvin unbuttoned more soberly. Yes indeed, he had heard a rumour about this little *momser*. An abomination no doubt – but so pretty. He must calm himself. He spoke again.

'You must try and understand about my family. And about me. You've noticed I have a limp?'

'Yeah. I guess. Quasi – Quasimo – what's his name . . .?'

Marvin turned around and saw Bobby lying on the bed as if his figure was lit by a sudden flash of sheet lightning. The body lay outstretched like a sacrificial victim with one long, black-denimed leg crooked. His hair fell like feathers over the rough pillow and his beautiful eyes were half closed. His skin seemed pearlized in the soft light. He looked so frail. One thin hand fumbled at his fly, trying unsuccessfully to unzip it. The cats were grumbling on the floor. Marvin was overcome with compassion and tenderness. His anger and tension vanished. Bobby would understand everything. He was a gentle, sympathetic boy. Marvin started to undress.

Bobby watched him covertly, through his lashes. His own family had access to every means, medical and financial, with which to perfect their human incarnations. He had never seen a naked primitive before.

Such shape-changing abilities as Marvin might have possessed were no match for the raging chaos of his genes. Bobby had absolutely no understanding of what a seriously decayed family could produce. The recessive genetics, the cross-breeding, the generations of incest – Marvin's DNA resembled psychedelic macramé. Outwardly, in his voluminous tweeds, he could pass. Under them, Vonderhyde had been strapped and tortured into a facsimile of a human being. It was a real DIY job, the work of a born bodger. Marvin shucked his jacket and shirt revealing women's foundation garments of uncertain age and provenance, designed for the fuller figure. They were a grubby pink and insanely restricting. Marvin loosened the strings.

'This corset was my grandma's. I like to keep nice, you know. And decent. You never know when you might get run over.' The flesh gushed out in sweaty rolls. Marvin appeared to have several breasts as well as a vestigial limb, a small, pink, nubby arm and hand extending from his belly button.

'Good foundation wear is what sets a woman – I mean a person – apart.' Bobby covered his mouth and groped in his shirt pocket for his Ray Bans.

From the waist down Marvin wore the bottom half of a black rubber diving-suit, specially customized. He had to cut it open with scissors and more flesh roiled out, nearly reaching the floor fore and aft. The pendulous buttocks were rough and scurfy, the texture of a cow's tongue, covered in nodules and sprouting clumps of hair. The heavy stench of long-unwashed orifices filled the room. The layers of the lower belly completely obscured the sexual organs and were thickly matted with coarse, damped-down hair.

Marvin's genetic inheritance was so scrambled that it had never really decided how many individuals Marvin was, or of what gender, or even what species. All his energy went into maintaining a passable public face while the directionless maelstrom of his genes churned away beneath the tweeds. Marvin's legs were the hind-limbs of a beast. Beneath the rubber they had been crudely splinted and clamped with screws and vices so that they were tortured out of shape, enabling Marvin to walk upright. The bones were winched backwards to breaking point and he walked – or rather limped – with considerable pain.

Bobby looked on as Marvin loosened the screws and took off his shoes to reveal cramped pads with horns of yellowed nail and dropped gratefully to all fours. Marvin wallowed about on the floor using his vestigial flipper to root around in his belly looking for the sexual parts which seemed to have got lost somewhere in all that incontinent flesh.

Bobby closed his eyes. He didn't know quite what to do. He could hardly refuse one of his own kind, particularly someone so pathetic, so desperate. God knows, he'd never been particular before and Marvin obviously had enough money with which to indulge him. But – *really* . . .

Marvin seemed to have shed his inhibitions and overcome his shame. He seethed over to the bed.

'Phew,' he said. 'It's nice to relax. I never usually undress in winter, just loosen the screws when I get home.'

To Bobby, Marvin's horn-rimmed glasses looked incongruous atop the rolling mountains of flesh some of which had started to decay during its long confinement. He nearly laughed.

'Why don't *you* relax, Bobby? Regress a bit?'

'I can't. I've forgotten how.'

Degenerate.

Marvin looked worriedly at him. 'I've trusted you, Bobby. I've trusted you with everything. You can't know how I feel but – oh, be good to me.'

He presented, a little shyly, a split-head penis, pink as wax, bubbling with anticipatory lubrication. He angled it towards Bobby's delicate mouth.

'Two grammes,' said Bobby. 'No – half an ounce.'

'Anything.' *Anything.*

Buried in that noisome groin, Bobby thought hard about his drugs, until he gagged on a ropy syrup of professiorial come.

'Turn over.' Bobby felt several eager hands slide his jeans over his hips. Pinned to the bed by the great *membrum virile* he listened hopelessly to the shrieking of the wind and to someone chanting, far away, the day's racing results.

Finally, sated, Marvin enveloped him in a damp, octopoid embrace. Bobby couldn't see his head but it spoke.

'I love you.'

... When the professor was safely strapped up again, he reverted to a look of academic respectability although he was in a wildly expansive mood.

'That was absolute bliss. I have never known anything like it. How was it for you?'

'Total bliss.'

'Now, Bobby, I have many plans for you. I have so much to teach you, so much to tell you. Now that we have found each other, you will never leave me, will you? I know I'm ugly – no one knows it better than me, but ... You think I'm ugly, don't you? Don't you?'

'Of course not.' Bobby flashed a curious, mocking glance and Marvin shrank.

Inwardly, however, Bobby sighed. Work, work, hustle. Still, things could be worse. He could wheedle a lot of money out of the guy – what did he *do* with his salary? And, anyway, he had nowhere else to go. Richer men were not always so accommodating about drug use. Sexually, Marvin was terminal, he was *the pits* but as Bobby's taste ran to pre-adolescents, so was everyone else with money. He would stay – for a while. Bobby had the infinitely flexible nature of the natural courtesan and the whore's ability to divine unspoken needs. This wasn't really about sex anyway. And Marvin was of course – in his grotesque way – a kindred spirit. Fundamentally, they were the same. Indeed he could even be useful in reconciling Bobby with his family. Low-life had rather palled by now.

And so their strange life began. Marvin was on sabbatical and typed an academic paper all day. He bought Bobby a Walkman and a battery television and a Ralph Lauren green and white silk robe. He bought ice-cream and liqueurs and smoked duck with kiwi fruit and *crème fraîche* and take-away *tapas* and white chocolate. Bobby's contacts came to the door and hesitantly handed in their packages. Bobby was in heaven. He lived on the bed, stoned out of his mind on coke and smack, playing with the kittens. Marvin could rarely be bothered to take off his undergarments. It was a major undertaking and usually he was content to kiss and cuddle which was fine with Bobby. He'd got used to the old guy anyway. Marvin told him a little of his background.

'You know, ever since universities were established in medieval times, there have been some of us placed there to monitor the work and to ensure that no one was engaged in Dark practices. We had some close calls – Descartes, Dee. My family were at Heidelberg for centuries and now – I continue the tradition in Gower Street . . .'

However, Bobby dimly perceived that Marvin's mood

was blackening as he sweated over his paper. One evening, he spun around in his swivel chair and announced: 'Bobby – I need your help. I now know that the Dark has been summoned by academics all over the world. We are in peril.'

'Nonsense. What have novels and poetry to do with the Dark?'

Marvin looked strained. Spittle dribbled down his chin. 'You see me as an Associate Professor of Literature. *Enfin*. But – I am a critical theorist. I know whereof I speak. You must take me to some powerful mediator – I no longer have the contacts I had – and I must warn them. It is my job. Perhaps it can be stopped.'

'No one will see me.'

'Give them my message.'

'They won't listen.'

'Of course they will. It is part of our *raison d'être*.'

'Our what? Oh – all right. I guess I owe you. There's only one person who'll speak to me, though. A relative, a social worker. He's, like, a total creep.'

Silently, Marvin handed him the new cellphone.

Alcott Alzheimer was more than thrilled to hear from Bobby. Bernadine Peste was always begging for news of her son.

'Bobby!' he breathed, 'I *knew* you just needed some space. I *knew* you'd work things through. Adolescence is a very tricky period and conflicts are not unusual . . .'

He was even more ecstatic when Bobby turned up in his office, fiendishly attractive in a new six-button Armani suit with Marvin in tow.

'Bobby – you look wonderful! Have some decaff! I can tell you've matured beyond your – sociopathic episode.' Al punched Bobby roguishly on the shoulder. Bobby stepped back and lit a Gauloise in a sullen, James Dean sort of way.

'Lighten up, Bobby, lighten up! I know a great hyno-
therapist for the little nicotine prob. And you can come
to my Thursday night "Rediscovering Our Feral Selves"
group – or perhaps not, in your case!'

Fuckin' faggot. Bobby said, aloud, 'Al, this is Dr
Vonderhyde from the University. He needs to see
Grandpa Canker – can you fix it up?'

'So you're in the groves of Academe at last Bobby!
Glad to hear it. As for Beau – that's a tall order, a very
tall order. He's at the European Summit this week – but
I'll certainly see what I can do. I'll have to come along
though. Now, how about some ping-pong with my teenage recidivists?'

'I *told* you,' said Bobby, in the cab, 'I *told* you he was
excrement.'

'It doesn't matter. How else would I get to the main
man?' Marvin's vocabulary had become more idiomatic.

They went home and played snap in the kitchen with
Alice who was delighted to have some company and
did a number of music-hall turns.

By the day Al was due to collect them Dr Marvin was in
an acute state of nerves. How could he possibly explain
to this august elder statesman – Beauregard Canker
himself – admittedly one of a renegade clan but powerful beyond belief in worldly affairs, how could he explain what was actually happening in the universities?
Few enough academics could grasp it, let alone anyone
else. Marvin had lost so much weight that he barely
needed his foundation garments any more. Bobby persuaded him to snort some coke 'to give you confidence'
but it made him more jittery than ever.

Beauregard Canker, who had inherited the ancient
English title of Lord Debris, lived in considerable, if

idiosyncratic state. He had served in various far-flung outposts of the Empire before the sun went down, inciting the indigenous peoples to riot and uprising, and now affected orientalism in his Eaton Square town house. He kept an Indian swami and a Chinese sage in his household and the parrots and monkeys should have made Marvin feel at home. Actually it was difficult for anyone to feel at home in those marbled halls, thick with incense.

Canker, dressed in white ducks, sat in a chair made out of elephant tusks, drinking whisky and playing backgammon. He was very, very old with the same high cheekbones and ice-chip eyes as Bobby. His white hair streamed beneath his pith helmet and his long fingers were as hard and yellow as the ivory.

'Great-grandpa Beau? Can you hear me?' started Al. 'I see you are making a positive adjustment to retirement –' Canker clicked a counter into place and motioned to Al to shut up.

'Sit down, sit down,' he said and his voice was like a whisper through the savannah grass.' Ah – Bobby. I knew you'd come back. But you're still a very sick boy. Don't think I can't tell.'

The Indian mystic brought them all some whisky.

Bobby wasn't going to be intimidated.

'Sir – this is Dr Vonderhyde. He's a Professor of Literature. He says the Dark is coming back.'

Canker gestured to his manservant, 'Bring me my pipe.' The half-naked servant-boy knelt over a spirit-lamp. He pierced a black pellet with a long needle, warmed it and plugged the pellet of opium into a heavily jewelled, ornamented pipe and handed it to the old man.

What a degenerate family, thought Marvin. And they call us decayed. Canker's eyelids, as fragile as eggshells, drooped over his cold eyes. Bobby passed Marvin a heap of coke on an ivory letter-opener. Startled, Marvin sniffed it and broke into a sweat.

'Come here, Dr ... er and tell me all about it.' Canker motioned to a footstool.

Marvin found himself sitting next to Canker and muttering disconnectedly. 'It's deconstruction, my lord. In the universities. Everything is mediated through language, particularly through written text. Firstly, deconstruction threatens an oral culture like our own. Secondly it threatens everything. Words have no intrinsic meaning, these people say. Words slip about. Without meaning there is nihilism.' As if very far off Marvin could see Bobby and Alcott seated on an ottoman. Alcott was edging closer to Bobby. Bobby kept moving away. Sweat poured from Marvin's brow. He felt small, grubby and insignificant. He struggled on. 'Language controls everything. We are controlled by language. Language, not knowledge, is power. Speech behaves like writing. Words speak to us. The world is text. History is fiction. So is our own oral history. We can have more control if we desert it. We must have text, to have power. These deconstructionists have more power than ourselves and they are abusing it and condemning us all to nothingness. We must stop them. This is the worst magic ever.'

Marvin halted, on the verge of tears. Why couldn't he give a better account of himself? But – surely – Canker could see that language was everything, was all-powerful? Canker was looking at him benignly.

'My dear young man, I can see how much you care. It is good of you to go to all this trouble. I see you have the same vices as my great-great grandson there, eh?'

Marvin blushed. Damn Bobby.

'No matter. I understand that you are a decent, respectable man. Now, what is it you say? That we – our people – must have written text in order to control? I seem to control well enough anyway ... Words have power, is it? Ah – it recalls to me the poor, dear Zulus. Well, let us try it out.'

He pulled a pad of rather tacky Basildon Bond from under the backgammon board and took a Mark Cross gold pen from his top pocket.

'Now I shall write something totally improbable and we shall see how much power it has. Let's see now ...' He started on some shaky capitals. 'DR – how do you spell it? – VONDERHYDE IS A RAGING PSYCHO-PATH AND UNABLE TO TEACH.'

'That's not quite what I meant,' murmured Marvin but Canker scrawled on. 'BOBBY FEVER IS NOT A DRUG ADDICT.' He pulled the page off.

'There we are. Fair trial, fair trial. Now, do those words have power? Do they speak truth?' He looked at Marvin, standing meekly by his side and at Bobby, nodded out on the couch, one hand clutching his fly. 'Well, sir, perhaps we'll stay with our oral tradition for now. Goodnight, all. Hamit, another pipe.'

As they trailed out Marvin saw the Chinese and Indian wise men conferring anxiously. They, at least, had listened with attention.

'I told you it was pointless. Anyway, even *I* don't know what you're on about.'

'You least of all. Why can't the fool see that we *are* language, we *are* text and without that knowledge we are doomed.'

'Try someone else.'

But Marvin did not know anyone else. He had long lost touch with other Weerde academics and did not know how to go about finding them. He went into a decline. His Assistant Professorship time was up and

was not renewed mainly due to his opposition to deconstruction which continued to rage like a brushfire
through academia. Marvin returned to teach on a lowly
Reader's salary. Bobby had just about cleaned him out
financially. The honeymoon was over. Bobby would
have to cut right back on his expensive habits.

'Why should I? I know a perfectly good way of getting
all the money I need.'

'No! I couldn't stand it. You wouldn't come back.'

Bobby shrugged. He'd got quite fond of the old boy
but his affection stopped far short of penury.

'Your family would give you money. Your mother.'

'Not to live with you they wouldn't. It'd be all on
their terms – sanatoriums in Switzerland, sessions with
Al – save me.'

And, soon:

'What the fuck am I supposed to do all day? Lie
around here like a dildo listening to your ghastly relatives crack bones?'

'You could come to college with me. Enrol.'

'Don't talk balls. I'm a party girl.'

Bernadine Peste circles her chilly rooms, endlessly. She
rubs her hands together. The curtains are always drawn
now. Alice goes to the book-makers, the off-licence and,
on sunny days, to Kensal Green cemetery. Their sons
continue to battle it out.

Marvin started to study late into the night. The bright,
modern paperbacks on his shelves were replaced by
heavy, dark volumes, crusted with leather and metal,
closing with keys and hasps.

'What are those awful dirty black books? Diction-
aries?'

'They are called – don't make a joke – *grimoires*.

There must be a way to convince the tribe. There must. I'm trying something very risky –'

'Dark practices?' said Bobby, hopefully.

Marvin looked scornful. 'Who remembers our own Dark practices? *We didn't write them down.* However, there are other sources . . .'

Bobby stretched. 'It's all crap anyway. Don't bother. Forget it.' Marvin glanced coldly at Bobby.

'You don't understand. You see, if we had written everything down too, we'd have access to our own occult history. We wouldn't have this half-remembered mish-mash of odds and sods and we'd be able to use our ancient powers and abilities coherently. As it is, I have to depend on these others. It's my last chance. If I do something really spectacular, they'll listen.' He put down *Culte des Goules.* 'I'm prepared to try anything. Fight fire with fire. If I don't, we're doomed. The old ones forget and youngsters like you just aren't inter-ested in maintaining even the oral history. We'll lose everything.'

Bobby yawned. 'You're an important guy.' His eyes were fixed on the tiny television. He was chewing gum and occasionally blew a perfect, translucent, rainbow bubble. 'Can I have some money?'

'There must be a way to convince them. To show them how the power – old and new – can work. Should work, could work together even. I could give our race mastery, security. If they'd only listened to me. I'd teach them how words work.'

'*Et ta soeur,*' said Bobby rudely. He'd learned a few things from his mother.

But, late at night, when the winter winds rattled the casements Bobby could hear Marvin mutter endless, disjointed words and phrases as though all his learning had scattered and fragmented. They made no sense at

all and even when Marvin lay silent, Bobby knew that
he was not asleep.

Marvin's behaviour became more erratic. Once he
brought a homeless alcoholic home – *why?* – and Bobby
had to throw the derelict out. Another time Bobby had
come into the room to find Marvin had shaved two
parakeets and crudely clipped their wings. Bald and
bleeding they staggered over the desk, picking feebly at
themselves and each other. Marvin was holding a
syringe.

'I've given them some of your stuff,' he said without
looking up. 'And some rum. They're not pretty now, are
they?' He started to laugh.

'Oh my God,' cried Bobby, 'the poor things. Put them
out of their misery. What's wrong with you? Sometimes
I think Grandpa Beau was right. You're crazy.'

'It's an important part of the ritual.'

The end came suddenly. The first night – it was a
Friday – that Dr Marvin returned home to find Bobby
gone he had a violent attack of asthma. He then went
into the kitchen and started to eat all the junk food that
Bobby had left lying around. Cheerios, Cheezits, Tortilla
Snax, Phileas Fogg cinnamon and garlic poppadoms,
Nachitos, Twixes, Picnics, Topics and a lot of small
sweets shaped like milk-bottles. He crammed them all
into his mouth, washing them down with gin, gagging
and choking. He ate some cans of Pal, Kennomeat, Pedi-
gree Chum and some Whiskas salmon-flavour for the
gourmet cat. His eyes were resting thoughtfully on a rare
plumed cockatoo when he snapped out of it and went
upstairs to wait. (*Bobby is waving goodbye from the deck
of a ship. He flourishes a vast wad of money and with an
extravagant gesture, kisses it. Bobby is walking out,
closing the door. He is bathing in a river of molten gold,*

his head encircled by fireflies, he is swinging high in a beribboned cradle pushed by several heavily muscled men in sailor suits. They are singing 'Mad about the Boy'. Bobby is leaving the room, closing the door. A tall man embraces him on a balcony, thousands cheer, Bobby is leaving the room –.) Marvin started to sob.

When Bobby came in at 2 a.m. Marvin threw a potty full of urine over him and then embraced him forcefully, smothering him with ardent kisses.

'Leave it OUT!' Bobby twisted like an angry cat. 'I can't take this. You're all sticky. God – I'm soaked. Gross. I didn't go anywhere *anyway*. I just went to Paul the Dog's, see if he *had* anything, but he didn't.'

'I'll wash,' said Marvin humbly.

'Don't bother, fuck-face.'

By the following evening Bobby was really sick. He sat shivering on the corner of the bed, his arms wrapped round his knees, wearing his Ray Bans against the desk-light glare.

'Get something out on your cashcard.'

'No. Anyway the bank took it back.'

'Cash a cheque at the Queensway bureau de change. I don't need much.'

'What difference does it make? If it's not today it's tomorrow. I'm nearly – what do you say? – skint as it is.'

'It makes a difference to *me*. I'm like, sick NOW. Not tomorrow. I'll think of something by then.'

'No.'

'Asshole, pig-face, cunt, deformity.'

By about midnight Bobby had had enough. He got up and lit a cigarette from a candle.

'I don't have to take this sort of treatment. Someone'll help me. You just don't care. You don't know how

much you disgust me, fuckin' shit-sack, fuckin' heartless, immoral —'

Bobby walked unsteadily towards the door and
turned on Marvin again.

'You ought to try it, you ought to just fuckin' *try* it,
you try throwing up and then shitting in your pants, oh
I forgot, you do anyway. Sorry, Miss Mess.' He narrowed
his eyes.

'You'll never get anyone else you know. You're just,
like total repulsiveness, you know that? No other boy
would be crazy enough to touch you, you're just a dead-
end faggot freak — me, I'm straight — I can go home and
marry a rich girl, so there, penis-breath!'

Marvin swung round in the swivel chair. His face
was mottled red as though he had been slapped.

'We'll go up to Queensway,' he said, quietly.

'What?'

'Queensway!'

'Sweetheart!'

Bobby ran down the stairs singing 'The One and
Only'.

It was a cool spring evening. There was a light, misty
rain falling as they walked, hand in hand, up the street,
crushing broken blossoms under their feet. Marvin
cashed his cheque, handed the money to Bobby and
waited patiently outside a Bayswater squat. When
Bobby returned his hair was combed and he smelled of
soap. They caught a night bus to the Embankment and
walked, slowly for Marvin's sake, towards Hungerford
Bridge.

'Look at the river.'

'Sweet Thames run softly till I end my song,' said
Marvin automatically, 'It's always there. It's an old
river.'

'Older than you?'

'Bitch.'

They smiled at each other and climbed the steps to the bridge. The rain was coming down more heavily now, like an ink wash over the city dawn. Bobby looked far into the distance. The familiar cityscape lay, as if blessed, shot through with shafts of light from beyond the heavy clouds. Beneath them the river moved like a nightmare; shadow and bones, liquid and light. The church bells were ringing. They had been ringing for centuries. *I do not – know ... Said the great bell of Bow ...*

'A city,' murmured Marvin, 'half as old as time.'

'Romantic, yeah?' Bobby turned round. 'You can suck my knob if you like. I don't care.'

Marvin shook his head. 'Your language – it's always been terrible.'

Marvin placed his heavy, red hands on each side of Bobby's face – *You're so beautiful I hate you, it's too late* – and gently stroked the dampened cheeks. He started to lick them, hungrily sucking at the flesh. Bobby jerked back – 'Leave it out' – and Marvin punched him, hard in the eye. Marvin tore at Bobby's shirt with his teeth. Swiftly he pulled some piano wire from his cuff and bound one of Bobby's wrists tightly to the railing before reaching up and encircling his neck with the wire, then bringing it back down to encircle Bobby's other hand, the wire cutting cruelly into the pearly flesh. All the time he was muttering, huffing and puffing and trains kept rumbling and squealing over the bridge, their lights sweeping over the struggling figures. Bobby could hear nothing.

'Disrepair – disregard – disinter – disintegrate; humiliate, destroy, damnation, abomination, break on a wheel, out like a light. Far from home, remember the ways, the path to the caves, deeds not words!' Marvin was sobbing as he tore the skin from Bobby's abdomen with teeth and nails.

A passer-by approached. Marvin loomed over Bobby, biting his lips shut before he could cry out and grinding his own groin lasciviously into the sagging figure. The footsteps quickened and faded away. Marvin started to moan and chant. He could feel his engorged penis throbbing and pounding behind the hot black rubber. He started cracking the bones. 'Show the world, take the mantle, steal the skin, quick the soul, engorge the essence, assume the other –' Half-remembered, scattered phrases rushed through his brain, he was lost, he was shunned, he parted the clouds and swallowed the sun – worrying furiously with his teeth like a terrier he sought sorcery and eternity, found only frail flesh and splinters, pierced the heart with a gush of black blood and dragged it out with his incisors. Chewing, gagging on gristle he stood up slowly and with both hands pulled the heart from his mouth and raised it to the morning. Heavenly music crashed around him, loud as thunder, and a sudden gust of rainy wind showered him with confetti, petals and scraps of lace. Gradually his breathing calmed and he began to walk thoughtfully away, the heart now tucked close to his own. Bobby was left, splayed on the bridge, a sacrifice to the city.

Marvin began to breathe freely, deeply, intoxicated by the bright air. He was tall, sleek as a greyhound, he glided down the steps, a ghost, a swan. Bobby – *pssst.* He spat. An outcast amongst outcasts, too human by half.

Now he – as beautiful as the day, as dark as the oldest night – he knew what to do with beauty. First – a lavatory; he needed to smell the soap, to stare deep into his own chipped-diamond eyes and feel the rich

sweep of his soft black-auburn hair through the comb.
Then, calmly – no more asthma, ever – he strolled north-
wards, smiling seductively at each passer-by. Blinded
by the light they turned away in confusion.

Marvin put on his Ray Bans. It was the morning of
the world. He had rediscovered the long-lost rites and
forced them to a resolution. He must tell someone – no!
He just needed to stand here – or there – in ornate
rooms and the caressing, loving gaze would always fall
on him. They were born to serve him. His mind felt
sharp as an adze. With such beauty, with such brains –
what might he not do? He had emerged ... *almighty* ...
victorious. What grace, what favours, what futures ...
what now ...

My love
The waste
My life
For ever and ever
My self ...

Dr Marvin limped slowly towards the Strand, a rotund,
placid figure, remorseless in his respectability. A police
car streamed past, its siren shattering the morning. The
city was waking up. He felt free and light-hearted for
the first time in his life.

He started to whistle.

He knew that there was one last rite he must perform.
He had ingested what he needed of the heart to complete
his transformation and ensure its permanence – oh yes,
they would listen to him now when they saw what he
had done. He had made the words work. He had brought
ancient rituals to life and now, he and he alone, had the
knowledge to unite these glorious powers with the new
world. He would offer a sacrifice to the new gods – O
Belial, O Barthes! – to the most powerful gods now in

the world. The Gods of Language. He must carry the heart to the books. He alone could unite the old and the new, complete the cycle and in doing so, transcend it and achieve immortality for himself and his tribe. He would break into a library, a very large library and once safely inside he was going to crawl right up into the middle of the warm, warm text and there he would rest for a while until the world came to claim him for its own.

RED, HOT AND DARK

Charles Stross

Moscow: Monday morning, 20 August 1991:

The soldiers on the back of the personnel carriers stared around, wide-eyed, clutching their rifles like drowning men hanging on to buoyant life-rafts. They were out of their depth, teenage conscripts from the sticks being trucked in by the grey men in the Kremlin, none of them sure what they were meant to be doing there. The *émigré* group seemed to be taking it quite well as the BMPs rumbled past their hotel. They clustered in the bar, talking quietly in small groups, occasionally pestering a vodka out of the distracted staff. Reporters swarmed and darted everywhere, like wasps around a rubbish bin in summer. And Oleg Meir . . .

Oleg Meir ignored the soldiers as he left the temporary safety of the hotel. The phones were down, only international calls from the city's contingent of foreign correspondents getting through. *They must be crazy*, he thought, *cutting off communications at a time like this.* Trembling with a chill, he thrust his hands deep into his coat pockets as he walked back towards the University. He glanced up at the clock jutting from the face of one of the office buildings on the opposite side of the road. It was almost ten o'clock! He'd have to hurry. Oleg increased his pace until it was little short of a trot. *Got to get the papers, destroy them or something. Change myself, get lost in the crowd. That way they*

*won't find me. If I can do it before Andrei catches up
with me . . .*

Yesterday's events had brought everybody out on to
the streets; everyday life had ground to a halt. The air
was filled with tension, as if an abscess was about to
burst. Never had he seen crowds of people who all
looked so *angry*; it scared him almost as much as the
horror of a remembered guilt, the phone call in the early
hours from his mysterious patron – just before the
public lines went down.

Tanks were drawn up in the square outside the University, their engines ticking over, soldiers milling
around uncertainly in front of a throng of defiant
youths; they made no attempt to detain the bespectacled
professor as he made his way past them towards the
concrete monolith of the Institute of Space Sciences.
Nobody stopped him as he went in, but he noticed a
few anomalies: a distinct shortage of staff, a surfeit of
students milling around the foyer, chattering.

Can't be good. Oleg made for the elevator, half-
remembered skills blending him with the shadows like
a third element of light and darkness. *Too many people
about.* The elevator began to rise. He yawned uncontrol-
lably. The elevator stopped; its brass gate slid open.
'Professor Meir?'

Oleg jumped. 'Who is – oh, Anatoly. What is it?'

The student stared at him. 'You looked a bit preoccupied, that's all,' he said. 'About the course work, I know
it's overdue –'

'Don't worry about it.' Oleg looked away. 'Heard the
news?'

'What news?'

'Don't worry.' Moving down the corridor towards his
office, the student following him, Oleg had things on
his mind. 'Have you got a few minutes?'

'For you, Professor?' The student's elaborate shrug was wasted. Oleg was too busy unlocking his office to notice.

'These filing cabinets. Do me a favour, get everything out of the top drawer there, stacked in order, and put it on the table. Please? I'll make it worth your while.'

'How worthwhile?' Something nudged Oleg's attention, but when he looked up Anatoly looked back at him innocently. 'A regrading?'

'You said it, not me.' Anatoly turned to the filing cabinet eagerly. 'Now if you will excuse me –'

The terminal on Oleg's desk was an antique, but it still connected him to the machines in the basement. To his surprise, Oleg found that his palms were sweating as he sat down and logged on. *This has gone too far.* He shivered and glanced over his shoulder. *If Andrei gets his grubby hands on these there won't be an excuse under heaven that'll save me!* Still he hesitated. Something in the air tickled his nostrils; scent of wood smoke and gasoline far away, screams remembered in the moonless night. *From her.* Behind him, Anatoly was systematically stripping his files from their steel nest. *Oh well. It had to happen – now or later.*

Oleg began to type, carefully – the sluggardly machine could barely keep up with his key pressure – a short e-mail message. He stared at it for a few minutes after he finished it, trying to understand what he had done. *To KGBVAX*, the police monitor on the net. *User: Valentin016.* An anonymous label. *Danger.* He'd been sweating before he started. Now he pressed enter, consigning the message to the invisible guts of the connected mainframes, where it would find it's way eventually to the destination –

To Valentina. Who'd know what to do, if anyone did. Oleg logged out and turned around, stood up and stretched, and stared at the student working on his files. *Time to think about avoiding Andrei. Why did I ever let it get this far?* he wondered. Hands deep in pockets, he wandered over to the window and stared out towards the distant Kremlin. *Dancing with the devil* ...

Twenty five years ago:

Oleg had first met Andrei back in sixty-three, maybe sixty-four, back when he had been a young student of astrophysics, fresh in from the sticks. Always the terrified compulsion to look up at the stars — attending Shklovskii's bull sessions about intelligent life in the universe made him feel out of control, his thin veneer of sophistication in danger of cracking open to reveal the depths of his superstitious fear. The feeling had a shuddery attraction to Oleg, who was unable to join in the merry banter of his colleagues.

'You see, comrades, if we are not alone in the universe, the very fact of our lack of uniqueness has implications for our way of life! No longer are we part of an isolated, unique trend. Other intelligences, once their existence can be proven, would provide a powerful stimulus to our exploratory tendencies. Such intelligences, should they be more advanced than us, may be expected to be in constant communication even if physical interstellar travel is impossible — yes? What is it? Meir, again?'

Oleg cleared his throat. 'I think you overlook something,' he said, suddenly aware that his heart was pounding. 'Perhaps, all is stillness and quiet not because we are alone ... but because they are scared. After all, ideas can be dangerous, can they not? Just as socialist ideas are considered dangerous by the capitalists, so may there be *darker* things lurking among the stars. Things that listen, like us, for the transmissions of the unwary ...'

'Like Voice of America?' some wit interrupted, and the whole room burst out laughing.

Oleg sat down, his face turning beetroot. He looked round, searching for support against the hilarity – there was a man he had never seen before at the back of the hall, and his expression was set and thoughtful. Something about him was vaguely familiar, like a half-remembered family photograph. Oleg looked away rapidly, and tried to ignore the good-natured joshing he received after the lecture from those who believed that the laws of dialectical materialism applied to interstellar communication. But somehow the face stuck in his mind; and he was not surprised when, two days later, he was awakened by a peremptory rap on the door of his room.

Struggling out of bed, Oleg made his way to the door. 'Who is it?' he called, half-hoping that it was the apartment warden about to complain again about him lying in on a perfectly good Saturday –

'Open up!' called a voice outside. 'We haven't got all day!'

Oleg tensed, shivering with more than cold – muscles bunching and coiling like ropes beneath his skin – then opened the door a crack. 'What's it about?' he asked. 'I was in bed –'

'Never mind that. You can get dressed now. You're going for a drive in the country this morning, how about that? Don't bother packing, you'll be back before sunset, I promise. Come along now!'

Goaded into sudden action, Oleg grabbed his clothes and began to yank them on haphazardly. 'You can come in,' he called when he had his trousers belted. The door opened. 'Have we met?' he asked politely.

The stranger shut the door behind him. 'Two nights ago, at the Institute, I was in the row behind you.'

Oleg's shoulders slumped with something like relief.

'I thought you were with the Cheka,' he muttered as he buttoned his shirt.

The stranger looked at him and smiled, exposing his teeth. 'You thought right – sort of. The people I'm with ... the KGB don't like us, but we don't have to put up with them. Do the initials GRU mean anything to you?' Oleg stared uncomprehendingly. 'Good. *Now* they do. We're going for a little drive in the country, and we'll have lunch at a dacha and I'm sure you'll enjoy our little chat; I'll drop you off back here this evening. How does that sound, comrade?'

Mouth dry, heart pounding again: 'You want me to be an informer?' Oleg pulled on his boots, not looking at the man from the GRU, whatever that was, trying to memorize his face in case he had to –

'Don't be an idiot. We're not the fucking MVD; we're the *army*. What you were saying about contact with extraterrestrial civilizations interests us ... we just want to ask you a few more questions, bounce some ideas about, see what you can come up with. And you know something else?' Oleg jumped round as a hand landed on his shoulder, then froze. A faintly familiar smell tickled at his nostrils like the memory of a forgotten sin. 'I was right,' said the stranger who had stolen his identity. Then, in a language far older than Russian – '*How long have you been living alone among the humans, my friend?*'

Moscow: lunch-time, 20 August 1991:

Cosmology and guilt and a blind fear of the unknown blurred together in Oleg's mind as he tried to concentrate on what he was doing. A trip to see the big military radar system at Semipalatinsk blurred into the dog-eared files he was lifting out of the back of his cabinet, vast banks of humming tubes meshed with the sleek

Western computer chained to his desk. Time was of the essence: panic was . . .

Possible. The big old radio beside the window was tuned to Radio Free Europe, but the MVD were jamming it again for the first time in years, the *pock-pock-whirr* of microwaves blasted into the ionosphere to stop the people learning of the crimes committed against them. *Radar stations in the hands of Andrei and his Dark-worshippers.* Oleg shuddered, uncertain. *Just as long as he doesn't know where to point them.* He looked up, clutching a sheaf of papers about Cepheid variables. 'Get me everything you can find under Krasnoyarsk,' he muttered.

'Under what?' Anatoly looked perplexed.

'Krasnoyarsk,' Oleg repeated. 'It's a radar installation. You know? One of the big ones the military let us borrow.'

'Oh, *that.* Isn't it one of the ones comrade General Secretary agreed with the Americans to dismantle?'

Oleg sniffed, bitterly amused by the way Anatoly still referred to Gorbachev by his title. 'I see. What do you expect to find there, boss? Is that where they're holding him?'

'Not on another planet,' Oleg muttered, thumbing through notes made years ago. The pile of paper was inches thick, held together with rough string and stale lies. Some of the documents were twenty, thirty years old: some were new, and of these a number bore CONFI-DENTIAL stamps. Oleg had removed these from his safe.

He sighed as he contemplated the documents with a mixture of fear and pride. *My life's work, and this is all there is to it?* Itchy fear made the skin in the small of his back crawl; his leg muscles twitched, aching to be elsewhere. *If Andrei gets hold of these . . .* they were the

originals, not the precisely-faked duplicates he had filtered to the GRU Colonel over the past years. Careful
cooperation, playing the useful idiot to find out how
much Andrei knew, who his friends were, that was one
thing. But this was for real; the probable coordinates of
the end of the world ... he stopped subvocalizing so
suddenly that he nearly bit his tongue. Maybe they
knew where he came from, what he had done. Frightened, he looked over his shoulder, but only a bust of
Lenin was watching. He scooped up the bundle and
began to squeeze it into his briefcase. Halfway through
the process he discovered that it wasn't going to fit
unless he emptied the case first; he up-ended it over the
carpet. Anatoly watched with what Oleg assumed to be
amused tolerance. He had to leave out the confidential
papers, the ones about Krasnoyarsk, but finally everything fitted together and he bent down to close his case.

Behind him, Anatoly cleared his throat. 'There's something you should know, Professor.'

Oleg turned to Anatoly, who stood behind him, and
sniffed, although he could tell perfectly well what was
happening. His guts loosened abruptly. 'What's going
on? Where did you get that gun?' He tried to conceal
his dismay as his companion stared at him. 'What's
happening?'

'This way, Academician.' The gun was small, oily-
looking, the hole in its muzzle horribly dark; he could
see the rifling in the barrel, which pointed straight at
him. 'Your services are required. Happenings more significant than the current ... ruckus, are being expedited
under cover of the confusion. Events of cosmic importance. You could say the trigger just fell into our hands.'
Anatoly – the being who wore the student Anatoly's
face – gestured Oleg backwards.

Oleg glanced left and right, but there was no way

out. He backed slowly towards the door. The stranger was holding his briefcase, and Oleg had a gut-deep feeling that his living cooperation was not essential. 'What do you want with me?' he whispered.

'Just cooperate. Through the door. Into the lift.'

The lift grilles rattled open behind him. The gunman crowded in close, thrusting the muzzle of his weapon into a coat pocket to conceal it from bystanders. 'Press the first-floor button.'

Oleg did as he was told, obedient, tense, knees trembling. 'What are you doing?' he mumbled.

'Taking you somewhere safe.' Anatoly sounded bored by the question.

'But – this is crazy! Why are you kidnapping me? Who are you?'

The rough walls of the lift shaft rose up on either side. 'Don't be naïve, Oleg. You made a bargain years ago: your research to continue, with our support, in return for obedience – when the time came. And what happens? You call your KGB kitten! That's not what I call obedience. And the falsehoods you've been feeding us this past year have not amused us greatly. Anyone would think you were trying to play a two-way game ... and you know what happens to people who get caught in the middle.'

The lift came to a stop. Oleg looked around frantically. The lobby outside the elevator cage was deserted but for four Interior Ministry soldiers, rifles at the ready. One of them crossed the floor and pulled the doors open. Anatoly gestured him back with his free hand. 'Forward, Professor. We have a long journey ahead of us.' He smiled as one of the guards opened the front door to reveal an armoured personnel carrier backed up against it, engine running. 'Glad you could make the party!'

*

Leningrad: Monday morning, 20 August 1991:

Valentina was waiting impatiently in the station lobby at the airport, a woollen coat pulled tight around her; when she saw the uniformed man she waved. He approached her rapidly. 'This had better be good,' she said.

He looked away from her. 'Maybe not,' he said, so quietly that the words were nearly lost in the omnipresent traffic roar. Louder: 'There's a message for you from Moscow, high priority. You want to read it here?'

Valentina stared at him. *Just another uniformed flunky.* 'Give it to me.'

He passed her the sealed slip and hung around, evidently pleased with himself. She hadn't bitten his head off, which was an unexpected bonus: Major Valentina Pavlova was notorious for expecting of her subordinates the same efficiency that she was known for herself.

She read the message quickly, face expressionless in the gloom. The officer glanced around, nervously; there were few people in the airport today, and when he looked at them they turned away pointedly. 'What's going on?' he asked. 'First the putsch, then this priority traffic –'

She stopped him with a brisk shake of the head. 'I wouldn't worry about the coup if I were you. It will all be over soon. I need to get to Moscow as soon as possible. Take a message! When you see me leave, tell Major Gromov I'll report back in three days, until then I'll be in deep cover.'

'You'll be –' she stared at the messenger until his eyes watered and he looked away.

'Don't ask. Tell him it's urgent. Is that understood, sergeant?'

He straightened up, saluted. 'Yessir!'

'Good.' She was already moving, walking towards the check-in desk, coat billowing out behind her.

'What is it?' he called over her shoulder.

'Got a plane to catch,' she said, hurrying through the door.

'Authorization –'

'No problem.'

'Papers? Channels?'

'No time.'

'As you say, Major.' They approached the milling crowd at the ticket counter together. The queue was long and agitated, worried travellers anxious to return to their own republics; but when Valentina produced her official pass everybody scattered to one side. Despite the resentful glances, some things never changed.

'Yes? What is it?' sniffed the clerk. She looked tired and irritated.

'This. Where is your manager?'

She thrust his badge under the clerk's nose. It didn't have the desired effect. The woman snorted, as if amused: 'You don't expect that to get you anywhere, do you? Chekist. We've had enough of your kind . . .'

Valentina reached out with a fluid motion and grabbed the clerk by one wrist. 'You do as I say,' she said quietly. 'Otherwise I break your arm. Do you understand?'

The clerk mouthed something silently, her eyes growing round with surprise and sudden pain. 'What – what do you want?' she stuttered.

'To see whoever is in charge here,' she said, 'of the air defence facilities. I have a plane to catch, to Moscow.'

'But no flights are scheduled!' protested the clerk. Valentina let go of her wrist, but continued to stare at her unblinkingly.

'*Now* there is. I repeat; where is the manager? I have a plane to catch.'

The clerk picked up a telephone handset and began to dial, glancing up warily at Valentina as she did so. 'I'll see what can be done, but I make no promises,' she said.

Valentina caught the sergeant's eye; he nodded imperceptibly. 'Tell Gromov,' she emphasized. 'It is essential.'

The clerk paused. 'But *why*?' she asked, curiosity getting the better of her fear. 'What's so important?'

Valentina glanced over her shoulder at her assistant. 'She asks what's so important,' she said quietly, all the time conscious of the crowd watching over his shoulder, not yet nasty but quite capable of turning if they saw something not to their liking ... 'What's important? I'll tell you what's important,' she said. 'If we don't get to Moscow by noon, both you and your boss can look forward to an extended holiday in Siberia ... whoever's in charge ...'

Moscow: three o'clock:

The ancient Kamov chopper she'd requisitioned clattered into the Moscow air defence region. The phones were down: whether it would have made any difference was questionable. Valentina sat in the middle of the narrow, glassed-in cockpit, beside the pilot. Her jaw was rigid, as tense as steel; her eyes were focused on a point a million miles away, replaying cinema reels of memory. Glacial, slow memories. Memories of an interview, not long after she'd come to Moscow: memories of a militiaman long forgotten, one of the kin, who'd helped her change her life ...

They'd been lucky to find her. Not so much gone to the dogs as abandoned to the humans ... twenty-nine, addicted to heroin, living as a street prostitute, a member of the officially non-existent underground encouraged by the Brezhnev faction during their twenty-year reign of hypocrisy. *My, but they did a good job of westernizing us fast! All the vices and none of the virtues* . . . lost in her memories, she blinked, astonished by the strange value systems her own mind was capable of throwing up. *Hey, live among humans for long enough, you even start thinking like one* –

It had been pure coincidence. One of the street-sweeps they'd been so keen on under Andropov; the Weerde who finally found her was a militia lieutenant assigned to mopping up the untouchables who weren't meant to contaminate the crime sheets of the squeaky-clean new order – after all, prostitution and drug abuse were Western problems, weren't they? She remembered the cigarette smoke rising in spirals from the ashtray on the scarred desk, the long interviews by lamplight as they tried to work out who she knew and why she had been tolerated for so long: unable to admit publicly that all cultures have a dark side, that everyone needs something to be afraid of, to lust after, some forbidden fruit . . .

The policeman looked at the woman in the fur coat, black minidress, tights and make-up that weren't even in the shops for people to queue for. The first thing that had caught his attention was how *attractive* she was. Thin, but not gaunt, young-looking but not a child. She shouldn't be pretty, not with the kind of lifestyle she had – a three-bag-a-day habit, not to mention the chalk mixed with the damned Afghan dust by her scum-bag dealer. 'We know all about you,' he said, tapping her folder meaningfully, and she had laughed at him like a wolf in the depths of a winter forest.

'No matter how much you think you know about me you will *never* know all about me,' she said. She stared at him with black, glittering eyes, ice-cubes that didn't melt under the lamp.

'*Really*?' he asked. To a human it would have sounded like something between a cough and a grunt.

Her eyes had widened, but not from fear: he had seen her fingers flexing to strike, and tensed. 'If my brother sent you to get me back,' she had said, 'you can tell him I'm not interested.'

The cop had leaned forward, exposing his throat: 'Really?' he asked. 'And why would your brother do a thing like that?'

'Because he loves me. Or he thinks he does. I don't think he would know love if it bit his throat out. All he's in love with is the Dark.' She relaxed her hands, looked down; noticed for the first time how bony they looked. As if her skin had become a translucent film, a winding-sheet for her skeleton, in the undead time since she came out of the forest. 'That's why I left. After our parents died.'

The cop had leaned back, the hardest bit of the interview over: making her decide to talk. 'And since leaving, is that when you began to hang out on the street?'

She shrugged. A certain tension had gone out of the interrogation; now it was more like a conversation. 'It's a living. I have no papers, as you may have noticed . . .'

'*That can be remedied.*' She blinked rapidly, surprised by a stab of resentment. *Trapped.* 'But first, it would help if you would answer a couple of questions. Strictly on a cooperative basis; it makes it look better on the record.'

'Like what?' she asked, forcing herself to relax. The sense of being caught in a trap intensified.

'Like beginning with when you last saw your brother?'

'Huh.' She snorted. It would have been a laugh if she'd been human. 'He wrote to me until a year or two ago; I burned the letters. He always knows where I am;

where he is I don't think even the KGB knows.' She stared at him. 'Do they?'

'Really!' The Kin who was also a militia lieutenant shrugged. 'Hey, don't look at me like that. The word has gone out from on high that people like you don't exist. So what are you going to do about it?'

'Why should I do *anything* about it?' she asked, feeling a chill run up and down her spine as she met his gaze. This was what she'd been afraid of for a long time, since the icy nights so long ago: the loss of her freedom of action. 'I'm doing very well as it is.'

'No you're not.' He had stared at her until she was forced to look away. 'You're ill. Your shit-head of a pimp is cutting your fix with chalk, you know that? Your apartment has slime on the walls and the residents hate you – that's why you're here. You were fingered.'

'So what business of yours is it, how I go about destroying myself?' she asked, mustering a calm as brittle as her paper-fine skin. 'Why do you want to stop me?'

The cop reached out and took her hand – gambling that nobody would be watching this interview, that it was not a hidden test of some kind – '*because you're one of us and you've been hurt by those fucking animals,*' he grunted. Her eyes flickered left and right, but she didn't pull away. She could feel his pulse against her skin, fast, like any other of her kind. 'How long is it since you had a proper meal?'

'What's one of those?' she asked. 'Hey, don't lay that shit on me!' *Now* she pulled away. 'I can look after myself. What are you after?'

The lieutenant glanced at the ceiling, abashed. 'Nothing,' he said after a moment. 'I don't want anything from you. At least nothing you can give me. I just thought –'

She reached out and touched his hand. 'OK,' she said. '*Comrade*. So that's what it is?' She looked at him askance. 'That's *all* it is?'

'And a full list of all your partners in crime,' he added, 'but that's no reason to run away from me. I'm not a monster. I'll settle for the humans.'

'Uh-huh.'

They sat in silence for a minute as Valentina collected her nerves for the next step in the process. There was an inevitability to it, a determinism, which scared and exhilarated her; *will everything begin to get better, now*? 'There is one thing, though,' she said quietly.

'What's that?'

'For the records, we need an excuse. I can't just disappear.'

'So?' The temperature in the cell seemed to drop a couple of degrees.

'I want to cut a deal.'

'Oh.'

Then Val leaned forward intently. 'My help,' she whispered, 'in return for yours. I'll need a hand afterwards, you see. I'll give you everything you want. But in return I need something.'

'And what would that be?' asked the cop, leaning back in his chair, staring at her with cool expectation.

She licked her lips. 'I've been thinking,' she said. 'This is no career for a lady. But tell me, do you know how easy it is to get a job in the undercover police?'

She was awakened by the change in engine noise as the chopper came in to land. From the military field it was a half-hour drive into the city. She was out of the police car as soon as it pulled up outside the Institute building; before she reached the doors some students emerged. They gathered in front of her, blocking the path. 'What do you want here?' demanded one of them, a fat, balding man with a beard and the look of an agitator about him. 'Who the hell are you?'

She stared at him, breathing hard. 'Is Academician Meir in his office today?' she asked, 'I need to speak to him urgently.'

'I'll *bet* you do,' began the fat man, only to be cut off by one of his companions, a woman. 'Wait! Who are you? Why do you want to see the Professor?'

'He's in danger,' she said simply. Nameless emotions threatened her control; she fought back ruthlessly, steeling herself for the big half-truth. 'I want to get him out of it.'

Almost at once the students crowded in. 'You're too late,' said the woman. 'Militia came for him oh, half an hour ago! In an APC.' She positively bristled. 'Fuckers threatened to shoot anyone who got in their way –' There was an angry rumbling from behind.

'Do you have any idea where they were taking him?' she asked, excitement and dread washing through her.

'No, but, hey! What –'

She pushed past the fat man. 'Where's Oleg's office?' she asked.

'Here. I'll take you.' It was the woman student again. They hurried indoors, then waited interminably for a creaking lift to arrive. 'We've barricaded the stairs – if they try to root us out we'll shut off the lift motor,' said the student. 'Who *are* you?'

'A friend of Oleg's. Not all the security forces are against you,' said Val. The lift doors opened and they crowded in. 'Where did they go?'

'One of them – an informer, looked like one of us – came and took the Academician downstairs. Oh, there's his office.'

'Looks like he left in a hurry,' observed Valentina, as

the student swung the lift doors open and darted into the room. 'Hey, what a mess! What . . .'

The woman leaned over the desk, concentrating. 'These are all his papers. Shit.'

Valentina stepped closer, her right hand thrust deep into her pocket. 'What are they about?' she demanded.

'This – these are all confidential! I didn't know Professor Meir worked for the army –'

She turned and made a dash for the lift; Valentina followed her, grabbed the back of her coat. 'Wait,' she hissed. 'What *kind* of papers?'

The student twisted round, then saw Valentina's expression. 'Uh –'

Breathe. Relax. Val forced herself to smile. 'What were they about?'

'Uh . . . oh. Something about the radar base at Krasnoyarsk. You know it? Big rocket forces base. They're going to dismantle it soon. Uh. I could have sworn you –'

But Valentina wasn't there any more, wasn't in the lift; was back through the office then halfway down the stairs and out to the police car before she stopped to think, before the student could even blink back afterimages of what she had *thought* she'd seen in Val's face.

'Airfield,' Val snapped at her driver, 'fast!' Rubber screeched. 'I've got a plane to catch.' *Why Krasnoyarsk?* she puzzled, consulting her inner oracle, her memory of her brother. But all he did was shrug and smile and say something: and all she could make out was one phrase. *Three thousand megawatts.*

Oleg Meir peered out of the small, dim porthole and tried to ease the pain in his wrists. The handcuffs were too tight, and the fleshy part of his hands tingled with

pins and needles. A simple exercise, thinning out his
own flesh, would ease it – but his captors knew who
they were dealing with, and there were limits to what
could be done in an hour or two. Besides, with fists the
size of a baby's he'd be in no position to put up a fight.

This is the worst part: the waiting. He looked down
across the white emptiness below, tried to ignore the
itching in the back of his throat and the pain in his
ears. Outside the fuselage, four giant Turmanskii gas
turbines howled across the tundra. The sky overhead
was the deep blue of an ice age. Pines clustered across
the low-lying terrain to the south, but the flight path of
the jet was carrying Oleg ever closer to the Arctic circle.
How long will this take? He tried to calculate it in his
head; assuming an air speed of five hundred knots, that
would make it ... seven hours. Give or take. To the
land of ice and sky fire, where nuclear-powered pyramids brooded beneath the eternal sun. Vast, many-
tracked crawlers bore fiery cylinders of nuclear death.
Oceans of ice beneath which submarines crept in cold-
war pursuits. Ancient tribes of ice-dwelling hunters,
bemused by the entry of the modern world into their
dream of ages, forced out of the wire-wrapped military
reservations. Solzhenitsyn had written about the Gulag
archipelago, the islands of prisoners locked in the sea
of Siberia, but this was something else. This was the
continent of the military, gripped in the paranoid embrace of an eternal winter of the soul.

I ought to stop them from doing it, Oleg told himself
for the thousandth time. It was a pathetic mantra, but
repetition made it seem more practical; if only the sense
of doing it would not so stubbornly elude him ...

Up front, a door banged open. Oleg looked up; it was
Anatoly, or whoever passed for him. The shadows standing out beneath his high cheek-bones gave him a lupine

appearance. Oleg turned his head away and closed his eyes. His captor ignored this; seconds later he sensed warm breath centimetres from his face.

'You don't have any choice in the matter, you know.'

Oleg opened his eyes. 'Don't I?' he asked.

Anatoly – whoever he was – seemed to find this amusing. 'Avoid the end of the universe? Huh!' He drew away a fraction and Oleg flinched, expecting a blow. It never came. 'We are not cruel, Professor. We are not the Dark. Our intentions are good.'

Oleg held up his chained wrists. 'Then why . . .?'

Anatoly shook his head slowly. 'You don't under-stand. We can't afford to take any chances. It has been many years since we tried and failed . . . too long ago. Our German colleagues who set the agenda at the Wann-see conference – now *they* were evil. In human terms, at least. But us? You do me a disservice.' He leaned for-ward until he was nose-to-nose with Oleg. 'We are here to help you.'

'Help me!' He snorted. 'How?'

'Help you –' Anatoly paused for a moment – 'help you do what you didn't have the guts to do on your own. Even though you've known how to do it for years, now . . . even though we gave you all the facilities you could possibly need. Don't play the innocent, *Professor*. You know what I'm talking about.'

'I do?' Oleg found himself unable to look away from Anatoly's dark eyes; the expression on that face, the shared fear of the pit over which he had been walking these past years, black as his worst fears . . . 'You really think that I can summon down the Dark?' His stomach turned over, a vast uneasy sense of urgency growing inside him. His heart raced, and the handcuffs slid around his slippery wrists as if on a thin coating of slime.

Anatoly leaned close to him. 'I *know* you can, Oleg. Because you *want* to do it, don't you? Otherwise you'd have turned me in long ago, to that Chekist major you can't leave alone, you think we don't know about that?'

Anatoly's face rippled slowly before Oleg's eyes, twisting into another shape that it had worn for a long time before it's owner had chosen to pass for a student; a visage at once familiar and frightening. 'I know you better than you think, Comrade Academician. You like your cosy office too much, and you're still afraid of the Dark the way they taught you to be. But part of you wants to get it over with very badly, doesn't it? You don't like human people, although you try to hide it — isn't that so? You don't even like your own kind very much. So you crouch in dark corners and search frantically for the key to the thing that scares you most, telling yourself that you need the information in order to *hide* better — such nonsense! I'll tell you what you wanted to know. You wanted to work out where the Dark had gone, in those long aeons since it first came, while the sun swung around the core of the galaxy — isn't that right? — because you knew better than most of us where the technology was leading the humans.'

Anatoly-Andrei turned sinuously and sat down beside Oleg. Oleg stared, trying to fix every tiny detail in his mind: the pores in Andrei's skin, the faint, acrid smell of the Kin, the slight, nervous way he fidgeted with his left hand. Andrei stared back, eyes wide in a display of inhuman concern.

'Another twenty years and their geneticists, they'll be able to pin us down everywhere. Have you thought of that? It would mean the end of us, the end of everything. But not if we have the guts to do what we should do, and use those three thousand megawatts, no? If we get our blow in first, we can be safe again. All of us. To sleep away another age without fear of interruption by the hairless apes.' Andrei – visibly Andrei now, still as youthful as when Oleg had first met him in the mid-sixties – stared like an obsessive, fear and calculation mingled in his gaze. 'Isn't that right?' he asked. 'Don't you know it's true? We *can't* let them carry on –'

'You're –' Oleg stopped, at a loss for words. *He thinks he knows everything.* Andrei blinked rapidly, as if looking for a further justification.

'The function systems, Professor. We've seen your interest in Lyupanov space and chaos theory. We even heard about those programs you ran – after you erased them and shredded the results. We can guess. You know *exactly* how to go about summoning the Dark; where to point the antennae, what message to send, how long it will take. The radar site at Krasnoyarsk interested you, so we *guessed.* Big, powerful transmitters. That's it, isn't it? You are our people's only hope, now.'

'Why? I don't understand. What's in it for you?'

'Nothing, probably. Freedom from fear.' Andrei shrugged, suddenly abashed. 'Come now, Professor. We're all afraid together, aren't we? Those who think the Dark will kill us, and those – like you – who fear it but understand the need. I just –' he sighed and looked away for a moment. Then: 'I just want to get it over with. The fear, not knowing. We live among animals who could turn on us at any time. What could be worse than that? Face it, Professor. When it comes down to it, we are all Kin. And that's all the humans will see if they learn of us.'

Oleg held up his hands again. 'With these, how can I trust you?' he asked, simply.

Andrei held up a key. 'How can *I* trust *you*, if you won't even tell me what you're running from?' he asked. 'Say it. You can't hide for ever.'

'Say what . . .' Oleg's mouth was dry, his heart pounding; he barely noticed that the tension of years was melting away from him as he let his real face peep through, let the darkness that had been raised in his childhood soul reveal itself to his captor.

'We know about the taiga.'

'The taiga . . .' Oleg swallowed, breaking out in a sweat. 'What do you mean?' He looked at Andrei, terrified beyond rational cause; he had expected them to kill him, not dig up his past.

'We know what you did. All we want you to do is do it again. How does that sound?' It was a plea rather than a threat, and it spoke to Oleg. 'Is it so bad that you must forget even who you were, what you did?'

'You're mad,' Oleg whispered, falling back on his last defence.

Andrei shook his head sadly. 'If I am mad, then so are you,' he said, turning away. 'Think about it, Professor: it's not so much. And you will do it, won't you? Because you want to. See you later . . .'

He left. And Oleg sweated out the rest of the flight, cold as ice and frightened as a ghost. Because, when he forced himself to confront the issue, Andrei was substantially correct. Nothing would please him more than to do away with these turbulent humans, except for the cost of returning to his own worst nightmare . . .

'They took off two hours ago, outbound for the Kola peninsula on a 192 with long-range fuel tanks and a detachment of military police. Looks like they're clear of you.'

'Shit.' Valentina thumped the table so hard that the telephone on it bounced. 'Can't you do anything about it?'

'Like what? Take them down?' The voice on the other

end of the line was sardonic. 'Be sensible! He's only a dissident –'

She hung up angrily. 'Well?' called the base political officer from across the room.

'Air Defence says no,' she muttered; 'Well fuck 'em!'

'You could follow them,' suggested the captain, complacent in his insularity. 'It's only a slow cargo plane.'

'No. I'd still be too late. All they need is the authorization to run a quick sky-search; that's what Oleg had. An astronomer. Then blast three gigawatts of pulsed microwave energy in the direction of . . .' she shuddered, searching for an excuse. 'The American early warning satellite.' *What a good lie. We should never have let them discover the wheel . . .*

'I didn't know it was that serious,' the base political complained. 'If they'd warned us, through proper channels –'

'Forget it,' she snapped. She stared out of the window of the office, towards the runway where the MiG-29s squatted on their landing gear like menacing green wasps. 'Those birds. Any of them ready to go? With a passenger?'

'But they're single-seaters –' the political stood up, paused for a moment of indecision – 'I think one of them's a trainer, though. You're going to requisition a fighter?'

Valentina turned and stared at him. 'Why not?' she asked, deceptively innocent. 'The man's got to be stopped. He's dangerous. I've got to get where he's going – fast. Can you suggest anything better?'

'Can *you*?' challenged the captain. 'I mean, it's all very well for you, but me – I've got to answer to the boss! Who will be unhappy, unless –'

'Name a price. Bill Department Seven Special Circumstances for the budget.' She was already halfway to the door when she paused. 'Where do you keep your flight suits?' she asked.

The base security officer was smiling. 'This way,' he said. 'You're really going after him? To get there first and arrest him?' Valentina nodded, unwilling to trust her own tongue. 'That's great! Just like in the movies!' And he held the door open for her as she went to collect her flight kit.

Six twenty-three:

Almost before it taxied to a halt beside the dispatch terminal, a personnel carrier drew up beside the jet. The evening sun scattered in orange shards from the truncated pyramids in the distance; a fine powder of snow dusted the runway beneath the aircraft's nose. An ancient military stairlift drew up beside the cockpit canopy as it swung open. As Valentina clambered down the ladder she discovered a welcoming committee. 'Major Valentina Pavlova? Major Rostopov, base security. I hope you have an explanation for this.' The spokesman wore a coat with major's epaulettes and a smile as charmless as a rattlesnake. His guards were decked out in full winter combat gear, rifles held at the ready.

'There's an explanation all right. Who are you?' Valentina shivered in her flight suit: it was a summer's evening, and the temperature had already dropped below freezing.

'Your papers –'

Valentina stared at him coldly. 'Contact Leningrad Central KGB. The exchange code is gold nine zero five. Ask to be connected to the office of Marshal Dmitri Yazov. Explain that Major Pavlova is here and you require clearance to proceed.'

Rostopov recoiled slightly, then caught himself. 'And

if I don't?' he asked sharply. 'This is a cold country, major. Have you noticed which way the wind is blowing?'

'Or you can contact Moscow Parliament. Ask for the office of the President. Tell Comrade Yeltsin's secretary to read you Presidential Emergency Decree forty –'

'Enough.' Rostopov raised his hands abruptly, as if surrendering. 'If you would care to get inside the carrier – I'm sure we can discuss this in my office –' He looked as if he had tasted something extremely bitter.

'No time. I want to go to the Priority Installation, not the airfield. Can you take me there directly?'

'The Priority ...' Rostopov stared at her. 'What *is* this? You've got the Emergency Committee *and* the President in your pocket and ... shit, I don't believe this!' He clambered into the body of the APC, still muttering vaguely. 'You *bet* I'm going to check your credentials, comrade, this is extremely irregular –'

Valentina followed him into the passenger compartment. As she did so she removed her right hand from her pocket. The Stetchkin automatic that nestled inside had not been needed – this time. *It's amazing how gullible the confusion makes them ...*

The carrier rumbled off towards the compound gates, under the gaze of the perimeter guards. She sat very still, waiting for the hot-air blowers to blast the chill out of the rattling metal box. It felt *unnatural*, in a way that she had never really learned to block out; too much living among humans numbed the senses, trained them to ignore alien smells and ways. She'd have told her brother it was a bad idea if he'd ever asked, back when they were young – but he wasn't likely to ask such penetrating questions, and she was not about to volunteer her opinion without it first being requested. That was the basis of all her relationships, after all. She remembered all too well where breaking that rule had got her in the past.

As they travelled, Major Rostopov tried to wheedle information out of her. This Valentina found vaguely amusing. 'What is going on, comrade, that can't wait until the current situation blows over? You nearly gave the Colonel a heart attack when he heard what kind of speed that bird of yours was doing – he thought it was a yankee F-111 coming down his throat – what gives?'

She yawned. 'It's been a long day, Major. And very unpleasant. Wet working conditions, if you take my meaning.' Rostopov blanched and shut his mouth with an audible *snap*, then scrambled forward into the driver's section.

The carrier rumbled through a tight turn and stopped while the outer gate opened in front of it. Rostopov reappeared. 'I can take you as far as the commandant's office,' he said. 'They won't let this vehicle go any further. You'd better have your papers ready.'

Valentina nodded. 'That will do.'

The diesel wound up into a full-throated howl and the armoured personnel carrier went to full speed. It was all she could do to prevent herself from being thrown from wall to wall like a rag doll; conversation was out of the question. For a gut-freezing moment she tried to remember whether she'd set the safety on her gun: a Stetchkin *looked* like a pistol, but it could discharge a full magazine in only a second, spraying white-hot lead around the whole compartment. That was why she'd chosen it. *I might only get the one chance.* Somehow the thought elated her at the same time as it scared her to death: it made her think of blood-red nights and flesh-hot mouths, of predatory passions that humans could not and should not understand. She'd come a long way for this, unimaginably far.

The one chance – she remembered her brother, the last night. He'd gone away when she was a baby, leaving her alone with their parents: gone away to school in the city where buildings of stone scraped at the sky until it wept stars of blood. Left her to years of cloying intimacy, the family that lived alone on the tundra in a hovel that froze from the inside out in winter: strange, inbred folk ignored by humans, shunned by everyone but the nomadic trappers ... it couldn't last for ever. When he returned from the unimaginably distant city she was older and wiser, but not old enough. He took her by the hand: 'I love you, sister,' he said, 'you're the only one.' Twenty years older than she was and he was right, there were no other kin within five hundred kilometres. When he touched her her skin caught fire and burned with an alien heat. 'Let me show you why,' he said.

They had gone outside in the woods, he and she, alone at dusk in summer, when the mosquitos bred in swarms above the stagnant ponds that lay among the roots of decaying pine trees. The summer tundra was stagnant and fetid, like a bloated corpse. He'd led her by the hand, deep into the woods along a path that human eyes could never follow, to a small glade surrounded by dead trees. There he set fire to her senses with his hands and body: it was not a new experience, for she was Weerde and fey and coming into adulthood in a land where the ice rarely melted. When she came she bayed like a wolf at the midnight sun.

Afterwards, as they lay side by side together, he said to her slyly: 'I have a secret, sister. Do you want to know what it is?'

Still warm from his embrace, she had said yes, she did. 'It's the humans. The trappers. Do you wonder why so few have visited us this spring?'

She'd nodded, mutely. Their absence had worried her unaccountably. 'They're not our people,' he said. 'Ancient, primitive ... they think they know it all. But we scare them. They mutter curses and keep their women behind the covers of their yurts because they think we possess the evil eye. Maybe they'd tell the communists, but they're afraid of us ... the hex is still stronger than the red star. You know something? They're right.'

He stood, naked, above her: shape melting into the trees like the ghost of something unimaginably ancient. No longer human, but raw and elemental as the winter. 'I hold the key, sister. I know where It dwells; the thing with no Name, of which the legends speak.' Leaning down, he helped her rise. Inhuman eyes glittered in the un-night. 'One day this will return, whether we will it or no. They sensed this, I think. I had no alternative.'

Together they walked deeper into the forest, where the trees wove overhead into a canopy of darkness and the ground was a rancid mulch of needles, he leading and she following. 'They came in the night to lead the kommunisti to us,' he said.

Deep foreboding chilled her to the core: 'What have you done?' she demanded.

'Didn't want to lose you,' he said, reaching for her hands. 'They were doomed anyway. In the nature of their people. Look.' She looked. Saw what he had done to the traders who had been their only contact with the outside world. 'I did it for you, my love. Didn't want to lose you. What's wrong?'

She remembered bending her head forward to kiss the dead thing that passed for an altar, no longer breathing, gagging on the stench of decomposition – '*One day this will return, whether we will it or no*' – striking out, changing her face, her mind, her memory to expunge the memory until the day a year later when she woke

379

up to see a letter lying on her straw-filled pillow – her fingers flexed involuntarily, opening and closing like talons. *Why did it fall to me to be born to the parents of a monster?* He couldn't leave her alone; through all the years he'd tracked her, from a distance, known where to find her. Bracing herself against one green-painted wall, she reached into her pocket for reassurance. But he'd never dared to face her down, to venture an explanation. *Happiness is a warm gun.* Yes, there it was: the sick feeling in her stomach subsiding momentarily. A flash of malice made her shudder with its intensity; *I hope he's still there, the bastard. So many lost years to answer for, and when he finally calls it's only to tell me . . .*

She noticed Major Rostopov was back. He was staring at her. She let herself smile back at him; let it all shine out, then closely observed the fear sketch livid shadows beneath his eyes.

Seven-fourteen:

Tracking Control was a cavernous chamber in a bunker deep beneath the permafrost, protected by layers of air defence missiles and interceptor squadrons against the day when the B-52s came over the horizon. Oleg Meir felt anything but safe, though. Even with Andrei behind him, smoothing the way at every turn and smiling-joking with the Colonel in charge, it felt *wrong*. Perhaps it was guilt. Oleg knew exactly what he was doing . . . and he had a feeling that Andrei, however strong his faith in the Dark might be, did not. Besides which, Oleg knew who was coming. Fear and guilt roiled inside him until he felt almost hollow. *What if she's right?* He worried. *What if she hasn't forgotten?*

'So I would like it if you could load the ephemerides and begin transmitting for a period of one hour as soon

as the message is loaded. Think you can manage that?'
asked Andrei.

The captain in charge of the post nodded. 'And bill
the Institute ... for SETI? Think we'll find anything,
Comrade Academician?' He seemed to be more bemused
than anything else.

Oleg shrugged uncomfortably, glancing at Andrei, who
smiled down at him with tight-pursed lips. 'It's a theory.
We need to complete it for a thesis, big international
conference, you know the sort of thing. Anyway, the
Americans haven't done it yet – they've listened, Project
Ozma back in the sixties was the first – but *transmitted*? If
this trial is a success we'll be able to get backing for a full
research project. Who knows? We might even get to keep
the big dish, whatever arms treaties they come up with.'

The captain's eyes glittered. Like far too many of the
hairless apes, Oleg realized, he thought of his machines
as being more human than other people. 'So what is the
text of the message, exactly?' he asked.

Andrei nudged Oleg surreptitiously. Oleg tapped a
couple of keys on the shielded terminal, calling up a
listing. He'd loaded it off tape barely an hour since,
under Andrei's wary eye. He hadn't given him an inch
of slack, whatever he might have said on the flight in;
Oleg was precisely as free as he had been before, handcuffed or otherwise. 'It's a fractal. Random looking, in
the most unimaginably deterministic way. There are
very few ways you can decode it, and all of them imply
that it is *no* coincidence ... the message is the medium,
in this case. With three gigawatts punching it out, it
should be quite deafening out to a couple of hundred
light-years' range. If I get the chance to repeat, we'll
need to sustain it for a full year.' *But we won't need to*,
thought Oleg. *Not if the old legends are correct. If
thoughts alone could summon it, even a fraction of a*

megawatt beaming the right message should be over-kill . . .

'That's settled, then,' said the captain. 'All I need is the authorization – oh.' He stopped, looked up.

Andrei leaned over Oleg's chair and turned the full force of his personality on the hapless officer. 'I'll see to that at once! I'm sure Colonel Blavatsky will agree; after all the project release has been signed by the ministry, hasn't it?' He smiled, baring spotless teeth, and the captain nodded back helplessly. 'Perhaps you'd like to load the transmission sequence now and run it through the modulator stage, just to check that there are no unforeseen problems . . . you're sure you can transmit on twenty-one centimetres? The, uh, water hole?'

'H-band, yes.' He nodded so violently that one of the technicians glanced round in concern before bending back over his diagnostic station. 'Of course. You want me to load it? Sure.'

He began tapping keys on his terminal at a surprising rate. Oleg watched, fascinated and terrified at the same time: his authorization on this system didn't extend to actually issuing commands. It was all automated – a phased array radar was nothing more than a series of pulses propagating through silicon, after all – but still it made him catch his breath, to see a pallid-looking captain sitting at a desk steer a billion roubles of electronics to point at an ephemeris from which no American missile could possibly originate . . .

There was a banging, some way off in the building. Oleg ignored it, watching instead the big wall screen that painted the beam path across a polar map of the Union. The highlighted strip jumped, suddenly, pointing inwards and upwards; a searchlight beacon of microwaves pouring energy out towards the stars. 'That's good,' he said, encouragingly.

The young officer grinned back. 'We can point it anywhere,' he said, 'even down here, if we wanted to fry our brains out. Hey –' He made as if to stand up, but Oleg caught his hand and held it.

'Sit down,' he said softly. 'Let the Colonel deal with it.' Behind him, Andrei was moving towards the door. 'You don't actually think this is a good thing to do?' he asked the captain, suddenly curious to hear this young man pronounce upon his own species' demise.

For a moment doubt flickered across the young man's features. 'What makes you ask that, comrade? Is this some kind of political thing?'

A shadow of exasperation crossed Oleg's features. 'They don't tell you anything out here, do they? About the coup? It'll collapse, you know, but the Union will go on in one form or another. No, not politics. Just ... think what might lie out there! What hideous evil we might be summoning down when you transmit that call sign ...'

But the captain shook his head and grinned. 'But you must be wrong, comrade! Look –' before Oleg could stop him he punched keys. 'I send it now! And you know, of course if they can understand what they are reading in decades' time from now, they must be *more* intelligent than us, more civilized! Mustn't they?'

Oleg stared at the anonymous soldier, utterly aghast. There was a staccato banging noise in the distance. For a moment ice water coursed through his veins instead of blood. *What have you done* ... 'Of course, if you are wrong, you might have killed the human race.' He felt a giant laugh, two-thirds relief and one-third terror, rumble through the back of his head like an echo of thunder, the humour of a mad god. Acutely aware of the guards, the guns pointing ever inwards, his guts melted to jelly. *You fool! The most important event in* the history of your species and you do it because of a discredited political theory! It's humans like you who screwed us over so badly that this is the only way out – a grand, manic hilarity bubbled up inside him, thirty years of terror set free in a single moment.

The captain, oblivious, shook his head and smiled. 'Rubbish, comrade! Any aliens sophisticated enough to read your message, of course they'll be good communists, won't they? I mean, it stands to reason that all intelligent life must be evolving towards –'

Oleg felt a sudden gust of cold air on his neck. The captain stood up, mouth hanging open, as Oleg spun round in his chair to face his sister, her frozen vengeful face, the ridiculously small pistol she clutched in her hands – 'You can't be serious,' he tried to say, smiling with embarrassment and fear – 'I didn't do it. They did it to themselves! After all these years I never even had to raise a finger!' Staring down the barrel of a loaded gun, he wondered as if for the first time if he might be held accountable: 'Won't you be reasonable? Talk to me!'

His sister took a step forward; and for a moment Oleg thought he saw her smile. 'What's there to talk about?' she asked.

'Everything –' he began.

But he was much too late.

Epilogue

RAISED VOICES IN A READING ROOM: II

Roz Kaveney

'I did not call you as a witness,' the scaly Lord of Stasis said in puzzlement as Valentina finished her story. 'I shall kill you, I think, in an exemplary manner, for this interruption of your elders and betters.'

'I am not interested in your prerogatives,' Valentina said. 'And I can face your threats with calm. Sometimes it is more important that the facts be known. It is not fear of your punishments that makes my voice tremble. You have got to understand, all of you. The Dark is coming.'

The scaly one towered over her, its great claws unsheathed for bloodshed.

'I have invoked,' Chepstow said, 'the Truce of knowledge. I believe that it holds for anything said or done in this council, though I am prepared to stand corrected.'

'You are, of course, correct,' the gracile Lord of Chaos said.

It turned to Chepstow's Ancient.

'I did not know you were part of the Shanghai business,' it said.

'Sins of my youth,' Chepstow's Ancient – who must, he realized, be the Saunders of Charlotte Matthews's stories – rumbled apologetically. 'Typical of humans to rake up old scandals.'

'Chaoticists and Progressives,' the scaly one bellowed.

'Revealer scum. I call on you to witness that there has to be an accounting . . .'

'Do shut up, my good man,' Chepstow said, 'you are not helping your case even slightly.'

The squat Ancient pulled at the scaly one's arm, and whispered into its ear. It subsided, muttering.

'Gentlepersons of the jury,' Chepstow continued, 'no case against humanity has been proved. More importantly, there is real danger now both to you and us. I suggest that this hearing be adjourned to consider the real crisis. The Dark is coming. You are concerned, all of you, with how your actions will look in the Fifty Lives, in the Songs of the Lines. And you cannot leave humanity defenceless before the Dark without risking condemnation and namelessness.'

The two small Ancients had moved to the front of the crowd.

'This is exciting,' one said. 'I could never vote for the extermination of humans. They are too much fun.'

'I still say we should kill them all,' the squat one said, but fell silent when it realized that none were offering him support.

'Remember,' Chepstow said, as if he had not been interrupted, 'the Dark is coming. If it arrives, and we apes are not here, can you rely on its slinking back into its intergalactic thicket unfed? The Dark is coming. Dare you face it alone, and risk the end of the Lives, the end of the Song? The Dark is coming. This, above all, is the time in history when Weerde and human must stand, or fall, together. The Dark is coming.'

He slumped exhausted. Around him, the Ancients murmured their way through a vote that was irrelevant, whatever its result. There was no pleasure in this victory. There would be no victories ever again, and, he feared, only the very grimmest of defeats. *The Dark is coming.*

THE WEERDE WAS DEVISED BY MARY GENTLE AND NEIL GAIMAN, AND EDITED BY MARY GENTLE AND ROZ KAVENEY:

Neil Gaiman is co-author of the bestselling apocalyptic fantasy *Good Omens*, with Terry Pratchett, but is better known for his work in the comics medium, particularly for his ongoing dark fantasy *Sandman*, which has won lots of awards. He comes up with quite a few of the ideas for Midnight Rose, while other people do the real work: Alex Stewart did all the heavy lifting on *Temps* (also published in ROC), and Mary Gentle and Roz Kaveney had to get their hands dirty with *The Weerde* and the ROC anthology *Villains!*

Mary Gentle is known for her science-fiction novels *Golden Witchbreed* and *Ancient Light*, and most recently for the Renaissance technoBaroque fantasies *Rats and Gargoyles* and *The Architecture of Desire*. She edits for Midnight Rose Ltd, and reviews for *Interzone*. She has an MA in seventeenth-century studies and continues with unrelated research. In her spare time she runs around a lot, swordfighting, and shooting people in laser-gaming events. She is a born-again redhead.

Roz Kaveney is probably best known as a journalist and reviewer writing on science fiction, comics and other topics for the *New Statesman*, *Foundation*, *City Limits* and *The Sunday Times*. At one time or another she has read for most of the SF lists in London, and edited the two *Tales from the Forbidden Planet* anthologies. In what would otherwise be her spare time, she is an anti-censorship and civil-liberties activist.

**Exploring New Realms
in Science Fiction/Fantasy Adventure**

Temps
Devised by Neil Gaiman and
Alex Stewart

At last, the cutting-edge of Superhero fantasy!

Danger: Talent at work

To the tabloid press the Department of Paranormal Resources is
a scroungers' paradise, issuing regular girocheques to a motley
collection of talents with questionable results.

But for the 'Temps' who place their bizarre abilities at the service
of the State in exchange for a miserly stipend and a demob suit,
life with a very British League of Superheroes leaves everything
to be desired . . .

Temps begins a startling new series in which a team of gifted Psi-
fi writers explore a strangely familiar world of empaths, precogs
and telepaths – with hilarious and terrifying results.

Contributors include: Storm Constantine, Colin Greenland,
Graham Higgins, Liz Holliday, Roz Kaveney, David Langford,
Brian Stableford . . . and many more.

Exploring New Realms
in Science Fiction/Fantasy Adventure

Villains!
Devised by Mary Gentle
and Neil Gaiman

Who needs heroes anyway?

These are the untold stories – the other side of the Legend. For in the Twenty Four Kingdoms lie those dark and dangerous places inhabited by halfling assassins, corrupt warriors and necromancers, evil princesses, and wickedly clever orcs ... the world of sword and sorcery as it really is!

At last the time has come to enter in their company the slums, mountains, cities and wilderness; to cross the boundaries of the Dark Land itself – and hear the *real* truth.

Because just for once the Dark Lords, mercenaries, money-grubbing dwarves and monsters are the stars of these new tales from Mary Gentle, Storm Constantine, Stephen Baxter, Keith Brooke, David Langford, Charles Stross, Alex Stewart, James Wallis, Roz Kaveney, Paula Wakefield, Molly Brown and Graham Higgins.

And just for once – the bad guys may even win!

**Exploring New Realms
in Science Fiction/Fantasy Adventure**

The Weerde
Book 1
Devised by Neil Gaiman, Mary Gentle and Roz Kaveney

In the Library of the Conspiracy many theories are pursued in rare books and documents supplied by a caste of white-gloved librarians. Many wild-eyed researchers piece together their elaborate nonsenses of Templars, Vampires and Illuminati.

But one such theory weaves like a constant thread of darkness through human history. The rumour of an ancient race, more powerful than we are: elusive, terrifying, offering sexual frenzy but bringing madness and early death.

These are the tales of the Weerde, the shape-shifting predators of which occult legend speaks. They are plausible, charming, different and very, very dangerous.

The Weerde contains eleven chilling stories that expose the terrifying truth behind the conspiracy. Their authors are Storm Constantine, Mary Gentle, Colin Greenland, Brian Stableford, Josephine Saxton, Charles Stross, Roz Kaveney, Paul Cornell, Chris Amies, Michael Fearn and Liz Holliday.